I0760950

She wasn't supposed to fall for me, but I should have known the second she walked into my town my life would never be the same. She claimed me. And I wasn't sure how long I could resist the temptation to make her mine.

Kelsey Summers never wanted to give her heart to Liam Castle, the wolf who'd been promised to her since birth, but the fates had other plans, and she could no longer ignore her feelings now that she'd claimed him as her mate.

Liam Castle would do anything to honor his pack. They're family, and as their heir prince, their safety is his responsibility. He never expected anyone could mean more to him than duty. And then she turned his life upside down.

Someone in the pack betrayed them, but the person the hunter points the finger at will rock the entire pack if accused. Not to mention what it will do to Liam. Together, Liam and Kelsey will uncover the truth at all costs—even if it means tearing their families apart.

Liam

Moonstruck Mates Book Two

By J.L. WEIL

Published by J. L. Weil

www.jlweil.com/

Edited by XterraWeb
Cover Design by MerryBookRound

Sign up for an exclusive first look at the hottest new releases, contests, and exclusives from bestselling author J.L. Weil and receive a bonus scene from the Raven series from Zane's POV, as well as *two free* eBooks, Losing Emma and Breaking Emma, bonus stories from my Divisa Series as a thank you!

Want to discuss what you've just read? Get exclusive teasers or connect with other readers and authors?
Join my reader group on Facebook!

Also by J.L. Weil

ELITE OF ELMWOOD ACADEMY
(New Adult Dark High School Romance)
Turmoil
Disorder
Revenge
Rival

MOONSTRUCK MATES
(New Adult Paranormal Romance)
Kelsey
Liam

DIVISA HUNTRESS
(New Adult Paranormal Romance)
Crown of Darkness
Inferno of Darkness
Eternity of Darkness

DRAGON DESCENDANTS SERIES
(Upper Teen Reverse Harem Fantasy)

Stealing Tranquility
Absorbing Poison
Taming Fire
Thawing Frost

THE DIVISA SERIES
(Full series completed – Teen Paranormal Romance)
Losing Emma: A Divisa novella
Saving Angel
Hunting Angel
Breaking Emma: A Divisa novella
Chasing Angel
Loving Angel
Redeeming Angel

LUMINESCENCE TRILOGY
(Full series completed – Teen Paranormal Romance)
Luminescence
Amethyst Tears
Moondust
Darkmist – A Luminescence novella

RAVEN SERIES
(Full series completed – Teen Paranormal Romance)
White Raven
Black Crow
Soul Symmetry

BEAUTY NEVER DIES CHRONICLES
(Teen Dystopian Romance)
Slumber
Entangled
Forsaken

NINE TAILS SERIES
(Teen Paranormal Romance)

First Shift
Storm Shift
Flame Shift
Time Shift
Void Shift
Spirit Shift
Tide Shift
Wind Shift
Celestial Shift

HAVENWOOD FALLS HIGH

(Teen Paranormal Romance)

Falling Deep
Ascending Darkness

SINGLE NOVELS

Starbound
(Teen Paranormal Romance)
Casting Dreams
(New Adult Paranormal Romance)
Ancient Tides
(New Adult Paranormal Romance)

For an updated list of my books, please visit my website:
www.jlweil.com

Join my VIP email list and I'll personally send you an email reminder as soon as my next book is out! Click here to sign up: www.jlweil.com

For everyone who's ever fought for love.
Even when shrouded in darkness, the moon still shines bright.

Prologue
LIAM

Thud. Thud. Thud. Shutters banged against the dark, run-down house if you could call it that. Shed would be a more accurate description—a room with four walls. The wind howled, shaking the trees surrounding me from where I crouched in the woods, staring at the faint light I swore glowed through the window. I couldn't figure out if I desperately wanted the speck of hope to be there or if it was a reflection of the moon.

This has to be it.

It fucking has to be.

If it wasn't...

I didn't want to think about how I'd react to another disappointment. It wasn't just me I worried for. My wolf suffered, tortured by the loss of our mate. Each day. Each hour. Each minute. Each goddamn fucking second killed a piece of our soul. I'd never endured a broken heart before, but the moment Kelsey was taken, the muscle pumping life into my body didn't just crack.

If fucking shattered.

Hell, it felt as if my heart had been obliterated.

We weren't meant to be apart.

There was a difference between spending a weekend with the girls,

going to the grocery store, or enjoying a day with her parents and having Kelsey ripped away from me.

It was not knowing where she was, unsure if she was safe, scared, alone, or in pain that drove me absolutely frantic. Without Kelsey, my life had no meaning. The world became void of all emotion, no color, nothing worth appreciating.

These were the ramifications of our bond and the consequences of being forced apart.

My link to Kelsey went deeper than the typical wolf mating.

She was more than my lover, my friend, my companion.

She was my damn soulmate.

My Moonstruck mate.

And I wouldn't fucking rest until she was back where she belonged.

By my side.

In my arms.

Sleeping in my bed.

No amount of time. No obstacle. No setback.

Nothing in this world would deter me. My mind focused on only one task, and I wouldn't stray from the path.

How could I have ever thought this girl meant nothing to me? How had I ever believed I could reject fate? How could I ever live without her?

I didn't plan to find out.

In my wolf form, I crouched lower in the brush, willing myself to melt into the coverage of night and the shadows of the woods. My eyes would give me away if I wasn't careful. A downfall of being a wolf shifter was the unearthly glow of our eyes.

I had to become darkness. Not an easy task when your fur shimmered pure as snow under moonlight. My mate, on the other hand, could have blended seamlessly with the night.

From the outside, the shack looked abandoned as if it hadn't seen life or had life living inside of its decrypted walls in years. Hell, decades. But I knew better.

Appearances were deceiving.

She was inside. I could feel her.

My heart beat in synchronization with hers.

The bond threading us together yanked and tugged, pulling me to her.

My mate.

A spear of lightning illuminated the sky. The outline of a figure flashed in the window. I blinked, my heart kicking up in my chest.

Lightning lanced again, and with it, the figure was gone.

It was time to move.

My paws trod lightly over the ground as I crossed the overgrown pathway toward the door. I took a long breath, assuring myself this wouldn't be another dead end, not like the last weeks had painstakingly been.

The door was slightly ajar when I stopped in front of it. I listened for movement on the other side, but my sense of smell caused my legs to lock up.

Blood. The sharp, metallic scent of it hit my nostrils.

Kelsey.

A low grow rumbled at the base of my throat, crawling up inside me with the vow of violence.

It took all my willpower to keep from bursting through the door in a panicked moment of revenge, hellfire burning in my veins. I needed to take a breath, fearful of what waited for me on the other side of the door.

Using my nose, I pushed against the cracked opening. The door moved with a slight groan like the beginning of a horror movie, but the howling winds and shutters hitting the house in a repetitive rhythm drowned out most of the grumbling door.

Darkness, moldy dust, and something potent like the smell of cleaning solution waited through the opened door. I took a cautious step inside, my eyes immediately drawn to the hallway where a faint light glimmered from somewhere.

Another flash of lightning burst behind me, lighting up the sparse room. Thunder followed moments later.

My eyes adjusted to the new degree of darkness as I made my way to the light. Silent and smooth like a hunter, I stalked down the uneven corridor. With each step my paws took over the dusty floorboards, tingles flourished within me like an internal map guiding me home.

Kelsey was my home.

Wherever she was, that's where I belonged.

I slid my tongue over my canines, bracing myself for what or who might be waiting for me in the shadows or behind closed doors as I passed by. There were three in the hallway, but only one concerned me.

The dim light seeped under the door at the end of the corridor. I couldn't just feel Kelsey's heart beating from the other side; I could hear it as well. Our link pulsed within me, spurring me forward, begging me to rush, dying to be reunited. And yet, I held back. Fear made me hesitate. Fear of what might wait for me.

Just a few more steps.

The door swung open before I reached it, and a wave of Kelsey swept over me. Dread pitted in my gut, a heavy weight that made my bones feel as if they were made of iron. My gaze panned the room, drawn to the grimy shelves lined against the walls.

A twisted sickness churned my stomach.

Vials of blood. Bottles of organs. Bloody, dirty surgical tools. It was a mad scientist's lab. A horror of experiments and torture.

And my mate lay lifeless on the operating table, a thin tube running out of her arm. Her dark hair spilled over the cold metal slab, waterfalling over the sides. I longed to see her unusual violet eyes, yearned for the way they captivated me, and yet, they remained closed, her long lashes touching the tops of her cheeks.

A whimper of agony lodged in my throat.

Pup. What have they done to you?

One
LIAM

His father. The prince. His father. His father.

Gunnar's words echoed again and again in my head, whirling like a deflating balloon spinning out of control. My father was responsible for the attacks on Kelsey? As much as I didn't want to believe this piece-of-shit hunter scum, part of me questioned the validity of his claim.

Rowan Castle, my father, was capable of so much worse that it wasn't hard to imagine him working with the enemy to gain something he desired.

My fucking mate.

Pieces of my life clicked into place or at least began to fit together. Loosely. It didn't mean they were true, but it did make me question aspects of my past. Like the possibility the treaty had nothing to do with what was best for me or the pack but with how it could benefit Rowan Castle. How Kelsey could enhance *his* power.

I glared at Gunnar, uncertainty warring with reason. Despite what my father was capable of, he was still my father. The pack alpha. The regional prince.

It came down to trusting my father or a hunter.

Right now, neither seemed fit to be trustworthy. Not with Kelsey's life.

The girl in question's body jerked when my father's name rasped from Gunnar's lips. She yanked the pointed nail embedded into the side of his neck, taking a step backward. His blood flowed like a stream from the puncture wound, cascading down his throat, and the air became tainted with the metallic tang of his blood.

Gunnar better freaking hope he got the healing abilities of wolves; otherwise, Kelsey just issued his death. She'd pierced a vital vein.

I'd be rather pleased if he didn't. He deserved nothing less than death.

Kelsey looked over at me, confusion and bewilderment taking up the lines on her face. "Liam?"

With my wolf eyes, I glanced at her, feeling as conflicted as she did. She could sense the struggle happening inside me.

"We can't trust him," I sent through our bond.

Conflict swam in her eyes, but she nodded, her magic still shackling Gunnar to the tree. The bonds around his neck loosened, and the hunter drew in a gurgling gasp of air. A hand flew to his neck, pressing into the hole left behind by Kelsey's claw.

"You lie," she spat, her violet eyes blazing.

The hunter's gaze shifted from my mate to me. He swallowed, struggling to speak.

I bared my canines, giving him an incentive to start fucking talking. I didn't give a shit if he bled out. Time was essential. My cousin was still tied up in the woods, and I wasn't certain how long Kelsey's powers could endure. The last thing I needed was this bastard to die before I got answers.

His blood-soaked hand dropped to his side, his labored breathing evening out.

Looked like someone could heal, and he wouldn't die after all. Pity.

I couldn't decide if letting him live was a good or terrible idea. The verdict remained in question.

"Do I?" Gunnar rasped, finally responding to Kelsey's statement calling him a liar.

She kept her chin high as she glared at him. "You'd say anything to save yourself. I don't even know why I'm listening to you. You've already proven to be deceitful."

His lips twisted. "The truth always comes out in the end."

"Too bad you won't be around to see it. I still plan to kill you. You can tell me that God sent you to hunt me, and I wouldn't change my mind," Kelsey said.

A howl rang through the treetops, and I shifted my focus to my pack. Over the rolling green hills covered in pines, oaks, and maple trees, my wolves sparred with Gunnar's rogue pack. The snarls, thudding of bodies, cracking of bones, and scratching of claws were faint, but the second howl of victory resounded.

They were driving the rogue shifters deeper into the forest.

With the threat contained, I wanted to shift and face Gunnar man-to-man. There was one problem. My clothes were shredded. Leith had spares in his car, which meant leaving Kelsey, and I didn't want to do that, even for a second.

I tried to judge the strength of her magic, but it wasn't easily seen, even with my enhanced vision. The power rippled in the air like heat on the hottest summer day but had no real color or shape. "*How long can you hold him?*" I asked, sending the question down our link.

It seemed unreal. I'd had no time to digest what Kelsey and I'd done. What *she'd* done.

A week ago, I never would have imagined she'd sink her teeth into my neck and claim me as her mate. I'd dreamed about it countless times, even before her coming to Riverbridge. Kelsey had been plaguing me with her smile, her beauty, and her striking eyes my whole life. She'd always been a temptation like Eve and the red apple.

Kelsey was the most complex wolf I'd ever met. I didn't know if that was true for all mates or females in general, but fuck me if she hadn't made me completely psycho from the moment she stepped foot into my town.

I'd never wanted to hate someone so much in my life and yet desired them with every particle of my being. No matter how much I tried to keep her at bay, to deny who she was, to reject the order of my father, I couldn't. The fates ultimately won.

"I don't know," Kelsey replied, her brows bunching together.

I brushed against the side of her leg, staring at Gunnar and sizing him up. "*Strip him,*" I said to my mate.

Her head whirled down to me. "What?" she shrieked, shock keeping her mouth open. "*Are you insane?*" she shot back, having the good sense to use our link. "*I'm not undressing the asshole.*"

Her reaction pleased me. "*Don't get all huffy. I need his clothes,*" I reasoned. "*That's all.*"

"Seriously, princeling," she hissed between gritting teeth.

"One of you want to fill me in on what this little disagreement is about?" Gunnar interjected, witnessing our silent exchange.

Kelsey whirled on him, her eyes lighting up the dark like purple flames. "Shut up, Gunnar." She forked a hand through the black tendrils of her hair. "I can't believe this," she mumbled.

"Don't make it weird," I said.

Her nose scrunched. *"Too late. It's already weird."*

She didn't want to touch him. And I didn't want her to lay a hand on the hunter, but we had few other available options.

"Fuck," she muttered, irritation flashing over her features. Straightening her shoulders, she stalked forward, and with purposeful movements, she unbuttoned Gunnar's jeans. When the button snapped out of the loop, she jerked back as if touching him literally caused her harm.

A flicker of surprise went through the hunter's eyes, which he covered quickly with snark. "Whoa, little wolf. I figured you were into some weird shit, and even though I'll admit I've fantasized about a threesome with you once or twice, it had always been with Hope."

A deep, ferocious growl rumbled up my chest, and I snapped my teeth at him.

She made a sour expression at the hunter. "As if you ever stood a chance with me. Hell, with Hope for that matter."

Gunnar smirked. "I wouldn't discount me yet."

"Shut. The. Hell. Up." Her fingers fumbled with his zipper.

"Hurry," I urged. I couldn't stand to see her hands on him or her being so fucking close to him. The fire flickering in my gut flared like it had been doused with gas.

Gunnar's leg twitched as her hands fisted into the fabric on the side of his legs, shimmying them down past his hips and leaving him in a pair of black boxer briefs. "Impressive, isn't it?" he boasted as Kelsey turned her head away from him, wiggling the jeans farther down his legs and pulling them off his ankles.

Her magic faltered.

I had to shift. Now.

Tossing Gunnar's pants to the ground at my feet, she straightened and narrowed her glare at the hunter. "You're still at my mercy. I'd be careful what you say next."

"If this isn't a kink, is it some kind of weird ritual before you kill me?" He was trying to distract her, force her to shift her concentration off her magic.

Kelsey flashed the hunter a wicked grin, backing up a few steps to put space between her and him, something I approved of. "At least you've come to terms with how this night will end."

Unwilling to push Kelsey's energy another second, I shifted, shedding my fur. Tingles radiated throughout my skin. I reached for the discarded jeans and tugged them on. They were tight, and I couldn't latch the button, but fashion and modesty came second to Kelsey's life.

We had bigger problems than the fit of my borrowed jeans.

Kelsey's gaze slid sidelong to me as I stepped up beside her, my shoulder brushing hers. My focus remained entirely on Gunnar, and the bastard watched me like a hawk, poised and waiting to see what I would do.

Crack.

His head whipped to the side from the force of my fist connecting with his cheek. "God, that felt good, but I'm just not satisfied."

"Good. Neither am I." Gunnar lunged for me.

I heard Kelsey's sudden intake of breath as she realized he'd broken through her wavering bonds.

Pivoting, I took Gunnar to the ground but not before he unsheathed a blade tucked under his shirt.

Shit. I should have had Kelsey check him for weapons before stripping the prick.

I'd been fast but not quick enough to avoid the sting of his dagger as it nicked my upper arm. Throwing my weight onto his chest, I went for his arm, intending to knock the weapon from his grasp, but before I could slam his hand into the grass, Kelsey's leg came hurling toward us, catching Gunnar in the back of the head.

The hunter's eyes rolled long enough for me to immobilize him and snatch the blade from him.

Christ, she's magnificent.

"Thank you" Kelsey responded, her sweet voice filling my head, a lick of humor lacing her tone.

I hadn't meant for my thought to project through our link. My thoughts weren't my own. Something I would have to get used to.

If I hadn't been straddling a hunter, I might have rolled my eyes at her, but as it was, I needed to deal with this asshole so I could get back to figuring out what to do with my mate.

One fucking problem at a time.

I held the dagger to his throat. "Let me guess. This is made of silver."

He didn't say anything, but he didn't have to. The confirmation shimmered in his eyes.

A silken smirk curled at my lips. "Seeing as you're part wolf, I hope this hurts like hell." My fingers flexed, readying for the killing swipe.

"Don't—" he rasped, swallowing despite the risk of cutting his Adam's apple.

Drops of hot blood dribbled down my arm as I angled my head to the side. "Why the hell shouldn't I kill you? Give me one good reason."

Kelsey loomed close; her body braced for trouble if Gunnar tried another escape tactic. Or worse.

I'd slit his throat first.

His eyes fluttered, pain probably ringing in his head from the force of Kelsey's foot. "I can help you," he muttered.

A wry chuckle tumbled out of me. "As if I would ever trust you," I fired back, pressing the weapon farther into his throat.

"Your father does. You can use that. Exploit his trust."

"Are you offering to double-cross an alpha?" My dark voice rumbled, strung with a temper that had been waiting for this moment. I hadn't been able to sink my teeth into him. Slicing him open was the next best thing.

"You need inside information," he reasoned like the snake he was. "I might be persuaded if the price is right."

Kelsey shuddered, a snort of disgust breezing through her nose. "Let me kill him."

Something like humor trickled into his features at Kelsey's not-so-subtle request. She amused him, and the little tidbit caused the shadows writhing within me to darken. "I take it you're into the murderess type," he bantered, but I wasn't in the mood to mince words, not with the lowest form of scum.

"Just shut the fuck up," I seethed, needing a moment to think.

If I killed him, would I ever find out the truth behind the capture order on my mate? I couldn't just take his word. He'd proven how little honor he possessed.

Keeping Kelsey safe had been a command not by my father but by my mother, the baroness. If it had been my father who made the demand, I probably would have tried harder to ignore the minx. Hell, who the fuck was I kidding. The promises I made to Mom wouldn't have mattered; the urge to protect Kelsey was ingrained in my genetic makeup.

Moonstruck mates.

The idea still flabbergasted me. I turned eighteen hours ago, and I already found the only girl I'd love. And believe me, I fucking tried to fall for other girls. All through high school, I'd dated and hooked up with dozens of girls hoping one of them would make me feel something...anything. It got to the point where I was positive I was dead inside.

And then Kelsey walked through the doors of Riverbridge High.

Shit, the truth of it was, I'd sensed her in the air the second she'd crossed into our territory. I'll never forget the moment when my chest squeezed like someone had their fingers wrapped around my heart with no hope of ever letting go.

And now it wasn't duty that spurred me to think of her life over mine. *I* wanted to keep her alive. We had so much shit to figure out, and to do that, I needed Kelsey unharmed and preferably by my side.

The question remained.

What the fuck am I going to do with him?

"Liam," Kelsey said, interrupting my internal struggle, but it was her tone that cleared my thoughts. Something in the way she said my name...had I picked up traces of fear? Worry? Panic?

"What is it? What's wrong?" I demanded.

"My father is coming."

TWO
KELSEY

Liam blinked, and the expression on his face said he wanted to believe he heard me wrong. He hadn't. "What?" It was barely a whisper.

Fuck.

My parents were more than I could handle in a single night on top of the hunter. Oh, and I couldn't forget bonding myself to Liam. I was having a damn eventful day. And it wasn't over yet despite exhaustion nagging at my bones. Holding the wards against Gunnar had stripped me of energy, and I would suffer for it. Sooner than later.

Sleep was far off.

I glanced at my hand, seeing the dry blood coating my fingers. "He and my mother are on their way with my pack. They'll be crossing the borders soon."

Reaffirming his threat at Gunnar's neck, he asked, "Do you know why?"

Boy, did I ever. I nodded. I'd rather not be having this conversation in front of a hunter, so I chose to take this topic to a more private means of communication. "*Because I claimed you. I need to go. I need to stop them before they reach your parents first.*"

"Kelsey," he growled. "*You're not going alone. We'll go together.*"

"Have you forgotten about him?" My eyes flared wide, shifting to Gunnar with a what-the-fuck-we-have-no-choice look. Having Liam in my head had its downfalls, like no private thoughts, at least until I learned to block him, but it also was damn handy, like now.

We stared at Gunnar.

The prick might not understand what was happening, but he took the opportunity to negotiate his freedom. "You could always let me go. We could deal with this issue at another date."

The heir prince didn't like his suggestion, and before I could utter a snappy retort, Liam planted his fist into the center of Gunnar's face with a sickening crunch. Liam packed quite the punch. He'd definitely broken the hunter's nose, and I was pretty sure he rendered him unconscious. Gunnar's head fell to the side.

I listened for a second to make sure his heart still beat.

It did. For now.

"What the hell, Liam?" Annoyance was clear in my tone.

Liam shoved off Gunnar's limp form, straightening to his full height. "Look, he's not a problem now."

I snorted. "Oh, and do you plan to bring his body with us as we go to meet my parents?" Apparently, having sex and bonding with him didn't instantly cure the tension between us, just proving it hadn't all been sexual vibrations. The heir prince still made me crazy.

Regarding Gunnar's body, Liam shrugged, seeming less concerned about the hunter and more worried about my parents, which might have been wise if I was honest with myself. "I'll get Riven and Colsen to take care of him until we decide what to do. They'll see after Hope."

Panic fisted in my chest. "When are your parents due back?" I asked, wondering what the hell we were going to do or say to mine when they crossed the border.

The heir prince bent down at the knees, grabbing Gunnar's arms and hauling him up over his shoulder. He did so without breaking a sweat. "I don't know. Not until sunrise at the earliest, but if word gets out the Hot Springs pack has crossed into our borders unannounced..."

I shouldn't have been impressed with the sheer strength Liam possessed, and yet, I couldn't stop my heart from flipping. Now was not the time for fated feelings. My focus had to stay on the problem at hand. Or in this instance, problems. "It will mean trouble," I finished for him.

As if I needed any more shit to go wrong tonight.

As he adjusted the hunter's body like a sack, Liam's hard gaze held mine. "I've come to expect trouble when you're involved."

I rolled my eyes, but there was some truth to his words. "Are you sure we shouldn't just kill him?" It seemed like a lot of extra work to take Gunnar prisoner. Not to mention, where did he mean to keep him? Especially, hidden from his father. And now we were involving Riven and Colsen, making it harder to keep this secret from the pack. Too many people involved. Too many voices that could slip within a pack that shared thoughts.

Liam started toward where we'd parked the car, carting Gunnar's extra weight over one shoulder. "I'm not saying we won't. Once I get to the truth, he's dead."

I sucked in my bottom lip. I shouldn't think about who might miss Gunnar, but it was a concern, and we needed to make sure his disappearance wouldn't come back to bite us in the ass. Other than Hope, I knew next to nothing about Gunnar's personal life or whether he had any family. He struck me as a loner, and I wondered, despite being nearly eighteen, if he lived on his own. It wouldn't have surprised me to learn he did.

I mean, he'd been experimented on, turned into something not human and not wolf either. Surely, his mother wouldn't have volunteered her son for such treatment. Perhaps Gunnar was an orphan or a runaway, making him the perfect candidate.

Sympathy wasn't something I could afford toward him. If Gunnar had succeeded tonight, I'd have been the one caged and experimented on.

"What are we going to tell Hope?" *Oh my god. Hope!* She was still out in the woods. Had the pack found her?

"Calm down. She's safe," Liam assured. "And we're not going to tell her anything. Yet."

I kept my pace in time with his, meaning I had to walk twice as fast. "I don't want to lie to her. She's my only friend here, and she deserves to know that this asshole isn't who he's pretending to be."

"Agreed," he grunted.

Look at us working together.

Riven and Colsen were waiting for us where we parked, leaning against Hope's car. Colsen pushed off the bumper at our approach, his brown eyes dark with fury. "What do you want us to do with him?" he asked, opening the trunk.

I scanned the car, looking for Hope, needing to see her for myself. Riven's green eyes followed me. "She's still unconscious," he murmured, coming up behind me as I peered in through the passenger side window.

I blew out a breath. "That's probably not a bad thing."

Riven shoved his hands into his pockets as Colsen helped Liam dump Gunnar into the trunk. "You smell different."

I held up my hands. "Blood. It's his, not mine," I replied, indicating with my eyes toward Gunnar.

Riven shook his auburn head, a strand of hair landing across his forehead. "No, that's not it." He craned his neck to the side. "You bonded."

My gaze narrowed. I wasn't altogether surprised, but I'd also hoped since it was only one-sided at this point Liam and I would be able to keep it a secret. But now with my parents coming, that dream was blown out of the universe. It wouldn't have mattered regardless if Riven could tell with my scent alone.

"Don't tell anyone," I quickly rushed out. "At least not yet. I need to talk to my parents before war breaks out." My connection to my parents was stronger than that to my pack, but I thought the distance might be enough to keep them from sensing the new link I'd formed with Liam.

Dumb.

Yet I clung to that slim chance, and when Liam and I had been alone in his bedroom, I hadn't been thinking of my parents or my pack. I'd only thought of Liam. Of me. Of what I wanted.

"This is a good thing, isn't it?" His brows lifted questionably.

"Depends on your perspective," I replied, staring at Hope lying in the back seat, her head turned away from me. My chest squeezed, guilt knotting inside me. She'd been in danger because of me. Gunnar had used her to get to me, used their friendship.

It made me sick.

Riven shook his head. "This is why I don't ever want to mate."

I could relate to his logic. Being linked to someone else meant you had another person to worry about—another person to protect—someone else who could be used to hurt you.

The trunk slammed shut with Gunnar tucked inside. Liam came to stand beside me. He put his hand on the small of my back. "You ready?" he asked.

I nodded. "I should clean up before we meet them. We both should."

"We can go to my house," he offered.

I shook my head, remembering the party we'd left behind. His birthday party. What a fucking gift. "Too many people. We can go to mine."

The heir prince didn't argue but shared a look with Colsen and Riven, silently giving them a command. I imagined it sounded something like *don't let him out of your sight.* And *keep her safe until I get back.*

Knowing Hope, we'd both have a lot of explaining to do about what happened tonight.

Liam ushered me to the BMW as Colsen got behind the wheel of Hope's car, starting the engine. Riven gave us one last glance before climbing into the passenger seat.

WHEN WE PULLED up to Nana's house, no lights shone other than the porch lantern she always left on. The elders, including Nana, were at a council meeting with the king. So, Liam and I had the house to ourselves. Assuming her visions hadn't given her an idea of what might have happened tonight. I thought back to when I'd left the house earlier. Nothing about her behavior struck me as odd, which I hoped meant she hadn't seen any of what went down, including me sleeping with Liam.

I cringed at the thought.

Nana's ability to see the future was often a burden I didn't know how she lived with, but I'd never considered her seeing me in compromising positions until now.

God, I prayed that was something we could both be spared. The embarrassment... I couldn't go there.

Shaking the thoughts from my head, I got out of the car and headed up the pathway to the front door. Liam followed me. I fumbled with the lock, my fingers trembling. *Keep it together, Kels*, I scolded, forgetting Liam was also in my head.

The heir prince put his hand over mine, taking the key from my unsteady hand. His shirtless chest warmed my back as he leaned over me. "Everything will be fine. I promise," he murmured, unlocking the door.

My whole body sighed, and for a moment, I allowed my back to rest against his chest, needing the comfort of touching him. His other hand came to my hip, sliding around to my lower stomach.

I didn't want to move.

I wanted to stay like this, wrapped in Liam—encompassed in a bubble of our making without the outside world.

I wanted to turn in his arms and press my lips to his.

Then I remembered I smelled like shit, covered in dirt, blood, and who the hell knew what else I picked up in the woods. It was bad enough that his birthday was tainted. I didn't want to associate Liam's lips with blood and tragedy.

Finding an inner strength I didn't know I possessed, I stepped out of his arms and opened the door. "We don't have much time," I said, walking inside. My connection to my pack intensified. They were gaining ground, closing in on the borders of Riverbridge.

Darkness greeted us along with the fragrance of lavender, eucalyptus, and sage. Nana's house forever smelled like a garden of herbs and flowers, pleasant and homey.

Calmed by the familiar scents, I reached for Liam's hand, not bothering to flip on a light. "This way," I said, leading him through the house to my room. Only then did I hit the switch on the wall, flooding my bedroom in a soft yellow glow.

I'd left my room in a state of disarray, but I didn't have the luxury to care or be concerned about what Liam thought of it.

This was the first time he'd been in my personal space.

I stared at the heir prince. "We should shower," I suggested, only to wince. Crap. That came out wrong. It was as if I suddenly forgot how to act around him. Hell, be alone with him. "Separately," I added for clarification, snatching a shirt I'd left on the bed and tossing it into my closet. We didn't have time for any of this after-sex awkwardness. It would have to wait. We'd already pushed it aside once tonight, a few more hours wouldn't make things any less weird.

Liam stood inside the room, his gaze panning from wall to wall, taking in the cream-colored paint, the unmade, wrinkly bed, the bra strewn on the top pile of clothes, and his lips quirked. "So, there is a softer side to you."

"Now is not the time to dissect the multiple facets of my personality. Do you want to go first?" I offered, thinking it would give me time to pick up my room or at least remove the undergarments discarded on the floor.

He shook his head. "Go ahead. I need to make a few calls."

"Suit yourself." I went to my dresser and pulled out clean clothes, scooping up the bra off the floor as I headed to the en suite bathroom. Pausing over the threshold, I turned around. Liam had his phone out. "Don't touch anything," I warned.

His aqua eyes lifted. "Don't worry, pup. I won't go through your panty drawer. Unless you ask."

How could he still give me shit at a time like this? Better yet, how the hell could he enjoy it?

I flipped him off, the banter easing a bit of the tension rocketing within me.

Discarding my grimy clothes into the garbage, I stripped and cranked the shower to hot. I didn't need to just get clean. I needed to sanitize. Not to mention, suppressing the urge to ask Liam to join me.

Going through a crisis the same night you mated was a torture I didn't recommend. My body couldn't figure out what the hell to do. The newly formed link to Liam made me want to always be close to him. Not just in the same space but touching and other intimacies.

I shoved my head under the steaming water spraying, banishing all thoughts of Liam Castle.

"It won't work, pup." His voice sounded in my head, followed by a toe-curling chuckle.

I let out a long growl, dropping my head against the shower wall.

"That was so unfair. Stay out of my head," I said as soon as I flung the bathroom door open, emerging into my bedroom. And then my eyes landed on Liam spread out on my bed like a delectable late-night snack.

What the fuck.

It hadn't even been twenty-four hours, and I was seriously regretting my reckless, impulsive, lust-hazed decision to mate the heir prince.

I couldn't do this for two months. My birthday was at the end of December. Like literally the last day of the year.

"You're not the only one who can't wait for your birthday," he said softly, his heated eyes never leaving mine.

I was staring, and I couldn't stop. Liam in my bed did shit to my body that should be illegal. It didn't help the bastard was shirtless, and the button of his borrowed jeans was still flipped open. Squeezing the towel into my hair, I ripped my gaze off him, ignoring the warmth staining my cheeks. "Your turn."

At some point, Liam and I were going to have to set some ground rules. *After* we stopped all hell from breaking loose between our packs.

I waited until the door closed and the shower turned on before sinking onto the bed—the same bed that now smelled like Liam. *Fabulous.* Now I needed to wash my sheets. Or did I?

While drying my hair with the towel, I contemplated the pros and cons in my head of sleeping in a bed smelling like the heir prince. It kept me distracted from the impending meeting with my parents.

Knock. Knock. Knock.

I jumped at what sounded like knuckles rapping against glass, and my gaze reeled to the window. My heart thundered in my chest. I prayed it was only the wind or a branch hitting the window, but as soon as I glanced through the pane, I gasped.

A shadow stood on the other side.

"Open the window!" the shadow hollered, pressing a face into the windowpane.

My senses were slow, thanks to the exhaustion nagging at every part of me, and it took me a moment to realize it was a shifter.

Not any wolf. Leith.

And I was going to kill him for startling my already frantic heart.

Rushing to the window, I threw it open, aiming him a look of displeasure. "Leith, you scared the shit out of me. Why didn't you use the front door?"

He shrugged, his sandy hair disheveled from the wind. "I saw your light on, and I wasn't sure if your grandmother was at the council meeting tonight."

"She is. And don't ever let her catch you referring to her as a grandma. She'll tear your ear off."

His lips twitched. "Noted."

I shot a glance back to the bathroom door where the shower still ran before looking at Leith again. "What are you doing here?" I could smell the alcohol on his breath, reminding me we'd both been at Liam's birthday party earlier in the evening.

"Liam said to bring this." Leith slipped the straps of a black bag off his shoulders. "He said it was urgent and to grab him a change of clothes." He passed me the bag through the window, and my wolf sense picked up traces of Liam's scent.

Leith's gaze darted past me into my room. "What the hell is going on?" he asked, his eyes settling back on me as a serious frown tugged at his mouth. "Liam wouldn't say on the phone, only to hurry. Why did you leave the party? Where did you go? And why did he take my car?"

Of course, he would have so many questions, and Liam had left his brother to me to deal with. A colorful string of words flittered through my head that I hoped the heir prince heard. I put the bag on the bed for Liam to find. "I've got so much to tell you. Fuck, I don't even know where to start." Shoving the window frame up higher, I climbed through, dropping down onto the ground beside him. "It's better if we talk out here."

His gaze narrowed, a glint of concern in them. "You're starting to freak me out. I thought I got a whiff of blood from your room."

"Don't worry. We're both okay," I quickly assured. The fuzzy socks covering my feet crunched over a layer of dried leaves. "It wasn't our blood."

"That doesn't particularly ease my worries." He looked me over, matching his pace with mine. "Are you sure you don't want to throw on some shoes or a sweater?"

"I'm fine. Really." I started to walk away from the house into the yard. Liam followed, waiting for me to explain what was happening. Where did I begin? I thought an apology might be a good start. "I'm sorry we left without saying anything. I couldn't risk that Gunnar might be lying. He wasn't. But I didn't know that at the party." I was bumbling the explanation, my mind trying to make sense of everything.

Leith blinked, staying by myself as we continued to walk. "What does Gunnar have to do with this?"

I took a much-needed breath, the air cooling my lungs. "Everything." My gaze went to the woods bordering Nana's house, the memories of tonight fresh in my head, rolling through my memory like a film. "I didn't know at the party it was Gunnar who sent me the texts, who'd been threatening me since I got here."

"Gunnar?" Leith repeated, skepticism darkening his features. His feet halted in the grass.

I nodded, turning to face him. "He's the hunter. The one who's been following and attacking me."

He flinched as if my words were a physical blow. I understood the feeling. "You're sure?" he asked like he needed me to say it again for the truth to sink in.

A pang squeezed in my chest, the betrayal of someone I thought of as a friend too raw. "Unfortunately," I replied grimly. "He took Hope as ransom tonight. That's where Liam and I went."

"Alone!" Leith proclaimed, nibbles of anger gnawing at his tone.

"Like I said, I couldn't risk Hope's safety. It was a gamble bringing Liam, but he refused to let me go by myself."

Leith shook his head, tension tightening his stubbly jaw. "I told you he had a few redeeming qualities."

"Yeah, if you consider stubbornness redeemable," I mumbled, and I swore I heard Liam chuckle in my head. Learning to block the heir prince from all my thoughts might be priority number one once I defused tonight's problem.

I finished telling Leith the details about Gunnar and how he was made, making him not quite human or wolf. But when I was about to get to the part of who Gunnar claimed was responsible, Liam growled in my head.

"Don't tell him what Gunnar said. Not until I figure out the truth."

I understood Liam protecting his brother and even his father. Without proof, it would do no one any good to jump to conclusions. Accusing the alpha of something of this magnitude would have dire consequences. We had to be sure.

Leith took a moment to stare up at the moon, absorbing things I'd hidden from him for weeks. "Did he tell you who hired him?"

God, I hated lying.

I chose my words carefully. "Riven and Colsen have him. I'm not sure where. Liam wouldn't tell me."

Leith had unyielding faith in his brother. "He'll find out who sent the hunters. Don't worry. Liam is ruthless. One of his other qualities, but I can't necessarily say it's a redeeming characteristic."

"More like annoying." But in this instance, I was grateful. Knowing Liam wouldn't rest until he uncovered the truth alleviated a fraction of my unease. I had a lot to stress about, including what would happen to us if his father was behind the attacks.

Leith and I started aimlessly walking around again, listening to the crickets chirp. Through the open window, I heard the shower stop running. A good thing because we had to leave. Soon. It was hard to judge distance-wise how close my pack was, but I'd rather be waiting to greet them at the borders than have them barreling over the line, ready to fight.

And they were definitely on a warpath.

I might not be able to pick up their thoughts, but their emotions were clear through our pack link. Urgency. Treachery. Strife. And anger in the forefront, leading the race.

They were coming for revenge.

"Are you going to tell me what else has you on edge?" Leith asked, his eyes on me. "I can...sense things have changed with you. I assume my brother has something to do with it."

God, it might be easier for me to make a bulletin post about the change in my relationship with the heir prince. Maybe I should send out a mass group email to everyone in the Riverbridge pack rather than answer this question a million times. "My parents are on their way because they think Liam and I broke the treaty."

Leith's brows furrowed. "Why would they think that?"

My fingers massaged the knot forming at the base of my neck. "I might have claimed him."

His eyes widened. "Kels, you didn't." He saw the serious expression on my face and watched it remain unchanged. "Shit, I can't leave you alone for two minutes."

"It just happened." A feeble excuse even to my ears.

Dried leaves crunched under our feet. "Do you know what you've done?" he hissed, and it was odd hearing disapproval from Leith.

I grimaced. "Not what my parents think. I didn't break the treaty. Liam's eighteen."

"So, for his birthday gift, you bit him."

"Something like that," I muttered. "But the point is, Liam didn't claim me. The rules of the treaty are still very much intact."

Leith started to put together the pieces. "But your parents don't know that."

I shook my head. "No. And they're coming."

He sighed, glancing up at the moon. "When?"

I rubbed my hands over my arms, wishing I'd grabbed a hoodie after all. "In less than an hour."

"Shit," Leith whispered, understanding the depth of our situation. "I'm not sober enough to handle this."

"I wish I wasn't sober."

A hand touched the small of my back, tingles radiating over my spine as my body flushed. *Liam.*

His eyes connected to his brother's, a look passing between them. "We should go," Liam said to me, a coldness in his gaze that hadn't been there before.

It had been weeks since I'd seen my parents, and you would think I'd be excited. I wasn't. Not when the reason for their visit could mean trouble for Liam and me.

I nodded.

As much as my legs wanted to run, I couldn't flee from this problem.

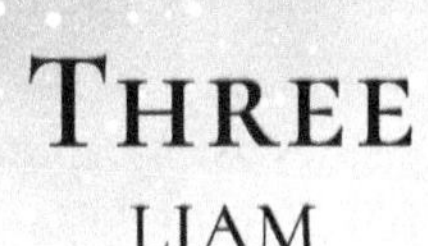

THREE
LIAM

"Leith, gather as much of the pack as you can," I ordered. "I already informed Dad." I could count on my brother, but Kelsey wasn't the only person I shielded. I'd been protecting Leith his whole life, and although we shared many secrets, the idea our father might be breaking shifter law wasn't one I was ready to unburden on him.

Leith's gaze shifted to my mate. "You and I aren't done talking," he told her.

I held back my wolf's growl rising in my throat.

Kelsey went back into the house to put on some shoes and a hoodie at my insistence. Her hair was still damp from the shower, and I didn't need her getting sick.

Leith arched a brow, watching me. "I can tell there's more to the story."

My chest drew tight. Leith and I might have our differences, but we were close. He never coveted the position I held as the alpha's firstborn, but I envied him and the freedom his life offered. "I haven't figured it out yet, but when I do, you'll know."

"I can live with that." A breath of silence passed. "So, Kelsey took the plunge but not you? I always knew you had unparalleled control,

but I'm impressed, bro. On your birthday too." He craned his head to the side, looking at my neck where two canine marks marred my skin.

Inside the house, I could hear Kelsey scampering about. "It was the hardest thing I've had to do so far in my life."

Leith shook his head, a look of sympathy on his features. "And you have to fight the urge to claim her for the next two months. Can you do it?"

My fists clenched at my sides as my spine bristled. "I don't have a choice. For the sake of the pack, I must." Duty first. My heart had never been considered in the decision when the treaty was signed. And now my heart was a tangled mess.

The only way to get through the next eight weeks was to put distance between Kelsey and me. Our connection was strong. At some point, my self-control would crack.

And yet my heart ached at the thought of staying away from her. A sharp pang seized my chest like being pierced with a silver blade.

My duty and heart would continue to war.

"You better not hurt her," Leith said with an edge, walking toward the driveway where his car was parked.

This wasn't the first, and I doubted it would be the last, time my brother warned me about hurting Kelsey. It wasn't physically he worried about. He knew I'd never harm her. His concern was for her heart.

Leith and Kelsey had gotten close over the last few weeks, and I couldn't deny feeling a shred of jealousy. She was *my* mate. I didn't want to share her. Especially now.

It seemed as if everyone else worried about Kelsey. What about my feelings? Despite how strong or heartless my reputation perceived me, I had a heart, and it could be broken. The vice around my chest squeezed tighter. "Right now, keeping her alive is more important to me than hurting Kelsey's feelings."

He considered my words. "Just try not to be a massive dick all the time."

I only made promises I could keep. "I'll see you at the bridge," I said, ending any further argument.

My dismissal wasn't immediately obeyed as Leith searched my face in the dark for another moment or two. "Be careful," he whispered before turning and heading to his car.

Kelsey came bounding out of the house, her long, dark hair getting caught in a gust of wind, blowing it out of her face and distracting me briefly from the turmoil coiling within me.

God, is she beautiful.

Like seriously breathtaking.

She didn't need makeup or fancy clothes to steal the air from my lungs. Who fucking knew I had a thing for girls in combat boots and hoodies.

It didn't matter what she wore. She looked good in anything. And even better wearing nothing.

"You ready?" she asked, stopping in front of me.

I brushed the back of my knuckles down the side of her cheek. The desire to kiss her beat strongly in my chest.

What the hell? Why shouldn't I kiss her?

We deserved a moment to ourselves before shit hit the fan. Depending on how things went tonight, I might not get the chance again.

She stared up at me with a tornado of emotions, and all I thought about was how much I wanted to quiet the storm.

Threading my fingers into her windblown hair, I tipped her head back as I closed the distance between us. The soft lines of her body pressed into me, and my lips took hers.

I sighed into her parted mouth, the first taste of her like coming home after being gone for months. My fingers cradled against her head, drawing her deeper into the kiss.

Her fingers curled against the front of my shirt as my tongue stroked and teased hers.

I hadn't meant for either of us to get carried away or lost, but her mouth was hot on mine. So. Damn. Hot.

The stirrings of desire danced down my spine, straight to other parts of me that had no business hardening, and yet, I couldn't stop my body from wanting her.

Knowing she tied herself to me only intensified my need, which I found both terrifying and exhilarating.

Kelsey always seemed to kiss with a reckless edge that made my wolf want to howl. I had to pull away before I walked her back inside her house and closed the door, consequences be damned.

Fuck, the way I was feeling tonight, the way I needed her, we wouldn't even make it inside. Taking Kelsey under the moonlight was a fantasy I planned to live out.

Just not tonight.

I broke off the kiss, both of us panting and clinging to each other as the light from the moon shone over our faces. My wrist tingled, and I knew without looking that the mark of the moon shone.

"Liam," she murmured, dropping her forehead to my chest.

"It will be all right," I said, allowing my chin to rest on the crown of her head for a moment. One more single moment.

And then...

Steeling myself, I flipped the switch, turning everything off.

I had no choice but to be the heir prince. I couldn't show any weakness in front of her parents. They needed to believe I was capable of protecting their daughter—that she would be safe in our pack.

The problem? I no longer was sure she was.

I wished I could go into this meeting assuring her parents I'd taken care of the hunter. It wouldn't be a complete lie. I did have Gunnar. He wasn't dead...yet, but he also wouldn't be the only hunter. Others would come once they realized Gunnar was no longer in commission.

The hunt for Kelsey was far from over.

KELSEY HAD the window open with her face turned toward the cool, evening breeze rushing inside. My fingers flexed on the steering wheel.

Leith would meet me at the bridge after he gathered as many of our pack members as he could. Half the younger ones were passed out in our house or on the front lawn.

Not exactly the eighteenth birthday party I planned.

Hot Springs was only a few hours away, just over the Wyoming border into South Dakota. It didn't give us much time to prepare, and my parents wouldn't make it back from the regional council in time.

Coincidence?

It was difficult to ignore destiny.

Perhaps this was a twisted test of fate.

I wanted to offer Kelsey words of comfort, but I didn't know what to say, so silence continued to fill the truck.

We weren't the first ones to arrive at the bridge. Relief at the dozen other pack members lingering about, including Leith, expelled from my chest. Many chose their wolf forms in case the discussion with her parents turned feral.

Kelsey toyed with the hood strings hanging from her sweatshirt, twisting and knotting them around her fingers as we waited. I didn't need to be bonded to tell that nerves were getting the best of her.

More of my pack arrived. The lesser-ranked wolves stayed in the trees' shadows, waiting for a command. The night drew on, and in only a few hours, the first rays of sunrise would peek through the trees.

Someone's cell phone rang, blaring through the relatively quiet woods. Kelsey jumped.

"You need to calm down." My voice came out clipped from where I relaxed against the bridge railings.

She turned her eyes to me, narrowing them. "Why aren't you freaking out more?"

I rested the back of my elbows on the wooden beams. "What makes you think I'm not concerned?"

"The fact that I literally can feel your emotions," she snapped, a frown marring those delectable lips. "You're way too collected, and it's getting on my nerves." Her eyes panned the towering pines. The damp ground from an earlier storm gave off an earthy aroma.

"It doesn't seem to matter what I do. I always get under your skin, pup."

She scoffed. "Ain't that the truth." Letting out a puff of air, she came to stand beside me, the river flowing under the bridge trickling beneath us. "People could get hurt," she whispered.

It was true. "Not you. I won't let anyone touch you."

She rolled her eyes. "It's not me I'm worried about. No one in my pack would dare harm me."

My jaw tightened as I did a mental check-in with the shifters who came to defend our pack. "Let's hope your parents are feeling reasonable tonight." I didn't want bloodshed. I didn't want to fight. Not after what I'd already been through with Gunnar, but I would do whatever it took to make her parents understand the treaty hadn't been broken. Colored outside the lines a little, yes, but still within the rules.

She pinned me with a look I'd rather have directed at someone other than me. "Have you ever known a pack to enter another's borders unannounced just to talk?"

She had me there. "We'll make them listen."

"You don't know my parents," she scoffed. "They've been waiting for any excuse to wage a war against your father. He isn't the only one harboring deep resentment for what went down between our parents."

"Something else we have in common." If my father was here, the outcome might be different than what I hoped to achieve tonight. I had no intention of fighting her parents or her pack. "But they support the treaty?" I asked, trying to figure out the best approach to soothing this shit situation before it unnecessarily escalated, harming both packs.

"Trust me. I don't understand my parents either. On one hand, they've pounded into me from the day I was born that my duty was to marry you. On the other, they never hid their dislike for your father. He was always a sore topic in our house."

I could relate all too well. Duty before anything else, especially when it came to orders issued or sealed by the king. "We're not our parents, pup. You and I might not have had a choice in our partners, but we can choose to be better than our parents. We can end the animosity between our packs."

A glint of hope entered her troubled eyes. "Do you really think you and I can make that happen?" She kept her voice low, looking at me expectantly.

It wouldn't have mattered what Kelsey asked of me at that moment. I would have promised her anything. I gave her the truth as best as I could. "I don't know, but we can try."

She wrapped her arms around herself, battling the cold biting the evening air.

I longed to pull her into me, securing her against my chest and offering her my warmth, but I couldn't drop my defenses. Not yet.

If there was one thing I'd learned since Kelsey came into town, she weakened my resolve. Her eyes had a way of penetrating the iciness I erected, making me feel vulnerable, an emotion I hated.

The alpha's heir had no place for vulnerability.

"Are you okay?" I asked, thinking she looked as if she could lie down on the bridge and fall asleep within seconds.

Blinking slowly, she nodded.

I'd feel better having Colsen and Riven by my side, but I didn't trust Gunnar to be left alone, which meant I had to do without my two most trusted allies.

At the end of the bridge, Jacy, my father's second-in-command, stood with his beefy arms crossed. He had the kind of muscles that could snap a person in half. He was my uncle, and despite the tough exterior, he was a whole lot more fun to be around than my father.

Guilt kicked me in the gut as I remembered Hope. I hadn't had time to check on her, other than a quick text from Riven assuring me she was fine. Pissed but otherwise unharmed.

I doubted Uncle Jacy had an inkling what happened to his daughter tonight, or that his brother might be directly responsible.

I didn't want it to be true.

Not because I thought my father was a stand-up guy because he wasn't. I didn't want it to be true for Leith. For my mother. For Jacy. For the pack.

And if it was true, I didn't doubt for a second that my father would have a valid reason—that it would somehow be for the benefit of the pack. He could talk his way around any problem. Some might say he was clever with words. I always thought his tongue was slick.

Minutes dragged on, the pack growing unsettled and fidgety. "*Anything?*" Jacy inquired through our pack link.

"*Not yet,*" I sent back.

"*Should she be here?*" he questioned about the girl beside me.

A muscle in my jaw ticked. "*Do you want to try and make her leave? By all means, I'd like to see you try.*"

Jacy's hard eyes met mine from across the bridge. "*You know not a single wolf in the pack would touch her.*"

"*Exactly. She's safe beside me.*"

Kelsey noticed the scowl lines that formed over my brow during my internal conversation with the beta. She angled her head to the side, regarding me. "You're acting different. Your emotions changed."

"How so?" I asked, shifting my weight, the wolf within restless. I didn't want to admit that when Jacy suggested Kelsey not be here a flare of jealousy barreled into me, unbridled and wild.

At least she'd stop pacing, even if it was to glare at me. "I don't know. Cold. Indifferent. Like the asshole I first met."

"I've always been that asshole," I reminded her.

"So being a dick is your default setting."

My lips twitched despite me trying to keep a straight, unaffected expression. I couldn't afford to be swayed by her. What my pack needed was for me to be the cold and calculating heir prince. With my father gone, the leadership of the pack fell to me.

I quickly banished the inkling of humor, deepening my scowl. "Stop distracting me."

Her lashes batted, and for the first time since my party, a hint of a smile touched her lips. I ignored the warmth blooming in my stomach, focusing on the cold, but it was so damn hard when my eyes wouldn't stray from her lips.

Only hours ago, that mouth had been so damn hot on mine, doing the most sinful things to me.

Kelsey's spine stiffened, those mesmerizing violet eyes widening. "They're almost here."

No sooner had the words left her did my ears picked up the faint pounding of a pack traveling.

They were here.

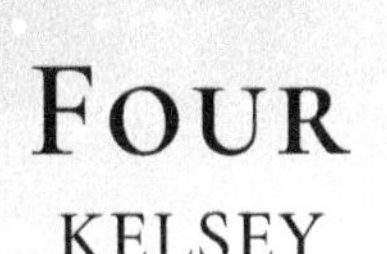

FOUR

KELSEY

Tingles of apprehension danced in my stomach, and regardless of the dread, a glimmer of excitement poked through. Weeks had gone by since I'd seen my parents, my friends, my pack, and a part of me shone in elation, eager to see their faces.

But fear kept my feet planted.

Liam's shoulder touched mine as he stood beside me at the center of the bridge. A precarious position and done deliberately, putting the heir prince and me directly in the middle of two packs, basically a metaphor for our relationship—caught between our parents.

The closer the stampede of paws thundering into the forest floor got, the faster my heart raced. A dense fog moved in with the dropping temperatures, curling over the damp earth and brush. The ground rumbled under my feet, shaking the leaves. My fingers wrung together until I caught the first glimpse of something glowing.

In the dark corners of the woods, the gleam of wolves' eyes cut through the mist. One after another.

They were my father's scouts, the wolves he trusted to observe ahead and relay any threats present. I could feel them in my link to the pack, but I noticed it wasn't as strong as it should be.

I snuck a glance at Liam, his muscles coiled for the first sign of an attack.

My bond with Liam weakened the connection I had to my pack, and soon, I would lose the tie altogether. Nothing would join me to the wolves I grew up with. I'd belong to another group completely—an outsider.

I couldn't imagine.

Scanning the forest, I picked out the familiar wolves. Dane. Sherice. Lucas. Ethan. Mia. CT. Justin.

The erratic beats of their hearts pounded with mine, each wolf tipping their head slightly as my eyes passed over them. I was their hope—the one who claimed to bring peace between two warring packs.

I'd always despised the responsibility and duty I was born with, but for the first time, I held my head high and accepted my fate. To reject the treaty now would mean rejecting my own heart, and after what I'd done earlier tonight at Liam's party in his bedroom, I couldn't deny how much I wanted him.

The other stuff, the politics, the titles, the burden of leadership, I could have done without.

It was Liam I wanted.

Not the heir prince.

A woman in a white, flowy dress came through the trees, a trio of wolves flanking her on both sides. She didn't look a day over thirty. Beauty had never been a trait she lacked.

"Mom," I murmured, my heart breaking into a gallop. I might not have the closest relationship with her, but she was still my mom, and she tried as best as she could.

She opened her arms, and I jogged into her embrace. "Kelsey." She sighed, squeezing me tight. The scent of her shampoo and sweet wild bluebell perfume sent a familiar lump of emotion into my throat.

Something about seeing my mother and the comfort of her arms after a really fucking shitty day broke my walls. Tears welled in my eyes as she looked me over.

Her fingers came to frame my face, and she pulled back to look at me. The eyes so much like mine glistened with water. "You're okay." She brushed my hair with her hand. "You're really all right."

I bit back a sob, nodding. The sight of her blurred through the tears that kept falling. It was as if seeing her fractured the dam holding back weeks of emotions, and now they flooded my system, pouring out of me.

She hadn't changed. But the same couldn't be said for me. And she saw it in looking at me, her gaze sharpening.

"Nana advised me of the attacks. I feared when I felt a thread of our connection snap tonight something had happened," she explained, the worry evident in her soft tone.

She wasn't far off. Something had happened. A lot of somethings, but I didn't know how I could trust anyone. As much as I wanted to tell my mother about Gunnar, about us capturing the hunter tonight, Liam's voice was in my head.

"Don't, pup. Not yet."

It wasn't the hard edge of his voice that prevented me from confiding in the woman who gave birth to me. I already decided not to say anything. Besides Liam, the only person I could trust was Nana. I needed to speak with her first.

From the corner of my eye, I saw another shifter approach. Unlike my mother, he had no guards. Just him.

Dad.

He might not be as brawny as Rowan or as tall or a brute, but like most alphas, Lincoln Summers had an aura about him. To me, he represented safety and home. We shared the same humor and loved the same scary movies. If we were deciding where to eat out on a Friday night, Chinese was always our first choice.

I might look like my mother. I'd inherited her family's powers. But all those little personality quirks came from my father.

Taking his time, Dad strolled up the arched bridge toward me. Not a friendly bone in an inch of his body. His focus went past me to where Liam stood.

Only when he stopped directly in front of me did his gaze shift down. He engulfed me in a massive bear hug. "Hey, whiskers," he greeted in a brisk voice, letting me know he was unhappy. The childhood nickname struck a chord in my chest, tugging on my heartstrings.

My nose wrinkled as it had all the other times he used the endearment. "Hey, Dad."

"Where's your father?" he asked Liam over my head.

"At a council meeting with the king," the heir prince replied, the response icy.

My dad sidestepped around me, putting himself between Liam and me. My mate didn't like the insinuation of our positions, and surprisingly neither did I.

I belonged at Liam's side, something I never thought I would believe.

Spinning, I stared at my father's broad back. He was like a mountain erected to keep me from Liam. I stepped to the side so I could see the heir prince.

Liam's aqua eyes flashed, his wolf coming to the surface.

I had to step in before things went awry, but before I could dash in front of Dad, Mom put a hand on my arm, halting me. "Kelsey," she whispered sternly.

Liam's jaw tensed.

"Don't," Dad thundered. "Stay back. This is between the prince and me."

Like hell, it is.

"He's right, pup. Don't interfere," Liam warned.

I shook off Mom's hand and dashed around my father so I was directly in his path. "You have it wrong. Liam didn't do anything. It was me. So, if you're going to be pissed at anyone, your anger should be directed at me."

Dad steeled. His eyes remained fastened on Liam. "Max." One name bit out from his clenched mouth. One. Fucking. Name. Yet, I knew precisely what he ordered.

I shook my head, backing up. "No. Your sentinels won't stop me."

"If he touches her, he'll lose a leg," Liam threatened with a deadly calm that nearly made me shudder.

"Kelsey," Liam called through our bond.

I understood and backed away from my father as one of his sentinels stepped onto the bridge, golden eyes glowing. Maxtyn Evans. He wouldn't hurt me, but he would shred apart anyone who tried to interfere. It was his job. Max was a guard, one of my father's most ruthless wolves.

"Kelsey," my father growled, his eyes warning me not to take another step.

The three wolves at my mother's side bared their teeth at the heir prince, a deep, ferocious warning. Hurt shimmered in Mom's gaze, but they weren't leaving me a choice.

Liam's warmth grazed my back. "*I'm here.*"

I exhaled as the pressure in my chest lessened with my mate close.

The reunion was over.

"They're communicating," Mom whispered, her hand touching Dad's shoulder.

His features darkened.

This had gone off so much better in my head. How naive of me to think two alpha hotheads would be reasonable for one minute. It wasn't in their blood, just as it wasn't in mine to be a docile female.

The bridge after which the town had been named was neutral ground, but once any of my pack crossed over, they would be officially stepping into enemy territory.

I had to stop that from happening.

If I had to throw up a barricade of magic, I would. My powers were bound to get out eventually, and it wasn't like there weren't already whispers among wolves about my family.

Max's lip curled, his canines shining under the stars. Behind me, an answering rumble came from a few of Liam's wolves, but the heir prince held up a hand, silencing them.

"It's not what you think," I quickly said, hoping I could get an explanation out before my father gave any orders. "Well, it is, but it's not," I added, bumbling completely.

"You're not helping," Liam said.

"Shut up. And let me think," I fired back.

In front of my pack, I retreated a step, aligning with the heir prince, and laced my fingers with his. I wanted the statement to be very clear. This was my choice.

Liam was mine.

I chose him.

Chaos erupted.

I shouldn't have been surprised, and I couldn't say which side attacked first. One minute the trees surrounding us were silent, the next the woods swelled with gnarling, jaws snapping, and the unmistakable stench of blood.

The rocky shores on either side of the shallow river became a battleground. Liam shoved me behind him as Max moved forward to protect me, the heir prince's canines gleaming under the waning moonlight.

"We need to stop this," I projected to Liam, clenching the back of his arm behind him.

"Right now, all I care about is you not getting hurt."

"None of them will harm me."

"Release her," Max growled at Liam, his gold wolf eyes flashing at my mate. "She isn't yours to protect."

"The fuck she isn't," Liam snarled in return, the muscles under my fingers coiling.

On either side of the bridge, our wolves continued to fight. It sickened my stomach to see them tearing into each other. The sounds alone twisted me up into knots. Liam and I were supposed to be what brought our packs peace, not cause a bigger strife between us.

I sliced a glare at Max. "Call them off." Only two wolves had the authority to cease the attack from my pack. My father and Max. For the Riverbridge pack, it was either Liam or Jacy. If I couldn't get through to my father or Max, my only other choice was the heir prince.

"Liam!" I shouted through our bond. *"If you don't do something, I will."*

"Don't make matters—"

I darted to the side and hurdled over the edge of the bridge, jumping into the river.

"Jesus Christ," Liam grumbled as I fell.

"Kelsey!" my father hollered seconds before my feet splashed into a few inches of water.

Someone landed in the behind me. A second splash followed. Liam and Max had both jumped into the thick of trouble, except Max had shifted, his massive wolf glowering at Liam.

"What the hell are you doing?" the heir prince growled in my head.

I moved before either could grab a hold of me, heading straight for a trio of wolves. Canines bared and lips curled, they gnashed at each other, circling off the edge of the freezing river. *"Ending this before someone gets seriously hurt."*

"Goddamn it, pup."

Interjecting myself between the wolves, I held out my hands. "If you want someone to fight, you'll have to take on me." I flashed my violet eyes at them, spinning in a circle to keep track of the trio.

They stared at me, uncertain what their next course of action should be. "Don't tell me you lost your balls already," I taunted, not believing any of them would lay a hand on me, which made me stupidly brave.

"Stop!" my father boomed, his command also vibrating through my pack bond. He cursed as his eyes found mine in the mayhem. It took a few long heartbeats for the disorder between packs to halt. My father didn't speak again until he could be heard over the valley without projecting his voice at me. "Kelsey, do you know what you've done?" It was a rhetorical question he didn't really expect an answer for.

I craned my neck to look up at the bridge. "Everyone needs to take a breath. There doesn't need to be any bloodshed if you would just listen."

Liam kept his glower fixed on Max. If he so much as moved a muscle in my direction, the heir prince wouldn't hesitate to attack the guard. I very much wanted to avoid that fight.

My mother stepped up beside my father. She put a hand on his shoulder, giving him a light squeeze. His chest rose and fell before he replied. "You made your point. What is it you need to say that is so important you put yourself in danger?"

"You left me no choice." As usual. I was never given a say in the treaty, in who my mate was, in my future. Nothing had changed.

Except I had.

His brows furrowed as he stared down at me. "The terms have been broken. You're coming home."

Liam was suddenly at my side, his body making a clear statement. He wasn't letting me go anywhere.

"No, they haven't," I replied without thinking. This might not be a conversation to have in front of our packs, but it's too late now. "Not by Liam. And I am home," I added, my chin lifting.

The look my father aimed at us soured my stomach. I hated disappointing my family, and whether he meant for me to see the disapproval in his eyes or not, the damage was done. "Are you saying *you* violated the terms?"

I tucked in closer to Liam. "Yes."

Mom looked horrified for a second before regaining her royal composure.

Liam's fingers weaved with mine, lending me some of his strength, knowing I needed it. "It was my choice. I claimed the heir prince tonight, but he didn't reciprocate. He hasn't dishonored the treaty."

A collective gasp reverberated through the woods and over the trickling river at my feet. "You're saying you bonded yourself to him without Liam's claim? That it's only a one-sided bond?" He made it sound unfathomable and disgraceful.

And a seed of what-the-fuck-have-I-done sprouted in my stomach. "Yes. The heir prince has every intention of waiting to claim me until I turn eighteen as is directed in the treaty."

His fingers tightened on the wooden railing. "Why? Why would you do such a thing?"

I doubted my father wanted to hear it was lust that made me bite Liam on the neck and take his blood into my mouth.

Liam made a choking sound I prayed was only in my head, probably hearing my thoughts.

Annoyance took root in my chest. "Because it was what *I* wanted." I didn't know how clear I could make this point. But I would say it over and over again.

With my mother frowning at his side, Dad shook his head, his shoulders dipping slightly. "It doesn't matter, Kelsey. The treaty says *you* need to be eighteen."

"Liam is. He turned eighteen today. Actually, given the time, it was yesterday," I corrected, not that either of my parents cared about semantics.

"This is a problem neither Rowan nor I saw coming," my father stated.

I searched the wolves, looking for Tess, but she wasn't among the pack. My father hadn't brought the younger members, whereas, behind me, a dozen or more of the wolves in Liam's pack were my age.

Disappointment ribboned around my heart. I really wanted to see her. We still talked on the phone a few times a week when we could, and sure, FaceTime gave me the chance to see her, but it wasn't the same as being able to hug my best friend.

"What's wrong?" the heir prince demanded, and I felt his gaze shift to me.

"Nothing," I grumbled, his fingers still warming mine. My feet on the other hand were frozen, and I was about to lose some toes if I didn't get them dried off.

"Pup?" he prodded like the annoying wolf he was.

"It's stupid. I know this isn't a friendly visit from home, but I just really wanted to see my best friend."

His fingers squeezed against mine. *"It's not stupid."*

My father sighed, drawing attention back to him and my mother. "I need to speak with Rowan. I assume he is still at the summit?"

Liam nodded.

"My wolves and I will stay in neutral territory until he returns. You have my word that no one will cross over your borders during our stay except for one of my guards," my father added.

Liam's body stiffened at the same time my stomach dropped in dread, an unsettling feeling working its way into my body.

"What's the reason for the guard?" Liam demanded gruffly, his features darkening. Like any born alpha, he didn't like to be told anything.

"Until my daughter turns eighteen and the claiming is complete, one of *my* guards will stay with you." The statement my father declared was unmistakable. He didn't trust Liam or his father.

"No," I argued, anger chasing the cold from my veins. "I don't need a babysitter." Unfairness made my voice sharp.

But my father didn't budge. His jaw set in a firm line. "This isn't up for debate, Kelsey. It's for your protection as much as it is for the pack."

I turned pleading eyes onto my mother. She gave a slight shake of her head, her gaze telling me to accept this, that there was no way to change my father's mind.

Dad turned his gray eyes on Liam. "To ensure no other rules are bent, I request you allow one of my sentinels to stay within your borders. He will not interfere with pack business."

A request. I almost snorted. It wasn't a request he put forth to Liam. It was an order.

If the heir prince refused, the fighting would be more than a few scratches and punctured teeth marks. "I doubt my father would oppose, but it will be his decree. Until he returns, the guard can accompany her."

I snapped my eyes at Liam. It was one thing knowing my father put him in a delicate situation and another to hear him agree I should have a shadow at all times. I was pissed, not at Liam but at this whole fucked-up circumstance.

My father jerked his head, giving a silent order. Max's wolves moved through the ranks, and I watched, waiting to see who the unlucky asshole would be. Max joined my father at his side. Dark-brown fur covered his powerful form, ripples of gold streaking down his back.

It took me a moment to realize the meaning behind the exchange my father had with Max.

He wouldn't.

Not Maxtyn Evans.

Anyone but that asshole.

Max shifted into his human form again, taking the shirt and sweatpants my mother offered.

I refused to take my eyes off him. For one, I didn't want to see anything below his chest. And two, I wanted him to witness the displeasure and bitterness on my face.

Not that he gave two shits.

A smile curved the harsh lines of his face as he slipped the gray sweats over his hips.

Fuck. My. Life.

FIVE

LIAM

Fury and jealousy swam in my blood. If the wolf named Maxtyn kept looking at my mate, I might very well go back on my word and rip out his jugular. I didn't like him. Didn't like the look of him. Or the way he eyed Kelsey with amusement.

I could take him. There was no question.

But if I acted on emotions, my pack would suffer, and a handful of our wolves weren't in top form, thanks to my party. The peaceful way to end this meeting without any further violence was to let the arrogant prick through our borders.

Didn't mean I had to like it. Or him.

I cracked my neck to the side, the tension between Maxtyn and I building to a palpable thing.

"Your mother and I will be staying in Stars Lake for a few days," the alpha told his daughter. When Kelsey avoided his stare, he sighed and shifted his gaze to me. "I'll need to speak with your father when he returns."

I nodded, eager to get Kelsey out of here and somewhere warm.

Too angry to say anything to her parents as they turned to leave, Kelsey stood with her arms crossed and watched them disappear into the woods.

The pack followed, drifting deeper into the trees until only a few warriors were left. They would be the last to leave, while the scouts ran ahead. Everyone had their place in the pack—their role.

Maxtyn shoved his hands into the pockets of his sweatpants. "Come on, Kels, I'll take you home," he said in a deep, gruff voice.

Who the fuck does this asshole think he is? He might have been ordered to guard Kelsey, but that didn't mean he was responsible for her.

That job was mine.

"She came with me, and she'll leave with me." I had half a mind to order someone to get this asshole a shirt. I was done looking at the ripple of muscles I swore he flexed whenever Kelsey's narrowed gaze landed on him.

My fingers squeezed hers, but she didn't move. Hell, I didn't think she blinked. *"Are you okay?"*

Her eyes lifted to me as if she suddenly realized her pack was gone. *"Yeah, just tired."*

I frowned at her excuse, knowing it was only a partial truth. *"Let's go, pup. I'm taking you home."*

She followed obediently, and that was telling. I didn't wait until we got to the edge of the bridge. Before she passed out from sheer exhaustion, I scooped her up into my arms.

Her head immediately dropped into the space between my neck and shoulder with no resistance. *"This is the only time I'll thank you for manhandling me in front of the pack."*

I chuckled lowly.

She yawned. *"No one got hurt?"* she asked, her voice weakening through our bond as fatigue took over.

"No," I assured as I approached my truck. I hesitated, my arms unwilling to release her yet.

The guard opened the door, and I barely spared him a glance. It's all I could do to keep from knocking his teeth into the back of his head. He wouldn't be smirking then.

She was asleep before I tucked her into my truck.

Turning around, I glared at Maxtyn. I had two choices. I could leave the bastard here and make him find Kelsey's house. Or I could keep an eye on him and offer the outsider a ride.

"Get in," I ordered.

I had enough to deal with. Now I also had to watch this jerk. His duty was to protect Kelsey, but Maxtyn and I both knew he had a secondary goal. To observe our pack and report anything suspicious. As well as make sure I kept my word and didn't claim Kelsey until she turned eighteen.

With Riven and Colsen already stretched thin with guarding Kelsey and now Gunnar, I couldn't add to their responsibilities, especially since those orders came from me, not my father.

I had to bring someone else in, someone who was loyal to me first. Being the heir prince, I didn't lack friends within the pack, but that didn't mean they were all genuine or trustworthy, not with the secrets I'd been keeping lately.

My eyes lifted to the rearview mirror, glowering at the figure in my back seat. "Just so we're clear, you aren't the only wolf with eyes on *my* mate. Don't interfere with my guys, and we won't have a problem."

"I'm not here to step on your toes, but I will if it means keeping *my duchess* safe."

Duchess.

Kelsey was a luna duchess, the daughter of the pack's luna. It was her title within the pack, and yet it was so weird hearing it. *And* hearing it off *his* lips made me want to hurt him. Bad.

I tightened my fingers on the steering wheel, my knuckles going white. "She's no longer yours," I growled, making it known I'd already staked my claim.

"Not yet," he murmured as my truck jostled over the rough terrain toward the road.

If Kelsey hadn't been in the car, I would have slammed on the brakes and sent him sailing through the windshield.

I HATED HAVING to compromise when it came to my mate's safety. My ego believed I was enough to keep her alive. I'd been doing an okay job so far. If he wanted a guard on her, I had plenty of wolves available.

I didn't know dick about this Maxtyn. Let alone trust him with my mate.

As the prince, it was my duty to put the pack first, and agreeing to allow one of his wolves onto Riverbridge soil to avoid further fighting was the smart decision.

But...the overprotective alpha in me didn't want Maxtyn anywhere near my mate.

It might be in the best interest of the treaty, but fuck me, if I wouldn't lose my shit on more than one occasion between now and December thirty-first. The second I claimed Kelsey, I'd kick Maxtyn out of my fucking town, and hopefully, he landed on his ass on the way out.

I still had to deal with my father. It was hard to guess if he would be proud of my actions or fuming.

Shit. All this trouble had me momentarily forgetting about Gunnar's little secret condemning my father.

Dad and I had a lot to discuss when he returned from the summit.

Not an ounce of me looked forward to it.

After tucking Kelsey into her bed and checking on Riven and Colsen, I went home, intending to crash.

Kelsey and I both needed the rest.

What I hadn't bargained for when I finally laid my head down was the longing my wolf had for his mate. It didn't matter how exhausted my bones and muscles were. The wolf paced restlessly within me, prodding me to go to her.

A bad idea.

What I needed was the opposite of what my wolf wanted.

Space. A lot of it.

I couldn't think of another way to diminish the wanting. If we were alone, the craving to claim her would only intensify, and if I had any chance of surviving two months without making Kelsey my mate, I had little choice but to distance myself.

This seemed like a next-to-impossible task. Overcoming challenges usually gave me a thrill. Not fucking this time.

I wanted to destroy my room, claw at the walls, shred the bedding, or tear down the ceiling. The beast stirred like a wild frenzy within me.

She would choose this moment to pop into my head. *"Calm down. I can't sleep with you and your damn wolf arguing."*

The beast in question whimpered at the sound of her voice. *Traitor,* I scolded. I hadn't meant to wake her, and guilt slashed through me. *"Go to bed, pup. I can't handle you inside my head right now,"* I grumbled in response.

Her scoff came through loud and clear.

Once I allowed my body the necessary rest, my priority became finding a way to block our link. I couldn't afford Kelsey intruding into my thoughts at her whim.

Rolling over onto my side, I groaned into the pillow that smelled like her. I slammed my eyes shut, trying to divert my mind from reliving those moments in my bed, when she'd been under me and I'd been inside her. What it had been like to stop dreaming about stripping her bare and worshiping every inch of her delectable body but actually touching her.

I'd never touched skin as soft as hers.

This isn't fucking helping.

With a rough hand, I ripped the covers off me and tossed them to the ground before I tackled the pillowcases. If I didn't get rid of her damn scent, I'd go mad.

All I wanted was sleep.

But my body...it had other ideas.

I gave up any pretense of sleep and headed out of the house without a shirt or shoes. I had no need for them. When I stepped onto the porch into the crisp air, I stripped. The sun glistened at the edges of the mountain, warm light poking through any available holes in the trees covering the rocky incline.

The familiar tingles enveloped me completely, traveling from head to toe during the shift to wolf, and my thoughts were fixated on only one location.

I took off, my paws pounding the ground. The morning breeze tousled my white fur, transforming the tips into a shade more gold than silver. With only a few miles between our houses, the forest yielded to me swiftly in my wolf form, and I emerged into her yard.

The house stood silent, the sun's ascent casting reflections off the windows. Birds chirped and flitted away as I approached the window of the girl sleeping inside. With each step, my wolf settled, and I cursed his persistent nature. *One night*, I told him.

I couldn't let this become a recurring issue. Spending every night outside her bedroom window was already too close. I could discern the gentle rhythm of her breath and the soft, steady thump of her heart.

The temptation to crawl through the window was there, inciting me. I ignored the urge and nestled under the tree closest to her window, finally falling asleep.

☽☽●☾☾

"AHEM." A throat cleared, drawing me out of sleep. I didn't want to open my eyes. They were far too heavy and felt as if I just shut them moments ago. Something told me to ignore whoever disturbed me and go back under—a defense mechanism because once I fully woke, there would be no pretending the last twenty-four hours hadn't happened.

The intruder showed unwavering persistence, their presence preventing me from being able to tumble back into the dream I hadn't wanted to wake from.

I swore, if Leith was messing with me…

With my eyes closed, I reached for a pillow to toss across the room except it wasn't a fluffy down pillow my hand connected with but a patchy bit of what felt like damp grass.

What the hell?

Cracking an eye, I peeked to see I was indeed not in my fucking room but outside. *Shit.* Fully awake, I glanced up to see the sun haloing around Penelope Nightingale in a warm glow making her look more angel than a wolf.

This had to be a dream. Strange…but a dream all the same. Mrs. Nightingale had the sight. Perhaps she could invade my sleep. Was she here to warn me? Had something happened to Kelsey?

Bolting upright, I shoved a hand through my hair, brushing out a few leaves. "What happened? Is she hurt?"

"Good morning," she greeted, a warm smile on her lips. "I let you sleep in while I tended my garden. You looked like you needed it." She tossed a T-shirt and a pair of sweats to me. "And my granddaughter is fine, relatively speaking."

Too many memories came surging to the forefront of my mind. Including where I'd run through the woods to Kelsey's house. I remembered.

This wasn't a dream.

Crap.

And fuck. I'm naked.

"Thanks," I mumbled gratefully. If Mrs. Nightingale was home, that also meant so was my father. A groan of dread pitted at the base of my throat. I was surprised he hadn't summoned me. "I'm sorry, I didn't mean to still be here." I pulled on the shirt before moving to slip on the pants and stand.

Her lips pursed. "A lot has happened. Would you care to join us for lunch?" she asked. "We have much to catch up on it seems."

I should refuse and go home. My father would be waiting, not that I was eager to see him.

Mrs. Nightingale shifted the basket to the side of her hip. "I let your mother know you were here and told her I'd send you home after I fed you."

I nodded, convincing myself it wasn't a chance for a glimpse of Kelsey that propelled me to accept. Lies. All lies.

The paisley print of her teal skirt blew in the wind, dancing around her ankles as she walked toward the porch. "Hopefully after a full stomach, you'll have a clearer head."

Mrs. Nightingale had a gift like her granddaughter yet not the same. I didn't question how she knew about the turmoil spiraling within me.

Bracelets of silver and gold jingled up her arm as she reached for the screen door. Remembering my manners, I quickly moved to open the door for her.

Inside, my wolf picked up traces of Kelsey, and he was damn pleased to be in the same vicinity as her. I followed Mrs. Nightingale into her kitchen where Maxtyn sat at the table. He eyed me with the same distrust and disdain I sent him.

With her bracelets chiming, she set the basket on the counter and faced Maxtyn and me. "Which one of you wants to tell me why I have two wolves from two different packs sleeping at my house?"

Maxtyn and I shared a tense look.

"Where's Kelsey?" I asked instead of answering.

"Still sleeping. She's safe," Mrs. Nightingale added as if she knew I needed to hear it. I did. "Have a seat," she gestured to the table, dragging the basket of fresh produce to the sink.

My shoulders relaxed as I sunk into the chair opposite Maxtyn.

He scooped a helping of pasta salad on his plate alongside the sandwich already there, his frown never slipping. "Why are you here?" he asked me.

Mrs. Nightingale handed me a plate. "Help yourself to as much as you'd like. There's plenty more for when my granddaughter decides to crawl out of bed."

I waited until Mrs. Nightingale went to fill a pitcher of tea before I answered Maxtyn's question. "None of your concern," I retorted, refraining from swearing when I really wanted to drop the F-bomb.

"If it has anything to do with Kelsey, it does," he countered, an arrogant smirk playing at his lips.

My fingers smashed into the sandwich I grabbed from the platter. "That's where you're wrong. You're here to make sure the hunters don't get within a hundred yards of her. That's all."

With his mouth full of pasta, he said, "Someone has to pick up your slack."

If he only knew what I'd done to keep this girl safe. "Don't get too fucking comfortable."

We'd both forgotten where we were and whose company was among us. He arched a smug brow. "Afraid I might steal your girl?"

My stomach twisted at the thought. "Not possible. She's already mine." I bit into my sandwich, hungrier than I knew.

His gold eyes pierced mine. "Bonds can be broken."

A muscle along my jaw ticked. He riled me up, and I was letting him. "So can every bone in the body."

Max chuckled.

And I fought against the itch to smash his face in.

A pitcher of tea appeared in the middle of the table, rattling the wood. Mrs. Nightingale stood over us, dusting her hands off on the apron tied at her waist. “Good, now that we got that out of the way, let’s chat.”

Six
KELSEY

"What's she doing here?" Liam hissed, pinning his closest friends with daggers of fury.

I smiled sweetly at my mate, caught between wanting to throw my arms around his neck and kiss his scowling mouth or telling him to fuck off. I guessed those mixed feelings edging between loving and hating the heir prince hadn't gone away when I claimed him.

Colsen looked down to the dusty cabin floors, avoiding the heir prince's glare from where he lounged on a couch that looked like they plucked it out of the dumpster. Smelled like it too. Or maybe the entire cabin just reeked like shit.

Riven, with his hands shoved into his pockets, rocked back on his heels. "She just showed up," he retorted. "It wasn't like we could kick her out."

"The hell you couldn't," Liam fired back. "I thought I made it very clear she wasn't allowed anywhere near this place."

The fact I was in the room and he talked around me as if I wasn't boiled my blood. We were about to have our first fight as half-bonded mates. "They don't answer for me," I snapped at the heir prince. "If you have a problem with me being here, *princeling*, you're going to have to take it up with me."

He looked at me then, and I almost wished those icy eyes weren't directed at me. "How did you even know where he was?"

"You talk in your sleep," I replied with a grin.

Liam's brows furrowed, his mind searching for how what I said made any sense. "*Damn it. Last night.*" I heard him make the connection to when he'd slept outside my bedroom window. "Only when I'm overtired," he muttered. Like he'd been when he lay down under my window.

Regardless that I'd just fallen asleep, I'd been jolted awake when he arrived, my heart racing, and the tingles...the damn tingles, they'd been stronger than ever in Liam's presence thanks to the claiming. Without looking through my window, I'd known Liam was out there. "Yeah, well. I'm still figuring out this connection."

"*You and me both,*" he grumbled through our link. "You need to go home, Kelsey."

He only used my name when he was serious. Never thought there would be a day when I'd rather hear him call me pup. "I'm not going anywhere." Annoyance sprouted inside me. "This concerns me whether you like it or not. I have a right to the truth, same as you."

"She has you there," Colsen said, risking his balls as he shoved a handful of dry cereal in his mouth, the open box resting beside him on the couch.

Liam whirled on Colsen. "I don't remember anyone asking your opinion, and if you know what's best for your pretty face, you won't side with her."

I gaped, unable to believe he just said that. "*I'm so kicking your ass for that.*"

His eyes bore into mine. "*Later, pup, when we don't have any audience.*"

"*I'm not flirting with you, heir prince,*" I sent back, using my eyes to convey the sarcasm I hoped came across through our link.

"Where's your shadow?" he demanded, his eyes flicking over my shoulder as if he expected Max to burst through the front door.

I hadn't had a good look around when I first showed up at the cabin. Riven and Colsen had bombarded me as soon as I walked in. Not that the place was much to look at. Clearly, no one had stayed here in months. Years, probably. The layers of dust tickled my nose, and I fought the sneeze crawling up my nostrils. "Please, give me some credit. I lost him."

Liam's lips curled with a ghost of pride shining in his aqua eyes. "What happens when your father hears about this?"

I shrugged. "I'm not letting you deal with this alone." Just because Liam hadn't died in the woods last night, it didn't mean he was safe from the hunter's arrows. I couldn't be sure my dreams were nothing, and when it came to Liam's life, I wouldn't take any chances. Whether he liked it or not, I was glued to him.

"I didn't ask for help, pup," he gritted out, walking back to the door and swinging the squeaking thing open. "Now get in your car and go home."

A gust of autumn blew into the house, sending dust particles dancing in the air. "If I don't listen to my father, what makes you think you're any different?" I poked him in the chest with my index finger. "I'm not about to start now. Just because I claimed you doesn't mean I'll bow down at your feet."

Colsen and Riven chuckled, only to be cut off sharply by Liam's icy stare. I even heard a snicker come from one of the bedrooms, and I assumed could be from none other than Gunnar.

He was listening. And enjoying himself.

Liam heard it too. The hard lines of his body went rigid, and his jaw locked up. "Fuck." The curse breezed through his teeth.

Riven must either still be drunk from last night or had lost his ever-loving mind. He draped an arm over my shoulders, grinning like a total shithead. "Hell yeah, Kelsey. You gave your guard the slip on the first day. I knew you had it in you, little rebel."

Colsen stuffed another handful of cereal into his mouth, crunching away as he grinned at me. "I'd love to see his face when he realized you gave him the slip. That's our girl."

"She's not your girl," Liam snapped, killing the buzz in the room. "And stop touching her."

"She will be," Riven boldly reminded him, squeezing my shoulder before stepping mindfully away from me. "Or have you forgotten that she'll be our luna?"

Liam groaned, irritation flaring in his handsome features.

A luna was the highest female in the pack, the alpha's mate. And once Liam became the alpha, I'd be the Riverbridge luna. Weird to think about. Riven and Colsen would be my wolves. Assuming I'd live to see the moment happen.

The heir prince was in rare form today. Lucky me. "Will the two of you stop encouraging her? She doesn't need any help in the causing trouble department."

Colsen turned to me, forcing his lips into a straight, serious line. "Your dad's going to be pissed."

"Exactly why she's leaving," Liam said, staring some intimidation into me, but it didn't work.

We could argue about this for hours and get nothing accomplished. I had to take matters into my own hands. "We're wasting time." And it wouldn't be long until Max tracked me.

Liam shoved a hand into his hair, and I could feel him wavering.

Taking that as a sign, I darted past Riven and entered the small hallway. I had to make a quick decision. Left or right. My senses told me right.

I flung open the door at the same time Liam bellowed my name, the front door slamming shut. I didn't look over my shoulder to see who followed, not when I couldn't take my eyes off the sight in front of me.

Cuffed to the wall by his hands and feet with silver chains, Gunnar sat on the dirty wood floors with his knees propped up and elbows resting on top of them. Strands of dark hair fell forward, his head bent, concealing most of his face.

His clothes were the same as I'd seen last night but covered in blood, grass stains, and dirt. My nose wrinkled. He smelled too. Like all of the above.

Metal bars sectioned off the room, making more than half of it into a cage meant to house wolves. I couldn't tell what the compound makeup of the bars was, but I also didn't feel like touching them to test my theory. They had to be strong enough to contain a wolf; otherwise, the prison was useless.

There were several reasons a pack might have a place like this, and none of them I wanted to think about.

Especially when I thought about Rowan being behind the order to kidnap me. It could have easily been me on the other side of the cage instead of Gunnar. If last night had gone differently—gone in *his* favor… I shuddered.

Gunnar's head lifted, his condescending gaze meeting mine.

The prick smirked.

Irritation itched under my skin, and the power in my veins stirred. I was far from ready to be wielding any magic, my energy still recovering, but it gave me courage. I tipped my chin. "For someone who's a prisoner, you don't look awful."

Gunnar's mouth twitched. "Funny. You look like hell."

If I'd had something in my hand, I would have hurled it through the bars at Gunnar's head. I was well aware of the dark circles under my eyes, the tiredness clinging to my bones, and my body sapped of energy. "At least I'm not the one in a cage."

"Not yet, little wolf. You'll have your turn." The determination in his eyes frightened me, as did the sheer conviction in his tone. He fully believed he hadn't lost, which told me Gunnar would take the first opportunity he got to take me.

Perhaps Liam was right. Maybe I shouldn't be here. It was obviously dangerous even with the asshole behind bars.

I wrapped my arms around myself, cold coursing through my veins.

Liam appeared behind me, his hand slipping to my waist. Heat moved into my skin, chasing the frost away. Liam's proximity gave me courage and hope. Any annoyance he felt before vanished in front of the hunter. Here, whether Liam liked it or not, we showed a united front.

It was inside my head where his lingering annoyance lived.

"I told you to go home."

My jaw clenched. *"I need to see this through,"* I responded.

Liam's fingers at my hip moved to the skin peeking out between my jeans and sweater. *"Have it your way, but I'm warning you it won't be pretty."*

I bit down on my lip to counter the other reaction my body had from his touch. My chin firmed in resolve. *"You don't have to worry about me, princeling."*

His sigh came through heavy in my mind. *"All I fucking do is worry about you."*

"Hasn't anyone told you it's rude to talk about someone behind their back? Or in your case, it would be inside your heads," Gunnar interrupted.

Liam pulled me back, putting himself slightly in front of me. "You want to talk? Fine, let's talk about why you think my father's a traitor."

Gunnar laughed, a short, clipped sound. "*Think*? I don't think. I know," he stated with bitterness.

"Why should I believe anything you say?" Liam spat.

Gunnar stood, moseying toward the front of the cage like he had all the time in the world. His chains dragged along the floor, leaving behind a mark in the dust like an invisible snake. "How about I let the source convince you? He should be calling me any minute for an update about last night. Or to find out what the fuck went wrong if he's already heard Kelsey's still very much walking around Riverbridge instead of tucked away in a secluded cabin chained up."

Liam moved so fast I didn't notice he had moved until I saw him grab Gunnar by the front of his bloody shirt, and he snarled in his face. "If you were smart, you would have left the last bit out."

The hunter smirked. "Touchy. If you give me my phone, I can prove it."

Liam snorted, releasing Gunnar with a shove. "I destroyed it."

Gunnar's face fell as he took a step back. "Then I guess we're both screwed."

"I never give up that easily," Liam retorted, malice darkening his already stormy eyes.

Anger swirled in Gunnar's features. "How long do you think you can keep me caged? Someone will eventually notice my absence."

"Good. For your sake, you better hope they show up sooner than later. How long can a wolf go without food or water?" Liam tossed over his shoulder to Colsen and Riven leaning in the doorway.

I slid a sidelong glance at Liam. He wouldn't? Would he?

The taut lines around Liam's mouth said he most certainly would. Besides, why did I care if the heir prince tortured him?

And yet, a tiny voice of reason countered, hadn't he suffered enough at the hands of wolves? Or maybe the person who made him was human? Did it matter?

I refused to let sympathy weasel its way into my heart.

I would not feel sorry for the hunter who tried to kill me. On more than one occasion!

Firming my resolve, I hardened the empathy trying to make its way inside me. There was no place for those emotions here in this cabin.

Liam's voice dropped, a slightly evil twist curving his lips. "You seem to be a fan of experiments. Why don't we have one of our own and see just how long you can survive without the necessities."

"You think this is the first time I've been locked behind bars?" Gunnar chortled. "It's going to take more than a cage to break me. This is like a regular Saturday night."

"Is that why you hate us?" I asked, interrupting the pissing match I sensed was only beginning.

Gunnar's features softened a sliver when he glanced at me. Or maybe I imagined it. "I don't hate all wolves like most hunters. Just the opposite. I really only despise one."

"The wolf who made you?" I guessed.

Silence followed, and I knew I hit a sensitive button, one I planned to push. Repeatedly if necessary. Gunnar's silence revealed a weak spot.

"What happened to him?" I asked.

"He's dead," he said tersely.

I didn't have to ask how. It was written in the tight lines of his face and the darkening of his eyes.

Gunnar had killed him.

"Where were you supposed to take Kelsey?" Liam demanded, circling back to questions that might help verify the identity of the culprit who hired Gunnar and if it truly was Rowan as Gunnar claimed.

Toying with the chain dangling from his wrist, Gunnar relaxed his features into a picture of boredom. "I was to call him once I had her. Only then would he tell me where to go next."

"Are there any other hunters looking for her?" Liam pushed.

He shrugged. "We don't exactly sit around bonfires drinking beers and conversing. If there are other hunters, I don't know who they are. Part of the code."

Frustrated, Liam scowled, shoving a hand through his hair. "God, you're turning out to be useless baggage."

"Do you at least know if there are others like you?" I inquired.

"Metamorphosed?" A grim sadness descended into Gunnar's face. "Or meta as we like to call ourselves. What do you think? Do you believe they would stop at just one once they succeeded?"

"Shit," Liam cursed under his breath. "How many?"

"Who knows? Hundreds at this point. I only went back once, and I didn't stick around. The creator might be dead, and his work burned with him, but I doubt it ended the creation of super hunters."

Super hunters. Wonderful.

Let's pile that onto the growing list of shit we had to deal with.

Seven

LIAM

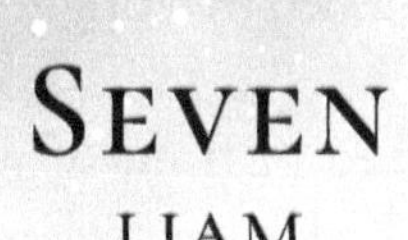

We were in the truck for three minutes tops before Kelsey's head fell to my shoulder. She snuggled against me, a soft sigh tumbling from her as if this was the first time she'd let her guard down all day. I should keep driving, but her gentle breathing and slightly parted lips lulled me like a damn drug, tempting me.

I needed just a fucking minute.

Just one fix of Kelsey Summers, then I'd be able to concentrate on something other than her.

Pulling the truck off to the side of the road, I took a breath and glanced down at the girl sleeping peacefully on my shoulder. It was a relief being able to give my full attention to looking at her instead of dividing it between her and focusing on the road.

I lifted my hand, carefully brushing tendrils of dark hair off her face. Giving in to just a moment of pleasure, I rested my head on top of hers and inhaled her scent deeply. I wanted to pull her into my lap, but I also didn't want to wake her.

A yawn pulled at my lips, my body still working at only fifty percent. Kelsey and I both needed more time to recharge than the measly few hours we managed to scrape this morning. A damn nap would be glorious, but I knew the moment I drifted off, Kelsey might

try to do something reckless. So, I forced my heavy eyes open, which wasn't a hard feat when I stared at someone as beautiful as my mate.

Longing nipped inside me. I ached for her, to drag her across the seat in my lap, but it wasn't what either of us needed. I only meant to close my eyes for a few minutes, however, the next thing I knew, a horn blared in my ears, my eyes blinded by a bright light.

What the fuck?

Another truck was parked in front of mine, its headlights casting beams into my windshield. Beside me, Kelsey stirred, gradually awakening. She rubbed at her eyes, appearing utterly sexy, rumpled from sleep.

"What's happening?" she muttered, her voice alluringly raspy, making me desperate to be alone again with her.

A string of swear words went off in my head. "We're not alone." I recognized the truck, and a lump knotted in my throat.

Kelsey blinked. "Who is it?"

The driver's side door opened, and the forbidding figure stepped onto the road. "My father," I murmured.

"Fuck," she whispered, her eyes suddenly wide.

My thought exactly.

I straightened as Kelsey sat back in her seat, combing her fingers through her hair. Rolling down the window, I waited for him to approach. His stern gaze shifted from me to Kelsey before fixing solely on me. "Looks like we have a lot to catch up on. Why don't you come to the house? Both of you." It wasn't a request but an order.

I nodded, staring at the man who had always been such a strong leader to me. When I was growing up, my dad had been larger than life, and I couldn't deny I didn't want to believe Gunnar's claim.

And yet...

Staring deep into his eyes, past the ruthless hardness, I feared he might be the traitor the hunter declared. I needed proof.

Instinct warned me to keep Kelsey away from my father. "She's tired. We both are. It's been a hellish twenty-four hours. Let me take her home. You and I can talk after."

"This involves both of you. She can stay with us for the night. I'll inform Penelope. And besides, her guard is waiting for her at our house. It's why I came to find you." I recognized the firmness set in his features.

Kelsey groaned, pinching the bridge of her nose as she closed her eyes.

Dad smirked, but the amusement didn't reach his eyes. "You're not the only one displeased by the outsider," he said to Kelsey. "But as a father, I also understand Lincoln's motivation. I underestimated this hunter. I won't make the same mistake."

Something in his tone changed, making him more callous, and it set off a warning through me.

From the corner of my eye, I noticed Kelsey winding her fingers together in her lap.

Nodding to my father, I met his gaze. "I'll follow you home."

His face softened, and for a moment, it was impossible to believe he'd ever betray me. Despite being a hard-ass most days, he'd been a decent father. When the pack wasn't involved. When duty was shoved aside. When it was just father and son, that's when he seemed the most genuine. But he had another side—the alpha, and it was the shifter I doubted.

"Are you okay with this?" I asked using our bond as I rolled up the window, watching my father's brawny figure stroll to his car. Using our minds to communicate was safer. I didn't have to tell her the risks. Kelsey knew.

"I don't think we have much of a choice."

My fingers curled around the steering wheel. *"You say the word, I'll take you home."*

"It's fine, Liam, really," she replied. *"I promise I won't blurt out and accuse your dad of being a traitor. I might be reckless, but I also don't have a death wish."*

I shifted the truck into drive. *"This is a fucking mess."*

"Do you think he'll let us share a room?" She'd deliberately changed the subject, probably because she felt the rise of my blood pressure.

Truthfully, I wasn't ready to face my father. Not when I didn't have any proof, and so far, Gunnar as a hostage was worthless. *"Don't tempt me, pup."* She was concerned with our sleeping arrangements, whereas I stressed over whether she'd be safe under my roof.

Not quite ten minutes later, I pulled into my driveway behind my father. He guided his car into the garage, and I parked mine next to Leith's Jeep.

We both sat in the car, neither of us itching to get out. "It's okay to be scared," I finally said, breaking the silence.

A sad, soft smile touched her lips. "I'm not. You're here."

I didn't know if I deserved her confidence, but I hoped I could live up to it.

Together, we walked up to the house, and the front door opened. Mom greeted us with a smile. This was her way of trying to ease any apprehension Kelsey might have. "I just made some hot tea. Let's get you a cup. I know I could use it." She squeezed Kelsey's hand before ushering her inside. Leith lingered in the entryway, his hands shoved into his pockets, waiting for me.

I shut the door and kicked off my shoes.

"Where have you been?" my brother asked from where he leaned against the stair banister, not an ounce of humor or warmth in his usual aqua eyes.

"None of your business," I testily snapped. He had to know how much stress I was under. Now was not a good time to push me, no matter what his feelings were about Kelsey claiming me.

I hadn't really talked to anyone about it and barely had time to think about it myself, but I could no longer shove the issue aside.

A kernel of mischief sparked in his eyes. There it was. The impish jerk he was known to be. "Heard you slept outside Kelsey's bedroom window last night."

My gaze narrowed. "Does the whole pack know?" Not that it would surprise me. Gossip traveled fast.

He tossed me a cheeky grin that would normally earn him a punch to the gut. "That our hard-ass young prince is pussy whipped? Yes."

My hackles rose. "Unbelievable. Can I for once not have everything I do broadcasted through the pack?"

"Unlikely. You are the next alpha. Besides, you still haven't told me where you've been." A calculating observation descended into his features.

"And I don't plan on it." I brushed past him.

"Liam."

The serious tone halted me in my tracks. I sighed, glancing over my shoulder at him.

"Are you going to tell me what's going on? And why all the secrets? Something else happened last night, and I want to know what. Everyone is acting weird. You. Kelsey. Hope. Riven and Colsen are avoiding me. Neither will return my texts or calls, which I know they'd only do if you gave them a direct order. Did you?"

"Yes." I owed him that much of the truth. I hated lying to Leith, but the further he stayed from this mess, the safer he'd be, and one less person for me to worry over. "I can't talk about this. Not here." My eyes held him, sending a silent message.

He nodded. "On another fun topic, guess who showed up? Kelsey's guard. He lost her his first day on the job." His eyes sparkled with amusement and pride.

"I heard," I replied flatly.

My brother grinned. "This should be fun."

I shook my head. "The fact you get pleasure from my torment is disturbing."

He clapped me on the back. "We can't all lead lives as exciting as yours, brother."

Leith and I walked into the kitchen, finding Mom and Kelsey sitting at the table. My gaze immediately went to my mate's until a body stepped into my path, blocking her from my sight.

A frown carved on my lips, deepening. I cut Maxtyn a sharp glare.

Shadows veiled his dark eyes. "You broke the agreement you made with my alpha."

The hell I did. "It's not my fault you suck at your job."

No kindness shone in his eyes or respect, for that matter, which he was going to have to show unless he wanted *me* to become a problem. "You were at her house last night," Maxtyn pointed out as if it were a criminal offense.

I scoffed. "Get used to it. I'm around a lot."

Leith chuckled behind me. "No one said this would be an easy job. If you knew anything about Kelsey, you would have figured it out already."

My lethal focus remained on Maxtyn, but I sensed Kelsey's irritation through our bond. She didn't like being cut out of the conversation, and she was about to make it known. I waited.

From the corner of my eye, I saw Kelsey grab a cookie from the platter and hurl it across the kitchen at Maxtyn, hitting the guard on the back of the head. Leith caught the cookie before it hit the floor, crumbs falling to the ground. Maxtyn turned around to stare at the cookie-throwing culprit. She gave him a sarcastic smile. "You might not like it, Max, but you and I both know I'm the one to blame. My father might have assigned you as my detail, but I agreed to nothing."

The guard's ears got red. "This might be a game to you, Kels, but this is my job, and I take it seriously."

"This is my life," she shot back. "I didn't ask for this."

"So, you want your beloved heir prince to answer for your actions? It won't be you who your father faults," Maxtyn counters, playing on my mate's compassion.

Her jaw tightened.

"I think we all need to take a breath and figure this out," Mom quietly interrupted, her fingers curling around her tea mug. "There must be an agreement everyone can live with."

Kelsey gave Mom an apologetic glance across the table. "I'm sorry about the cookie. I'll clean up the mess."

Mom waved her off. "I'm guessing he should be lucky it was only a baked good and not something sharper."

"He can leave," I stated, wishing Mom would let me throw his ass out of the house.

"Liam," Mom said, sternness in her features.

My father appeared in the doorway. "As much as I agree with my son, I also understand Lincoln's position." His voice boomed across the kitchen, commanding the room.

Maxtyn and I both straightened our spines at the same time, whereas Leith continued leaning against the counter, his body unchanged by our father's presence. Kelsey spilled a bit of tea over the rim of her cup.

I kept my eyes on my father but projected my thoughts down our bond. *"Try to stay calm. We can't let anyone know we have him."*

Her knee bounced under the table, tapping the chair leg anxiously. *"I know. It's just that your father always makes me nervous."*

Too far to touch her, I did the next best thing, keeping my emotions calm and level. She didn't need to feel my turmoil. *"He has that effect about him. Look at me, not him, if it helps."* I shifted my eyes.

Her gaze collided with mine.

"We've kept up our end of the treaty," my father continued. "And yet, Kelsey remains in danger. This hunter has become the pack's top priority, and until he's dealt with, Maxtyn stays."

No one argued. Even Leith didn't have something smart-ass to say for once in his life.

Going to the fridge, Dad pulled out two cans of beer, passing one to Max. The can in his hand hissed as he popped the top. "Now that we have that cleared up, let's talk about what happened while we were gone. As I understand, your party got a little...out of hand."

That was putting it mildly.

Kelsey swallowed.

This time, Leith couldn't suppress his grin.

Mom always had impeccable timing. "Leith, why don't you show Maxtyn around the grounds and the guesthouse where he'll be staying for the night while we talk."

My brother no longer grinned. He straightened up, eyeing the guard. "Sure, why not."

Maxtyn didn't move, his attention on Kelsey as if he didn't want to lose sight of her again.

Dad took a long pull from his beer. "Don't worry, Ms. Summers won't be going anywhere for the remainder of the night. You have my word," he assured Maxtyn.

The shifter glanced at me.

"My son also gives you his word. Liam?" Dad prompted.

There was nothing I wanted less than to agree to something that would make the guard's job less stressful. "She won't leave the house tonight," I said, not for Max's sake but for my peace of mind.

Kelsey rolled her eyes, and I could tell it took everything in her not to speak out. She didn't like anyone answering for her.

Maxtyn shot a sidelong glance at my mate. "All due respect, but I need to hear it from her."

Dad's brow lifted.

Kelsey narrowed her eyes at her guard. "I don't like to tell lies."

My lips twitched while Leith chuckled.

The corner of my father's mouth quirked into a smirk. "Spoken like a future luna."

When the guard didn't move, Kelsey let out an audible sigh, her fingers spinning the mug on the table. "If promising I won't leave tonight is the only way you'll *leave,* then you have my word as the alpha's daughter."

Maxtyn nodded and followed my brother out of the kitchen, leaving Kelsey and me alone with my parents.

Joy.

This conversation won't be awkward at all.

Dad cleared his throat as he took a seat at the informal kitchen table beside Mom. Kelsey sat across from him. I walked to the empty spot next to her and sat down.

After taking a drink from his beer, he set the can down. "I don't need to know the details of what happened last night at your party. I can put the pieces together. I imagine things got out of hand and neither of you was thinking clearly. What I need to know is if it's true. You claimed my son as your mate."

Kelsey didn't hesitate. She nodded. "I did."

"And he didn't try to stop you?" he asked.

She squirmed slightly in her chair, showing the first visible signs of unease. Through our bond, I sensed trickles of fear. They weren't as vibrant as my emotions would be to her, but even before she claimed me, I'd had some sense of Kelsey. "No, not really," she confessed.

"Your parents are concerned this might be viewed as a violation by the king. I have to explain to him what happened, but since the king wants this union as much as the two packs do, I don't see him viewing it as an infraction of the treaty. In fact, I believe he will be pleased to know how... eager you are to become mates," my father said.

Did the king have any involvement in the attacks on Kelsey? If

Gunnar was telling the truth and my father was the one giving the orders, could it be he was only following directions from the king?

A part of me wanted to grasp at any reason, but my gut couldn't get past the alpha I knew and his thirst for power. My father was one to push and push until you broke.

"Is this necessary?" I asked. "She'll be eighteen in two months. And we have bigger problems to worry about."

"The hunter," he said. The vein on the side of his neck ticked. "I agree. He will be dealt with. I'm meeting with your father tomorrow to discuss what we can do to ensure your safety until you're fully part of the pack and connected. We don't want any more trip-ups between packs."

"It's my fault," Kelsey spoke up. "I know no one got seriously injured, but they could have it. I hadn't thought about my link or how my parents would feel our bond weaken. It was reckless of me."

"I like your recklessness, Kelsey. It's what someone like my son needs."

Kelsey blinked as if she couldn't believe my father had just complimented her. "Still, I feel as if I owe both you and Sydney an apology. I came here so angry and determined to make Liam hate me, but I never wanted to hurt either pack. I didn't expect to have a strong bond with your son, and it's made me act irrationally. More than usual. I'd like to tell you I won't be the cause of any further trouble, but I think we all know it would be a lie."

God, she played her part perfectly. I wanted to kiss her...but I couldn't. Not just because we were in front of my parents but because I wouldn't stop.

The magnetic pull luring me to claim my mate pulsed brighter and more vibrantly within me.

My father leaned back in his chair, looking pleased like a prince on his throne. "You'll make a powerful luna, Kelsey. Your ability to know your faults and your strengths will be tools you'll use well during your reign."

His choice of words hit me like a punch to the gut. *Powerful.*

Kelsey was powerful. Perhaps more so than either of us comprehended. If I had no knowledge of Gunnar's accusation against my father, I still would have seen the hunger in his eyes. He wanted Kelsey in our pack. Not because she was my mate or that we were blessed by the moon. No. He wanted her for selfish reasons. His ambition to have the strongest pack, which allowed him to move up the political ranks, was a driving factor behind possessing Kelsey.

She was a tool to him.

We both were.

My hands fisted under the table, sparks of fury flickering deep in my gut. He hadn't outright threatened her, but my wolf growled inside, ready to protect his mate. I sensed the danger concealed, and it came from my father.

EIGHT
KELSEY

Anger licked through my link from the heir prince. My head whirled to Liam. *"What's wrong?"*

"I'm fine," he ground out, doing a pathetic job of convincing me.

I wanted to roll my eyes, but Sydney and Rowan were watching us. Was he upset I apologized to his parents?

Just because I had a direct line to Liam's emotions, it didn't mean I had any clue what was going on inside him. He kept a tight lock on his thoughts. Or blocked me out with skill.

Had he figured out how to do that?

I wasn't sure why, but the idea annoyed me. It wasn't that I wanted to be in his head twenty-four-seven. Just the opposite. I wished to keep him out of mine.

Walling off Liam's bond to me wasn't the same as the pack bonds. I could turn those off without thinking like flipping a little internal switch. My connection with Liam was stronger, and blocking him took effort and energy I didn't have at the moment.

"It's been a long weekend. Why don't we let them get some sleep, Rowan," Sydney said before I could push Liam further on what troubled him.

I'd wait until we were alone.

If we got the chance to be alone.

"I'm going to level with you both." Rowan glanced at Liam and me. "This won't get any easier, so if you think the hard part is behind you, you're wrong. The fight is only beginning."

Sydney let out a sigh as she folded her hands together on the table. "I wish your father was wrong. Keep each other safe. Your bond is special. More than any of us realize, and because of that, we also don't know what to expect. Liam, show Kelsey to her room." She reached over the table and squeezed my hand. "You'll be safe here. Rest."

I wanted to believe Sydney and let my guard down, but the restless doubts inside me wouldn't go away. "Should I stay at the guesthouse as well?" I offered, not wanting to disrupt the household, plus the idea of not sleeping under the same roof as Rowan appealed to the uneasiness tightening in my chest.

Liam's eyes flew to mine. "No!" he barked, the question hardly off my tongue. "You're not sleeping with Maxtyn."

He made it sound as if we'd be sleeping in the same bed, which we most definitely would not be.

Rowan shot his son a look. "I understand my son's reservations about you sleeping in the same room with your guard, and regardless that I think a little space apart would do you both good, I doubt either one of you will stay put in separate rooms."

A burst of color rushed into my cheeks.

Rowan sighed. "Can I trust you?" he directed to his son.

An ironic question. Liam had my trust. He was the most disciplined wolf I knew, but did he have the same faith in himself? I could feel the wavering of emotions from him.

"Probably not," he admitted, surprising me.

Sydney laid a hand over Rowan's, giving it a gentle squeeze. "The guest room you stayed in prior will be fine for the night."

"I don't want to cause trouble." My eyes shifted to Liam. If it was difficult for me to be so close, I hated to make things harder for him.

"You could never. You're family now, Kelsey," Sydney said, her smile warm and welcoming. She had a way of alleviating some of my apprehension.

"Besides, your parents will be here in the morning. I'm sure they would like to see you again before they go home," Rowan said.

I blinked. "They're leaving?"

He lifted his beer. "Yes. After we iron out a few more details."

Of course, they couldn't stay. Responsibilities waited for them at home. An entire pack. My little brother. Selfishly, I wanted them to stay a little longer. I felt safer with them close.

"What about the hunter?" Liam inquired.

"I have wolves patrolling the woods nightly. We'll get him, and when we do, we'll get the answers we need."

I wanted the tightening of Rowan's jaw to be my imagination. The alpha sounded so damn confident that I believed him. If only Gunnar wasn't tied up in the cabin. But he was...and my doubts lingered.

I LEFT Liam in the kitchen with his father, eager to put distance between the alpha and me. Keeping up the façade wore on me. I could only pretend and be fake for so long, not that I convinced anyone, but I hoped they assumed it was the stress of my parents and the claiming.

But honestly, everyone around the kitchen table had been hiding something.

So much had unfolded that it was difficult to fathom we had to return to school on Monday. The significance of education paled in comparison when confronted with life-and-death challenges.

Alone, I padded to the bed and sat down to check my phone. No calls. No texts. I didn't know why I thought my parents might reach out. When it came to pack business, my brother and I came second. They loved us. I didn't doubt that, but their titles came with sacrifices.

It was one of the reasons I wasn't thrilled with stepping into the same position as my mother—why I fought against the treaty. In the end, my efforts were futile. I would end up like my mother, which wasn't a horrible thing. I just pictured a different life for me. One where I wasn't tied down by bullshit shifter rules.

If I was going to end up in a position of power, I planned to use it to change those bullshit rules. I never thought too hard about having kids.

The concept seemed so far away, but if I did become a mother, I vowed to put them first.

Sniffling, I smeared a hand across my eyes. *Don't fall apart.* I had no intention of crying and fought at the lump of emotion crawling up my throat.

And yet as a single tear tracked down my cheek, my breath hitched, and I lost it. The key locking my feelings away turned, setting the pesky bastards free.

Bottling shit up did no one good. That was what my therapist would say if I had one, but I wasn't ready to deal with all that had happened.

My body no longer gave me a choice. *Deal with it*, my wolf screamed within me.

In a house full of shifters, crying in private didn't exist. I didn't want the Castles to hear me fall apart, so I did the only thing I could think of. I locked myself in the bathroom and cranked on the shower.

The tears streaming from my eyes were as hot as the water hitting the tile, clouding the air with steam. I surrendered, purging my heart and letting go of the chaos swirling in me.

I shouldn't be here, not in this house, and yet, leaving would only raise questions. I could lie, but I didn't have the energy to muster up a good lie.

Or maybe it was being close to Liam that kept me here.

I thought about calling my parents and telling them everything. Staring at my phone, I wondered what they would do. Anything? Nothing? Would they believe Rowan was capable of what Gunnar accused him of?

Did I?

I shut the shower off when the tears were mostly dry without ever having gotten in. In the mirror, I glanced at my puffy eyes, red and glossy.

What are you going to do next? I silently asked the girl staring back at me.

I had no answers.

Wandering out of the bathroom, I noticed my phone light up on the bed where I'd left it with a notification. I padded over to check the text. It was from Nana.

Are you safe? I had a vision.

God, I knew what she'd seen.

I'm okay

I sent back, wishing she wouldn't worry.

Soft knuckles rapped on the door, and I twisted as the knob turned. Liam stood in the doorway. He'd changed into comfy clothes, a pair of sweats and a T-shirt, and yet he had never looked better.

His eyes took in the sight of me, searching mine, and then he was striding across the room to the bed with long, purposeful steps. "Why are you crying?" he demanded, jaw locked like he was ready to kill whoever hurt me.

Did he have to ask?

There were too many people responsible for my pain. Including me.

"It doesn't matter," I replied, roughly swiping under my eyes with the back of my sleeve. Annoyance rippled in me. I hadn't wanted Liam to see me like this, to catch me upset and crying.

Having him in the room would only make gaining control of my feelings harder.

"Do you want to leave?" he offered, thinking that staying in his house with his possibly psycho father bothered me. He wasn't entirely wrong. "I'll take you home right now."

As I gazed into his concerned aqua eyes, the confusion and gloom pressing on me became diluted. It didn't matter where I was as long as he was there, I realized. His proximity did something to me, regulated those overwhelming feelings. When he stood at my side, he made the world...right.

I could breathe easier, the pain in my chest lightened, tingles radiated over my skin, and, most noticeably, my heart quickened...but so did his. I couldn't say for sure, but I had this theory that when we were together our hearts synced up, matching in rhythm. From what I knew about bonded mates, that wasn't a normal trait. It had to be due to our Moonstruck link.

We knew little about the moon's blessing bestowed upon us by the fates. Why us?

What would happen when we were fully bonded? How much closer could Liam and I become?

I shook my head at Liam's offer to take me home. Looking at him, I very much did not want to leave. "No." My hand lifted, reaching for his. "I just don't want you to go." I laced my fingers with his, my gaze shifting to stare at our joined hands.

A different awareness moved into his body, and for us, it wasn't any less lethal or dangerous than the hunter chained up in the cabin. "Kelsey." My name was a warning on his lips, and yet he didn't untangle his fingers from mine. He clung tighter.

I stood next to the bed, bringing our bodies closer. I needed his nearness, his warmth, and his strength.

"I shouldn't be here," he murmured, his thumb stroking the inside of my wrist, right where our matching moon marks were.

My pulse skipped. "No," I agreed. "You should probably go." I didn't mean a word of it, and he knew it.

His gaze stayed locked on mine as his free hand went to the small of my back, inching me closer toward him until our bodies were flushed.

I leaned in, our intertwined fingers falling to our sides. "Why aren't you leaving?" My tongue skimmed my lower lip, heat rushing into my body as his gaze moved to my mouth, and his eyes darkened.

"Pup," he groaned, melting my insides, and then the bastard did the impossible. He took a step away from me, retreating. "I can't." His head shook, his fingers unweaving from mine as he lifted his hand to ward me off when my body moved forward of its own accord, seeking more than his warmth. "You stay there. Don't come any closer."

Disappointment ribboned in my chest at the loss of space I'd just managed to close between us. I angled my head to the side, regarding the heir prince with new light. "Are you afraid of me?"

"Yes." The single word contradicted the fire in his eyes.

"Liam," I whispered, knowing it wasn't just the kindling between us I needed.

He studied me with an intensity that had me swaying toward him. "The last time we were alone, you attacked me, bit me, and claimed me in a span of seconds."

I smiled, unable to stop myself. "Such good memories. We should relive them, don't you think?"

"Kelsey," he growled, retreating another step.

"You can't blame me. It's your fault. If you weren't so damn irresistible, I could have gone on hating you." The emotion swelling in me was heady, like the feeling I got when I used my power. It was the knowledge that I unsettled him, made his control slip.

And I loved it.

He continued to retreat. "You might be onto something. Do something to make me hate you." His back touched the wall, and I had him right where I wanted him.

Trapped.

My head angled to the side, a ghost of a smirk on my lips. Who would have thought teasing the heir prince would pull me out of my slump? "Like sleep with you brother?"

"Yes. No," he quickly corrected, shaking his head as my suggestion sunk in. "I don't want to kill you or my brother, for that matter. I just need to hate you for both our sakes."

This time when I advanced, Liam had nowhere to go. I ran my fingers up his chest, my eyes locked on his. "Or you could kiss me."

"Pup," he groaned. "You're the one trying to kill me."

I rested my hand over his heart. "It's not me. It's this bond."

His lips twitched, the scar on his bottom lip beckoning me. "Nice try. The bond only amplifies what's in your heart and soul."

My fingers curled into the soft material of his shirt. "My heart has issues if it chose you as my mate."

"I can't argue with that." His voice was low and strained. How could someone fight so hard with their basic needs? An unfathomable thought.

I lifted on my toes, aligning our lips. "Liam."

"Fuck it," I heard him say through our bond as his gaze dropped to my lips.

Joy splintered within me, anticipation surging. It had only been last night since the heir prince kissed me last, and yet, it felt like weeks.

His fingers dove into my hair, taking a handful as his mouth slanted across mine.

Yes. Yes. Yes.

I needed this to chase away the confusion, hurt, and anger constantly assaulting me. Only when Liam's lips were on mine did everything else stop. Only the sensations he created with his mouth and hands existed.

The perfect distraction I desperately wanted. Instead of wallowing in tears, I'd rather be flying in his arms.

My lips parted eagerly, inviting him to take the kiss deeper. Liam didn't disappoint. His tongue met mine halfway, sliding along mine with skilled strokes that made me shiver.

"Kelsey," he moaned, the fingers in my hair tipping my head back farther.

Half afraid he would stop kissing me, I sucked on his lower lip, scraping my teeth over him. He kissed me harder, my body singing, edging toward the line of recklessness I was so known for.

How ridiculous it was to think I had control of the situation. I was so wrong.

Liam grabbed my waist firmly, switching our positions my back dug into the wall, and I was the one falling deeper, thoroughly losing myself in the kiss.

Little electric sparks danced through my veins like magic. Maybe it was my powers or my bond with Liam.

My fingers dove into his hair, sliding through the sandy, silky strands as he explored my mouth, fully devouring me until my knees were weak. Thank God, he was more or less holding me up with his body because I didn't trust my legs to support me.

He broke away from my lips, and I was so ready to complain—to draw his mouth back to mine—until he dragged his lips over my jaw, pressing a kiss to my neck. My head fell against the wall, letting the sensations Liam enticed consume me.

They moved and settled between my legs where I pulsed with need. I wanted Liam. I had to have him. Desire gripped me. It blew me away how much I wanted one person. Only him.

Why did it have to be him? The damn heir prince of Wyoming.

I'd never live that quiet life I dreamed of. Then again, with or without Liam as my mate, I'd never live a simple life. I was the target. I was the one who put Liam in danger, and once he claimed me, his entire pack would also be in jeopardy.

If his father was involved, it would be easier to get to me.

Being like this, Liam made me forget my troubles, if only for a few minutes, and I didn't want the bliss he created to end. Not after the emotional roller coaster I hadn't fully gotten off yet.

He chased the grim shadows threatening to absorb me like the moon casting light on the darkness.

With as much impulse as he had taken my lips, he broke off the kiss, wrenching a moan of protest from me. I tightened my fingers in his hair, keeping him from pulling away.

"No more. We have to stop." He breathed heavily, his eyes lighting up the dark room.

Struggling to catch my breath, I dropped my hands to my sides. I couldn't touch him, or I'd ignore the plea in his gaze.

"I have to go," he said stiffly, countering the heat still blazing in his eyes.

Panic trembled within me. I didn't want him to leave. All the emotions I was avoiding would come barreling back. My head shook. "Don't. I can't sleep without you." I hated how vulnerable I allowed myself to be.

He retreated a few feet. "Me neither. But I'm not climbing in the bed with you." His words had a grit I couldn't muster.

The sudden lack of warmth left me empty. "I never asked you to."

"But you want me to. I can see it in your eyes." The heat in his contradicted the coldness of his tone.

"What else do my eyes tell you?"

He raked both his hands into his disheveled sandy hair. "That sleeping on the floor is a dumb idea. That I should leave now while I still have a shred of restraint left."

I rolled my eyes as I shoved off the wall. "Boring."

He watched me walk toward the bed like he didn't quite trust me not to accidentally trip and tumble into his arms. "Just throw me a damn pillow and go to bed, pup," he grumbled roughly.

Giving him a perfect view of my ass while I climbed onto the mattress, I felt his eyes on me and smiled in satisfaction. "I can't believe I claimed you."

Liam's husky chuckle cut through the dark. "No one was more shocked than me."

I unfolded the bedding, pushing it aside to get underneath. "I'm still pissed off at myself."

"Do you regret it?" his voice asked moments later.

I tossed a pillow to him. "Do you want the truth?"

He grabbed the knitted blanket draped over the foot of the bed. "Yes."

My head snuggled deeper into the pillow as he curled up into the corner chair near the window. "As much as admitting it bugs the shit out of me...no, princeling. I don't regret claiming you." I rolled over on my side so I could see him better, our eyes locking together. "If I hadn't bitten you on your birthday, I'd sink my canines into you right now."

"Kelsey," he rumbled roughly. "Keep that up and I'll leave."

I wanted him lying in the bed beside me where I could wrap my arms around him and rest my head on his chest, but having him close was enough...for now. "You said you wanted the truth. And the truth of it is, princeling, I think about biting you all the time."

His eyes flared in the dark. "The point of me staying here was for us to sleep. Now I'm more restless than before."

"So, a goodnight kiss is out of the question?" I teased because I was morbid and loved the scowl that formed on his mouth. It made me want to crawl across the bed and tug him in.

He shifted forward as if he intended to stand up. "I'm leaving."

"Liam. Don't go," I whispered, all playfulness dropping from my face. "I really don't want to be alone."

He settled back into the chair, his gaze finding mine. "You'll never be alone. Now close your eyes." His words were like a caress, and I doubted either of us would get any sleep.

☽☽●☾☾

I WOKE up Sunday morning curled in Liam's lap with no recollection of climbing out of bed in the middle of the night. But the fact remained, I found my way into his arms.

God was he gorgeous. I fully understood why I was attracted to him —why I claimed him. I just prayed my rash decision didn't come back to nip me in the ass. Besides, if Liam chose to reject me, I'd feel more than a nip. I was pretty damn sure it would kill me.

Literally.

My position wasn't the most comfortable, and yet, I'd never slept so deeply.

Facing each other, we lay on our sides, legs tangled together. He had an arm tossed over my waist. My gaze roamed his face, taking in the details of his chiseled jaw, the sharp angles of his cheek, and his full mouth. The scar located on his bottom lip only made him ten times hotter.

A streak of sunlight filtered through a crack in the curtains, hitting Liam on the side of the neck, right where my canines had pierced his flesh. Two tiny prick points were visible—my claiming marks.

Liam was mine.

My heart fluttered.

I stared at him, unable to believe that this arrogant, stubborn, disagreeable wolf belonged to me.

Half afraid to move and risk waking him, I stayed still, but the longer I gazed at him, the stronger the urge to touch him became.

I couldn't stop my lips from brushing his in a whisper of a kiss.

My wolf purred.

The arms around me tightened.

"Kelsey," he murmured.

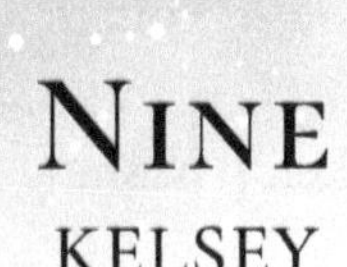

Nine
KELSEY

Liam insisted on sneaking out of the room, but I highly doubted the entire house didn't know where the eldest Castle sibling spent the night. Scent and hearing gave it away easily enough, and the heir prince's scent was all over me. Hell, I was drenched in the essence of him. And him in me.

I considered showering before heading downstairs but found comfort in my clothes smelling like him. It was like carrying traces of Liam with me, and with the day I had in front of me, I needed a bit of extra strength.

And if I was being honest, I didn't want to wash off the woodsy notes. I liked it too fucking much, which scared me.

Claiming Liam wasn't the same as being in love with him. The lines were blurry for sure, and most people assumed being his mate would mean I was in love with him. Fuck, maybe I was.

But I sure as hell wasn't ready to admit that to myself, let alone to him.

I wanted him without question, but lust didn't equal love.

When I trotted down the stairs, voices drifted from the kitchen. I followed them, recognizing my mother's laugh as I drew closer, meaning my father was also somewhere around.

This would be one very awkward meeting. I couldn't remember the last time my parents were together with Liam's. The history there made me want to turn away from the kitchen and head straight outside. I craved a run in the woods more than the bacon I'd whiffed or the freshly brewed coffee.

"Where do you think you're going?" someone asked as I stared down the hallway.

I turned and frowned at Leith, hushing him. "Do you have to be so loud?" I hissed.

A brown brow lifted. "Are you running away?"

I didn't bother to lie. "Maybe."

"I'd love to join, but I don't think we'd get too far. Your hunky guard is outside the front door." He directed his gaze to the foyer behind him.

My eyes rolled at the mention of Max. "If you like him so much, why don't you go distract him for me?"

A sparkle glimmered in the youngest Castle's eyes; his lips pursed thoughtfully. "Tempting."

"There's more than one way in and out of this house, I assume," I grumbled, toying with the ring on my thumb.

"Your best bet would be to jump from a window."

"Leith, this isn't funny."

He wrinkled his nose. "You stink."

"I thought you liked my scent. I distinctly remember you telling me I smelled like cotton candy." God, the memory of my first day at Riverbridge seemed like a lifetime ago instead of just a month.

His normally humorous eyes studied me. "I do, just not when you reek of my brother."

I raised a brow. "That bad?"

Leith's lips twitched. "Nauseating."

I grinned. "Good, I hope you choke on his scent."

His chuckle was quiet as his mouth twisted. "Evil. Now I see why he's so enamored by you." Leith walked to my side, tossing an arm over my shoulders.

"Who?" I blinked, wanting to hear him say it. A part of me needed reassurance that other people saw what I did in Liam.

"Hell, at this point, everyone. But I meant Liam."

Like his brother, Leith had a sturdiness about him. The difference, Leith made it easy to lean on him—effortless. I didn't have to think about it. "Are you going to help me or not?"

Leith started to lead us down the hall. "What are friends for?" Then the traitor spun me toward the kitchen.

"Some friend," I mumbled, flirting with the idea of bolting.

Leith gave me a grin, flashing his dimple. "Would it persuade you to know Liam's in the kitchen?"

My mouth tensed. "Not really."

He squeezed my shoulder. "Liar. I heard your heart pick up."

"It's irritation you're sensing," I mumbled, dread pitting in my stomach.

"As soon as I get you alone, you and I are going to have a chat," he murmured in my ear. "Someone's going to tell me what the fuck is going on."

I swallowed, entering the kitchen alongside Leith who produced a smile with little effort. I didn't know how he did that, shoving aside what he felt and replacing it in a snap with a convincing fakeness. He was good. Too damn good at hiding his true self.

My scowl deepened as I locked gazes with Liam.

Sadness and loneliness hung over my head the rest of Sunday. Saying goodbye to my parents generated conflicting emotions. It hurt to see them go, leaving me with another pack. And yet, relief pushed just above the pain. If they weren't in Riverbridge, then they weren't in danger.

No one volunteered information about the discussions Rowan and my father had outside. It was apparently above my station despite being the topic of conversation.

I made my parents promise to give Noah, my little brother, a hug from me, and tell him that I'd see him soon.

Liam drove Max and me back to my house. Nothing else happened between the heir prince and me. Max, the third wheel, made sure of it.

The drive had been quiet, and when we pulled into my driveway, the only thing Liam said had been see you tomorrow. I'd just nodded, trying not to be disappointed or hurt.

What had I expected from Liam? For him to kiss me goodbye? Walk me to my front door? We weren't a couple. Other than the fact that I'd claimed him, I didn't know where the heir prince and I stood.

Just add that to the list of shit I needed answers for.

"I'm home. I don't want to see you for the rest of the day," I spat at Max, feeling cranky.

He grabbed my elbow before I could step inside. "We need to talk. It's clear after today we need to set some ground rules."

"Fuck off." If he thought for a second I'd make this easy for him, he was sorely mistaken. I slammed the door in his face before he could walk inside.

Nana lifted a brow when I stormed into the kitchen. "Did you say goodbye to your parents, then?"

I opened the fridge and pulled out an open bottle of wine. Nana liked to indulge in a glass in the evening. Twisting the cap, I drank right from the bottle, letting the chilled, fruity liquid coat my throat. "More like good riddance," I mumbled, closing the fridge door and taking the wine with me.

Nana only looked at me, not batting an eye. "And Maxtyn?"

I sunk into a bar stool. "Hopefully he took the hint and went home."

Max appeared in the doorway and leaned against the frame with a smooth smirk that made me want to give him a bloody nose. "Still here."

Nana beamed. "Good, you can both help me with dinner."

The last thing I wanted was to be alone, so regardless of my loathing Max's company, I was grateful for the distraction. It kept my mind off other things.

Gunnar.

Rowan.

Max.

Leith.

Hope.

So many loose ends.

But most of all, Liam. He occupied the largest amount of space in my thoughts.

The wine helped.

And Nana put us to work.

Chewing on my lip, I cut veggies for a salad and tossed them into a wooden bowl. If Max wasn't here, I wondered if I would have opened up to Nana about everything going on and sought her advice. She would know what I should do. Nana would be objective, unlike my parents. If she thought Liam's father had any involvement with the hunters, she wouldn't think twice about reporting him to the king.

Which was why I couldn't tell her. I didn't want her involved. I had to protect and shield her from any danger. I wasn't sure me living here was a good idea. Maybe I could convince Max to look out for Nana. I would feel a million times better knowing she was safe. Gunnar might be locked up, but the threat wasn't contained.

☽☽●☾☾

The last thought I had before I drifted off to sleep was of Liam. The first thought I had when I woke up was of Liam.

It was maddening.

I checked my phone, attempting to add a semblance of normalcy back into my life. Six in the morning on a Monday. I groaned at the time. I had an hour to shower and get ready for school.

How much more normal could you get than that? Oversleeping and rushing to get ready was pivotal high-school shit.

Showered and dressed, I felt halfway human when I trotted into the kitchen for my first cup of coffee, but someone had stolen my favorite cup. I scowled at the guilty party leaning against the counter with his lips on my mug.

I blinked, wishing I would wake up from this nightmare. "Shit, I forgot you were here," I mumbled.

Max's dark hair was slightly damp, and he smelled like soap. "I don't know how that's possible. I have such a presence about me."

I brushed past him to grab a different mug. "Or lack of."

"Do you want me to drive?" he asked, sipping on his coffee, the steam seeping into his cheeks.

Even with my arm extended, my fingers barely brushed the cup on the top shelf just out of reach. "Liam's picking me up."

The front of Max's body grazed my back as he arched over me, securing the mug. "Is that a good idea?"

I stiffened. "He's my mate," I said, whirling, intending to shove him away.

Max retreated a step, smirking at me as he offered the cup. "Spending so much time with him will only make it harder for him. What happened to the girl who vowed she'd rather be human than claim Liam Castle?"

After snatching the mug, I filled it with coffee. "Have you seen him?"

Max snorted, leaning back against the counter. "He's nothing special. And you used to think that as well, as I recall." He reached out, tugging at a piece of hair that fell over my face.

I knocked his hand away. "Yeah, well, that girl grew up. And stop touching me. You're here to do a job. That's it. You and I aren't friends."

With a cocky grin, Max dropped his gaze to my mouth for a second. "I can help you if you change your mind. Just say the words."

I pressed my lips tightly together and glared at him. A few days ago, I would have leaped at the offer to run away with him. Now, it made me sick to my stomach. "Jump off a cliff."

Taking my coffee, I grabbed my bag off the counter and headed down the hallway. Max was on my heels. "When was the last time you stepped into a high school?" I asked over my shoulder. He was only a few years older than me, but giving him a hard time made me miss Liam a little less. Just a little. Like minuscule, but it was something to do.

"It wasn't that long ago," he grimaced.

My ears picked up the familiar rumble of Liam's truck. He was almost here. "I wouldn't want you to stand out."

He opened the door before I could do it myself. "Oh, I'll stand out, Kels," he assured as if he was God's gift to women.

I cut him a sharp glare. "Don't flirt with me. It's not cute."

The corner of his mouth twitched. "I wouldn't dream of it."

Liam's truck pulled into the driveway, and through the windshield, the heir prince's eyes found mine. Our gazes locked. The world faded. There was only him. I wondered if this feeling of no one else existing would go away after he claimed me.

It used to annoy the hell out of me.

Now...I looked forward to the moments when it was only Liam and me.

"Kels," Max called. From the weird tone of his voice, I guessed it wasn't the first time he'd said my name.

Exhaling, I stepped off the porch. "Get used to that. It happens frequently."

"What the hell was that?"

I shrugged. "Some kind of effect from being Moonstruck."

Max had nothing more to say, and instead of riding in the back seat of the cab, he hopped into the truck's bed. His boots clambered onto the metal, shaking the car.

"What's his deal?" Liam asked as I buckled my seat belt.

"Who knows." I didn't want to talk about Max. What I wanted to do was stare at my mate while he drove and perhaps distract him.

He must have sensed my gaze. A full minute had gone by, and I'd said nothing. "Are you okay?" he asked. "You seem...quiet."

My heart fluttered at the concern in his voice. "I'm trying to figure out how this works. You and me. I know we have bigger problems, but I don't know how to act around you, especially at school." Sure, all wolf shifters at Riverbridge High would have heard I claimed the heir prince, but what about the rest of the population?

He shrugged. "It doesn't matter what anyone at school thinks."

I rolled my eyes. "Okay, fine. Then what am I supposed to say to Hope?" I couldn't very well tell her we had her best friend chained up at some cabin in the woods. It was the extent of what I knew about Gunnar's abduction.

He glanced at the rearview mirror, a tense line appearing on his forehead. "Nothing. She doesn't need to know where Gunnar is."

Snorting, I shook my head. "And how's that going for you? She's going to have questions, princeling."

His lips twitched.

Irritation flared within me. "What the fuck is so funny?"

He guided the truck into the school parking lot and glanced at me. "Nothing, I just really like it when you get snarky with me. The way you call me princeling it makes me wish we were alone."

Max pounded on the back window. "I can hear you," he growled.

I sunk lower in my seat.

Scowling, Liam glared at Max through his rearview mirror. "Good. Then you'll love this," he replied, shoving the truck into park. The heir prince leaned over the seat, his lips brushing my neck as he whispered, "I missed you last night."

I shuddered at the wisps of his hot breath on my skin.

My door wrenched open, a scowling Max waiting on the other side. It was too damn early for a pissing match between wolves.

Liam's eyes lifted, a hint of his wolf glowing brightly in the center as he glowered at Max.

I put my hand on Liam's chest, angling my head so he stared at me, not Max. "We're going to be late."

We left Max to survey the perimeter of the school; he wasn't allowed inside for obvious security reasons. They didn't let just anyone within the school's walls, but regardless, I still always had a shadow.

Liam, Leith, Colsen, Riven, and basically every other wolf who went to school followed me everywhere. Since only Liam's closest circle knew we had Gunnar locked up, appearances had to be kept as well as precautionary measures.

If there was one hunter, there were likely more as Liam often reminded me when I grumbled about the constant eyes on me.

"Did you see *him* this morning?" I asked as we strolled inside the double doors, careful not to use his name.

Liam nodded, a tightness forming around his mouth. Anger trickled from our bond. "Yeah, Colsen and Riven are alternating shifts."

Gunnar was a triggering topic of conversation, the betrayal and threat too fresh. "Are they going to be able to keep up with school like that?" I asked, worried about Colsen and Riven missing classes. I didn't need them to fall behind and be unable to graduate with us on my conscious.

The noise from the crowded halls masked our voices. "Not for long. Their parents are bound to find out, which will get back to my father."

I glanced up at him as we stopped at my locker. "What are we going to do?"

He leaned a shoulder on the row of metal lockers, trouble stirring in his eyes. "I'm not sure yet."

"Kelsey," someone called, sounding out of breath.

I turned just as Hope reached me. She looked ragged, eyes puffy and tired, not a stitch of makeup on. My heart sank, but I forced my lips to smile. "Hope. Hey, how are you?"

She grabbed my hand and pulled me away from my locker and Liam. I glanced over my shoulder at the frowning heir prince.

"Don't say anything," he warned in my head.

I wanted to argue with him. I hated lying to the only friend I had here, but I understood Liam had his reasons, and she would be safer not knowing. I thought.

Hope dragged me to the girls' bathroom, which wasn't unoccupied. Holding the door open, she glared at the trio of freshmen. "Get out," she ordered, looking and sounding a tad frantic.

My friend was unraveling, but I couldn't blame her. I felt like shit for not having reached out to check on her this weekend. I had no excuses. I should have for one minute stopped and thought of someone other than myself.

What happened Friday night hadn't only happened to me.

She'd also been a part of it—a victim.

God, she had to be a mess. Conflicted and torn up inside.

I tried to put myself in her shoes and didn't know if I could come close to imagining what she must be going through. Or what she knew.

Hope flipped the lock and faced me. "What the hell is going on? Where is he?"

I assumed the he she referred to was Gunnar, but I couldn't be a hundred percent sure. "No one told you." The plan was to skirt around the topic without giving any details until I discovered how much she knew.

"No one is telling me shit."

So not helpful. We didn't have time to beat around the bush. "What do you remember?" I asked straightforwardly.

She got this sad, far-off look in her eyes that tugged at my emotions. "That's the fucked-up thing. I don't. Well, at least, I don't think I do. I remember getting ready for Liam's birthday party and Gunnar picking me up. Then nothing. Just a giant black spot. The next thing I know, I'm at home, in my bed, fully dressed, as if I never left." Lifting her gaze, she looked at me, and I hated the confusion in her features. "I thought maybe I got so drunk that I basically blacked out, but it doesn't make sense why I can't remember any of the party. Regardless, my dress had dirt on it, and I found leaves in my fucking hair."

I didn't know what to say. I could fill in most of the blanks she was missing. "It will be okay, Hope."

She started to pace from one side of the bathroom to the other. "How is any of this okay? I know something happened. I can feel it. Plus, Liam is acting weird. And Gunnar's just disappeared. I haven't been able to get a hold of him since Friday night."

I swallowed.

Halting, she angled her head at me. "Why did your heart rate increase when I mentioned Gunnar's name? Liam's I get. He always gets your heart going."

Shit.

What the hell do I say?

I can't tell her the truth, yet I wanted to.

Her usually soft brown eyes narrowed, suspicion inching into her features. "Why do I get the feeling whatever comes out of your mouth will be a lie?"

A curse tumbled out of my mouth with a whoosh of air. "How are you so good at reading people?"

"I'm not always, but with you..." She shrugged. "I felt this instant friendship. I figured it might be because you were to be part of the pack."

I reached out and took her hand, expecting to offer her the comfort of a friend, but the moment our fingers touched, something flashed behind my eyes.

It was Hope in her wolf form, an arrow protruding out of her side, blood staining the snow-covered ground crimson.

She threw her head back and howled.

A scream cleaved through the air, part wolf, part human.

And then it was gone, and I stared at Hope's face, slightly paler than it had been a few moments ago.

"What just happened? Where did you go?" she asked, concerned etched on her face.

"I-I'm not sure." My fingers came up, pressing to the side of my head where a dull throb started.

"Kelsey, tell me what's going on? Does it have anything to do with you and Liam? Oh, I heard," she added, noticing the way I flinched. "Sabrina told me, and you know how I feel about her. She was all too pleased that my best friend hadn't told me she claimed my cousin. Are you avoiding me?"

"No." I shook my head, regretting the movement instantly as a spike of pain lanced through my brain. I winced before continuing. "Not intentional. It's been a crazy fucking weekend with my parents here and dealing with the whole claiming business."

"What else happened, Kels?" she insisted.

I looked into her eyes and knew I couldn't lie to her. I just hoped it wouldn't be a decision we both could live with. "Liam's going to kill me. But I think it's better I show you than tell you. Are you free after school?"

Ten
KELSEY

I made it through six classes, and I didn't learn a single thing. It had nothing to do with the teachers or the material being taught, but it entirely fell on my lack of concentration.

It was nonexistent.

How could I concentrate on differential equations, the US Constitution, or whatever the hell topic in my macroeconomics class when my life was going to shit?

At the tail end of my sixth class, my chest seized, and I gasped. Numerous gazes glanced my way, and Leith gave me an are-you-okay brow raise.

My hand pressed to my heart. *What the hell was that?*

It happened again, this panicky feeling that eerily reminded me of having an anxiety attack. And boy did I have a lot to be panicky over except I wasn't.

Not to this degree.

My heart raced. My breathing became labored. And I couldn't sit still.

What is wrong with me?

Perhaps a cold or illness, but wolves rarely caught human sickness. It could be something else.

Fidgeting in my seat, I barely made it through class, my eyes watching the needle tick on the clock like a hawk. Seconds before the bell rang, I jumped out of my seat and rushed to the door.

"Kelsey!" Leith called after me, but I was already sprinting down the hall.

I needed fresh air, a moment to clear my head. Taking the stairs, I headed for the rooftop. It was closer than the courtyard and far less crowded considering the area was restricted from student use. Not that a rope and a warning sign stopped any of us from wandering where we weren't supposed to be.

In high school, a "Do Not Enter" sign was like an invitation.

I burst through the door, the cold air slapping me in the face. It had rained earlier, and dampness clung to the earth, moisture filling my lungs as I took a deep breath of crisp air.

The expectation that being outside would alleviate the unease prancing within me proved futile. If anything, the tension constricting my insides intensified.

I inhaled greedily, forcing my lungs to take the air in slowly and then release it with the same tempo. A few tries later I felt marginally better, and my eyes fluttered closed.

I continued the breath pattern until something stole the air from me and I was suddenly pressed against the door. Not something. Someone.

Warm lips were on mine, kissing and coaxing a response from me.

Liam, my wolf purred.

Tingles radiated everywhere like an explosion of stars burst from my heart. My brain was slow to catch up, but once I did, I kissed him back with everything I had, thrilled to have him alone.

My wolf purred again, content to be close to her mate; however, it didn't take long for my greedy wolf to want more. My life felt dependent on this kiss, and stopping would end us both.

Dramatic? Definitely, and yet dramatic summed up my relationship with the heir prince.

Liam broke off the kiss, our panting breaths mingling. His luminous eyes held mine, streaks of his wolf close to the surface, and my blood raced. *"What took you so long?"* he asked, a finger tracing along my chin.

"That was you?" I send back, recalling the panic that had gripped me and what had ultimately sent me dashing up here.

"Hmm," he murmured, his lips dipping to claim mine in another soul-splintering kiss.

This was madness, and yet I felt wholly right. Liam and I belonged together. This was how it should be between us. None of the rules or stipulations of a paper. Free to do what we wanted when we wanted.

Why the hell shouldn't Liam claim me right now if he desired? All because a stupid document said I had to be eighteen. As if two months would make any difference.

To stop kissing seemed more insane than to keep our lips sealed. I was willing to risk insanity if it meant his mouth stayed on mine.

Liam hauled me against him, spinning us away from the door seconds before it swung open. A low rumble vibrated at the back of his throat, the muscles underneath me tightening.

Max stepped out onto the roof, his gaze landing on me wrapped up in the heir prince's arms, quickly assessing the situation. "Let go of her."

Perhaps not the wisest choice of words.

Liam's arms didn't so much as budge, and he made no indication of releasing me. "Why are you here? Does she look like she is in danger? Do I look like a fucking hunter?" The coarse texture of his voice matched the storm brewing in his eyes.

Max said nothing, only continued to stare at Liam. Underneath my fingers, Liam's muscles coiled like a wolf about to kill. I had to find a way to defuse the fight I sensed concocting.

"You're here to protect her from the hunters, not me," my mate reminded.

Max lifted his chin like a fool. "I'm here to make sure you don't violate the treaty and that she lives long enough for her to make a choice."

"She's mine." The possessive words rumbled from deep in Liam's chest. I swore I felt the roof tremble under my feet.

Max's canines gleamed. "Not yet."

Liam exploded.

Not like in a frenzied rage, because he was plenty pissed off, but as in a burst of fur and rippling muscle.

Fuck.

The heir prince shifted at school.

He landed on four paws in front of me, placing his wolf in the direct path of Max. Liam curled back his lips, snarling at the guard.

I blinked, unable to believe what was happening. Liam, the epitome of self-control, had just lost it over being baited by another wolf.

"Liam!" I called through our link, attempting to calm him down. This was bad.

He ignored me, his focus centered solely on Max.

My guard's eyes rimmed a bright gold. "I'm not afraid of you."

I refused to have two wolves shift on the school's goddamn roof. If I'd been closer to Max, I would have shoved him in the chest. I settled for throwing my hands up in the air. "Then you're a bigger idiot than I give you credit for. Do you really think you're stronger than the alpha's son?"

Max sidestepped, moving away from the door and toward the center of the roof. His eyes never left Liam's. "I guess we'll find out."

"I'm going to enjoy telling my father he's down a guard," I replied smugly, no longer giving a shit if Max got hurt. It would be his fault for acting like an egotistical idiot.

Liam lunged.

Backing up, I pressed into the wall, knowing better than to get in the middle. My stomach twisted as I watched, uncertain of what the fuck I should do.

Max's canines dropped down, his fingers shifting into claws, but he didn't fully turn wolf as the heir prince flew at him. My guard pivoted a second before Liam's massive paws could hit him. The ground shook when my mate landed, whipping his head toward Max with a nasty snarl.

Violence swam through our link at an alarming intensity. I covered a shriek as Liam swiped his claws in Max's direction, connecting with his chest enough to rip through his shirt and slice the surface of his skin. Lines of blood stained the front of his long-sleeved tee.

Without a single breath, Liam pounced, and this time, my guard didn't have time to avoid the hit. He knew it too, his golden eyes narrowing as he braced for the impact. It knocked him back, too close to the edge of the roof, his arms wrapping around Liam's muscular back, taking him to the ground with him.

Max landed on his back. The hit would have knocked a normal person out. He managed to maintain his hold on the heir prince, and they rolled, Liam snapping and growling.

My guard delivered an uppercut into Liam's chest, and I gasped, annoyed at both. If they thought I would tend to either of their cuts and bruises, they were sorely mistaken.

Screw this.

Liam must have had a similar thought. He twisted his head, sinking his sharp teeth into Max's shoulder. The guard groaned, grasping Liam by the throat and digging his claws into flesh. He ripped them out with the same force as he had jabbed them in.

The sight of Liam's blood coating the tips of Max's nails and running down his fingers made me faint. It also caused a surge of protective instinct in me. My wolf surged to the surface, ready to defend her mate at all costs.

I took a step, and Liam's voice thundered in my head. *"Don't you think about it, pup. This isn't your fight."*

"You're bleeding," I replied, defending my motives.

"It's a scratch. Stay out of this."

I huffed as Liam rammed Max to the ground, landing on top of him, with his front paws pinned to his chest. He bared his teeth in Max's face, the low growl a reminder of who the heir prince was. Max stood no chance of overpowering the alpha's son.

"Liam!" I called.

His body froze.

"Don't," I begged through our bond. It wasn't Max I tried to save but Liam.

The heir prince kept his teeth touching Max's throat. One move and my guard would be bleeding out on the roof.

"What are you waiting for?" Max taunted like he had a fucking death wish.

His aqua eyes blazing, Liam panted in his face. I stopped breathing like I was on the edge of the roof, teetering and waiting to see which way the wind would blow.

I saw the moment he made a choice and unhappily growled before easing off Max. I stepped toward the white wolf, but he didn't look at me. Instead, Liam galloped off toward the side of the building, leaping to the stairwell. I ran to the edge. Seconds later, I spotted his white fur racing into the woods. I heard a few gasps and a girl shriek from the grounds below before the dense trees swallowed him whole.

I whirled and marched up to Max, shoving him in the chest. "What the fuck was that?"

He pulled at the collar of his shirt, revealing the teeth marks Liam left behind. They looked wicked, but I wasn't overly concerned considering it would heal. "That was me putting my life on the line for you," he retorted, eyeing the injury.

The feelings pulsating inside me weren't entirely mine, but I was past giving a shit. "You're pushing him. He doesn't need your shit on top of everything else."

Max let his shirt fall back into place, wincing slightly as the material rubbed over the wound. His upper stomach looked to be fairing just slightly better than his shoulder. Although, he clearly needed a new shirt. "He needs his boundaries tested."

"That's not for you to decide!" I raged, or maybe Liam's fury still affected me. "He could have killed you, and if Liam doesn't, I just might."

He arched a dark brow as a streak of sunlight caught his golden eyes. "Are you threatening me, Kels?"

I scooped my bag off the ground. "If you keep poking my mate, I won't go easy on you. Next time, I won't stop him. I'll stand by his side and fight you alongside him." With that parting promise, I left, unsure what the hell my next move would be.

Eleven
LIAM

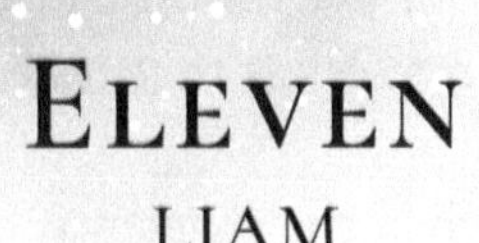

My paws flew over the damp ground, dirt and leaves kicking up behind me. I hurdled over a fallen log, not breaking my stride. I pushed my wolf despite his insistence I turn around. He wanted to go back for the girl.

For Kelsey.

For our mate.

Not yet, I argued.

Not yet. Those were Maxtyn's words, and they taunted me. Even now, miles from both the guard and Kelsey, the unruly jealousy still burned in my chest. I hadn't wanted to just hurt Maxtyn. I wanted to end his life due to pure jealousy.

I'd never been so possessive before that I lost my shit. I couldn't figure out who drove me crazier. Her or him. Regardless, it shouldn't have happened. Definitely not in front of him, but everything about the guard got under my fur.

He was staying in the house with *my girl*.

He was protecting *my girl*.

And if he made one implication that she could change her mind, that she could choose *him*, or that she would be better off with *him*, I'd rip his throat out with pleasure.

Consequences be damned.

I'd never lost control like that before especially not at school. Kelsey drove me mad. The more time I spent with her, the weaker my restraint became when she was involved.

These reactions I experienced weren't normal. Not for most wolves. Did these feelings stem from our Moonstruck connection? Everything was heightened, intensified to levels that tested us and made it impossible for us to be apart.

If I had to pinpoint when the chaos was created, it started the day Kelsey came to Riverbridge, but it had been tolerable. These irrational feelings were magnified after she claimed me.

It was as if the moon continued to push us together, a way to seal the bond. Our link was unfinished, and the fates didn't like loose ends.

Neither did I.

We had less than sixty days until her birthday, and it couldn't have felt farther away than if it were a year. Each day that passed, the gap seemed to stretch instead of moving closer. I ran and thought long and hard about how I would survive the next two months. Just as the full moon called to the wolf. Kelsey called to me.

All the fucking time.

I cursed the treaty and its stipulations. Why should a piece of paper dictate my life or how I choose to live it?

But it did.

And the burden of being the alpha's heir. I had to make choices I didn't like. Decisions that would literally tear me in half. Or in this instance, make it feel as if my heart was being yanked out of my chest.

For my pack, I would sacrifice the one thing I wanted above all other things.

Kelsey.

At least until the night she turned eighteen.

We would both suffer, but we were already suffering. How much more could a conflicted, aching heart add to the torment?

I had to stay away from her.

No more sneaking off to sleep beside her.

No more kissing her on the school rooftop.

No more moments alone with the temptress.

It all had to stop if we had any hope of making it to the end of the year.

My first mistake had been sleeping with her on my birthday. Now that I'd had her and knew how sweetly addicting being inside her was, I craved my next fix.

It wasn't only her body I coveted. To my surprise, I enjoyed her company, her dry, sarcastic humor, her smile, and her wit. Hell, I even loved the way she argued and contradicted everything. Her recklessness shouldn't have been a turn-on, but damn if it wasn't.

Discipline had always been my strong point, and no one tested me like Kelsey did. I wouldn't be able to have her a second time without sinking my canines into her flesh. I'd claim her. There was no doubt in my mind, considering it was all I thought about.

Coming to a trot, I decided to tackle one problem at a time. I had to throw myself into dealing with the hunters and uncovering the truth about my father.

The less time I spent with Kelsey, the better for both of us. She had Maxtyn to look out for her, much to my annoyance, but that did free up some of my time, and I could put it to other uses.

Gunnar being my top priority.

I wasn't far from the house where we stashed the hunter. It could be my subconscious had already come to a decision and led me to the dense part of the woods. I finished the last few miles of the trek to the cabin and shifted on the small wooden porch. From inside, the TV played an episode of *Survivor*, one of Colsen's favorites. This was as close as he would get to living completely off the land.

My hand stretched toward the door, but before I could reach the knob, the door flung open, Colsen's broad frame darkening the doorway. "What happened?"

I shook my head even as a slice of pride went through me. He'd been on guard. "Nothing. I just...needed to get away. You got any spare clothes?"

He studied my expression a moment before stepping back and replied, "Always. Do I want to know what happened to yours?" He moved through the cabin's main living area and tossed me a stack of clothes from a bag in the corner.

I caught them. "Fuck." I tugged the sweats on first. "I went wolf at school."

Colsen blinked. "I'm sorry. You did what?"

"Exactly," I mumbled, putting my arms through the school football tee. My tone made it clear I didn't want to expand on any details, and Colsen didn't press. He knew me better than to push when I was in a mood. "Any problems?" I asked, my gaze sliding to the closed door down the hall.

Colsen's gaze followed. "I wish. It would give me something to do if he did anything other than sit in the middle of his cage with his eyes closed like the bastard was in some sort of meditation state."

My lips turned down, but it felt as if I'd been frowning since I left school. "That won't do."

A grin split Colsen's rugged face. He'd been growing out his facial hair the last week and it suited him.

"Go take a break. Get something to eat. Sleep for a few hours. I got this covered," I said, making it more of a demand than a request but at the same time stressing I wanted him to leave.

He lifted an unsure brow. "Are you sure, man?"

I nodded. "Yeah. The hunter and I need some time alone."

Hesitation had him lingering, and he shoved his hands into his pockets. His job was to protect me, and leaving me alone with a hunter, even one behind bars went against his nature. "Okay, but if you need me—"

"I know how to reach you," I cut in. The one great thing about pack life was our connection. A distress signal was only a howl away. Literally.

I waited until Colsen's truck started up, the tires crunching over gravel as he backed out of the cabin's driveway, leaving me alone with the hunter. He might have been gone three whole seconds before Kelsey's voice entered my head.

"Where are you? Why have you been ignoring me?" Annoyance, worry, and a touch of panic wove into her questions.

My brows pinched as the wolf in me perked up at the sound of her voice. What was she talking about? Ignoring her? *"I haven't been ignoring you."*

"Then what do you call not responding?" she fired back.

It didn't matter that I was miles away in the woods; the urge to run back to her remained. If anything, the distance made the ache stronger. A flare of irritation sparked at my wolf's one-track mind. *"This is the first time I've heard your voice, pup."*

"Well, it's the fiftieth time I've communicated how much I hate you."

My lips twitched. *"Fiftieth, huh?"* I moved into the kitchen, opening the fridge to check if anything was left inside.

"I'm so not up for your charming humor," she grumbled.

What was going on with our bond? Did I even want to know? *"So I'm sensing."* I scanned the contents of the fridge, which were scarce, mostly drinks and some leftover pizza. I grabbed a beer and the cardboard pizza box, setting it on the counter.

"If you weren't ignoring me, then why couldn't you hear me?" she asked, and I went to reach for my phone to check what time it was, curious what class she was in.

"Shit," I grumbled. My phone was sitting in my pants pocket on top of the roof. Hopefully, Kelsey grabbed my stuff. *"I don't know. Maybe it has something to do with the fact I was in my wolf form,"* I suggested, not having any real answers for her. Understanding the differences in our Moonstruck bond would take time as well as experience. We wouldn't know the extent of our connection without testing its parameters, not unless we found another couple with the moon's marks.

"It never was a problem before," she pointed out.

She was right. The first time we communicated through the bond, I'd been a wolf and she'd been in her human skin. Why was this time any different? Had I done something? *"Well, I can hear you perfectly now. Are you okay?"* I unscrewed the beer cap.

"I should be asking you that," she snapped.

"You don't have to worry about me, pup," I assured, taking a long pull from the bottle.

She snorted. *"Oh, so it's okay for you to be concerned about me but not the other way around?"*

Having a conversation with her inside my head at least freed up my mouth to do other things like eat cold pizza. I grabbed a slice and bit off the end. *"Correct."*

"Whatever. I don't have time to argue with you. Are you sure you're okay?"

A tightness drew in my chest, and she could probably feel it. *"Yeah, I went for a run. My head's clearer."*

"Fine," she said, and I could sense she pouted.

I took that to mean the discussion was over. With Kelsey, I never knew when she would pop into my head. Another problem I needed to figure out. But first...

I faced the closed door.

After polishing off another slice of pizza and finishing the beer, I padded down the hall barefoot and flung open the door. Pretty much as Colsen described, Gunnar sat in the middle of the floor, his back rod straight, hands palm up resting on his knees.

His eyes remained closed. He didn't flinch as I cleared my throat. Perhaps *he was* in a deep meditative state, but I didn't give a shit. I leaned against the door frame with my arms crossed. "Stop with the feng shui bullshit. It won't save you."

"So you've decided to kill me," he said, lacking any feeling. We could have been discussing what we were going to have for dinner instead of his death.

"If you were in my position, what would you do?" I countered.

He opened his eyes and stared directly at me with darkness. "I'd kill you."

I felt the sizzle of his rage despite the relaxed façade he put on. Deep down, the hunter waited to get his hands on me again. "That's right because you're a killer," I stated.

"And you're not?" he scoffed as if he had me all figured out.

"We don't hunt humans," I replied with a callous quiet.

Unfolding his long, lanky legs, he stretched them out in front of him, leaning back on his hands. "If you believe that, then I don't think you and I are living in the same world."

Shifters fought each other, hunters, and only humans out of self-preservation. If our life was being threatened, then we could defend ourselves. These were shifter laws. If we broke them, we had a council that governed punishment. "I'm not here to debate the rules of shifters. Your opinion matters little to me."

"Did you want to talk about what happened that drove you here instead of at school where you should be?" He sniffed, wrinkling his nose. "You reek like wolf."

This prick was too damn perceptive. It raised my hackles. "I'm here to weigh my options."

A slow, sinister smile spread across his face. "Could you at least tell me how Hope is first?"

This was the first time he showed any interest in my cousin's well-being. "Why would I do that? Especially after what you did to her? You don't deserve to know anything about my cousin except she is better off with you gone."

"You really think so?" he snorted. "Knowing Hope, she has a lot of questions. Who do you think she will go to for the answers? She's too smart to think you'd tell her anything yet too damn persistent to give up. She'll pick at the truth like a scab, bit by bit."

Anger bristled my spine. "You seemed to be under the impression that you know my cousin better than I do. She's *my* family."

He pushed leisurely to his feet as if he had all day and this was a spa instead of a jail cell. "I know it's hard for your pea-size brain to process, but I never wanted to involve her. Kelsey left me no choice."

I surged forward, my fingers clenching the bars so hard my knuckles turned white. "Don't you fucking say her name!" Violence trembled through my muscles. *God, what the fuck is wrong with me today.* I rarely went from zero to a hundred in seconds.

I needed to relax, or I'd end up wolfing out again and killing him. I was so damn on edge. Showing Gunnar how much Kelsey affected me was equivalent to revealing my weaknesses, something no enemy should be equipped with.

His head angled to the side, strands of his black hair sweeping over his forehead. "Someone's a little sensitive and out of sorts today. Does your wonderful disposition have anything to do with your one-sided bond?" Gunnar hit a nerve, and it bothered me that he was so easily able to read me. Most couldn't.

Why him?

What I wouldn't give for two seconds inside his cage to backhand the smug smirk off his face. "Shut the fuck up. I'm asking the questions, and I'm only going to warn you once. Kelsey nor my cousin are your concern. Not anymore."

He stepped forward. "Unfortunately, they are," he pushed.

I shot him a glare equivalent to plotting his death. "If this is an attempt for me to end your life, you're doing a pretty good job."

"Do you believe wolves are the only beings capable of mating?" he asked, cocking a brow.

My grip loosened on the bars, taken aback by the sudden shift in conversation. "Are you implying humans have mates? You know it's not the same bond. And why is any of this relevant?" I hadn't come here to discuss the differences between humans and wolves. I didn't need a fucking lesson, but perhaps he did.

"Just thinking out loud. I don't exactly fall into either category, do I?"

"Your ability to mate or not is high on my I-don't-give-a-shit list. Hell, why consider it when there's a good probability you won't live to find out." I dropped my hands from the bars and took a step back. "But I do have something you can test since you seem so curious. If my father is responsible for the attacks on Kelsey, you're going to prove it."

His arms swept out. "And how do you propose I do that from within here?"

The corner of my lip tipped up. "Ever heard of a collar?"

Finally, Gunnar showed an emotion other than his I-don't-give-a-crap attitude. The superior smirk on his lips faltered, and I swore he stopped breathing.

Satisfaction entered my features. "So, you do know what it is."

Color blanched from his lips as his unholy dark eyes widened. "If you have access to a collar, then you have every right to distrust your father. Where do you think he got such a tool?"

I wanted to scare him. Mission accomplished. "Right now, it doesn't matter to me where it came from."

"I guarantee your mate doesn't know they exist. Or what it can do. How do you think she would react if what made her special was quashed, stripping her of not just her wolf but her powers?"

I fucking hated that he made me think of such a scenario. Murder. That's how she would feel—how I would feel. She'd kill whoever ripped her soul from her. And I'd do the same. Without the wolf, we were a shell in human skin. "I'd never let that happen."

"I never thought you'd keep me in a cage, and yet here we are," he reasoned in a desperate attempt to prevent me from using a weapon that took away a wolf's free will.

Unclasping the black chain from around my neck, I let it dangle from my fingers. "I'm not giving you a choice. You were right. I do need you. With you alive, I have a better chance at luring out the ones responsible, regardless of how close or how high up this goes."

He inched his way to the far wall and pressed his back against it. "What will you do once you have your proof? Go against your father?"

"I'll figure out my next move when we get there. I'm still not convinced my father's the villain you're claiming him to be."

"I never said he was a villain. What he does with Kelsey and her powers isn't of my concern. I'm not her mate."

My jaw ticked, the collar's power thrumming against my fingers. It made me want to hurl it across the room. Keeping it with me all day had probably been a mistake and magnified my bad mood. I should have realized it sooner when I stole it this morning from the vault. "You see my dilemma as her mate."

His eyes locked on the chain dangling from my fingers, the frown on his lips deepening. "Are you certain the collar will work on someone like me?"

Gunnar was human with wolf DNA that had been forced into him by means I didn't want the details of, but the outcome had altered his genetic makeup, making him not quite a shifter but no longer human.

In my eyes, he was a fucked-up experiment gone horribly wrong, and when this was over and when I no longer needed him, I damn well planned to extinguish the hunter.

"We're going to find out. I'm willing to take the risk," I said with a gleam in my eyes.

His expression became a thing as unfeeling as a rock. "I thought you didn't break the rules." He grasped at straws, looking for any excuse or weak point to get me to change my mind.

My honor was hardly enough. If he knew me, actually knew me, then he wouldn't have led with duty or morals. I could be as contemptible as anyone else when the situation called for it. "It's amazing what you're willing to compromise to protect someone you care about."

"Your father would be proud." Spite and rawness laced his words, and I couldn't blame him. If our roles were reversed, I'd do my damnedest to kill him before he got the collar anywhere near my throat. I expected nothing less from the hunter. "Once the collar is on, you'll be at my mercy and no longer a threat." The only way to remove the necklace once I activated the power inside was through my blood—only my blood. "It's the only way you're getting out of here alive."

"I'd rather have death than be someone's slave." Again. He didn't say it, but the unspoken word hung in the air. Specks of fear trembled in his eyes.

I had found what the hunter feared most. My lips curled. "Then I can't think of a better punishment."

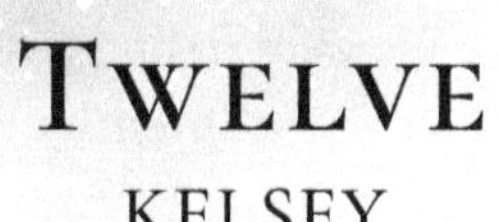

TWELVE

KELSEY

Liam didn't come back to school for the rest of the day, and damn it, if I didn't miss him. I had a very good idea where he'd run off to, but if he was at the cabin, it screwed with my plans.

I had Max. I couldn't exactly bring him with me to the house where we had a hunter chained up.

And I promised Hope an explanation. It wasn't a matter of trust that worried me about confiding in Hope. I was afraid of involving her more than she already was.

The vision in the bathroom... It meant something, and if that was Hope's fate by telling her the truth, then I'd be issuing her death warrant.

I hadn't anticipated the fight on the roof when I told Hope we'd talk after school, and now all I wanted to do was find Liam. This damn bond was both a curse and a godsend. It had saved my life on more than one occasion, but at the same time, I had mixed feelings about the heir prince. Wanting him was not a problem, and I didn't foresee our attraction dimming. Our Moonstruck link ensured we'd have no problem making baby wolves in the future.

The very distant future.

The final bell rang, and once I stepped out of school, I had two

different problems waiting for me. I had to find a way to tackle them both. All while also preventing Liam from evading my thoughts. The one good thing about having a single-sided bond—there weren't many—was thankfully he couldn't sense my emotions. Not like I could his.

I'd bombard Liam with all the turmoil circulating within me. It was bad enough sorting through my own emotions, let alone his too.

Today they were easier. We were feeling two very different ways, and for reasons unbeknownst to me, the intensity of those emotions wasn't as prominent as they'd been at first. Perhaps we were settling in, or maybe it was something else entirely.

Riven kept sneaking me funny looks as he escorted me through the building. I chewed on my lip, debating whether I should ask for his help in distracting Max, but that would lead to me having to tell him why I was looking to ditch my guard, a topic I most certainly wanted to avoid.

We were almost to the double doors, lost in the sea of students rushing for freedom, when I spotted Colsen coming toward us from the other side of the hall. "What's Colsen doing here?" I asked Riven. "Isn't he supposed to be at the—"

"Yeah," Riven said before I could finish, a frown building on his brow. "He is."

"If he isn't at the cabin, then who is taking care of our...guest?"

Riven's green eyes darkened. "Good question. I'm guessing Liam sent him away. It's the only reason Colsen would have left," he said, coming to the same conclusion I had.

"Have you spoken to Liam?"

The shifter shook his head. "No, not since before he took off. You?"

"Only for a minute in class," I admitted as a cluster of football players bypassed us.

"Is he there?" Riven asked Colsen as the three of us walked out of the school together.

"He's in a mood." Colsen's eyes shifted to me, accusation in them.

"Why do you automatically assume it's my fault?" I tried to look offended.

Colsen lifted a brow while Riven covered a cough with his signature boyish smirk.

"Okay, yes," I conceded, fixing the strap of my bag higher up my shoulder. "I had something to do with it, but I can't control Liam going off the rails every time Max decides to open his mouth and be an asshole."

"I'll take that as a compliment," Max said in his deep voice from my left side. Max shoved off from the corner of the building, weaving through the crowd toward me.

I rolled my eyes and shot my middle finger up at him. Problem number one arrived.

"Kelsey!" Hope called, and my head swung in the opposite direction. And problem number two showed up seconds later.

"Which one of you wants to help a girl out?" I muttered to Riven and Colsen.

Dipshit one and two grinned. "See ya, Kels," Riven said, saluting me as he and Colsen took off to the parking lot.

"Assholes," I mumbled under my breath.

Hope and Max reached me at the same time, and they stared at each other. Hope obviously heard about my father assigning me one of his guards, but this was the first time they'd met.

"Hey," I greeted her, moving with the crowd or we risked getting trampled. "I just realized I don't have a car. Liam drove me this morning, and he left school early."

Hope's gaze darted to Max, her expression a blend of curiosity and wariness. "I heard. It's no worry. I can drive. Where are we going?"

I squinted against the sun. "Change of plans. We need somewhere we can talk alone without anyone else eavesdropping. Or a lot of noise. Got any suggestions?"

Max leaned down and murmured in my ear, "What are you up to, Kels?"

I sent my elbow into his hard abs. "You're here to make sure I don't get an arrow in my back, not butt into my social life."

"I got a place," Hope retorted before Max and I could start bickering.

"Thank God." I sighed. "I need to get away from him."

"You wish, Kels," Max boasted. "Where you go, I go."

I groaned. "I hate my life," I grumbled.

Hope drove us to downtown Riverbridge, better known as the

square, because it was just as the name sounded, a square block of shopping and restaurants, basically the hub of Riverbridge.

She parked her car in front of Nick's Pizzeria, one of the busiest establishments Riverbridge had to offer, known for its exceptional pizza. I approved of Hope's choice. It was like getting a two-for-one special. We got to talk in a crowded, loud space that would drown out our conversation and stuff my belly.

I hadn't eaten much at lunch, so I was particularly hungry. More so when we walked in and the aroma of freshly baked dough and the tang of tomato sauce with spices hit me.

Max started to follow Hope and me to a table, but I spun and put a finger into his chest, halting him. "Nope. No way. You can sit at the bar, far enough away that I can't see your face but you can still keep an eye on me."

The guard opened his mouth, but I shushed him.

"There are no ifs, ands, or buts in this request. I'm having pizza with my best friend. That's it. We're catching up and talking about how much I hate you."

Max grinned. "Now I know you're lying."

I snorted and turned to find which table Hope had been seated at. A back corner booth. Perfect.

Packed with mostly kids from our school, Nick's brimmed with chatter. The restaurant's speakers cranked out the tunes at a volume that made having a decent conversation difficult unless you were a wolf with superior hearing like Hope and me.

Sliding into the booth, I did a quick scan, counting how many shifters I could spot. Other than Hope, Max, and me, only two others in the pizzeria were supernatural. A guy and girl who looked like they were on an after-school date, too absorbed in each other to give us a second glance.

We ordered drinks and a pizza to share. "Tell me what happened," Hope said once our server delivered our sodas.

My mind went back to Friday night. "You didn't get drunk, Hope. You never made it to the party."

She closed her eyes briefly, her shoulders going slack. "I knew it, but why did I wake up with what felt like damn close to a hangover?"

I didn't relish what I had to say next. "You were drugged."

She blinked, the hand stirring her drink halting. "Did you just say drugged?"

I nodded, confirming what she thought she heard. "It's a long story and pretty unbelievable, but I wouldn't lie to you."

The slight narrowing of her eyes assured me she was suspicious enough to listen. "How?"

Taking a breath, I paused. This was the part I dreaded, telling Hope her best friend was a hunter and he had used her as bait to trap me. Too bad I wasn't twenty-one because my Coke could really use a shot of something strong. Rum would be great.

This was one of those truths I had to rip off like a Band-Aid. Stretching it out wouldn't make it hurt any less. "Gunnar's a hunter. He's the one who's been attacking me. He drugged you so he could lure me into the woods to kidnap me." I rushed it out as quickly as I could.

I had no idea what her reaction would be. She could laugh. Get mad for accusing her best friend of something so outlandish. Or she could believe me. The latter would be harder than the others.

She blinked, sinking into the worn leather booth. "You're serious."

Toying with my straw wrapper, I gave her a sad frown. "Trust me, I wish I wasn't."

I could see her process the few memories of that night she had and put together how Gunnar could have drugged her. He was the last person she remembered being with. "He can't be. I would know."

Denial was the first step. "He fooled us all. There's more you need to know."

"More?" she squeaked, slumping into the leather booth.

I skimmed through the restaurant, double-checking we hadn't caught anyone's attention. Max sat at the bar, his eyes on the big screen replaying a football game that had been on earlier in the week.

I explained how Gunnar's DNA had been altered and manipulated, giving him traits of a wolf. "He isn't the only one. There are others according to Gunnar, but being made into a shifter seems to have one hiccup. Gunnar can't shift."

She took a moment to let it all sink in. "How can I possibly have not known he was a wolf or part wolf? Whatever he is."

I wish I had the answers to give her to make sense of it all. "None of us saw it. Part of his abilities is he's able to shroud his scent. I don't know how; maybe because he smells like a human."

"I can't believe it. It doesn't seem plausible."

I understood her disbelief. I had trouble believing the shit that happened in my life daily.

She stared at me with a puzzled expression. "Why is he hunting you?"

This was a big step for me, and I wasn't sure it was the right one. For so long, I'd protected this secret, but maybe shielding my power wasn't the way to live. Perhaps the women in my family had it wrong. Perhaps we weren't meant to conceal our magic. Would it be so wrong to trust Hope? I'd trusted Liam with the truth. My long pause was telling. "The same gifts my nana has were passed down to me." I studied her reaction to see if she understood what I was trying to convey.

Her brows squished together. "You have magic?"

I nodded. "And someone hired Gunnar to capture me."

She frowned from across the table, the severity of what happened sinking in. "For what?"

Indignation tapped up my spine. "I don't know. Experiments most likely."

"The same ones that were done to him," she guessed, connecting the dots more effortlessly than I predicted.

"I don't know," I murmured, tearing the straw wrapper into little pieces and tossing them on the table.

"This is so fucked up." Her shoulders dipped as a long sigh left her. "Why didn't you tell me about your powers?"

Guilt settled in my stomach. I crossed my legs under the table, finding a comfortable position. "You have to understand. I've spent my whole life keeping them hidden for this reason. It's been a coveted secret in my family for generations. Further back than I can trace. Few are trusted with the knowledge within the pack."

She tucked her hair behind her ears. "The rumors about your grandmother have circled within the pack since before I was born. I can't believe they are true. And Liam knows?"

I nodded. "He does. I had no choice. He could have been killed if I hadn't exposed my sixth sense."

Emotion flashed through her features. "By Gunnar?" she asked softly, disbelief making her sound raspy. "Did you—?" She gulped, her voice giving out, unable to bring herself to contemplate that perhaps the reason she hadn't seen or heard from Gunnar was because I killed him.

I didn't expect her to roll over and blindly except my word. I had to show her. Time for the big reveal. I shook my head. "He's alive. Liam has him locked away at a cabin in the woods. That's why he isn't responding to you or at school today."

A hand flew to her mouth. "Oh my god."

Our pizza arrived right then, interrupting a tense moment, and we waited until our server set it down in the middle of the table and left before continuing. My stomach rumbled at the sight and smell of gooey cheese, pepperoni, onions, and green peppers, I dug in, scooping a slice onto my plate.

"Which cabin?" Hope asked, her initial shock wearing off.

I had my pizza halfway to my eager mouth when I paused from taking a bite, a quizzical expression crossing my features. "There's more than one?"

Hope nodded, sliding a piece of pizza onto her plate. "My father is usually the one in charge of overseeing any wolves who need to be contained. What does Liam plan to do with him?"

"He hasn't decided," I answered, chewing with my mouth full.

She nibbled on the end of her pizza while I was about to take my second slice, scarfing it like I hadn't eaten in days. "What about you?" she inquired as if I had any sway over Liam.

If she had asked me on Friday night, I would have said without hesitation to kill him. But now... "I don't know," I admitted. "I can't trust him."

"I want to see him," she stated, my heart dropping.

If I were in her shoes, I'd have a million questions for the guy who posed as my best friend for years. That took a certain type of dedication that scared me. I swallowed. "I figured you would say as much. Liam will be a problem, along with my guard. We'll have to think of a way to get up there without either of them knowing." Ditching guards was my specialty. I could handle Max. It was Liam who would be the difficult one.

She dropped her barely touched slice of pizza onto her plate, little flecks of sauce falling onto the table. "I just can't wrap my head around Gunnar being a hunter. This is Gunnar we're talking about. He acted so surprised and interested when I told him what I was. God, I feel like such a fool. And I also want to slap the shit out of him."

I couldn't imagine how confused and betrayed she must be feeling. All I could do was be a friend, one who wouldn't hurt her. "I'm sorry, Hope. I hate that I'm the one to tell you." The guilt in my stomach doubled. I couldn't help but feel partially responsible for the betrayal weighing heavy on her. I couldn't say how much of their friendship was real or what percentage was because of me.

Hope shook her head. "Gunnar should have told me a long time ago. When I spilled my secret, he should have revealed his."

"I can't argue with that, but weirdly, I think he was trying to protect you."

She scoffed. "By drugging me? He has a funny way of showing it."

I snuck a glance at Max. He sipped on a half-drunk glass of beer while still watching the TV. He gave no indication he was listening in on our conversation, but I wasn't foolish enough to think he wouldn't try. The girl behind the bar stopped by him and looked to be asking if he needed anything else. She gave him a flirtatious smirk.

A snort breezed through my nose. If she only knew what an annoying, jerk he was behind the pretty face. I wasn't about to tell her. As long as she kept distracting my guard, I was happy.

"Is it weird having him around all the time?" Hope asked, following my gaze.

I shrugged. "Yes and no. This isn't the first time I've been assigned protection detail. You kind of get used to it when hunters are always showing up trying to end you."

Her elbow rested on the table, and she brought her hand up and leaned her cheek on it. "You really are a bundle of trouble."

Truer words were never spoken. Prior to coming to Riverbridge, I would have taken that as a compliment, but I swore nothing bad would happen to Hope. Not again. And not because of me.

☽☽●☾☾

HOPE SLID into the seat beside me thirty seconds before the bell rang. She dropped her laptop onto the table and faced me with tired eyes. It appeared neither of us got much sleep last night. "Tell me you came up with an idea because I got nothing," she said, keeping her voice low.

Our teacher stood in front of the whiteboard, writing out notes for today's lecture with a black marker. Last night, Liam and I slept apart, and the distance stretched between us, making the restlessness crowding within me unbearable. It took everything in me to stay planted in my seat and not go classroom to classroom searching for the heir prince for a glimpse of him. Not that it would do any good. He wasn't here. Not yet.

Liam hadn't picked me up this morning. He claimed he had something to take care of and would be at school later in the day. The one good thing about our telepathy was text messages weren't necessary. If he had to tell me something, poof, his voice popped into my head.

Alarming occasionally when I was naked in the shower or going to the bathroom.

"Depends on if you are up for detention," I replied, matching my volume to hers.

She grinned. "Do you even have to ask?"

I appreciated the smile even if it was forced. "Before fifth period, meet me in the bathroom on the first floor near the gym."

A glint appeared in her eyes. "I already like the sound of this."

By the end of my fourth class, I still hadn't felt the familiar tingles and began to worry about Liam. What was he up to? I couldn't shake the sneaky suspicion it had to do with Gunnar, but the heir prince wasn't filling me in on any details, which irked me.

Ever since the incident yesterday on the roof, I couldn't help but feel as if Liam had taken a step away from me. He created this distance, and I was trying to respect his need for space and to figure his shit out. I should be doing the same thing, but it was damn difficult to think with a rational mind when all I could fucking think about was *him*. Liam consumed ninety percent of my thoughts. It was exhausting having my brain whirling with concerns, fears, wants, and annoyances all centered around Liam.

Leith even mentioned something this morning about his brother's surly mood when he drove me to school. Surlier than normal, Leith added. He'd already heard about Liam wolfing out at school. By the end of the day yesterday, every shifter at school knew.

Keeping secrets from Leith was wearing on me. I didn't know how long I could continue with the façade nothing was wrong. I'd already broken down and involved Hope, but she'd already been involved. Keeping Leith in the dark might be the best way to protect him, a decision I hadn't yet decided would end up being more hurtful than helpful.

"If you were in trouble, you would tell me, wouldn't you?" Leith asked as we meandered down the halls.

He didn't know it, but I was about to abandon him at school and take off with Hope. The deceit ate at me. I wanted to drag Leith with us and bring him into the fold, but then I'd have a pissed-off Liam to deal with. Not that I was concerned with angering my mate. Annoying the heir prince was a favorite pastime. I loved to ruffle his fur, but this felt different.

The stakes were higher.

Regardless, I only had a minute to decide.

"How do you feel about detention?" I countered instead of answering his question.

His brows rose. "What are you up to?"

"Being reckless. You can thank me later." I grabbed Leith's hand and tugged him down the hall.

Next to Hope, Leith was my closest friend. He had welcomed me on my first day at Riverbridge High, and I owed him the truth. Liam might not agree with my decision, but my instincts were telling me Leith would be safer if he knew what we were up against. Knowledge could be a weapon, and I didn't want Leith in the dark when the storm hit.

And a storm was brewing.

I could sense it.

"Kelsey, wait—"

It was too late. I'd already pulled him inside the girls' bathroom, and his protest died when he saw Hope.

"What are you two up to?" he asked, eyeing us as I stepped in behind him.

"Tell me you've never wanted the chance to see the inside of the girls' bathroom," I said, moving to the far wall of the bathroom with the window.

"Who says I haven't?" he replied, watching me with eyes so similar to Liam's.

Only Leith. "We're sneaking off campus," I tossed over my shoulder before turning back to further inspect the window and what I was working with.

"I'm assuming the drastic measures have something to do with the hunky guard outside," Leith speculated.

Turning around, I gave Hope an apologetic look, hoping she didn't mind I brought her cousin along. She gave me a small smile, and I faced Leith. "He's a pain in my ass, which now that I'm thinking about it, I should have had you distract him instead of coming with us."

Leith crossed his arms over his chest, the black sweater pulling tight against his muscles. "Uh-uh. Not happening. I'm involved now."

"In that case, help me pry open this window," I said.

He glanced at his cousin who held up her hands in an I'm-innocent stance. "Don't look at me. I'm as clueless as you," she insisted.

"Not quite," I corrected, flipping the lock undone. "He doesn't know about Gunnar."

Hope dropped against the sink counter, her features saddening. "Oh."

I wished I had the kind of magic that could take away pain. "I figure we can give him the lowdown on the way to the cabin," I explained, straining to shove the window open. It was stuck, but if I applied any more pressure, I'd break the damn thing.

"Here, move out of the way," Leith said, bumping me with his hip as he wedged himself in front of the window.

It took him a few good shimmies, but the window gave and groaned as Leith shoved it open. Dust sprinkled the air. Clearly, no one had opened it in a very long time.

Flashing us his dimples, Leith stepped to the side, linking his fingers together into a makeshift step. "Ladies first."

I put my boot into Leith's hands. "Hope, did you park in the gym lot like I asked?"

Shoving off the sink, she walked toward Leith. "I did. I got a spot near the corner of the building."

"Good." I hiked my leg through the opening. "We should be able to get to your car before Max detects us."

The bell rang as we climbed out of the window, raced to Hope's car, and jumped in like we were criminals escaping jail. I looked over my shoulder, staring behind us while Hope steered out of school to the main road. Only when we'd turned onto Station Road did I flip forward in my seat, fastening my belt. "Take this to Crystal Bend and make a right," I advised.

I continued to give her directions while also filling in Leith with as many details as I could cram into the drive until we were nestled deep in the woods and her tires rolled to a stop in front of a small cabin.

"Are you sure this is the place?" Leith asked, closing the car door behind him.

I couldn't deny it looked abandoned. No signs of life emitted from within the house. Plumes of smoke didn't billow from the chimney. The gravel driveway was empty, no other vehicles were parked in front, and only tire tracks remained behind. Where were Colsen or Riven? One of them should have been here.

My eyes squinted. "I'm sure."

Leith climbed the steps, putting his nose to a dirty window, and peered inside. "I'm not doubting you, but there's no one here."

He was right. My wolf sense picked up no traces of life from within the cabin. If Gunnar was where I'd last seen him, I should be able to hear his heartbeat or his breathing.

My ears picked up...nothing. Only the sounds of the surrounding forest.

I took off, a sickening pit sinking in my gut. What if Gunnar broke out and hurt Colsen or Riven? It had been hours since I last spoke with Liam. What if...?

I burst through the door, half expecting to smell the sharp, metallic remnants of blood.

“Kelsey!” Leith called after me.

Darkness and lingering fragments of burning wood greeted me as I entered the cabin. Hope’s and Leith’s footsteps were right behind me, but I didn’t stop and made a beeline straight for *the room*. The door was opened, and I stood in the entryway gawking at the empty cell. Chains were scattered on the floor, but no one occupied them.

“What the fuck?” I muttered, dread choking my voice.

“Kelsey?” Hope called gently.

I whirled, Hope and Leith hovering in the doorway. “I swear he was here.” My voice weakened.

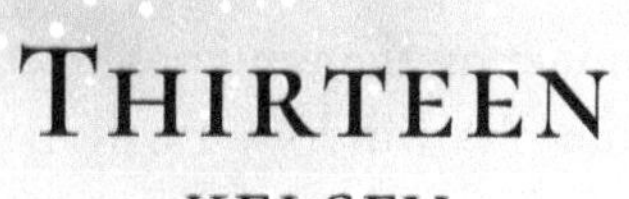

THIRTEEN
KELSEY

Hope took a step over the threshold into the room. She eyed the cage that took up three-quarters of the space, landing on the empty chains on the floor. "I've heard my father speak of this place, but I've never been here. Do you think he broke out?" she asked, and I swore I detected a fleck of hope in her tone.

"I don't know." The bigger question was how I planned to tell Liam Gunnar escaped and how I came to know this. Then again, perhaps it was me who was the last to know.

My fists curled, nails digging into my palms as a combination of fear and fury spun inside me.

I tried to think rationally.

If Liam didn't know about Gunnar's escape, I had to warn him.

"Kels, we should leave," Leith said, his eyes brimming with worry. "This was a bad idea. You're unprotected."

My chin lifted. "I can take care of myself. And I'm not alone. I have the two of you."

"We should leave," Hope echoed, her arms wrapping around her middle. "This place is giving me the creeps."

"I can't believe this is happening." Now it was my turn to repeat the

game of disbelief. Yesterday, it had been Hope. Ten minutes ago, Leith. It looked as if we would just keep passing the torch.

"Come on," Leith coaxed, laying a hand on my shoulder. "If he's out in the woods, I don't want you anywhere near him. Let's not give him a second chance to get what he wants."

Me.

None of us spoke much on the way back to school. I chewed on my nails, blankly staring out the window. Partly because I was trying to connect with Liam, but the prick wasn't responding. All I wanted to know was if he was safe. How hard was it to reply with a simple yes?

The anxiety tightening my chest intensified the closer we drew to school and the longer our bond stayed silent. I jumped out of the car before Hope shifted it into park.

"Shit," Leith mumbled, dashing after me as I raced toward school.

"What period is it? Still fifth?" I rattled off as my legs moved, eating up the ground.

"Fifth ended a few minutes ago," he said, catching up to me, the wind blowing his sandy hair around.

Explained why so many students were in the parking lot and lounging around the building. It was the first lunch period. "What class does Liam have?" I should probably know his schedule, but memorizing what classrooms he was in hadn't been high on my priority list.

"PE, I think," Leith replied.

My pace increased, going from a sprint to a run.

Leith reached out, his fingers curling over my forearm, hauling me to a stop. "Kelsey, you can't just burst into his class. We don't even know if he's here."

I stared up at him. "He's here. I can feel him."

"If he's at school, then he's safe," Hope reasoned, finally catching up to us and attempting to calm me down.

"Valid point," I agreed, yet it wouldn't stop me from having my way. "But I need to see him. I can't explain it. I have this feeling inside me that won't go away until I see his face."

Leith shook his head, releasing a breath at the same time his fingers unfastened from my arm. A dimple appeared on his cheek. "Glad to see you haven't lost your spunk."

I took off again, drawing closer to the school and making the tingles dancing up and down my spine multiply, but as I jumped the curb onto the sidewalk, a shadow of darkness gathered behind my eyes, momentarily blinding me.

I came to a sudden halt, Hope bumping into me. "Oomph," she said as her hands landed on my back.

"Something's wrong," I muttered, and then Leith stiffened, his muscles coiling beside me.

"Looking for me?" someone asked.

I whirled at the sound of that particular voice.

It couldn't be.

It wasn't possible.

But then I remembered the empty cell, and shit, the idea seemed very fucking plausible.

How the hell…?

My gaze landed on Gunnar's smug, grinning face.

"Miss me?"

"Gunnar," Hope gasped. "Where the hell have you been?" Then she launched into his arms as if she'd completely forgotten everything he'd done. And maybe she had. The hug could be an instinctual reaction. One didn't forget years of friendship overnight.

The hunter didn't immediately embrace her, and his hands stayed hanging at his sides for a few moments before they came up around Hope. I swore flecks of relief sparkled in the center of his dark eyes.

I had a different reaction to seeing him, a sort of chain reaction that went something like…

No fucking way.

Goddamn it.

Holy shit.

Is he going to kill me?

How did he escape?

The balls of this asshole to show up after what he did.

Oh my god, Hope! No!

Hadn't she heard anything I said yesterday? Did she not believe me?

I'm going to rip his lethal hands off her if he so much as touches her,

I hated that fear hit me first before the anger, but once the red-hot fury entered my veins, I held on to it. A growl started deep in my chest, vibrating until Hope backed out of his arms and turned to look at me. Gunnar's gaze was right behind Hope's, except his brows lifted in mocking intrigue, whereas Hope's drew slightly together in confusion, her mind catching up.

I couldn't care less we were at school, that it was lunch, and people were everywhere. I didn't need a mirror to see that my wolf eyes had surfaced, shining brightly.

"What's going on? Why am I getting waves of anger from you? It's making my temperature rise."

Now Liam decided to suddenly pop into my head. Fucking convenient. *"Because I'm about to kill someone."*

"Kelsey," he rumbled.

I ignored the heir prince, my focus solely on Gunnar. "How are you here?" I asked, finally finding my voice, but it didn't sound normal. It came out gravelly and not quite human.

"Kelsey," Hope hissed under her breath, backing out of Gunnar's arms and putting space between them. Space that didn't go unnoticed by the hunter. "You're showing," she added.

Ice trickled into my blood. "I don't care," I gritted between clenched teeth, my glare solely for Gunnar. "Explain why I shouldn't slice your throat right now. And as I've already stated, I'm past giving a shit about consequences or audiences."

Smugness mottled in his eyes and made me want to jab each with a scalding poker. "Ask your boyfriend," he replied.

My jaw started to hurt. "He's not my boyfriend. Shit, I don't know what he is, and it doesn't matter. What does Liam have to do with this?"

"Everything, little wolf," Gunnar said, his hands going into his back pockets. "And before you go feral on me, I can't hurt you."

Hope's gaze volleyed between Gunnar and me, a desperate look in her eyes. I could tell she very much wanted Gunnar to say this was a big misunderstanding, that he wasn't a hunter, that he hadn't used her, that he hadn't tried to injure Liam or kidnap me.

"What do you mean can't hurt me?" I asked. Gunnar said that he couldn't hurt me, not that he *wouldn't*, and his choice of words struck me as odd. I could be reading too much into it, but the hunter didn't do or say something that wasn't with purpose.

Gunnar took a step forward, and Leith lunged between us, becoming a barrier between the hunter and me. "Come any closer and I'll carve your heart out. I don't care what you are. Every creature needs a beating heart to live."

"You told them." Gunnar's gaze accused me of treachery when he had no right. I never promised him anything. He snorted. "I guess I deserve it, to lose the only thing I care about, considering I tried to do the same."

Damn right.

My chin jutted up.

Hope's hands flew to her hips like bat wings. "It's true. Everything that Kelsey told me. You're a-a hunter?" she stammered.

Gunnar tore his gaze from mine, his features softening when he glanced at Hope. "We should probably talk."

Hope took a step away from him, shaking her head. "It wasn't a fucked-up dream, was it? What Kelsey told me was true. Every bit of it. You drugged me."

I figured it was best to let Gunnar dig his own grave with her. He wouldn't need any help from me. What he'd done would be enough to put a giant fissure in their friendship, maybe too big to repair as I sensed Gunnar wanted.

"Yes," he admitted, head hanging low. "But you need to understand. I didn't have a choice."

"We always have a choice. How many times did you say that to me?" She shook her head, tears pooling in her big brown eyes. "I can't believe you tried to kill my best friend."

"I wouldn't have hurt her," Gunnar said, pleading with Hope's compassionate side.

I tried to comfort myself with the theory that he wouldn't try anything with so many people around, but I couldn't be certain. Gunnar represented a fear I hated—the fear of being caged.

I felt Leith's heat warm me, and it gave me a boost of confidence, melting some of the ice forming in my veins as I moved to Leith's side, rather than staying behind him. "Right, he wanted to kidnap me so other people could hurt me. Your hands are still dirty as fuck. You have nerve showing your face here after what you did," I hurled with a disgruntled rumble.

His gaze never wavered. "Like I said, I didn't have a choice."

My eyes flared. "What does that even mean? What does Liam have to do with it?"

A gust of wind blew out of nowhere. Strong enough against my back to shove me forward. I stumbled straight into Gunnar.

FML.

I reached out to break my fall, catching his arms, and a flash zapped behind my eyes, the world before me vanishing.

THE BRIGHT LIGHT FIZZLED OUT, and I blinked, gaping at the towering trees surrounding me. What the hell? Where was I? What happened to my school? To my friends?

It was the quiet that gave away my sudden abandonment.

Or maybe it was me who abandoned them.

Regardless, I stood alone in unknown woods without a clue how I got there or how to get back.

Joy.

A howl rent the air, and at the top of the hill, the shadow of a wolf appeared, yet as my eyes cleared, the figure wasn't animal but human.

Meta.

I'd never seen a human have the reflection of a wolf.

He was like Gunnar.

Hell, was he Gunnar?

My gaze swept over the rows of trees, rendered immobile as one meta became a dozen. A dozen became fifty.

I stepped back, my boots crunching over a bed of dried leaves and fallen sticks. The sound crackled through the sleeping forest.

There was outnumbered. And then there was fucked.

I was fucked.

Even with my powers, I wouldn't be able to take on this many altered humans with wolf abilities. I might be able to hold them off for a spell, but eventually, I'd run out of steam, my magic would deplete, and I'd be left at their mercy.

If I thought one mutated hunter in Riverbridge was a problem, fifty was damn terrifying.

The one leading the pack stepped out of the shadows, a slice of moonlight hitting his gaunt face, and I gasped. His features were distorted, a mixture of human and wolf. Bright glowing red eyes, sharp cheekbones, and elongated nose and mouth. Pointed canines descended as he opened his mouth and snarled.

He wasn't someone I wanted to meet in a back alley or the woods at night for that matter.

Power stirred in my blood as if the sight of him awakened it, sensing the trouble about to befall me.

Behind me, a growl thundered the ground underneath me. I didn't want to take my eyes off the meta, but the prickle on the nape of my neck warned me we weren't alone.

Taking a risk, I pulled my eyes from the hilltop and glanced over my shoulder.

Wolves.

So many of them. Their glowing eyes sliced through the darkness, pinned on the meta. War brewed in the air, turning the cool evening into something so cold it froze inside my lungs.

They'd come to fight the mutated.

And leading the pack was...

No. It couldn't be. No. No. Fuck no.

My head shook over and over in denial at the wolf who broke through the pack first.

Liam.

My pulse leaped.

Where was his father? He was the alpha. He should be here leading his pack into battle. Not his son. Not my mate.

He could die. They could all die.

Beside Liam stood out a form that didn't belong in a group of wolves —a human.

Gunnar.

He had a bow strapped to his back and a pair of daggers glinted in each of his hands.

"Liam!" I screamed. "Run!"

The heir prince didn't so much as flinch at the sound of my voice.

I started to run at the same time Liam's wolf threw back his head and howled.

The pack charged, filling the woods with the thunderous pounding of more than a hundred paws hitting the earth.

I had to intersect. I had to stop them.

But my efforts were futile. I wasn't fast enough. The net I cast with my power was useless. The pack barreled through like my magic was nothing but smoke and mirrors.

I could only watch as the boy I never got the chance to really love risked his life to take on those who threatened us.

Was this all because of me?

Was I the reason they were here?

Snarls, snapped bones, teeth gnashing, torturous cries, whimpers of pain, and blood soaking the earth unfolded before my eyes.

I couldn't take it anymore. I couldn't watch them die.

An arrow flew toward me, but I detected it too late. The silver tip sunk into my chest, piercing my heart. Pain erupted and I fell to my knees.

MY FINGERS DUG into firm biceps as the vision playing out in my mind slowly dissolved. I wavered on my feet, my head whirling and my eyes blurring the two worlds, until I stared clearly into a face no longer speckled with blood.

Gunnar. He stared down at me, brows knitted together and his hands steady on either side of my arms. He shouldn't be touching me, and for a few seconds, I couldn't remember why.

It was the rush of tingles over my skin clearing the fog, and I jerked out from Gunnar's hold too fast. My head wasn't quite stable, and I stumbled, the ground tilting on its axis.

Shit. I'm going to pass out.

"Kelsey." My name was a familiar growl on the heir prince's lips as he caught me.

A swarming relief blew through my body. The pain, the fear, and the confusion all disappeared, and I sighed, throwing my arms around Liam's neck, and burrowing my face into him.

"I got you," he murmured, holding me tight to his sturdy chest.

"They're coming," I whispered.

His fingers combed through my hair, and his hands framed my face as he pulled back to look at me. "Who's coming?"

Tears clouded my eyes. "I saw them. So many. Like the hunter."

"You saw them?" he echoed.

I nodded.

A shadow moved into Liam's features. It made me believe he'd already considered this possibility. Before I could question him, a movement distracted me.

Max halted at my side, having jogged across the parking lot. "What happened?" he demanded with a glare of accusation pointed at Liam.

"Nothing," I replied. He was the last person I wanted to be involved in this mess. My chest hurt so badly that I rubbed at the spot where the arrow had pierced, half expecting to find the silver stem sticking out of my heart.

Max's gaze narrowed on me. "Where the fuck were you? Why aren't you in class?"

"She left school without you knowing." Liam's nostrils flared, and I feared he might shift again. "Your job is to guard her, and yet you seem to fail to do so."

"Damn it." My guard raged, shoving a hand into his dark hair. "You left?"

My lips pressed into a thin line. "I don't need a lecture. So save it."

Max's scowling eyes lifted, cutting Leith, Hope, and Gunnar a not-so-friendly glance. "You helped her?"

"I'll deal with them. It's not your place," the heir prince barked. I was beginning to think Liam loved pulling rank around Max and not so subtly reminding him of my guard's position. The pissing match between them grew tiresome.

"How did you know she wasn't here?" Max hurled at Liam as if he would catch the heir prince in a lie.

Liam kept a hand secured around my waist. "She's my mate. I don't just feel her presence, but I know when she's in danger. From the time she stepped into Riverbridge, I've been able to sense when she was in trouble because she's mine. Do you see? The only person who can truly protect her is me."

I struggled to keep from rolling my eyes despite the truth that rang in Liam's words.

Something flashed over Max's features. Surprise perhaps, but it was quickly replaced by a mask of impassiveness. "Not possible. You haven't claimed her."

"That would be true if we weren't Moonstruck." The confession was a snarl from Liam's lips.

A range of emotions crossed Max's features, and I tried to recall if I'd ever mentioned my unusual link to Liam. Apparently, my parents hadn't either. Packs were tight-lipped among each other, especially when it came to secrets. We were exceptionally good at keeping them.

As far as Max knew, I was his alpha's daughter who needed his protection. He had no idea of the depth of his duties or why he truly protected me.

"Moonstruck," Max repeated. "It's a myth. No one's ever seen a pair of Moonstruck mates in decades. Probably longer."

"Until us," I said, confirming Liam's claim.

Max looked at my friends, expecting them to back him up.

"It's true," Leith said. "We've all seen the marks."

Hope's features brimmed with worry and confusion. "Are you okay?" she asked me.

The heir prince's arm continued to support me. "Yeah. I'm fine," I assured, regardless that my insides were nothing but disorder.

"What just happened was not fine," she countered. "You passed out."

"You fainted?" Liam asked in my head, eyeing me from the corner of his gaze.

I gnawed on the inside of my cheek and replied, *"No, I don't think so. I think I had a vision."*

"I'd feel better if you were certain, pup."

Me too. I faced Gunnar, suppressing the icky feeling I had at being in his arms. "How many are there?" I demanded.

A speck of light flared in his gaze, just a fraction, but it was enough to know he understood what I referred to. "How many what?" he replied like the skilled liar he was.

I nailed Gunnar with a glare. "Hunters *like* you."

A muscle along his jaw popped. "This is not a discussion you want to have here," he retorted, his gaze circulating through the parking lot behind me.

"Answer her," Liam ordered with no kindness.

I don't know who was more surprised when Gunnar obeyed. Me or the hunter. "More than either of you can fight."

Leith, Max, and Hope stood there gaping at us, soaking up what information they could while trying to piece it all together.

"When?" I blurted.

The hunter pulled at the collar of his hoodie as if he couldn't breathe. "I don't know."

I bared my teeth.

"It's the truth," he insisted.

"Kelsey, what's going on?" Leith asked, breaking his silence. The younger Castle looked to me for answers.

Liam scowled down at me. "I'd also like to know."

Gunnar's response did nothing to alleviate the clenching of my stomach. I chose my words carefully with Max listening. "One of the rogue wolves escaped the pack Halloween night. They know we've caught Gunnar, and they're coming for him." Or for me. I didn't know.

"That's what you saw," Hope whispered, her eyes widening.

I nodded.

"Fuck," Liam said.

Fourteen
LIAM

I couldn't deal with another problem. Not of this scale, despite them being connected, but it didn't look like I had a choice if what Kelsey saw came to light. I didn't know shit about her gifts, of how much she was capable of, or how much power flowed in her veins, but if it was as much as suspected, then we should all be very fucking worried.

Not of Kelsey, but for what was coming. We might be putting out little fires one at a time, but soon our whole world would burn if I didn't figure out how to protect her.

A war was coming.

I thought it would be internal. Father and son. But looking into Kelsey's terrified eyes, I began to wonder if the battle would be on a scope that didn't just involve the pack.

Damn. It would have to wait. And hopefully, I had the time, but it wouldn't hurt to give my father the heads-up just in case. It would also be an opportunity to see what his reaction would be to learning about the meta.

I'd be bringing a guest for dinner.

Should be another interesting family meal, keeping with Castle tradition. I'm not sure we'd ever had a quiet dinner in my life as much as my mother tried.

I shoved a hand through my hair, my eyes darting from Hope to Leith before landing on Kelsey. "Where have you been? I got to school and you weren't here. What trouble were you causing, pup?"

Her gaze swung to Gunnar. When they returned to me, a spark of suspicion and anger clouded those violet irises. "You let him go," she whispered, a dawn of understanding passing over her stunning features. "Why would you do that?"

This was not how I planned to tell her, but I should have known with Kelsey nothing goes according to plan. Of course, she would run into him before I could explain. "If you had been where you were supposed to be, I would have told you first."

Her head shook. "Nope. You don't get to turn this around on me. It doesn't negate the point that you made this decision without me."

I kept my eyes on her but spoke to everyone else. "You'll have to excuse my mate and me. We need to talk."

Kelsey chuckled sarcastically. "Talk. Is that what you call it? Let's say it like it is. We're about to have a fight, princeling."

My brother coughed.

Hope shifted on her feet, staring at the ground.

And Gunnar smirked.

Max just stared at us, scratching his head and looking utterly perplexed by what was happening. I didn't blame him. He'd walked right into a shitstorm. He needed to walk right back out.

"As much as I'd love to stick around for this, I'd rather not get caught in the middle," Hope said, giving Kelsey a wave.

"I'm with Hope," Leith agreed, shooting my mate a wink and taking off after our cousin.

"Well, this is awkward. I've got a lot of schoolwork to make up," Gunnar said, shoving his hands into his pockets as he strolled past us toward the school.

That left just Kelsey, Max, and me. I gave the guard a pointed glare, making it obvious three was a crowd. "You want me to leave," he said, stating the obvious. His gold eyes radiated.

"If you're waiting for me to ask politely, we'll be here all night," I said, my tone sharp like a dagger carved of ice.

Kelsey huffed, but at least the coloring in her cheeks was coming back. When I'd seen her in Gunnar's arms, an unbearable heaviness had squeezed my chest.

If I'd been thinking rationally, I would have realized she wasn't hurt, but the sight of her lifeless in another guy's arms clogged all logical reasoning.

"I don't remember high school being this dramatic," he mumbled before walking off, finally leaving me alone with my mate.

I turned to Kelsey, calling forth on my control. I needed all of it to keep from throttling her. "Get in my truck."

She stiffened. "I'm not sure you want to be locked in a confined space with me now."

"Okay, the hard way then." She anticipated my move and side-stepped out of the reach of my arms. I smothered a grin, humored that she thought she knew me so well. The second time I reached for her, I changed direction at the same time she dodged, my arms sweeping around her waist. Seconds later, I swung her over my shoulder and hauled her ass across the parking lot to my truck.

I lost track of the numerous cuss words she heaved. Her temper shouldn't amuse me. I shouldn't find it cute, yet I did.

After planting her into the seat, I slammed the door closed and jumped into the other side. It was an effort not to use my wolf speed and keep my pace at human levels. Kelsey was known to not stay where I put her.

She crossed her arms, shifting toward me. The only reason she stayed in the car was because she itched to fight. I could be accommodating when need be.

I captured her gaze, and my heart did that damn stuttering thing in my chest. "You went to the cabin." The thought alone raised a storm of fury in my veins. She purposely put herself in danger.

Her eyes sparked with violet fire. "I had to. Hope needed to know."

The anger fueling within me flared. "I should reprimand you for going back to the cabin as well as involving my cousin and brother."

Energy crackled in the car. "You'd like that. Would you bend me over your knee and spank me?"

I pinched the bridge of my nose. Why did she have to make it sound so damn sexy? If I didn't tread carefully, all this turbulence in my blood could turn into something as dangerous. Lust. Need. Desire. "We'll get to the spanking later when we're alone."

She scoffed. "So you can ignore me some more."

"I'm not ignoring you."

"You're keeping secrets from me," she chastised.

My fingers flexed against the steering wheel. I needed something to do with them. "I'm not the only one breaking the bonds of trust, pup. I specifically told you not to involve Hope and Leith. You did exactly that behind my back."

"If you'd stop shutting me out, I could have told you. Since we're sharing, why did you let him out? It was you, wasn't it? That's where you've been all morning."

"Yes, but it's not what you think. He isn't free," I said with quiet steel.

Confusion built on her brow. "What do you mean?"

Four of my football teammates were fucking around in the parking lot, tossing a football over the cars. The ball sailed passed the top of my truck and into Brody Nieman's hands. I waited until they moved a few feet further down the parking lot. "Have you ever heard of a collar?" I asked.

Her brows drew closer together. "They're archaic. *And* banned. The king had them destroyed, deeming it an inhumane practice."

"Not all of them were destroyed," I revealed, waiting to see her reaction.

She twisted the ring on her thumb, understanding dawning in her eyes. "Your father."

I nodded.

"And it works on the hunter?" she asked,

"It does," I confessed. "He has just enough wolf DNA to make it functional." I'd taken a gamble, and luckily it paid off...so far.

Her pretty features darkened in a look I recognized. She was mad. "You should have told me. I won't be the kind of mate who sits by and lets you make all the decisions. If that's the kind of partner you're looking for, then you shouldn't claim me." She swung the car door open and rushed out of the truck.

I knew exactly who she was. How headstrong and proud she was.

How feisty and reckless. She was so damn powerful. I caught her at the back of the truck. Latching onto her wrists, I whirled her around to face me. "We're not done here."

She shook her head, a curtain of dark hair swaying. "I don't have anything else to say to you, *princeling*. You made your position very clear. You want a wife who blindly obeys," she spat.

Her emotions gave me whiplash. I couldn't keep up. "That's not what I said."

Her chin went up. "Same difference. I don't like being blindsided."

A sigh of exasperation left my lungs. "And yet you didn't talk to me about involving my cousin and brother," I reminded. She hadn't been the only one blindsided today.

"Fine. We both fucked up," she compromised. "Happy?"

Nothing about her tone or facial expression indicated she was "happy." I wasn't sure there was any way I could win this argument that I never really wanted to have in the first place. I lifted her hand and ran my thumb over the inside of her wrist where the faint outline of a crescent moon glowed. I heard her heart beat faster at my touch. "I missed you." Was I using a cheap trick to defuse the situation?

Yes. Shamelessly.

Her palms flattened on my chest, and she shook her head again. "Oh, no. You don't get to do that and smooth things over. I'm still mad at you. I still hate you."

"I hate you too, pup." My lips grazed her cheek. "Every glorious inch of you," I murmured in her ear.

She shivered in my arms, slowly melting into me.

I slipped a hand around to the small of her back and applied a bit of pressure, encouraging her to close the distance separating us. "Last night was torture."

The stubborn wolf that she was she didn't sink immediately into me but glanced up with a wistful look that edged the thin line of sadness. "How long will it be like this? How many nights do we have to suffer?"

My intent hadn't been to erase her anger with anguish. I wanted to tease her, to draw out her smile. Instead, I gave her the truth. It's what she asked for. "Until I claim you."

Her lips curved downward. "I know all the reasons we're supposed to wait, but I don't see why. I want you to claim me. Don't you want it as well?"

When we were together, completing our bond felt necessary. Not just the right thing to do but the only thing. My pulse quickened. "You make everything so damn difficult, pup. If you keep looking at me like that, I'll risk a potential war, not just between our packs but with the damn king himself."

They were words that could get me killed.

"Maybe this was a mistake," she whispered.

A knot twisted in my stomach. The harder Kelsey shoved me away, the more I wanted her. Explain that logic. I didn't even try to understand my feelings for her anymore. They weren't reasonable or rational. "We both know you don't mean that."

She stepped out of my arms and leaned against the back of my car, slivers of regret sparkling in her eyes. "Maybe I should."

I moved quickly, grabbing either side of the truck bed's edge and boxing her in. Her eyes stayed on mine. As usual, an overwhelming connection to her burned within me. Just staring at Kelsey made me feel different.

I saw it then. Something I'd never noticed before. A fleck of power like a tiny moon shone in the center of her eyes. "Something's changed."

She gave a weak shrug. "I don't know. You're still a jerk."

I suppressed the tug of amusement at my lips. "No, not me. With you."

Her head angled to the side. "What do you mean?"

"I'm not sure." I zeroed in on the glint in her eyes, and my other senses picked up on other differences. Minuscule, but when you were as in tune with someone as I was with Kelsey, those minor changes were noticeable if you paid attention. "I can...smell it too."

Her nose wrinkled. "I smell different?"

"Not really, just a hair of something...more, I guess. And your eyes..."

"Maybe it's because of the claiming?" she suggested.

"Probably." And yet her eyes betrayed her. She didn't believe the excuse any more than I did. And knowing Kelsey, she would pick at it and pick at it until she discovered the source.

She swallowed. "What do you plan to do with him?"

We were back to Gunnar, a smooth transition away from herself. Duly noted. She didn't want to talk about it, but at some point, we would. "I understand his presence makes you uncomfortable, but his disappearance would bring up questions, and I don't want to alarm his boss. I have to know if it's my father."

She nodded. "Having him free will lead us directly to who is responsible. I don't like it. I don't trust him. But I understand."

"Stay close to Maxtyn." I winced at the words. It physically hurt, but the more eyes on her, the safer she'd be, I reasoned.

Her lips twitched. "Orders I never imagined would come from your mouth. You want the hunter to work with us. I can see all sorts of problems manifesting, but I also think we have little choice. Working with the enemy might be our best hope."

Or it could bite us in the ass. I fucking prayed I hadn't made a choice that would hurt her. I had a feeling the road ahead would be bumpy and full of pain. Tough decisions waited for me, and I'd do whatever it took to keep Kelsey out of the hands of those who wanted to use her. Even if that meant staying away from me.

I could be the one who's putting her in danger. As much as I always wanted her by my side, it might just be the deadliest place to be.

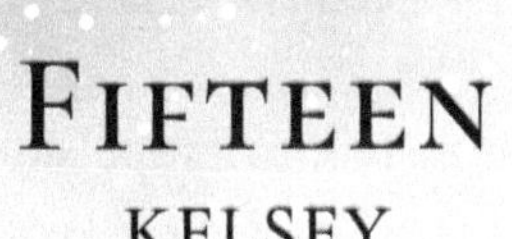

Fifteen

KELSEY

My conversation with Liam stayed with me for the rest of the day. Yes, I was upset about Gunnar, but I also understood the logic behind his decision. It was a risky plan; however, it might be our best shot.

What stuck with me was the mention that something was different about me. I felt it too, but with everything else going on, I shoved any awareness I had of it away to deal with later. After the fainting spell in the parking lot, I needed to unscramble the messy tangle of stuff happening within me.

Was it a byproduct of claiming Liam?

I wasn't sure.

Was it because we were Moonstruck? Did the strength of our bond alter parts of us? Or just me?

The change wasn't only physical. I'd anticipated some of the changes that occurred after I mated Liam. The shared emotions, the telepathy, and the closeness were traits all mated wolves acquired. Another reason I hadn't questioned this off feeling with me.

Yet, it was more.

My magic felt unstable and sporadic. I no longer had control, and I didn't know where the root of the change began.

Liam was right. Something was different. And I needed more information.

Only one person came to mind who might have the answers I needed.

Leith drove Max and me home after school. Liam had football practice with Colsen and Riven. Half the time, I forgot he played, let alone was the quarterback.

I hadn't had a chance to talk to Hope since running into Gunnar. Sending her a quick text, I checked if she was okay. It didn't matter what excuses the hunter came up with. What he did to Hope, using their friendship, crossed an unforgivable line, but Hope wasn't one to hold a grudge.

Still, I hoped she made him suffer before she forgave him. He deserved to be on his knees begging for mercy. The worry, the tears, the confusion, the ghosting her for days, using her as bait, and most of all the years of lies. It made her question the entirety of their friendship, whether it was real or a means to get close to me.

Hell, I questioned it.

I'd give him points for determination. Waiting as long as he did took commitment.

"You okay?" Leith asked, taking his eyes off the road for a moment to check on me. "You seem awfully quiet after the day we've had."

I stared out the window, the latticework of trees off the road blurring by. "Still processing."

"Get some rest, Kelsey. Your body needs it," he advised as a friend who worried about me. I was sure seeing me faint earlier hadn't looked good. Of course, my friends would be concerned.

"I will," I promised and climbed out of his car when he stopped in front of my house. Max, my silent shadow, followed me.

After grabbing a drink from the fridge, I informed Max I needed to speak to Nana.

He nodded. "I have to check in with your father."

The glass of iced tea paused at my lips. "You're not going to tell him about what happened today, are you?"

Max smiled. "Which part? You skipping school? Ditching me yet again? Or the part where you collapsed?"

"Collapsed is a strong word. I got lightheaded. No big deal." *Please don't make this into a big deal.*

"It's my job, Kels."

I frowned. "Being referred to as someone's job doesn't make me feel good."

He brushed past me and grabbed a drink. "It's not your feelings I'm worried about. It's your life."

"Whatever." Taking my glass of iced tea, I stomped out of the kitchen and went in search of Nana. If she wasn't in the house, there was only one place left to check.

I found her in the garden, pruning and preparing her flowers for the impending winter. Many of the fall plants still flourished with vibrant colors and perfumed the air. The breeze carried their floral traces to me as I strolled down the stone pathway. The summer plants also showed signs of hibernation. Shivered and dried petals hung melancholy, all the beautiful colors sucked out of them.

I hadn't spent as much time out here as I would have liked. Her gardens were a peaceful place where life flourished. When she came to visit in Hot Springs, she always brought gifts she'd grown or made—bundles of flowers, mint leaves to chew on, baskets of fruits and veggies, or baked goods. It was something different each visit, depending on the season, but always homemade. Half the excitement of her staying with us circled around what she might bring.

Pulling the sweater down over my hands to chase the November chill, I smiled up at the sun, allowing a moment to bask not just in the warmth but the freshness and liveliness of nature. The air tasted purer in my lungs like I could almost inhale all the vitamins and nutrients growing in the soil.

From where she sat on a little wooden stool my grandpa had made her, she turned as I approached. Rays of sun haloed at her back, highlighting the few strands of silver in her long, black hair. It was tied at the nape of her neck, wisps framing her face. Whether she dressed for gardening or going out, Nana looked the same. A periwinkle flowy dress with long sleeves billowed over the ground at her shoeless feet. She was a firm believer in feeling the earth between her toes. Nana believed we could absorb natural elements into our body just by connecting with the ground for a few minutes.

Eyes the same color as mine twinkled at me. "Did you come to help?"

After taking a sip of my tea, I nestled the glass into the grass and slipped off my shoes and socks. The ground colder than I imagined felt nice against my feet. "What do I do?" I asked.

She handed me an extra pair of shears. "Gardening is great for thinking and working out problems."

Nana always knew when something was on my mind. I wouldn't doubt if she'd been waiting for me.

"Pruning helps promote new growth for the next season, but not all flowers need to be cut. It could cause more harm than good. But for these here"—she lifted her fingers, brushing the dried petals—"you want to make the snip right under the first set of leaves." She demonstrated and I watched, paying close attention.

With delicate fingers, I lifted the stem, searching for the last set of leaves before I trimmed off the shriveled flowerhead.

"You're a natural," she said with a smile.

The bracelets on her wrists clanged together like wind chimes blowing in the wind as she worked, and the sound comforted me.

Five minutes or so went by. "Can I ask you something?" I inquired, interrupting the peaceful quiet.

"You can always talk to me, dear."

I cast a wary glance at the house. We weren't quite far enough away where Max wouldn't be able to listen in. "Would you mind if I gave us some privacy?"

A soft smile touched her lips, and she winked. "Might be a good idea."

I hadn't used my power since Friday night, and it was keen to come out and play, requiring very little effort on my part to cast a dome to drown the outside world and protect what was said.

Nana's eyes followed the line of power as it arched around us. Invisible except for a scatter of sparkles glinting off the sun. "It's been so long since I've seen your gifts. They're lovely."

"They don't always feel that way," I confessed, sitting down on the ground and laying my clippers off to the side.

She swiveled in her stool to face me. "It can be a blessing, but even those come with their own burdens. Ours is a high one with much responsibility."

"Something's changing in me. My power feels off—unstable. Like when I was younger and hadn't yet conquered control."

Nana pursed her lips. "I meant to have this conversation with you before the claiming ceremony on your birthday, but things have shifted as they are known to do. I should have told you sooner so you could have been prepared. I'm sorry for that and my oversight. I couldn't be sure which path you'd choose, but I'm proud of your decisions, Kelsey. Know that. The heir prince isn't like his father. He doesn't have the same ambitions or hunger the alpha does. He will make you a good mate, but I think you figured that out on your own just as I suspect you have an inkling of what caused the disruption in your powers."

"Liam," I guessed, reaching for my tea and taking a sip.

"In a sense. I speculate it's a combination of things. You claiming your mate, the heir prince's strength as a wolf, and the grace of the moon. Together and individually, these are impacting your magic. And yet you still haven't come to your full potential."

I blinked. "There's more?"

"I'm afraid so," she said sympathetically. "Our abilities are strengthened by the partners we choose to mate. It's our link from the claim that amplifies what's in our blood. The stronger your mate is, the greater the impact."

"And I would just have to bond to a future alpha," I muttered, picking at a blade of grass. It made me wonder if Liam's father knew this information when he pushed for the treaty between our families. I couldn't entirely blame him. Regardless of the treaty, Liam would still have been my mate. It wasn't the arranged marriage that made us Moonstruck. Our connection was inevitable.

Just how much power would being mated to Liam give me? Could I handle it? Control it?

I suffered so much growing up. The last thing I wanted was to repeat those experiences of finding and learning to dominate the magic swirling in me.

"How are your abilities changing?" Nana asked.

"I can't be certain, but I believe I've been having visions, glimpses of the future. It's only happened twice."

"Twice since Friday?"

I nodded.

Her expression turned contemplative. "They're manifesting. Interesting."

I didn't like the sound of interesting. "Did you have the same reaction when you and Grandpa mated?" What a fucking strange question to ask your grandmother. I internally winced.

"My visions became clearer. The flashes lengthened, developing into mini films that could last for minutes," she explained.

I frowned. "New abilities didn't unfold or evolve?"

She offered me a gentle, supportive smile. "No, but our situations are different. What's happening to you isn't wrong. There's no right way to mature, and that's what your magic is doing. Maturing and coming into its full extent."

I tossed the few blades of grass I'd plucked from the ground. "Fun. I can't wait to see what happens next."

Her eyes grew serious, and for a few moments, she stared over my shoulder, a far-off gleam in her gaze. I didn't ask what she saw. She didn't often volunteer the information her sight gave. "What concerns me is how much power you're gaining at once," she said quietly when the haze cleared over her eyes, and she focused back on my face.

By the change in her tone, I could tell the vision had been about me. "Does your sight ever overwhelm you?" I inquired. As far as I knew, she never fainted from her gift.

A ribbon of wind fluttered through the garden, picking up loose strands of her hair. "Not in the way you seek. I've never had as much power as you have or will have."

No doubt, another premonition she'd seen. "How do I find my balance again?"

She reached out and took my hand, her bracelets twinkling. "You have the potential, dear. But you don't have to do it on your own.

Remember the people in your life who love and care about you. Lean on them for support and fortitude. They hold the key. The magic isn't something you work against but exist with." Her fingers squeezed lightly.

What would I do without her insight or having her by my side? Both were vital. Just talking to her, despite not always liking what I heard, gave me the peace, inner strength, and clarity I desperately needed in my life. Maybe some of this sudden calmness in my heart was from being surrounded by flowers that had healing properties of their own. Knowing Nana, we were deliberately pruning flowers to soothe a conflicted and anguished heart.

Their sweet, earthy aroma tinged a bit of Zen into the air. A part of me didn't want to release the shield I'd erected around us. I wanted to stay a little longer in the bubble and stretch out this temporary inner peace, for when I left the garden, all my troubles and worries waited for me.

I couldn't escape them. No matter how hard I tried.

I STAYED with Nana for another hour chatting about school, my grades, college, and all those normal topics that had nothing to do with conflict while we tended her garden before coming inside to start on dinner. Upstairs, homework waited for me. My schoolwork lately had suffered, and unless I wanted to repeat my senior year, I needed to put effort into passing my classes regardless of the storm swirling around my life.

My mind found it difficult to concentrate on writing an essay or working out math problems. Those were the worst. A jumble of numbers and words on a page that I couldn't get to come together. I stared at my screen, my finger tapping the same key over and over again until I had rows filled with the letter L. Didn't take a genius to wonder what it stood for or who occupied my thoughts when I should be concentrating on what the derivative of the function was.

Taking a break to grab a cup of hot tea Nana brewed, I leaned out the window and gazed up at the moon. For some people, it might be strange to have part of their life dictated by a bright, shining orb in the sky, but for me, it was a way of life. Some wolves resented the power of the moon. I'd always been fascinated by it. Even after knowing it was the moon's fate who chose my mate. The moon also chose me—picked us out of thousands of shifters.

Why?

Was it my powers that attracted the fates?

Speaking of magic...nothing like a little plot twist to spice things up. If my bond with Liam gave me a direct line to more power, what else would I be able to conjure? I'd be a liar if I continued to believe my power didn't frighten me. Moving through life with unexpected visions and passing out everywhere was scary.

Unless I figured out how to steer this newfound power, a lot of bumps and bruises were in my future. I wondered if I would see those beforehand.

The tea was herbal and hot as I sipped, frowning out the window in the dark kitchen. I hadn't bothered to turn on the lights. My best thoughts came in the dark.

And they turned to the heir prince. If I'd waited until I turned eighteen to claim him, would my experience with power be different? More controlled and contained than this wild and reckless humming within me?

The vision I'd had earlier weighed heavy on my heart. It might be nothing, but on the off chance an army of meta invaded Riverbridge, we had to be prepared. It wasn't just me in jeopardy. The entire pack would be in danger.

I should go to bed, but if the images I'd seen played in the back of my mind were real, I could only imagine the nightmares I'd have when I went to sleep. Or worse. Another vision. Hell, maybe two. My mind seemed more susceptible when I slept.

Only two solutions came to mind. Enough sleeping pills to knock me out for a week. Or...

"Can you come over tonight?" I sent to the heir prince through our bond.

I didn't have to wait long for his rough voice to respond. *"I'm not sure that's a good idea."*

Liam and his goddamn badge of control. "*You can't avoid me forever.*"

"I'm not avoiding you. I'm protecting you."

"It doesn't feel like it," I grumbled, setting the mug on the counter.

"Isn't Max there?"

I frowned up at the moon, staring at the dark shadows covering its surface. *"He's always here, but he's not you."*

"I should hope not, pup," he retorted, my attempt at jealousy failing.

I didn't want to beg or come right out and tell him I was afraid to sleep. He would worry, and the heir prince worried enough about me. *"Do you want me to ask him to sleep in my bed? Because that's what I need tonight."*

A long pause stretched through our bond before he replied, *"Don't toy with me. Not tonight."*

Sighing, I picked up my tea and spun away from the moon, pressing my back into the counter. *"I promise not to touch you, happy?"*

"But I won't make such promises. I'm already thinking about putting my hands on your body."

Blood rushed into my cheeks.

"What are you doing?"

I jumped at the sound of Max's voice, spilling a splatter of hot liquid down the front of my oversized tee. "Son of a bitch," I hissed, staring at my shirt before I glared at him.

A smirk curved on the guard's lips. "Don't blame me. If you weren't so preoccupied, you would have heard me coming or noticed my scent," the smart-ass said.

True, but I refused to admit that to him. "Don't you sleep?" I put the mug into the sink and grabbed a towel to dab my white shirt with.

He moved past me, reaching over my head into the cabinet. "I just came to get a drink."

"Whatever," I complained. "I was about to leave anyway." I flung the towel onto the counter.

Max's fingers wrapped around my wrist, and I turned my head toward him, my brows lifted in irritation. "Are you okay? Earlier tonight when you—"

"I don't want to talk about it," I quickly cut him off before he could finish. "It's the last thing I want to talk about." Especially before bed. I'd been looking for a distraction from such thoughts, not to dwell on them.

In the dark, Max leaned against the counter across from the sink where I stood. "What should we talk about then?" His lips tipped at the corners, a sudden heat glowing in his gold eyes.

The moon shone at my back through the window, and I realized my shirt was partially see-through as Max's gaze shifted lower off my face. I also didn't have any pants on, which normally wasn't a big deal, but with my guard staying here, it wasn't the smartest attire to be traipsing around at night in.

My arms quickly crossed over my chest. "Nothing. You're the last person I want to talk to. You'll just run to my father and tattle."

His lips quirked at my obvious attempt to cover my nipples peeking through the thin material of my shirt. "If you can't sleep, you know where my room is." His dark voice traveled after me as I shoved off the counter and left.

"Pup?" Liam's voice traveled down our bond.

"Goodnight, Liam," I huffed, letting my irritation seep into my voice, annoyed at all men.

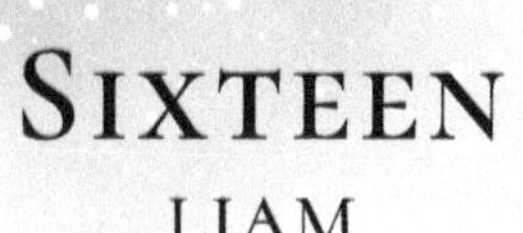

Sixteen
LIAM

Kelsey was trying to kill me. The phrase love kills had meaning now in my life. Why did she have to ask me to come over? And right before bed. Now I couldn't stop thinking of her.

I hadn't gotten a full night of sleep since before Friday night. And thanks to the little minx, tonight would be just as fretful. It was easy to blame Kelsey, but it wasn't her fault. Not entirely. We both had a hand in this predicament. She happened to live up to her reputation. Besides, I found her wildness and recklessness sexy.

I was just as much the problem.

Shoving a hand through my hair, I gazed out my bedroom window. The moon glimmered in the clear midnight sky, so close I could see the shaded dark spots. Nights like tonight made me wonder why I resisted. I knew what I wanted.

Before I could do something stupid like jump out my window, my phone buzzed on the bed. I turned to see the screen light up with a text from my cousin.

What did you do to him?

Hope's question stared back at me.

I typed back a response.

Why do you care?

I watched the three little dots on the screen until her message popped up.

Who said I did?

What the hell is with the females in my life tonight?

You wouldn't be texting me if you didn't.
He's not your friend.

She shouldn't be tangled up with him, but I didn't know how to get across how dangerous he was.

Don't start caring about my feelings now.
Besides, I never said I forgave him.

Arguing over text was annoying, but calling her was also something I wanted to avoid.

He hunts wolves,

I pointed out. Why was it so hard to grasp that Gunnar was the bad guy?

You of all people should understand that we
can't always control who we fall in love with.

My fingers tightened against my phone. *Love! She loves him*. Was she delusional? Loving a hunter was completely different than my situation with Kelsey. Mostly. I mean she did have moments where I wanted to wring her neck. Still, not the same.

You don't love him. It's forbidden.

I don't give a shit about rules. I'm not you.

Fuck. I couldn't handle a dysfunctional cousin right now.

What do you want me to say?

Promise me you won't hurt him.

I refused to make such a promise.

I need his help. That's all. If you know what's good for you, Hope, you won't fuck with him.

What about everyone else?

No one in the pack knows. Just us. Meaning Kelsey, Leith, Colsen, and Riven. And they answer to me.

How long do you plan on keeping him as your dog?

Until I get answers. He's lucky to still be alive.

I made a mental note to have a chat with Gunnar about spilling his guts to my cousin. He'd involved her enough in his schemes. That shit stopped now. I should have ordered him to stay away from her, but I couldn't prevent my cousin from seeking out the hunter.

Between Kelsey and Hope, the women in my life drove me insane.

My phone stayed silent. I took that to mean Hope had given up... for now.

I went to the bed, tossing my phone aside, and lay down. Two minutes went by, and I frowned at the pull inside my chest again, this nagging pestering me like a two-year-old in a toy store. It nearly felt like my wolf was about to have a temper tantrum if I didn't give in. He wanted his mate, and I wanted to keep from bringing hell down on the pack.

This was Gunnar's first night free and under the control of the collar. The hunter had already proved he was exceptionally skilled at deception. What if he only pretended to do my bidding? What if it was all an act and the collar didn't work at all? What if he was at Kelsey's house right now to finish the job? Did I trust that Max alone could protect her?

Hell no.

Like I was his parole officer, a random home visit was in order. I needed to see if the hunter was where I ordered him to be. Gunnar was cunning. He wouldn't sit around like an obedient bitch. He would search for loopholes or a chink in the chain around his neck, any spot of weakness he could find, and then he would exploit it.

I had to be smarter. I had to be a step ahead of him. I had to always be on guard.

Fuck it.

I rolled out of bed, jumped from my window, and hopped into my truck without a second thought, choosing my truck instead of shifting, and my wolf protested at being contained.

With my headlights off, I backed out of the driveway and flipped them on once I hit the road. Gunnar lived alone in a small house close to town. Secluded enough so his neighbors wouldn't question the hunter's late-night activities. He didn't have parents. Convenient for his job but also depressing. It was no wonder he was a loner at school, doing his best to not draw attention to himself.

And my cousin was drawn to that sad-boy, lone-wolf persona like a moth to a flame.

His very average and seen-better-days car sat in the narrow driveway. I killed the engine on my truck and got out, running my hand over the hood of Gunnar's car. It was cold. As unused as the house looked. Not a light shone through the windows, but the asshole was in there.

He appeared in the doorway before I reached the porch, an apple in one hand, a paring knife in the other. "What a pleasant surprise," he said sarcastically.

My eyes immediately went to the black chain at his throat. He still had it on. Short of cutting off his head, he wouldn't be removing it without the key.

To activate the collar, I'd added drops of my blood and Gunnar's onto the onyx stone set in a pendant. The order of the blood was a vital piece. His first and mine layered on top because I was the dominant controller, and he was an omega bound by orders. A collar could only be used once. My father would be furious when he figured out I'd stolen and used it, but I had few other choices.

I remained at the bottom of the porch steps, glaring up at him. "Stay away from my cousin."

Leaning against the post, he carved out a slice of apple. "You drove all the way here in the middle of the night to warn me off my best friend."

"She's not your friend anymore, or have you already forgotten you're the enemy?" My breath clouded in front of me from the freezing temps that continued to fall.

He lifted the knife to his mouth, biting the apple. The steel glinted under the moonlight. "I couldn't hurt her now if I wanted to. You made sure of it."

Darkness swept inside me, my wolf growling as my lips tightened. "Unlike you, I protect my friends."

He flinched. "Yes, well, we don't all have the luxury of being the alpha's son."

Did I detect hints of jealousy?

The wrath in my blood had been too easily provoked lately. "My position in the pack has nothing to do with you being an asshole," I retorted with icy coldness.

"But your kind does," he countered too calmly. He might not outwardly show the grudge he held against wolves, but it simmered under the surface. Years of practice hiding made him a master of his emotions.

"I'm not my father." My features remained merciless, as did my heart. "Don't go anywhere," I ordered.

A cruel smile curved on his lips, the kind that made me want to watch my back. "Wouldn't dream of it."

Leaving Gunnar, I steered my truck onto the road, telling myself I was going home, and yet the car went in a different direction. Minutes later, I parked at the end of the long driveway, killing the engine to avoid waking Kelsey, Maxtyn, or Mrs. Nightingale. An owl hooted as I jogged across the lawn, heading for the house.

The lure of our bond guided me straight to her window. Did I knock? Or just let myself in? What if she was asleep? I didn't want to wake her. I also didn't want to scare her either.

My eyes went to the spot under the tree where I'd camped out the last time. I wanted to feel the warmth of her body. It wasn't enough to be close to her. I should leave while I had a shred of control left in me. I got what I came for. She was safe.

Forcing my feet to turn around, my back to the window, I took a step away from the house. Leaves crinkled under my boots, but the soft moan of my name carried through the walls, and it stopped me in my tracks.

I inhaled, drawing in a gulp of brisk air before letting it rush out of my lungs. The coldness did nothing to sway my wolf.

Fuck it.

One night.

I wanted one night of sleep.

Tomorrow I'd worry about what to do.

Pivoting, I moved with stealth to the house. My fingers wedged under the gap between the window and the frame. Relief and irritation flared within me when the glass shimmied up.

She left her damn window open!

This girl!

My mate would be the death of me. How did she expect me to keep her from being kidnapped when she carelessly left her window unlocked? It was a fucking invitation to every stalker and hunter out here. She might as well put a sign on the glass that read, *Take me. I'm ready and waiting.* Or posted a fucking message in a hunter's forum that read, *powerful female wolf with crazy magical abilities. Would catch a pretty penny on the black market.*

A snarling growl vibrated behind me, and my fingers paused on the window while I looked over my shoulder. Under a pine tree a few feet away crouched a wolf baring his canines.

Maxtyn.

I narrowed my eyes at him.

The prick knew it was me.

Calling the beast in me to the surface, I flashed him my wolf eyes, a rumble vibrating in my chest. If Maxtyn wanted to fight, I was fucking game. Hell, I was more than ready for something physical. It would be a release for all my pent-up aggravation and repressed sexual tension. I'd love nothing more than to sink my fist into Maxtyn. Claws, teeth, fists, it didn't matter if I got to hurt the bastard.

The guard's presence should have alleviated some of the stress that came with protecting my mate.

It didn't.

Not when he made comments about her changing her mind, breaking our mating bond before it was complete, or implying I wasn't the right wolf for her.

Basically, my jealousy hit new heights because of this dickhead.

With a wry grin on my lips, I crooked my finger at Maxtyn. "Take your best shot, asshole."

Maxtyn charged, his paws heavy on the ground. I watched and waited for the moment when he shoved off the grass, lunging at me. That's when I struck.

I sidestepped to his left, pivoted, and put my clenched hand into his side. His wolf went to the ground, a whimper of pain leaving him as he hit the cold surface. I had to give him credit. His recovery rate was impressive. Not even a second went by, and he was back on his feet, snarling at me.

A squirrel nesting in the tree above scampered down the trunk and took off into the woods. Smart critter. It would be wise to stay clear.

He came at me again, but this time, I let him tackle me, and together we went down. I landed on my side with my arms wrapped tight around his middle. He rammed his paw into my chest, using it as leverage for him to gain space. I wasn't letting the bastard have an inch.

His teeth snapped at me, gnarling fiercely.

"You keep this up, and you'll get hurt," I grunted.

Maxtyn squirmed against my hold, his teeth doing their best to take a bite out of me. I had no intention of bleeding tonight, not when I wanted to crawl into bed beside my girl.

The wolf within me begged me to summon him. He craved the fight, and I wanted to give in, but if my animal instincts took over, I could do more than give Maxtyn a few bumps and bruises.

This had gone on long enough.

I shoved Maxtyn off me, sending him skidding on his side through the grass. We both came up at the same time, him on four paws and me crouched at his level.

I put a punch behind my growl this time, the growl that made lesser wolves bow. He would hate it, the use of my alpha power, but it was mine to use. The air trembled, and Maxtyn had no choice but to shift, shedding his fur for human skin.

My power could do so much more. It wasn't the same as Kelsey's. It didn't stem from magic but from dominance and leadership.

I stood, towering over him. "Do I look like a fucking intruder?"

Muscles coiled, he pushed to his feet, unashamed of his nakedness, but as a shifter, most of us weren't shy about our bodies. "Doesn't hurt to be safe."

"At least you're doing your job. A little late. If I hadn't been cursing Kelsey for leaving the damn window unlocked, I'd already be inside before you got here," I hissed, letting my anger loose. "Do you feel better?"

"No," he growled, bare chest rising and falling with his breaths. "I still want to kick your ass."

"The feeling's mutual," I rumbled, dusting off my clothes.

Max cocked his head, the tree hanging above shadowing most of his body. "Why are you here?"

My scowl carved deeper. "I think the reason is pretty obvious considering where you caught me."

He folded his arms over an expansive chest. "Is this going to be a nightly ritual? It would help me to know. I'd hate to mistake you again as a threat."

I snorted, my brows flattening. "I haven't decided yet, but I wouldn't want you to get complacent in your duties."

"Being a warrior is the only thing I know how to do," Maxtyn gritted out, flashing his canines.

"I've yet to see if you're any good at it," I scoffed.

He cracked his knuckles. "Maybe we need to go another round."

This fucking guy. "Not until you put some clothes on. And don't even think about cracking some stupid joke about your nakedness bothering me. I'm trying to spare Kelsey from being traumatized."

I swore his lips curled before he searched the yard for his clothes. He came back a minute later, tugging on a pair of sweatpants. "You're still here?"

Leaning my shoulder into the tree trunk, I eyed Maxtyn. "I've been contemplating whether I can trust you. You're loyal to her family, that much I can tell, which means something to me. Still, I can't be positive, but for her safety, I feel if you had this information, you'd be better prepared to protect her. I'd rather her father didn't know, which is why my hesitancy, but there will come a point where both our packs would benefit from this knowledge."

"What is it?" he asked, slipping the sweatshirt over his head.

I took a breath, going out on a limb. "There are hunters with wolf abilities. They can't shift, but due to their altered DNA, they received other traits like speed, strength, healing, and some new skills I've never seen before. I don't know how many there are; perhaps all of them have been mutated."

Skepticism creased over his forehead. "How do you know this?"

"Because I have one of them. He tried to take her from me." Even though it had been a couple of days, thinking back to Halloween night sent prickles of frozen fury racing down my neck.

"And you didn't kill him?"

I couldn't blame him for wondering why I let the hunter live. It was a decision I prayed I wouldn't come to regret. "Oh, I wanted to. I still do. But killing one meta hunter won't stop the attacks on her. I need to flesh out the boss. The one giving the orders. It's the only way to take the order off her capture."

He held my gaze unflinchingly. "And you want my help."

"At the very least your cooperation," I said with an edge to my voice.

The guard ran a hand through his black hair. "I need to think."

"If you make a decision, you know where to find me." With a twisted smirk, I crawled into Kelsey's room, shutting the window behind me.

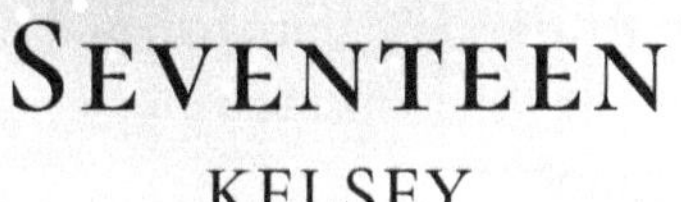

SEVENTEEN

KELSEY

My biggest fears were being buried alive, being trapped in small spaces, or being imprisoned. Wolves thrived in the wild, being free. Take those away from me, and panic set it, the kind of anxiety that did more than spike my blood.

I woke up pinned to the bed, and the first stirrings of uneasiness moved in me. Not the best way to wake up. I'd been deep in a pleasant dream for once. No nightmares of death, bloodshed, and war. No arrows pierced through Liam's heart. No field scattered with the bodies of my friends. It made the sudden weight pressed into me confusing but only emphasized the ribbon of terror tying itself around me.

Seconds away from flying out of bed with a scream lodged into my throat, I felt tingles dance over my heart. Warmth flooded against my back, a soft breath tickling my hair.

The weight draped over my hip shifted, tugging me closer to what I realized was a body behind me. The anxiety flipped like a switch to excitement and happiness.

A smile curled on my lips as I turned, facing Liam. Who would have thought having the heir prince in my bed would cultivate such elation? Not the girl who came to Riverbridge all those weeks ago. Such a

contrast to the disdain I felt for him then. It wasn't the wolf or the guy who I cursed, but what he represented, the stripping of my free will.

Turned out it went beyond a piece of paper signed by our parents.

Our fate had been sealed well before the treaty had been drummed up.

Unable to ignore his full lips, I brushed mine across his. Those long lashes fanning over his flawless face fluttered, and then I was lost in a sea of sparkling aqua. Liam had the most startling eyes I'd ever seen. Gazing into them was no hardship.

Nor was the sound of his raspy voice in the morning. "You're awake."

I rested my chin on his chest, staring into his face. "How did you get in?"

His arms tightened around me, and I relished being in his embrace. "Your window was open. You should keep it locked."

I blinked, retaining my serious face. "Then how would *you* get in?"

His groan was full of sleep and had less punch behind it than normal. "Someone else might sneak in beside me and snatch you from your bed."

I pinched his side, not that there was much flesh to grab. "Thank you for the vivid picture I'm sure I won't be able to get out of my head."

Light fingers trailed down my spine. "Good, something needs to scare you for you to take this seriously."

A delicious shiver danced on my back. "Who said I wasn't?"

He kissed the tip of my nose. "Lock your windows and your door."

"Would either of those keep you out of my room?"

Blinking his heavy eyes, he gave me a wicked grin. "No."

"My point exactly."

"Nothing would keep me from you."

And there went my heart, cartwheeling in my chest like a giddy girl in love.

Holy shit.

Am I falling in love with him?

No, it was far too soon for that.

People automatically assumed mating equaled instant love. For some, it did. For others, it was a gradual affection that grew and was nurtured over time. Our bond was unique.

When I claimed him, it hadn't been love spurring me to mark the heir prince. It had been pure lust. Wanting Liam wasn't a problem. My body responded to his, and I assumed I would fall in love with him. Our Moonstruck link made it inevitable. Love might not always be a factor among mates, but when lovers were marked by the moon as Liam and I was, the connection was solidified by more than emotions.

Our bodies, souls, hearts, wolves, basically every cell and crevice of our beings, were interwoven.

To keep from saying something utterly stupid early in the morning when he had my heart racing, I did the only other thing to keep my mouth busy.

I leaned down and kissed him.

A deep purr resonated in Liam's throat as his fingers shoved into my hair, lacking his usual skillful finesse. His lips pressed hard into mine, hot and demanding, giving me no choice but to respond equally or lose myself.

What I figured would be a sweet good-morning peck turned into something tempestuous. The space between us kindled with electricity, sparking under the sheets. Liam also found the inches separating us like a canyon.

I hadn't been able to take a breath yet as his hands moved to my hips and lifted me so I lay on top of him, my body sunk into every glorious hard line of his. It was then I realized he was only wearing a pair of boxers, and the thin material did nothing to hide the bulge pressed between my legs.

I'd heard of morning wood, but holy hell. He was so fucking hard. My fingers longed to wrap around him and experiment. Would he grow harder? Longer? What would happen if I used my mouth?

"Stop thinking about it, pup, and touch me." His raspy, tortured voice pleaded in my head.

"Not yet. I'm not done with your mouth, princeling."

I'd never had sex with someone when I could hear their thoughts and feel their emotions, and damn, if I wasn't beyond intrigued. I wanted to experience it all.

I chased the dancing of his tongue, kissing him back with everything I had while he used teasing strokes that made my body flush.

"More. I need more," Liam demanded.

My teeth sunk into his lower lip, inflicting enough pain to make him moan, and then I sucked his bottom lip into my mouth, adding pleasure to the sting.

"Kelsey," he groaned. His fingers dug into my ass as he ground his hips into me.

A burst of lust tingled between my legs, and I whimpered.

I was ravenous to have him. The taste. The feel. The smell. All my senses were buzzing. It was at the point where our desires blended, and I couldn't distinguish between his and mine.

My lips grew tender and swollen from the onslaught of his never-ending kiss, but like Liam, it was not enough for me. I needed more.

To anyone else it might seem like utter madness, felt like it too, this desperate desire for another person as if I'd die if I didn't have him right now.

My hips rocked against him, craving the friction only the hard length of him could create. My body remembered too well what it was like having the heir prince inside me, moving and stroking my inner walls with the very male part of him.

Need pulsed from our grinding bodies, growing to maddening heights. Liam consumed me in a way I never thought possible. Perhaps the bond I created with him made each touch like little fires on my skin. Made his lips taste like addicting nectar I couldn't live without.

His fingers skimmed the hem of my underwear near my ass cheek and so damn close to the hot spot of my core. My hips twisted slightly, inviting his fingers to invade. He didn't disappoint.

I melted into him as he slid one in, and I surrendered wholly to the heir prince. A gasp left my lips.

"Is this what you want, pup?" he asked.

I answered with my hips, grinding against his finger, my breath quickening. He inserted another finger, and I sunk down on them both, chasing the release already building like a rogue wave within me.

"God, you're so wet. So ready for me."

How was he able to think, let alone have thoughts? My brain hummed with yearning.

His canines descended, scraping up the column of my throat, and I angled my neck for better access. Rough hands tunneled into my hair and fisted to keep me right where he wanted me. At his fucking mercy.

"You're mine. Only mine."

I didn't just hear his possessive admission. I felt it in my bones—in my wolf—with such sheer conviction that went beyond our physical bodies.

"Yes." I agreed. *"God, yes."*

A flicker of the treaty burning on a stone shrine flashed behind my eyes. The vision had the same effect as a splash of cold water on my face.

Kissing Liam had been a mistake.

I'd attached my lips to his when he'd had his guard down and was still half asleep. The wolf instantly responded to his mate, a basic instinct, one Liam fought daily. The same one I'd given into on his eighteenth birthday because I didn't have anywhere near the control the heir prince possessed.

And now his canines were poised on my neck. The slightest fucking movement and Liam could claim me, breaking the treaty our families had waited eighteen years to fulfill.

I closed my eyes, trying to clear my head from the pleasure Liam's fingers created. It would pain me, but I had to pull away. I had to put a stop to the thing I wanted most in this world.

I had to find a discipline I wasn't sure I carried.

My hands went to his chest, and I shoved hard, moving away from him. "Liam, stop," I gasped, struggling to gain composure.

His eyes glowed like a predator in the night, bright and zeroed on me. I was his prey, but he wasn't hunting me. Not in the traditional sense. He wanted me for other more intimate means, and damn, if my whole body didn't buzz in anticipation.

I had no idea how I'd find the control to put an end to this, but for once in my life, I had to be the reasonable one.

He reached for me, and I had to put more space between us. A lot more. Hovering over him on his lap wouldn't cut it.

Jerking away from his hand, I rolled off him onto the bed. "Liam, you can't."

His brows furrowed as he stared at me, clarity slowly, very slowly, breaking through. He sat up in the bed and slammed his eyes shut, fighting against the desire coursing within him. I could feel the wild emotions swirling in our bond.

I stayed still on the bed, doing my best not to breathe his way, not to breathe at all. One whiff of me and we could be back on the bed, tearing off the measly amount of clothes we wore, and this time, neither of us would have the discipline to stop.

A full minute went by before he opened his eyes. A glint of his wolf still shone in them, but they were less bright and more human. "I shouldn't have come. This was a mistake."

Not what I wanted to hear, but I wasn't surprised. Liam took things to the extreme when it came to duty. "Nothing happened. There's no point beating yourself up about it."

He swung his legs over the bed and reached for his clothes, pulling his shirt on. "I should go."

"Don't ever make me be sensible again. I don't like it."

Liam's lips twitched. "I thought you wanted me to lose control." Standing, he shimmied his pants up over his firm ass.

I glanced up at him from the bed, capturing his gaze. "Precisely. Next time, I won't put a stop to it. I'll break the treaty without so much as blinking or having a regretful thought about it. I didn't do this for me. I did it for you."

He zipped his jeans but left the button undone. "And that means more, pup."

"I guess this is the end of future sleepovers?" It was meant to lighten the mood but only made me sad.

I SHOWERED and got ready for school after Liam left. With not a lot of time, I skipped breakfast and headed out the door, Max hot on my heels.

"I'll drive," he offered, holding out his hand as I briskly walked down the driveway.

A puff of cold air left my lungs as I sighed. "Sure, why not." I tossed him my key fob.

The guard wasted no time getting into the driver's seat and starting the engine. As he put the car into reverse, I buckled my seat belt.

"Don't drive like a dick," I said, thinking I had to make this car last through college.

Fuck. When was the last time I thought about extending my education past high school? Really contemplated my future beyond claiming Liam?

Before coming to Riverbridge if I had to guess.

I had no clue where I wanted to go to school. I'd filled out no applications, toured no campuses, and felt completely lost when it came to deciding on a career. Would Liam and I have to go to the same school? Could we manage to be away from each other? What if one of us went out of state? The idea of him being miles and miles away sent my wolf into panic mode.

"Did you have a nice night?" Max asked, interrupting my internal meltdown. Sarcasm dripped from his tone.

"Are you interested in the details? The way his lips devour me or how huge his dick is when he's slamming it inside me."

His features contorted in disgust. "Christ, you're a brat. If your father heard the shit that comes out of your mouth…"

"You're not my dad," I reminded. I had no reason to watch what I said around him. Besides, making Max uncomfortable entertained me.

He used one hand to maneuver the steering wheel, resting the other on the gear shifter. "Good thing, or I'd pull this car over right now and spank the shit out of you."

"You'd probably get off on that."

"You want to test me," he growled.

We both knew Max couldn't lay a hand on me. I was the alpha's daughter. No one touched me without my permission.

I grinned as silence stretched for the remaining car ride. My good spirits didn't last long. When you went to school with a hunter, it took the fun out of learning, not that I was a stellar student. I mostly went for the social game.

Tension radiated from every part of my body during my morning class with Gunnar. I could do nothing but glower at the hunter, watching and waiting for him to make one move out of place so I could pounce. I was looking for an excuse to attack him, but the prick gave up nothing.

He sat in class like a good obedient dog.

My eyes repeatedly returned to the black chain looped around his neck. Despite the meta sitting rows over from me, my arms tingled from the power of the collar. It made my skin feel like tiny spiders crawled across it. Now and again, I'd get this prick as if I'd been zapped.

My magic loathed the collar, nearly as much as my wolf. Being shut in a room with it made her feel caged, and she paced inside me, waiting for the clock on the wall to strike eleven. Seconds before the bell rang, I was out of my seat, rushing to the door.

Tossing my bag over my shoulder, I bypassed my locker, weaving my way through the sea of kids piling into the halls as I made my way toward the common area. I had to cut through the courtyard to save time and get to my next class one time. I burst through the doors, embracing the cold air as it nipped at my cheeks and nose. My blood had been churning for almost an hour. It needed to cool the fuck down.

Except, that wasn't going to happen.

I spotted the heir prince, and the tingles went haywire within me. Liam stood with a group of shifters unaware I'd entered the courtyard. He smiled and I felt it like a caress. A shiver rolled through me. I continued to stare, dazzled by Liam. How could a smile create this bubble of euphoria that floated in my chest, rising and rising until...it fucking popped?

Except...the smile hadn't been for me. My eyes followed the path in which Liam looked, expecting Riven's dumbass or even Colsen's, but his two best friends flanked him on either side. Neither lingered in front of him.

But Sabrina Thompson did along with the other pair of hags she called her *friends*. I used the term loosely. A fitting term considering how *loose* she was. Sabrina didn't know how to be a friend. She was a bitch to everyone.

Looked like my hope that she'd given up on wanting Liam was just that...hope.

As if I wasn't already on edge. Sabrina Thompson picked the wrong day to fuck with me.

My body remained frozen in place, a haze of red streaking across the backs of my eyes. I burned a hole with my stare into the side of Sabrina's face, my fingers digging into my palms. My wolf snarled.

People brushed past me, giving little thought to the new girl.

Seething, I watched as the group dismantled, taking off in different directions. Liam, Colsen, and Riven went to the opposite side of the courtyard, disappearing into the door. Sabrina, Jules, and Nora giggled as they came toward me.

Someone behind me bumped into my shoulder, but my glare remained on Sabrina. They mumbled an apology, but I barely heard the words over the buzzing in my head.

Sabrina glanced at me then, our eyes clashing, and the bitch had the audacity to smirk as if she knew I'd seen her with Liam. Her imperious grin stayed in place as she paused with her friends, eyeing me with a censoring look that implied I was underneath her.

Flipping the ends of her strawberry-blonde hair, she said, "I wouldn't bet on him claiming you. There's still time for him to change his mind."

The red spots in my vision darkened. I angled my head to the side. "Let me guess, you plan to sway him?"

Smugness gleamed in her eyes. "You're not the only wolf who's been underneath the heir prince."

That was it.

I lost my shit.

My bag hit the ground as I lunged, and I held nothing back as I swung my leg out, catching Sabrina behind the ankles and knocking her feet out from under her. The bitch fell on her ass.

"What the hell, you psycho!" she shrilled, shoving strands of hair out of her face to glower up at me.

We weren't done yet. Not by a long shot. "Don't act like you didn't deserve that."

She shoved to her feet, hair wild and expression contorted with fury. "You bitch," she hurled.

Her friends shrieked beside her, jumping out of the way so they didn't risk feeling my wrath.

I grinned. My hand struck out, and the tips of my nails were pointy like claws I hadn't realized I summoned. Not the smartest tactic in school; however, I was past reasoning.

Sabrina stumbled back, barely missing her cheek being shredded by my claws.

"I bet you wish you'd have kept your mouth shut," I taunted, circling her. Only slightly aware of the scene we created, I also didn't care. One more detention this week wouldn't kill me, but I might kill her if she didn't back off Liam.

Her lips pressed into a firm line, her gaze flicking to her friends as she looked for support. That was when I made my move.

I hit Sabrina full-on, slamming her into the ground and landing on top of her. My fingers dove straight into her hair, wrapping around the strands like a vise grip. "Cat got your tongue?"

"Are you crazy?" Sabrina gritted between clenched teeth while doing her best to ward off my attack and untangle my fingers.

"Yes," I hissed in return, my grasp tightening in her hair. I had my full weight restraining her to the grass. "I warned you what would happen if you didn't back off." I yanked, and tears sprang into her eyes.

The heel of her palm came up toward my face, but I jerked my head to the side, and she clipped me in the chin. Still didn't feel fantastic.

I winced. Using my free hand, I balled it into a fist and sent it flying at her nose. A sickening crunch was followed by a sharp ache radiating through my hand, but the pain didn't concern me.

Sabrina's expression morphed into one of pure shock right before blood gushed from her nostrils. "You broke my fucking nose."

"It will be fine in an hour. Your shirt, however..." I glanced down at the pretty white sweater with pearl detailing. "Looks like a horror prop."

"It's designer, you whore." She bucked, going wild underneath me. Her efforts weren't in vain. Sabrina managed to grab a hold of my leg and flip me onto my back, but I refused to let her have the upper hand.

We rolled over the damp grass, going back and forth switching positions, until I'd had enough.

I knew how to fight dirty.

But honestly, she asked for it. Sabrina should consider herself lucky I hadn't been able to shift. She wouldn't stand a chance against my wolf.

My canines dropped down in my mouth, and I sunk my teeth through her sweater into her shoulder. The warm, sharp, and metallic taste of blood touched my tongue.

Sabrina hissed as I unlatched my teeth. "You fucking bit me," she gasped in horror.

I rolled off her, sitting on a patch of grass. "It's the closest thing you'll ever get to a mating bite," I retorted lowly.

Looking like a mangled mess, she shoved to her feet, shaking leaves out of her curls. "You'll pay for that. I promise."

The dirt on my clothes, the leaves in my hair, or the blood staining my teeth mattered little. "If you don't learn how to respect me, the first thing I'll do as your luna is banish you from the pack."

Daggers pierced me from her dark green eyes. "You'll never be luna." Her threat was laughable. There would be no repercussions for my actions, not within the pack. The school was another story.

She whirled, storming off through the doors I'd entered from, shoving a pair of girls out of her way in the process.

I ignored the gawking stares and the murmurings traveling through the courtyard. What my peers thought of the crazy new girl had no meaning to me.

Eighteen

LIAM

I reached for the door when a commotion behind us broke out. Colsen turned first, and the curse under his breath warned trouble started. My first thought was Gunnar. Or one of the boys getting out of line.

What I didn't expect to see was Brina on the ground with Kelsey looming over her. I could tell by her eyes my mate was in the mood for a fight. They tussled, and Kelsey had a fist of red hair clutched in her hand as she snarled into Brina's face.

A slow grin spread across my lips.

"You're not going to put an end to this?" Riven asked, looking as if he was seconds away from interfering on my behalf.

I shook my head. "No, I told Brina what would happen if she didn't stop her games. Kelsey needs to handle this on her own, or it won't stop."

My mate was magnificent.

I didn't linger to see how the fight ended. I would find out in the next ten minutes regardless, and after this morning, I didn't trust myself. Not around Kelsey.

I'd been too damn close to doing the very thing I fought against my whole life. Losing myself fully to the wolf. At all times, I maintained a

certain level of control, even in my animal form. It was that degree of discipline that made me stronger.

To think, a single weak moment of waking up in bed with Kelsey nearly dismantled years of training. That was the power she had over me.

And right now, the best thing for both of us was distance. My focus needed to be on Gunnar and drawing out the one responsible for targeting Kelsey.

I had to come up with a plan. Get my head in the game. Or we'd be blindsided again when we needed to be a step ahead.

It needed to be foolproof, and I couldn't involve the pack. The risk it would get back to my father was too great. I didn't want to believe he would order my mate to be kidnapped, but I also knew better than to disregard all possibilities.

One of my father's policies.

There was a liar among us.

Gunnar or my father.

One of them would be exposed.

AFTER COMING SO close to ruining everything and claiming Kelsey, I spent the next few days contemplating my options. I had to figure out the best way to make it to the end of December without biting her.

It had only been a week since Kelsey claimed me, but every day became harder for me to ignore the basic instinct to take what was mine.

She was mine.

Each time I saw her, I grew closer to saying fuck the treaty. I promised myself I wouldn't see her all weekend, a test of wills.

I'd like to say it was going well.

It wasn't.

I made it to Sunday but not easily. If my wolf could climb walls, that was what I would be doing. I didn't trust myself to go for a run in the woods. My wolf would only end up at her house.

I glanced at the time on my phone. Sunday dinner was in less than an hour, and my *guest* should be on my doorstep soon.

"What's your deal?" Leith asked from where he lounged on the couch watching a football game. "You haven't been able to sit down for more than two minutes. If you miss her that much, I don't understand why you don't go see her. I know I sure as hell would love it if you got out of the house. Then I wouldn't have to see your moping ass pace in front of the TV."

I went to the liquor cabinet, reaching for a bottle of scotch Dad kept fully stocked. "I'm not moping," I insisted, my tone glum.

Leith shoved a handful of potato chips into his mouth. "That's all you have to say?" he asked, crunching away.

Taking my drink, I sank onto the couch beside him for what might have been the fifth time in the last few hours. I was driving myself insane. I could only imagine Leith's annoyance with me. "I can't."

My brother didn't often frown. "Why?"

"You know why." I confided in him what happened and why I was choosing to keep my distance.

He shook his head, his hand dipping back into the chip bowl balanced on his lap. "And I still think it's a stupid excuse. When have you ever let fear drive you?"

Fuck. He had a point.

I shifted my attention to the game, not really seeing the players as they huddled into formation. "Can we talk about something else? Anything but her?"

"Do you think her guard is seeing anyone?" he asked nonchalantly.

Not the topic change I'd expected. I slid a sidelong glance at my brother. "Don't tell me you're interested in that jackass."

His brows arched while he swallowed. "Still jealous, I see."

A rough snort breezed through my nostrils. "What do I have to be jealous of?" I knocked back the contents in my glass.

"I don't know, maybe the fact he gets to spend every day and night with your girl."

Anger licked through my blood. "Shut up," I snapped.

My brother grinned. "Bingo."

"I thought we weren't talking about her."

Leith shrugged. "I was asking about the guard."

The doorbell rang, thank fucking God.

I shot up off the couch, eager to be doing anything, even something as mundane as answering the door.

"You expecting someone?" Leith inquired, throwing a hand over the back of the couch.

"Yeah, Gunnar. Play nice," I warned.

His grin turned mischievous. "And to think I thought it would be another dull dinner without Kelsey. I'm excited for once."

I shook my head. "Watch what you say tonight," I cautioned, walking into the hallway. There was no room for mistakes or mishaps.

With his head down staring at his feet, Gunnar stood on the porch. His eyes lifted when I opened the door. So far, the collar appeared to be working like a charm. Or...the hunter could win an Oscar for his performance.

I crossed my arms over my chest, scowling at him from the threshold. The sun had disappeared behind the trees, taking the warmth from the air and leaving it brisk outside. "You're here. And on time."

Gunnar rubbed his hands together to keep them warm. "As if I had a choice." A puff of cold air came out with his words.

"I can't have you spending all weekend alone in that house. Not now that we've become such close friends." I kept my voice at normal levels to not alarm Mom anything was up. Dad wasn't home yet.

As instructed, Gunnar wore a black turtleneck to hide the collar. I considered the pros and cons of letting my father see the spelled object, but I chose not to show all my cards at once. Best to keep a few tricks up my sleeve.

I swung open the door and stepped back, inviting him in. This was the first time a hunter had ever stepped foot inside this house. Hopefully, it would be the last.

"So, this is where the great Liam lives," he said, his gaze sweeping over the foyer. The crystal chandelier lights above our heads twinkled.

After slipping off his boots, he followed me into the family room. Leith glanced over as we approached but diverted his gaze back to the game without saying a word. His hands clenched on his thighs, tension radiating from my brother. He was pissed Gunnar was here despite the jokes.

Classic Leith maneuver to cover his true feelings with sarcastic humor.

I went to the minibar Dad kept in the corner and refilled my glass and one for Gunnar. "Have a drink. We'll both need it." I figured having the hunter here would be difficult, but I underestimated how much. My instincts were screaming at me to kick him, my wolf engaged and ready to fight. It took more of a conscious effort to maintain control over my basic impulses against threats.

Gunnar was the epitome of a threat.

His threat to Kelsey was a direct threat to me.

Gunnar took the glass I offered. "No Kelsey tonight?"

My eyes narrowed on him at the mention of my mate. I loathed the way her name sounded on his lips. It made me want to rip out his tongue. "She's busy," I replied. "Have a seat, but don't get too comfortable," I added softly.

He took one of the chairs, avoiding Leith on the couch. Smart move. I returned to the spot beside my brother, sipping the scotch from my glass, and had my ass planted for a whole thirty seconds before the doorbell rang again.

Leith and I glanced at each other. "Expecting anyone else?" my brother asked.

"No, did you invite anyone?" I returned.

Settling lower into the couch, he gave no indication of getting up and grumbled, "I wish I had."

"Watch him," I muttered, shoving to my feet.

"With pleasure," Leith said.

As I strode around the couch, my wolf picked up the scent of another wolf.

What the fuck?

Why is Hope here?

I was going to kill her.

I flung open the door, a dark scowl sculpted on my lips. "What are you doing here?" I hissed.

My cousin grinned up at me. "Surprise. Aunt Sydney invited me." She didn't wait for me to invite her in and brushed past me, shaking off the cold once inside. It looked like her leg was bothering her more than usual.

My mom? "Why do I get the feeling you prompted her for an invite?" I accused.

Hope's smile brightened. "Is it so hard to believe I wanted to spend an evening with my cousins?"

"Yes," I said firmly. "You shouldn't be here. I don't want you getting involved." I kept my voice as low as I could, not wanting Mom to pick up on the tension.

Too late.

"Involved in what?" Mom asked as she walked into the room and moved to give Hope a kiss on the cheek. "Hi, Button. I'm glad you could make it. It's been too long since we've had you for dinner. I'm excited to catch up."

Button was Mom's childhood nickname for her niece that stuck.

Hope gave Mom a genuine smile that lit up her face. "I miss coming. No one cooks like you."

"At least someone appreciates me. How's your dad?" Mom inquired, making small talk. They chatted for a few moments as we strolled to the family room. Mom's eyes swept the room, noticing someone was missing. "No Kelsey?"

I shook my head. "She's busy tonight." I repeated the same excuse I'd given Gunnar.

"That's too bad. It would have been nice to have a full house." Mom turned a friendly face to Gunnar. "It's been too long, Gunnar. I see you're still hanging around my niece."

"She hasn't kicked me out of her life yet," he said smoothly as if being in a house full of shifters had no effect on him.

A round of coughs went through the room, and the hunter had the fucking nerve to sit in his chair and smirk.

Mom gave us all funny looks, reading the weird vibe in the room, but good manners had her biting her tongue. For now. "Dinner will be ready in a minute. I think I hear your father."

My knee bounced as I waited on pins and needles for my father to stroll in and see the hunter. His reaction would be a telling sign. All I needed was a single flinch, and it would be enough for me to keep digging.

He came in, barely sparing the lot of us a glance, and went directly to pour a drink. It wasn't until he emptied his first glass that he turned around. "Sorry, it's been a hellish day."

I studied his face as his eyes went around the room and passed over Gunnar without so much as a flicker of emotion on his features other than stress and tiredness.

Dimples flashed on either side of his sharp cheeks. "We have guests tonight. It's lovely to see you, Hope. Next time, drag your old man with you. It's been ages since your dad has come to one of your Aunt Sydney's dinners."

"I will. He hasn't been home much as you probably know. A decent meal would be good for him," my cousin replied as I kept my eyes trained on my father.

"How's your mom?" Dad asked, setting his drink on the fireplace mantel to add a log to the fire. Embers danced in the hearth, the wood catching flame moments later.

"Good. She's working the late shift tonight," she informed politely.

Who would have thought Hope would be the buffer at tonight's dinner? I couldn't tell if her presence hurt or aided my plight. So far, nothing was going according to plan.

Unfortunately for Leith, dinner didn't wield anything eventful, unless you counted Mom's baked lasagna as memorable. Everything was too cordial, and Dad didn't seem to give a shit I'd brought a hunter to dinner, and I couldn't help but wonder if Gunnar lied.

What if my father had nothing to do with the attacks on Kelsey?

What if Gunnar played us?

And this entire dinner was a waste of my fucking time.

"Hope, are you and Gunnar dating yet?" Mom asked while serving slices of her white chocolate raspberry cheesecake, a family favorite.

Everyone at the table, including my father, choked.

"What?" Mom blinked, setting a small plate in front of Hope. "You've been friends forever. It's only natural that things might progress in a different direction. How do you think I ended up with your Uncle Rowan? We were friends first."

I kept my mouth shut, but we were all thinking the same thing. Mom had been the consolation prize after the girl he truly wanted ran off with another alpha—Kelsey's dad.

"We're just friends," Hope assured.

As dinner drew to a close, my frustration compounded. I clenched my fists under the table, clamping my jaw shut or risking blurting out Gunnar's true identity...all the lies he'd kept from us. I was seconds away from shoving out of my chair and causing the spectacle Leith wished for. I needed something, anything more than this limbo of not knowing. I wanted the doubt to end.

When I surged to my feet, the chair scraped on the floor, but before I could hurl any accusations across the table, Gunnar stood as well, diverting everyone's eyes off me. "I should probably get home. Thank you so much for having me. I can't remember the last time I've had a meal this good."

"Let me pack some for you to take home," Mom insisted.

Gunnar smiled gratefully, and to my surprise, the jerk seemed genuine. "I won't turn down leftovers."

It occurred to me that he didn't have anyone at home cooking for him, let alone waiting for him to return, yet that didn't mean I would feel sorry for the bastard. Maybe before, but not after he tried to take what was mine.

"I'll come with you," Hope offered.

Gunnar shook his head, lingering awkwardly at the table. "Thanks, but Liam and I have something we need to do before school tomorrow. See you later?"

"Oh," Hope stated flatly, her shoulders drooping slightly. "Sure."

I couldn't fathom how she felt any disappointment at him turning her down. It went over my head, this unhealthy attachment she had to the hunter. My cousin and I needed to have a serious sit-down about the choice of people she kept in her life. I imagined that conversation going as well as if she were Kelsey.

A fucking disaster.

I pinned the hunter with a pointed glare once Mom left the room. Did he just save me from making a costly mistake?

I felt my father's eyes on me, the callous stare he used on our enemies, but I'd been wrong. The glare wasn't for me.

He glowered at Gunnar, and the hunter lifted a mocking eyebrow in turn, daring my father to do or say something. It was the first all night my father's posture cracked, a tiny sliver, but it added to my doubt.

Dad blinked, and the ruthlessness was gone, and I almost questioned if I had seen it at all, if I hadn't wanted it to be there.

No, I know what I saw.

I waited until Gunnar and I were outside and inside his car with the radio on to drown out our voices. "Why did you do that?" I asked.

An alternative song rocked from the speakers. "You mean save your ass from exploding in front of your father and ruining any chance you have at holding him accountable for what he plans to do with your mate? You're welcome."

Maybe I should thank him, but not for the reason he referred to. If he hadn't reacted, standing after me, I might not have ever caught a glimpse of my father's true feelings about the hunter.

He knew who he was. I was sure of it.

I didn't have all the answers I needed, but tonight had been a start. I loathed being unprepared, uncertain when the threat would strike. Should I confess to my father what I knew? Lay it all out in the open? Perhaps I could convince him what he had planned for Kelsey's magic wasn't worth it.

"I know what you're thinking. Don't. Nothing you say will change his mind," Gunnar said.

"What other choice do I have?" In the meantime, the ceremony for the treaty loomed near, and my intuition told me that if I didn't do something soon, another hunter would try to take Kelsey again before her birthday. The hands on the clock were ticking.

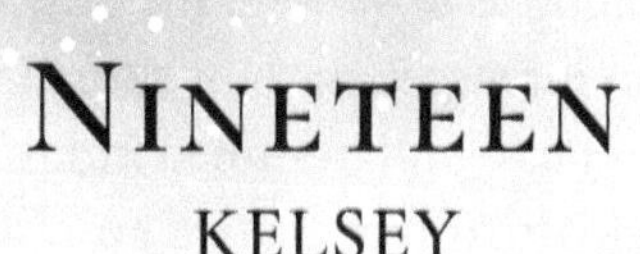

Nineteen
KELSEY

"Hey, I've barely seen you all week." How did I end up here? Chasing after the heir prince? If the girl who first arrived could see me now. She'd be so damn disappointed.

Where had my resolve to fight against the treaty gone?

One night in Liam's bed, and all my resolve vanished as it was never there.

It had never been Liam himself I was against, but the lack of free will neither of us was allowed in this situation. Our parents never considered our feelings or our wants but thought of only the pack. I understood their position as leaders, but to use your children as bargaining chips... It always made me feel less like a shifter and more like a chess piece. I was an object for them to move.

Deep down, I knew my parents loved me. This was pack life. Deals and treaties such as mine were signed every day. I didn't think either one of them relished in sending me away, but they had given their blood, which was an oath that couldn't be broken.

Besides, as I gazed up into the heir prince's stupidly handsome face, I felt lucky. He could have been grotesque *and* an asshole. He was just an asshole...well, in some ways. In others, like when his guard was down, he could be heartbreakingly charming.

Frighteningly so.

Liam Castle had the power to not just break my heart but shatter my soul into pieces so small they would be nearly invisible to the eye —dust.

My mate lifted his head, our gazes colliding for the first time today, and there it was, the feeling as if we were the only two people existing in the world. It was like an intense version of tunnel vision that also jacked up my heart rate. A magnetic pull hummed in my body. Every bone and muscle propelled me closer to him. I used to resist the feeling with all the willpower I had, which honestly wasn't much pitted against Liam's, but I no longer fought against it.

I gave in, moving nearer until the fronts of our bodies brushed. His eyes stayed on me the entire time, never faltering. The touch of my hand on his snapped the spell.

Liam blinked. "We need to talk."

"That sounds serious." I deliberately took the bottom of my lip between my teeth, and his eyes tracked the movement as I hoped.

Seeing his eyes darken made me feel alive. "The roof," he said, dragging his gaze away from my mouth. His hand attached to mine firmly, and he pulled me down the hallway toward the stairs.

The crowded corridors parted at the heir prince's approach. It was like that everywhere he went. Even the humans treated him like royalty, but they didn't know why. I guessed they considered it a popularity thing. Liam was the quarterback and deemed a god on and off the football field.

I doubled my footsteps to keep up with him, his strides so much longer than mine. He shoved the door leading out to the roof open. The middle of November drew near and had brought cloudy days with it. A light drizzle fell from the murky sky, and if it wasn't for my higher body temperature, I might have found the cooler air intolerable, but I loved days like today.

I lifted my face, inviting the crisp air into my lungs while the biting wind kissed my cheeks.

A bit giddy and a tad drunk on Liam's presence, I looped my arms around his neck as the door swung shut behind us. "If you wanted to be alone with me, you could have just asked."

He drew in a hard breath, his muscles tense instead of relaxing into me.

I angled my head to the side, regarding him. Something was definitely up, and I wasn't sure I wanted to know. An unnerving flutter entered my belly.

His fingers traced up my arms, unweaving my fingers at the nape of his neck. "This is hard enough as it is. I can't have you touching me, or I'll never get it out."

"Why does this sound like the beginning of a breakup speech?" I joked. We hadn't discussed what our relationship was or would be.

He didn't laugh, and uneasiness squirmed inside me.

I inched back, my hands dropping to my sides, and the reeling sensation from being around my mate slowly faded. "You can't break up with me. We're not even a thing. Not really."

"That's not what this is," he insisted, the frown on his mouth building deeper.

I tried not to be drawn by the scar on his lower lip, but damn, if my eyes weren't beckoned by it. "Then enlighten me, princeling. What is it you brought me up here to say?" My arms spread out wide, waiting for him to make his grandiose speech.

"You have to understand things from my point of—"

I cut him off right there. "What is it I need to understand? The suspense is killing me." My voice shrilled, growing higher with each word. I shook my head at the sadness in his ocean eyes and the fragment of regret I didn't want to feel through our bond. Before he said the words, I knew what would come out of his mouth.

"A break. We need to take a break," he struggled to say like the statement caused him physical pain to get out.

It made me sick to my stomach. "A break?" I repeated sharply. "From what exactly?" I knew I sounded like a crazy ex-girlfriend about to go mental on him, but I didn't give a shit. "From me? From the link I created? From the stress? From the danger? From the pressures of being the heir? Explain it to me?"

A rough hand dove into his messy hair, the wind whipping the sandy strands around his face. "I would if you give me a second to speak."

My lips slammed together in a scowl as I crossed my arms over my chest. I forced my feet to stay where they were when all I wanted to do was bolt. Run straight for the woods and keep going, never looking back like I should have done that night after the ceremony where it was revealed Liam and I were Moonstruck mates. Leith had stopped me.

A regret I had to live with.

I'd probably still end up here having my heart ripped out, stomped over, and then tossed away as if I meant nothing.

Liam waited a moment to see if I had anything else I wanted to get off my chest. Boy, fucking did I, but I would hear him out first.

He swallowed. "We can't risk another slip up like we had the other morning. You and I are already treading a slippery slope with the king and our packs. We can't afford another mistake."

"Are you saying my claiming you was a *mistake*?"

His chest rose and fell in a deep breath. "No, of course not. That's not what I meant. You might not like me much right now or in five minutes, hell, in five weeks, but regardless of your feelings, know that I want you. I'll always want you. Yes, even when you hate my guts. This isn't anything you did."

"If you even think of giving me the it's-me-not-you lecture, I'll fucking scream my lungs out." So much for not interrupting. I couldn't help it. The shit he said didn't make sense to me. I couldn't see how it did to him.

He dropped against the brick ledge. "Damn it, Kelsey, do you always have to make things so difficult?"

"Yes, *Liam*." I emphasized his name. "Life is difficult. Wolf or not, there are always hurdles to jump and obstacles to face, but we do it together. Not apart."

His eyes churned, and his proud shoulders dipped slightly. "I don't have the willpower to be around you. Every second, it chips away. We still have six weeks to go, and I don't know if I'll make it another day, let alone weeks. My entire being, wolf and man, want to make you mine."

My stupid heart cartwheeled. "You think I don't understand that sort of craving? Why do you think I risked claiming you despite knowing you couldn't reciprocate? You have the power to destroy me."

"That's not what I want," he whispered. "Hurting you is the very last thing I wish for. It kills me. Fucking kills me, pup." He was basically begging me to understand.

I shook my head and stepped to the edge of the roof, looking down at the river bordering the west side of the school. "This is so messed up. Being separated from you causes pains in my chest. Being close to me makes you mad with the basic instinct of mates. There's no compromise. We both end up in pain."

He turned, facing the same direction I did, gazing into the distance. "A conclusion I've recently accepted. I've tried to come up with a better solution, but the truth of the matter is, I can't ignore my wolf, not when we both want the same thing."

On one hand, I could sympathize with his struggle. I hadn't been restrained enough to say no to my wolf. And yet, the selfish part of me dreaded being apart. "What about school?" I asked, clinging to some part of my life he couldn't avoid me in.

"I switched a few of my classes so we won't be in the same room together until the second term after winter break." He'd already made up his mind before talking to me.

Anguish bit my heart.

I let it branch inside me, attempting to figure out what I would do or say next, but then it felt as if I couldn't breathe. I gasped for air, expecting to find relief, but it was as if my lungs stopped functioning.

Am I having a panic attack?

"Breathe, pup." Liam's calming voice filled my head.

And it was his voice that set me off.

Agony swiftly turned into rage like lightning cracking through the dark clouds. Hell, lightning could have very well struck, but the anger flooding my veins drowned everything else out.

My hand balled into a fist, and I whirled, sinking it into Liam's gut. "You're a coward, Liam Castle. I never thought you would run away with your tail between your legs. I thought you were a fighter." I didn't care if my voice lashed out like a dagger, cutting him with my words.

It was no different than how he made me feel.

Worthless. Alone. Unwanted.

His stomach flexed from my hit, but he didn't feel nearly enough pain as I wanted him to.

My hands were moving before the thought registered of what I was doing, beating against Liam's chest. He didn't stop me but let me pound on him, unleashing the fury, hurt, and pain working its way through me.

It didn't help.

And suddenly, I no longer wanted to be on the roof with him. He wanted distance. He wanted a break. I'd give him both. Backing away from him, I shoved the wild strands of hair off my face. "I don't want to see your face again. And stay the fuck out of my head."

I ran across the roof, flinging the door open to the school. The heir prince didn't follow me, no matter how hard I willed him to. Despite the anger, I longed for him to stop me, to change his mind, and pull me into his arms, an apology falling from his mouth.

Each step away broke a shard off my heart. The worst part was that his emotions compounded with mine, causing one massive, messy, tangle of feelings I couldn't sort through. It was too damn much to deal with.

I had to shut them out, wall them off. I had to block our bond, or I'd crumble. I'd lose myself to hurt tearing me up and the darkness threatening to consume me.

Love was supposed to smell like roses. Sweet and a bit like tea not like fear, pain, betrayal, blood, and death.

Those were the visions I had in my dreams, and Liam was well on his way to making them a reality.

☽☽●☾☾

I WOULD NOT CRY. I would not shed a fucking tear.

I'd get in my car, stop at the store, buy gallons of boys-are-assholes-mint chip or love-sucks-chunky-monkey, and go home to drown my misery in ice cream.

The halls were empty as I dashed down them with only escape on my mind. Classes had started, and of course, I should be in one of them, but I couldn't sit in a room, pretending to learn when such chaos spun within me. My emotions were too strong, and at any moment, I could burst.

Tears pricked my eyes, but I blinked them away. Temporarily at least. I just needed to make it to my car, then I could purge Liam Castle from my heart.

I hadn't wanted to admit it before, but the way my chest squeezed, it became clear I had feelings for the asshole. Strong feelings.

Fuck, close to love.

I'd been falling in love with the heir prince.

And that's why it hurt so damn much.

I wasn't going to make it to the car. *Fuck. Fuck. Fuck.*

The tears were back with a vengeance, threatening to spill, and a lump clogged in my throat. I looked around the corner and headed straight for the girls' bathroom.

I locked myself into a stall and flipped the lock. *Breathe, Kelsey. Just breathe.*

Hot, big tears tracked down my cheeks. My back collapsed against the partition wall, and I slammed the heel of my palm into the metal door, the force of the hit vibrating through my body.

I stopped fighting the swell of overwhelmingness and let the waterworks flow. My body needed the release because the alternative involved a whole lot of magic and probably would endanger the school.

Time got away from me. When the tears finally dried up and I had nothing left to feel but numbness, I unlocked the door and went to the sink. I splashed water on my face and glanced at my reflection in the mirror. My features were out of focus, and my violet eyes wavered in front of me.

Then I was falling.

I LANDED hard on my ass, shit falling over my face and in my hair. My mouth opened as I groaned, and the debris got into my mouth. I spit as I orientated myself.

The crap tasted like dirt, which made me think it might very well be just that.

Despite having a sore ass, I wasn't hurt anywhere, not that I could tell.

Total darkness surrounded me, but I picked up traces of damp earth like I was outside.

I glanced up where a small stream of light filtered into a hole I now sat at the bottom of.

Fucking hell.

Panic started to claw my chest as the reality of my situation unfolded. How the hell did I end up in a hole? Had I been running in the woods and stumbled upon a trap?

Shoving to my feet, I pressed my hand flat against the dirt wall and looked up to judge how deep this crater went. A knot tied in my gut, and I cursed. Even if I shifted, I wasn't sure my wolf could leap out of here.

Whoever dug this pit meant to keep more than a bear or wolf inside.

I backed up, searching for leverage to help me when my shoe bumped into something on the ground. I crouched down, using my hands to help identify what it was. It didn't take me long, not when I felt the outline of an unmoving body lying beside me. A silent scream rose in my throat. Were they dead? Please don't let them be dead.

The unknown person moaned, and I exhaled.

At least I wasn't alone in my misery.

Tingles radiated near my heart, fluttering throughout my limbs, and a different horror gripped me. The person trapped in the pit with me was Liam.

I shook my head. No. It couldn't be. There went my hope of the heir prince saving my ass.

"Liam," I murmured, wishing the moon was brighter tonight. I needed to see his face. Was he injured?

I didn't have time to dwell on the heir prince's condition. My ears picked up sounds in the distance like a stampede. A wolf howled into the night, and the dirt under my hands trembled.

Company was coming.

A lot of company, and my intuition told me they weren't friends.

We were being hunted.

"Kelsey," someone whispered.

The ground rattled.

My eyes were heavy, yet I had to open them. Someone kept calling my name, ordering me to wake up.

"Kelsey."

More shaking.

Hands pressed into my shoulders. It wasn't the ground trembling underneath me. Someone shook my shoulders, jostling me from this darkness that swallowed me up, trapping me.

I directed my energy to my eyes, willing them to open. I never thought I would have to use my powers for something as simple as blinking. My lashes fluttered, and a heavy sigh filled the room. Not mine.

An unnatural and blinding light beamed down on my sensitive eyes, making it uncomfortable to fully open them, but I forged on until I stared at the paneled ceiling with water stains on the white tiles.

My head twisted to the side. Hope crouched down beside me, watching me with cautious eyes tinged with relief. "Hope?" I rasped.

"Holy shit, Kelsey. You scared me. I was about to grab the nurse." She rocked down on her ass, sitting next to me.

I lay on the ground, the room around us coming into focus. *Am I in the bathroom? Lying on the floor?*

Gross.

"What happened?" I asked, but as the question left my mouth, I had a good idea, my memories coming back.

"I don't know," she admitted. "I found you like this, unconscious and spread out over the floor."

Wincing at the throb assaulting my head, I tried to sit up. Hope helped, her hands going under my elbows to guide me.

"Be careful," she warned, her gaze narrowing. "I think you hit your head."

I touched a spot at the back, and sure as shit, a wet substance warmed my fingers. Drawing my hand away, I stared down at the blood coating the pads of my fingers. "Shit."

"Are you okay? Should I get Liam?"

"No! Don't." The response flew out of my mouth. Taking a breath, I added, "I'm fine. Really. Just a bump. It will heal in a few minutes."

"I know you want to be fine, but you're not. This is the second time you've fainted this month. Something's going on and I want you to tell me the truth."

Staring at her, I thought about the reasons why I shouldn't share what I'd learned about my magic. I hadn't told Liam, and I probably shouldn't unload on Hope, but damn, if I didn't need a friend right now. "Remember I told you about my extra sense?"

She nodded, waiting patiently.

"It's been a little unsteady since I claimed Liam," I admitted quietly.

"Is that normal?"

"According to my nana, it is to some degree. There are factors that come into play like my claim to the heir prince. The strength of our mates nourishes our powers."

Hope blinked. "You're fucked."

"Thanks," I replied, dropping my head and staring at the disgusting bathroom floor. I tried not to think about the fact we were sitting on it.

"Outside of his father and perhaps the king, Liam is the strongest wolf I know," she said with wide eyes.

Lifting my head, I propped it against the wall. "Are you trying to freak me out?"

Her brown eyes seemed to be processing a thousand thoughts at once. "What happens when he claims you?"

I gave her a halfhearted shrug. "My power will probably consume me."

"How can you be so calm about this?" she demanded, her voice rising in outrage on my behalf. "What are you going to do?"

Today I didn't have it in me to contemplate the future. The grief, anger, agony, and confusion swirling within me were too strong. "I'm not sure yet. Learn to control the visions instead of them controlling me."

"Is there anything I can do to help?" she asked, leveling her tone.

I met her gaze, hating what I was about to ask of her. "Don't tell Liam. Promise me."

A contemplative line wrinkled her brow. "I don't understand why, but if it's that important to you, I won't."

I sighed in relief. "Thank you."

"Is it weird that we are still sitting on the bathroom floor?" she asked scrunching her nose and effortlessly lightening the tension in the room.

"Probably. I think I might need to go get a tetanus shot after this. Think the nurse has any stashed inside her office?" I joked, thankful for Hope's presence. I'd be curled into a ball if she hadn't found me.

Hope chuckled.

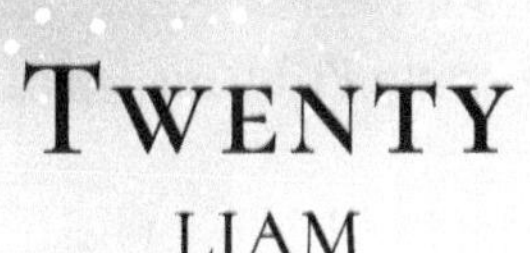

Twenty
LIAM

I didn't follow Kelsey, but I damn well wanted to. My wolf balked and whimpered inside me. A physical ache sprouted in my gut, blooming until I couldn't stand any longer.

Sinking to the hard, cold surface, I dropped my forearms to my knees and lowered my head.

I'd done the one thing I never thought I'd do. Hurt her.

Since Kelsey came to Riverbridge, this overwhelming protectiveness nagged constantly within me. It was as if she stepped over the town's borders and a switch flipped in me.

Neither of us asked for the intense connection we had, deeper than most wolves, but despite my loathing of the situation, it didn't take me long to want the girl, which infuriated me.

I hadn't understood how I could want someone so much without knowing them, and I convinced myself I only felt lust for her.

Pressing a hand to my chest, I rubbed at the pain spreading. *It's only for a few weeks*, I reminded myself.

I compiled a list of reasons why staying away from Kelsey was the best tactic. High on the list sat focusing on who hired Gunnar, and if it was my father, I needed to figure out what to do about it. Who could I trust?

Minutes dragged on, the school buzzer going off and on, but I never budged. My mind dwelled on the look on Kelsey's face when I told her I wanted a break—when she realized I was serious. Knowing somewhere she sat in pain and I couldn't comfort her killed me. Knowing I was the reason for her anguish destroyed me.

I stayed on the roof until I sensed Kelsey leave. She didn't stay until the end of school, and I couldn't blame her. I'm surprised she hadn't immediately fled.

Staying seated, I listened to her boots clamor over the blacktop as she rushed to her car. A second set of steps followed. Her guard, Max. Then the engine purred to life, and her RAV4 zoomed to the main road.

My ears followed the sound of her SUV for miles until I lost it and only the chirping of birds, the lapping of the river, and the slew of voices inside resurfaced.

THE FIRST WEEK was the hardest, especially the weekend, but I kept busy. If I wasn't with Gunnar, then I was with Colsen and Riven. I didn't trust myself alone.

Today the hunter and I were having a catch-up in the woods bordering his house, one of the safer places for us to talk without being overheard by anyone. "Has he reached out?" I asked, not expecting good news. My father was too smart.

Gunnar's jaw clenched. "Not yet."

Living under the roof with a man you no longer felt you knew was fucking torture. I wavered between disbelief and wanting to hurt him. "You're certain he will?"

A bed of stiff grass and frozen leaves crunched under our feet. "Your father doesn't strike me as someone who gives up, especially with something he wants, and he wants your mate. I saw the hunger in his eyes. He will stop at nothing to get her power," Gunnar said.

"I agree. My father isn't one to let things go or surrender. He's relentless. If he suspects you're no longer an ally, it explains why he hasn't contacted you."

Gunnar unearthed a pack of cigarettes from his pocket. "My guess is he's moved onto a new hunter."

And if that was true, then Gunnar's life was on the line. "But he put so much time and energy into you. He's not done with you. My father doesn't leave loose ends."

He offered me one, but I shook my head. "You've finally come to that conclusion, huh?" Tapping out a smoke from the pack, he put the slim stick between his lips.

He'd kill Gunnar before risking exposure, particularly when he had so much to lose. "Since you're so fond of using bait, you just became the lure."

The lighter in his hand flickered, producing a flame. He held it to the end of his cigarette, lighting the stick with a long inhale. A puff of smoke came out. "Using my tactics against me. Classic—"

Whizzzz.

My head whipped to the side at what sounded like...an arrow slicing toward us. It didn't just sound like it. It *was* a fucking arrow. "Get down!" I hissed, spinning back to face Gunnar.

He saw my expression and picked up the sliver of metal sailing through the trees. The hunter had good reflexes, but if he didn't move now, he'd be taking a hit to the chest.

Is he trying to kill himself?

The thought made me rethink my next move. Did he hate the collar enough to intentionally let himself get injured? Or worse?

Son of a bitch.

I understood hopelessness and feeling trapped with no way out, but the bastard wasn't about to get out of the mess he created that easily.

Shoving off my feet, I lunged at the hunter, tackling his ass to the ground. As we fell, I felt the sharp point of the arrow slash my hoodie. I waited for the tip to pierce my skin, waited for the pain.

With a hard thud, I landed on top of Gunnar with an oomph, dirt and grass spitting up into my face, but the only pain came from the ache of my fall and landing on Gunnar's bony ass. The hunter needed to pack on some fat if he planned to continue making trouble for me.

We had no time to waste.

Scrambling to my feet, I hauled him up by the neckline of his sweatshirt. "Run!" I ordered, not waiting for his legs to move. I dragged him through the woods, knowing he would have no problem keeping up with the pace I set.

Another arrow zigzagged past us. I couldn't be sure they wouldn't kill me in the process of hunting Gunnar. A growl vibrated at the base of my throat. I hated having my life threatened. They might not be commissioned to take me out, but the heir prince of Wyoming was quite an impressive target for any hunter's rap sheet.

We didn't get far when my wolf picked up the trace of other hunters in the woods, and they were racing toward us.

Gunnar detected them as well. "Looks like reinforcements have arrived."

"Fuck," I mumbled under my breath. It was bad enough having Gunnar in town. Now others? Who knew how many? How the hell could I keep my distance from Kelsey now, knowing the threat in town surged? I no longer had it under control.

Yanking Gunnar around to face me, I held his gaze. "You will fight for your life. Do you understand me? It's a fucking order. Do whatever is necessary to survive."

He rolled his neck from side to side. "As if I have a choice."

"You don't." I tossed him a knife from my pocket.

He stared down at the weapon, disappointment in his features. "This is the best you can do?"

"I'm sure you won't have a problem handling the blade. As I recall, you're pretty damn resourceful when you need to be."

"Game on," he mumbled, flipping the dagger between his fingers. Back-to-back, we faced our enemies. For once, the hunter and I were on the same side with a common foe. "Now might be a good time to call for backup," he gritted out.

I kept my focus trained on the trees ahead, poised for the slightest movement. "All you need to worry about is staying alive. I'll handle the rest. By the way, you should duck."

"Now?" he had the audacity to ask.

"Now!" I bellowed.

Another arrow came soaring toward us. Gunnar flung himself to the side, narrowly missing being shot in the back. I chose a different path, shifting into my wolf. My roar cleaved over the trees, shaking the leaves with the force of a wild storm.

"Finally," Gunnar muttered, squaring off, his feet planted firmly into the ground and my blade raised in his hand. "I was beginning to wonder if I'd ever get to fight again."

I scanned the woods until I found a target, and once I had him locked in, I didn't take my gaze off him.

Fangs flashing and fur bristling, I charged at the threat neither human nor wolf. Meta. *This should be fun.*

Rearing up when he was in front of me, I swiped out with my claws, slashing his throat into ribbons. Blood sprayed into my face, but I only pivoted, looking for my next target.

Seconds later, I spotted him.

The bastard gave me an unholy grin, canines gleaming, and nocked another arrow. I dodged out of the way as I took off, running straight for him. He readied and fired another arrow. Again. And again. But the mark never found its target, and then I was upon him.

A phantom breeze rustled my fur.

I came down hard, and the earth seemed to shudder underneath my paws. Lost in vengeance and rage, I leaped onto the hunter, bearing my full weight on his chest as he hit the earth. My canines sunk into his neck, hitting a vital vein as blood erupted into my mouth.

I risked a glance at Gunnar to see how he fared, pleased to see him still standing with a dead meta at his feet. His eyes were hard as stone as they met mine across the woods. He gave me a quick nod before whirling for the next attack, the bloody dagger clutched in his hand.

The woods grew eerily quiet as I listened. Not being able to track my prey with scent put me at a disadvantage I wasn't used to. Intuition told me there was at least one more lingering among the trees, poised and waiting to make his move, and I felt like a sitting duck. I was supposed to be the most lethal thing in these woods, not some genetically altered—

From the corner of my left eye, I caught movement, a blur coming toward me with blinding speeds that made me question if I could outrun him. Crouching at the last second, the meta slashed at me, knowing precisely where to strike, and if I had been a hair slower, he would have hit his mark.

With an impressive recovery rate, the mutated hunter used his momentum to spin around, coming back at me from a different angle. Not a killing blow, but still one that would hurt like a bitch.

I took a gnash in the calf, but nothing that wouldn't heal once I killed this bastard. They weren't using silver, which I found odd. Perhaps their orders weren't to kill Gunnar but to capture him instead.

No wonder he chose death.

Snarling, I bared my teeth, ignoring the stinging pain in my leg. I suppressed the urge to rip out his throat in one clean clamp of my jaw, wanting his death not only to be agonizing but also informative.

Launching at the meta, I slammed into his body with enough force to knock him several feet away, right into a tree. The crack of his back hitting the thick trunk almost made me wince. It was a fucking loud, beautiful sound.

Before he could push himself off the ground, I was there slamming him back into the earth as I roared in his face, my paws pinning him down.

Interrogating in wolf form was damn difficult when the culprit wasn't part of the pack. Lucky for me, Gunnar knew the drill. For once, the hunter and I were on the same wavelength, and communication was unnecessary. When it came to fighting tactics, our minds might have worked similarly.

The hunter strolled up and plunged the knife I gave him into the meta's chest. Not a flinch of hesitation in his movements. Just ruthless darkness in his eyes. Crouching down at the mutated hunter's side, Gunnar left the blade in his heart. "If you don't want to bleed out in these woods, start talking," he demanded.

I approved of his interrogation methods.

"The wolf with magic," he wheezed.

I snarled again and bared my teeth despite the wave of ice trickling down my neck at the mention of Kelsey.

"What about her?" Gunnar demanded, twisting the knife embedded in his chest.

The hunter cried out in an agony that echoed in my bones. Blood squirted from the wound, seeping from where the flesh had been only moments ago.

My mind whirled. Had a new order been issued for her kidnapping since Gunnar hadn't finished the job?

The meta laughed, a gurgling sound. "This isn't over. You shouldn't have left her."

My lip curled, a low vibration humming in my throat.

"Why?" Gunnar demanded.

I dug my claws farther into his shoulders, his eyes rolling back in his head. We were losing him. Fast.

"What have you done to her?" Gunnar tried again, ripping out his knife and sinking it back in. But it didn't matter if we threatened him or beat him to a bloody pulp. He wouldn't give me the answers I was desperate to have.

He was dead.

And Gunnar and I were the last ones standing, the forest floor surrounding us soaked in blood and littered with bodies.

☽☽●☾☾

I RAMMED my foot on the pedal, pushing the truck to its limits. We weren't far from school, but the few miles stretched like an endless road in front of me.

Gunnar wiped the knife on his jeans, cleaning off the remnants of killing. "We just barely escaped death, so why are you trying to kill us now?"

After clearing the area and getting useless information, Gunnar and I had rushed to my truck. I didn't waste any time, only quickly yanking on a pair of spare sweats from my bag. Then we were off, speeding toward Riverbridge High. "I need to see her." My fingers twisted on the steering wheel, dried blood staining them.

"Just use your bond," he said like I hadn't already attempted to reach her a dozen different times with no success.

I sent him a dry look. "You don't think I tried. She's not responding."

"She's probably still pissed at you."

I hoped he was right. The alternative would send me spiraling. My control already walked a razor-thin line.

He turned the blade back and forth, inspecting it. "For once, I'm glad I don't have a mate."

Could he mate? Honestly, right now, I didn't give a shit what Gunnar could or couldn't do.

I held out my palm. "Hand it over."

He hesitated, glancing at the knife as if it hurt to release the weapon. In a way, I understood. Whether by choice or not, at his root, he was a hunter. Without a weapon, I imagined he felt bare—incomplete—how I would without my wolf. "I could ram this into your heart right now and disable the collar."

For a split second, the organ in question tripped in my chest. "You could. But you won't, or you wouldn't have taunted me with the threat first. I think you want this to end as much as I do. Perhaps more, and you know I'm your best shot at taking out those who might want you dead."

"I'm a pretty fucking smart guy," he said with an unapologetic smile. With reluctance, he flipped the knife around and placed it into my hand.

Tucking the dagger under my seat, I hammered the gas and took the turn at full speed, Gunnar hanging onto the door.

"Kelsey," I gritted out, trying our bond again. It didn't surprise me I received nothing but silence in return. This break had been my idea. She was pissed, and she would punish me for it.

"Answer me, damn it," I growled, not believing a forceful tone would change her mind.

My fingers slammed against the steering wheel, the silence from our bond lingering.

"Here, toss this on," Gunnar said, flinging one of my spare shirts from the back at me.

I caught it with one hand, the other steering my truck into the school parking lot. "Don't tell me my bare chest is bothering you." I didn't bother to look for a parking spot or turn the engine off as I slammed the truck into park in front of the main entrance.

Gunnar unlatched his seat belt. "It would bother anyone. Maybe you should lay off the protein shakes."

Leaving the keys in the ignition, I flung open the door. "Park this damn thing and find Hope. Stay with her for the rest of the day." The hunter had pulled her into this mess. He could very well make sure nothing happened to her.

I didn't wait for him to respond. I wasn't interested in another snappy retort, nor did I want to waste my time. My bare feet flew over the concrete as I tugged the shirt on. I hadn't bothered with shoes.

Maxtyn hung out against the side of the building. He had his phone pressed to his ear. His gold eyes swung in my direction as I approached, and his brows furrowed at the expression I wore. I conveyed silently for him to get the fuck off the phone, or I'd smash it. He had two strides before I reached him. Maxtyn nodded once in response and hung up, shoving his phone into his back pocket.

One stride left. My fingers balled into the material of his flannel, and I thrust him into the brick wall. "Where is she? Where the fuck is she?" I demanded.

"What the hell has gotten into you?" Maxtyn snapped, shoving my hands off the front of his shirt.

"Just tell me where she is?" I seethed.

The guard's gaze drew cold. "Inside. You look like shit."

I'd just come from a fight, but damn, if I wasn't ready for another one. The combination of fear and fury made me volatile. "You're sure? You're absolutely sure?"

"Why are you asking me? Shouldn't you be able to tell? Use your bond." No mercy crawled into his tone as he gave the same response Gunnar had.

If I'd taken a moment to assess my connection to Kelsey when I pulled into the school, I would have felt the increase of tingles radiating inside my chest like dozens of fireflies, warm and fluttery, but my mind didn't have time to be rational. I had to see her. I had to know the meta hunters weren't inside.

I refused to admit to Maxtyn that Kelsey was ignoring my summons or perhaps she discovered a way to block me. I didn't doubt she had the powers to do so and the skill.

Without a response, I twisted around and bolted toward the school entrance.

"What the hell happened?" he called after me.

Inside, I rushed down the nearly empty halls, earning wary glances from a few students lingering about and a teacher on their way to the break room. I glanced at the clock hanging from the wall, checking the time. Third period.

I headed for the stairs, taking them three at a time as I jogged upstairs to the second floor. Room 234 was on the right side about halfway down the long corridor. I bypassed all the rooms, stopping at the class we had shared up until almost two weeks ago before I rearranged my schedule.

Forgoing a courtesy knock, I whipped open the door. If the teacher didn't like my interruption, she could take it up with the principal, who happened to be a pack member and a friend of my father's. I didn't perceive my disturbance would be a problem.

Mrs. Dutton's hand paused on the whiteboard, her gaze swinging to me. A hush fell over the classroom as my eyes raked over the seats, looking for one particular face.

She had her head bent over a notebook, a pen resting between her fingers as she doodled. Slowly, her focus shifted off the paper and onto me.

Our gazes collided.

She stared at me.

I stared at her.

Nothing else in the world existed.

Just Kelsey. The days separating us cut into me like a knife, leaving me aching and in pain.

I lost myself in the depths of her eyes as they widened. It felt as if I was dangling on the edge of a cliff, and she had the power to either reach a hand out and save me or shove me into the rocky ravine below.

My breathing stuttered.

Violet gleamed in her eyes. The tightness in my chest eased, and my heart started beating again.

She was safe.

No one had taken her.

I greedily digested every inch of her, unfazed by the awkwardness growing in the room as I did nothing but stare at my mate. My fingers clutching the door handle compressed harder. My nostrils flared, searching out her scent, and when it hit my senses, I detected the warm aroma of vanilla and a tinge of something sweet like cotton candy. The anxious wolf within me sighed.

She was mine.

My mate.

And more than anything in the world, I longed to sweep into the room, haul her over my shoulder, and carry her out.

I swore through our bond I felt a ripple of excitement, relief, and happiness, then concern. The sparkle of joy only lasted a few seconds before it was extinguished, ripped from our bond.

Mrs. Dutton called my name. Not once but three times. I slammed the door shut without a word to anyone just as I did the same with my emotions, closing the door on them. A gasp of surprise from the teacher followed me into the hall.

Maxtyn waited outside, pacing the side of the building that faced the river. Calmer than most days, the water trickled downstream. His gaze snapped to me. "What the fuck happened?" he pressed. "You reek of blood and death."

Shit. I'd forgotten about the blood on my hands. We were too close to the school. I walked down to the river, Maxtyn following as he waited. "Our town has a few more unwanted guests. I've added extra detail on Kelsey at school but wanted you to be prepared. They will try to get to her."

His gaze narrowed and hardened. A warrior stared back at me, his body stilling. "More hunters. How many?"

"I don't know. Too many." I shifted my eyes to the river down the bank, deciding how much I should tell him. Today in the woods had only been a warning. The bigger threat had yet to come. "Have you thought more about what I said the other day?"

"The meta hunter?"

I nodded, crouching down and dipping my hands into the icy water, washing off the grime. "He's here with me. Has been for days, and you never suspected him."

"Who?" he demanded, voice rough and brows pinched.

Gunnar stepped out from around the corner with a slick smirk. "That would be me."

Maxtyn's muscles coiled, his back going rod straight. "You?" Clearly, he wasn't impressed with the look of Gunnar. I could understand that. Gunnar didn't have the makings or appeal of the hunters we were used to, but I imagined that was part of what made him dangerous.

Shaking my hands off, I stood. "Why didn't you hear him coming? Why didn't you smell another human or wolf approaching?" I posed the questions that had also first boggled my mind.

Maxtyn's brows crinkled, eying Gunnar with a new light, a more critical eye. "How?"

"I told you. He's the hunter who tried to take Kelsey, and he isn't like the hunters we're used to fighting."

A gleam of his wolf lit his gold eyes. I watched as he struggled with who to fight first. Me or Gunnar. I won. Maxtyn pinned me with a glare. "You've known who he was this whole time? And you let him walk free? Why isn't he dead?" Waves of anger rolled off the guard, understandably.

Gunnar chuckled like he had a death wish.

Ignoring him, I gave Maxtyn the truth. "Oh, I considered it but decided he had better uses to me alive. Except that's not why I'm telling you this."

His wolf remained close to the surface. "Why are you?"

My wolf growled within me, restless. He wanted to deal with the threat now. Not later. "I need you to be prepared, to know what we're up against."

"There are more?" the guard guessed.

I nodded. "Yeah, and they're coming for her and to kill him. They will wage war on our packs."

"Let them kill him," the guard said with disdain, his glower indicating Gunnar. "He chose his side. He chose against us."

"I didn't have a choice," the hunter rectified. "They didn't give me one. I didn't volunteer or ask to be what I am."

Maxtyn didn't seem interested in the hunter's origin sob story. "How can you trust him?"

"I don't. But he won't hurt Kelsey. I made sure of it." Trust went both ways. Just as I had to trust Maxtyn, he had to offer me the same.

The guard had more questions. They darkened his eyes. "She isn't going to like the extra protection."

"All I care about is keeping her out of the enemy's hands," I retorted.

"Is that really all you care about?" Gunnar snarked.

I shot him a shut-the-fuck-up scowl. "If she gives you shit, tell her the order came from me."

Maxtyn grinned. "Better you than me."

"I think it would be good if we spent some time with Gunnar, learning his skill set and how to best kill them. It will also give us the chance to learn more about them. Discover any weakness we might be able to use against them. Particularly in detecting them, seeing as their masked scents mean they have a heads-up on us." I might not be able to stop them from coming to Riverbridge, but I could sure as hell make sure some of my crew was prepared, and the guard, as long as he fought to keep my mate from a fate worse than death, was an honorary wolf of my pack.

Maxtyn nodded. "It's been too long since I did any training. I could be down to kick his ass."

Gunnar glanced between us. "Just so we're clear. You're not actually killing me. This is practice, a learning session."

Maxtyn and I both smiled. "Doesn't mean it won't hurt like hell. I might actually enjoy this," the guard said, anticipation gleaming in his eyes.

I knew I would.

"WHAT THE FUCK WAS THAT?" Kelsey slammed her hands down on the table, rattling the trays of everyone who sat with me.

I had a handful of fries halfway to my mouth, smothered in ketchup. I glanced up, staring at my annoyed mate. After leaving Gunnar and Maxtyn by the river, I'd gone to the locker room to shower and put on clean clothes. "A wellness check," I replied.

The chair across from me was occupied by another pack member. Kelsey shifted her bright eyes onto him. "Find a new seat."

A glob of ketchup dripped onto the cafeteria table as Ozzy's chair scratched over the floor. I dropped my fries onto my plate, beside a half-eaten slice of pizza, and leaned back in my seat, watching Ozzy take his food and leave. Kelsey sat down after he vacated the table.

"You don't mind if I join you? Don't worry. I won't stay long seeing as we're on a *break*." She used air quotes around the word.

Clearly, she hadn't forgiven me.

Behind her, Riven folded his arms and smirked at me as he leaned against the table behind Kelsey. Leith sat beside her, and the stupid grin on his face told me he couldn't wait to see what Kelsey would do next.

"Why do I have not one but two idiots tailing me around school all day?" she demanded, clearly not caring how loud she spoke.

Leith chuckled, unaffected that he was one of the two idiots she referred to.

I ignored my brother as usual. "Have you had any other visions?"

She sucked in the corner of her bottom lip. Answer enough for me. She had despite not wanting to admit it. "Don't try and change the subject."

"Did you stop to think they might be connected?"

Her eyes searched mine, and I could see how badly she wanted to use our bond to communicate. "What happened? Did Gunnar go AWOL or something?"

I lowered my voice. "No. Some of his friends came to town." She'd find out anyway. If there was a mystery that needed solving, Kelsey wouldn't stop until she cracked the case.

She plucked a fry off my plate. "More hunters? Are they...?"

I nodded. "Yeah."

She sunk against the back of the chair, chewing with a frown. "Were you hurt? I saw the blood."

"I'm fine," I replied, my tone short. "It wasn't mine."

"Oh," she said breathily, our gazes locking. "I should go." She spun out of the chair, long strands of dark hair flying out behind her.

I got a whiff of her scent. "Kelsey," I growled, and my hand shot out and attached to her wrist before I could think about what I was doing. Her skin was so damn soft.

She froze, and it was a full breath before she turned around, a brow lifted in question. "Is there something else?"

Yes! God, yes. I fucking miss you. Can't you see how much this is hurting me? The pad of my thumb brushed over the inside of her arm, right where a faint outline of a moon marked her skin.

Violet eyes brightened, going glossy with tears. *"I miss you too,"* she said devastatingly in my head.

Agony speared like a lance through my heart. She'd heard me. I hadn't meant for her to hear my thoughts.

"Goodbye, princeling." She walked away and didn't look back.

Not even when I whispered her name.

I stared after her until she disappeared, willing her to turn around and, at the same time, praying she wouldn't. *This is for her own good*, I tried to tell myself. *For the pack.*

Still, it fucking sucked.

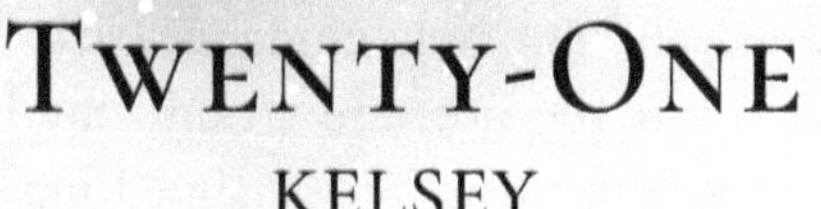

Twenty-One

KELSEY

Thanksgiving break arrived, and for the first time since coming to Riverbridge, I went home to Hot Springs to spend a few days with my family. Nana came with me as did my ever-present guard.

A heavy tightness squeezed at my chest as we drove over the town line, watching the "Thank you for visiting Riverbridge" sign fly by.

I cracked my window, needing the crisp, fresh air to keep my senses alert and give me something else to concentrate on other than the ache in my heart. It was my suggestion to drive, hoping it would distract me from the anxiety creeping in with each mile I drove.

Nana and Max chatted over the low radio in the background while I tapped my fingers on the steering wheel. I didn't hear a word they said, and as if the two of them understood I needed to be left alone, neither pressed me to be included in their conversation.

As an hour turned into two, I wished the ride would become easier. That wasn't the case. At one point, I swore I'd have to pull off the side of the road or risk having a panic attack while driving at speeds over seventy.

I didn't want to kill Nana.

Luckily, for all our sakes, my visions stayed at bay. Of course, tonight

would be a different story. I anticipated being riddled with restlessness and haunted by dreams of war, death, broken hearts, and agonizing suffering. All the fun stuff.

My parents waited on the porch when I pulled up the long winding driveway. Even in the dark, home washed over me in such a comforting way. It felt like the house, the yard, and the woods surrounding our property gave me one giant hug, welcoming me back.

I sighed in relief, but the pressure around my heart remained. It wouldn't ever go away. Not until Liam claimed me. *If* the heir prince claimed me. That doubt always lingered over my head like a damn dark cloud.

My feet were hardly out of the car and touching the ground when small arms flung around my waist. "Kels!" Noah squealed with a child's excitement.

"Hey, squirt." I ruffled Noah's dark hair and crouched down to give him a big hug. He smelled like lollipops and fresh soap. My little brother's scent engulfed me, and the binds around my heart loosened a fraction. "Did you miss me?"

"You were gone forever." His small arms squeezed tighter around me.

A few months to a six-year-old was forever. "Tell me about it," I mumbled, pulling back to look at his face. He might have my same shade of black hair and the same face shape, but our eyes differed. He had my father's bright gray eyes that shimmered like starlight. I'd always thought Noah would be quite stunning when he grew up, and I didn't envy the girl who fell for him. My brother might only be six, but he already had all the makings of a heartbreaker.

Too bad I wouldn't be around to see it happen or tease him about the girls falling at his feet.

His sticky fingers weaved with mine. "Mom made cookies," he said, pulling me along toward the house.

A smile spread on my lips. Noah had a sweet tooth. It ran in the family. I wanted nothing more than a warm chocolate chip cookie and a glass of milk with my little brother.

DAD TRIED to send Max home to be with his family for the holidays, but the stubborn ass refused. He said something about his family being out of town, and they might have been, but I knew Max lied; he still could have gone home and had a few days off from babysitting duty. Yet he refused. I suspected Liam had something to do with his decision.

After three cookies for both Noah and me, much to my mother's dislike and Nana's amusement, I dragged my bag upstairs to my room.

Standing in the doorway, I flipped on the light, a soft glow of yellow flooding the room. It hadn't changed. The ivy and fairy lights Tess and I strung on the wall above my bed still hung like a vertical garden. The suspended round chair I begged my dad to install into the ceiling swung in the corner, stuffed with pillows and a throw. Sage-colored walls gave the room a cozy aesthetic that years later I still loved. Mom had painted them as a surprise when I was at a sleepover at Tess's one weekend.

Everything was exactly where I left it. Every little bottle, all my little messes, and the discarded clothes I stuffed on the closet floor.

So many memories lived in this room, and they hit me all at once. Growing up was a burden and a wonder. The combination of wanting to cling to being a little girl while also desiring to be a woman made me feel all kinds of ways, confusion at the top.

I dropped my bag inside the doorway and plopped down on my bed. This might be the best part of being home, sleeping in my bed, except despite all the comforts and familiarity of being surrounded by my things, I didn't think I would sleep at all the first night. Maybe not even the second or third night.

I DID my best to keep my spirits high for Noah's sake mostly, my parents too, during my visit and especially on Thanksgiving, but for all the fake smiles and forced laughs, I didn't know if I fooled anyone but myself.

Without having slept in the past few days, I didn't feel up to being around a lot of people. For as long as I could remember, Tess and I had had a Black Friday shopping tradition. It started with our moms getting together and taking us out. And then as we got older, we broke off and went out on our own.

This year, I didn't feel much like shopping, but I very much wanted to spend time with my best friend. Tess was far too understanding and didn't badger me when I suggested we stay home this year. She could take any situation and turn it into something fun. So instead of shopping and crowded stores, she proposed takeout and a Harry Potter marathon. Nothing sounded better in my life.

She knew me too well.

I heard her car pull into the driveway, and I ran down the hall, my socks sliding over the hardwood floors, to the front door. Whipping it open, I hurried out onto the porch not bothering to wait for her to ring the doorbell.

We came together in the middle of my driveway, squealing, laughing, hugging, and jumping all while tears tracked down my face. "I can't believe you're here. In front of me and not on my phone screen," I shrilled, my words coming out rapidly.

Tess pinched me in the side. "Does that feel real, bitch?"

A watery laugh bubbled out of me. "I missed you."

Dressed in an oversized sweater with black tights, boots, and a short jacket, she hadn't lost her style. Brown curls framed her stunning face. Tessa was a natural beauty who didn't need a stitch of makeup. "So you haven't replaced me with some other prettier and friendlier wolf?"

I wrapped an arm around her shoulders, guiding her inside and out of the chilly late-November air. "Never. You're stuck with me for life."

"Okay, let's get to the juicy shit," she said once we were inside my bedroom. "Tell me about the hunk. And then we can talk about me. Oh, and I heard your father assigned Max fucking Evans as your guard." She fanned her face, placing a hand over her heart as if she would swoon at just the sound of his name.

I groaned. "Don't remind me. He's downstairs, you know," I warned. There was a good chance whatever we said in my room he could overhear.

She gave me her notorious wicked smirk that always got her in trouble. "It's no secret I want to jump his bones."

I rolled my eyes. "You have questionable taste in men."

Climbing onto my bed, she made herself right at home. "Speaking of taste. How does Liam Castle taste?"

The question dredged up a memory I'd rather not relive, but it was too late. The image of me biting his neck, the taste of his blood hitting my tongue, and the surge of warmth and power flooding my veins as I claimed him bloomed in my mind, and it wasn't going away anytime soon. *Thank you, Tess,* I thought sarcastically.

"Don't hold out any of the details. I want it all, including the naughty bits," she said.

Another memory I didn't want to remember, but I should have known better. Tess loved this shit. The more drama, the better. She thrived on chaos. And with my recklessness, it was no wonder the two of us were drawn to each other.

We were like Thelma and Louise, but our nicknames would be Reckless and Chaos.

"Do you have pictures? Pictures would be better." She nearly salivated at the prospect.

A ribbon of sadness untied inside me. I didn't have a single picture of Liam. Not of us together. Not of him. I could conjure the heir prince in my mind without any effort, but as I sat in my room with Tess, a part of me wanted to show him off. The other part still simmered in anger at Liam's choices.

"I'm not showing you pictures." I hoped my sarcasm masked my heartache. I crawled onto my bed, sitting opposite her so we faced each other cross-legged.

She scrunched her nose, making her features look like she was put out. "Stingy. If I had sex pictures, you know I'd share."

I rolled my eyes. "You haven't changed one bit since I left."

Her hazel eyes twinkled. "Did you think I would?"

God, she looked and acted the same. It was like being transported back to my childhood. "The thought crossed my mind," I admitted.

Leaning back on her hands, she studied me. "Are you going to tell me what has you so glum? You look like someone ran over your puppy."

"I don't have a dog."

Her leg snapped out, playfully kicking me. "That's not the point,

Kels. Tell me. What happened? And whose ass do I need to kick? Though I have a pretty good idea."

"You up for taking on an alpha?" I teased, keeping my voice light because the last thing I needed was for Tess to march into Riverbridge and call Liam out. She would it. She was the chaos to my recklessness.

"Liam, huh? What did the bastard do?" It was no question. If I hated Liam, so would Tess. That was the kind of loyalty she possessed. She would have my back without hesitation.

I'd already updated her on everything that went down on Halloween, Liam's birthday, but I hadn't told her yet about his decision to take a break from me. My hunch said she wouldn't take the news well. She would be outraged on my behalf, which was why I hadn't yet said anything.

Why did I want her to like Liam?

She'd been all team break-the-treaty when I left, but at the same time, she'd encouraged me to give him a chance before writing the entire prearranged engagement off.

Drawing my knees up, I wrapped my arms around them. "Apparently, he can't stand to be around me."

She flinched, her expression saying there was no way she believed the heir prince wouldn't want me. "He rejected you?" Her head shook. "Uh-uh. Not possible. No guy with a pulse would reject you."

"Thanks, I think." In a way, what Liam had done felt like a rejection despite understanding his reasonings. It hurt all the same regardless of how you sugarcoated it. "He claims he can't be near me without sinking his teeth into me."

She digested this added information and drew her brows together. "I fail to see how that is a bad thing?"

I pressed my teeth into my bottom lip. "It is when you've already claimed him, and it physically hurts to be apart."

"Hmm. I see your point. Are you afraid he won't honor the treaty on your birthday?"

My fingers fiddled with my bedding. "I have bigger problems."

"True, but it's this doubt that's weighing on you. I've never seen you so twisted up over a guy before. It's refreshing." She grinned.

I tossed a pillow at her head. "What's wrong with you?" And then I laughed at the smile on her lips.

She hugged the feather-filled square to her chest. "I'm here for your entertainment, to distract you, and for you to vent. Take your pick."

And that's what I did—let Tess be a friend.

We vegged out on Chinese and binged movies late into the night. She fell asleep sometime in the middle of the last film, and as usual, I couldn't or didn't want to sleep. I wasn't sure which.

Taking the empty cartons of food into the kitchen, I heard a low voice coming from the other room. No lights were on, and I wondered what Max was doing in the dark and who he was talking to this late.

Should I mind my own business and go upstairs?

Probably.

Was that what I did?

Hell no.

Tiptoeing around the kitchen island, I pressed against the wall outside the doorway and listened.

"Asleep. And no, I'm not waking her up. Not even for you," I heard him say, irritation evident in his response.

A stretch of silence followed, and I assumed the other person on the phone responded.

Max chuckled. "Are you jealous?"

I rolled my eyes, waiting to see what my guard would say next.

"If you're that worried, you should check on her yourself." A few moments passed. "She's safe here. Not a single trace of hunters. The same can't be said for Riverbridge." They hung up after that.

I stepped out of the kitchen and stood in the doorway, my eyes searching his form out in the dark. "Who were you talking to?"

Max whirled at the sound of my voice. His gold eyes dimmed in the dark when he realized it was me. "Liam," he stated dryly.

"What did he want?"

"To check on you obviously."

I crossed my arms. "What did you tell him?"

He kept moving closer until he stood inches from me. "That I'd take care of you."

I shook my head. "You shouldn't bait him. He'll snap one of these days, and I won't stop him from ripping out your heart."

To annoy me, he lifted his hand and wrapped strands of hair around his finger. "Are you sure about that, duchess?"

My eyes narrowed. "Flirting with me will only get you a black eye or a bloody nose. Possibly both if you're lucky."

He gave a tug on my hair before releasing it. "At least it keeps your mind off him."

I frowned. Is that what Max was doing? Distracting me? I hated to admit it worked. For a short spell.

His gaze dropped to my lips, and I didn't like the glint flaring in his gold eyes.

My hand flattened on his chest before he could act on any weird thoughts going off in his head. "Don't."

He inclined his head to the side. "Why not?"

"Because I'm bonded to Liam," I replied, stating the obvious.

"But you don't have to be," he dared to say.

Straightening my shoulders, I lifted my chin. "I'm only going to say this one more time. I *want* to be Liam's mate. I chose him. And if you try that shit on me again, it won't be what Liam will do you to that you'll have to worry about but what I will."

His gaze turned hard, unflinching. "He's going to hurt you, Kels."

My chest expanded. "You don't know that."

"And you do? For certain?" His brows lifted.

I hated the seed of doubt Max planted. As if I didn't have enough to worry about or didn't have plenty of my own trust issues. I didn't need to add his to the layers piled on mine.

The lights flipped on. In unison, Max and I swung our gazes toward the switch, spotting Tess watching us with a curious expression.

"What's going on?" she asked, glancing sharply at Max.

"Nothing," I said. "Absolutely nothing."

Holiday breaks used to be my favorite. I'd stay up late, sleep in until past lunch, shop with Tess, drink an exorbitant amount of peppermint mochas, and eat nonstop. For a week, I had no responsibilities, no homework due, no papers to write, and no after-school detention to attend, but this year, my break was fucking sad and depressing.

There were obviously contributing factors adding to my layers of misery. Lack of sleep. Wonky visions. Saying goodbye to Tess, knowing I wouldn't see her again for weeks, maybe months. And the biggest factor was this being the farthest I'd been from Liam, and the distance wasn't kind.

Not even my run in the woods with Tess helped. Shifting into our wolves and exploring the fields and forests had been one of our favorite pastimes. Yet instead of feeling exhilarated, a kernel of forlornness sprouted in my gut. That urge to bolt took root. But this time, I wouldn't be running away from something. I'd be running toward someone.

Every fiber in my body pulled and pushed me into the direction of Riverbridge. I dreamed night after night about returning. They were some of the most vivid dreams.

Tonight's dream in particular had been more lucid than any other I'd had.

I could feel the icy air slapping at my cheeks. The hairs on my arms stood up from the cold. Owls hooted from the towering trees. A wolf howled, and my heart raced. Rocks dug into the soles of my bare feet as I walked.

The wind lashed through the thin shirt I had on, and I couldn't help but wonder why I hadn't dreamed of warmer clothes. It didn't make sense to be traipsing around outside in nothing but a tee that only came to mid-thigh.

Dark hair fluttered around my face, hampering my view, and if it weren't for the slice of moonlight, I'd be walking down the road in the pitch-dark.

Every so often, a car zoomed by on the road, its headlights either blinding me or highlighting my back. No one stopped. I didn't want them to.

I didn't know how long I walked. Minutes. Hours. The dream kept going endlessly, almost parallel in time to how long my feet endured, and I continued to wait to wake up.

When it felt as if this night would never cease, I came upon a sign on the side of the road. My feet stalled, and I stared at the metal shape. *Now Leaving Hot Springs.* I read and reread the words as if they held weight—as if I stood on the cusp of a decision. To leave or not to leave.

All I had to do was walk over the boundary line, and I'd be a step closer to my mate. *Shift.* A whispery voice filled my head. *It will be so much faster if we run.*

True. It would be. The temptation was there.

"Kelsey." The wind carried a whisper of my name.

It gave me a second pause, but the wolf wanted to run—she wanted to go *home.*

"Kelsey," someone called again in my ear like a pesky mosquito buzzing around my head. I tried to swat it away, but the voice became louder and more insistent. My wolf grew annoyed at the disruption, a snarl climbing up my throat as I recognized the voice.

Max was becoming the bane of my existence.

Why can't he leave me alone? Let me sleep?

The sudden realization it was Max's voice cleared the fog hazing over my eyes. His face slowly came into focus, feature by feature. First, it was the golden glow of his eyes. Then the slim line of his nose and the sharp angles of his cheeks. My gaze moved to his lips, watching them form my name.

"Kelsey, snap out of it," he said, snapping his fingers in my face.

I blinked, a scowl of confusion broadening on my lips as I smacked his hand out of my face. "What are you doing?"

"I could ask you the same question considering I spent the better part of the night following you around," he said, leveling me with one of his firm stares.

What?

Before I got a chance to think too hard about what Max said, something warm trickled from my nose. I brushed it aside with the back of my hand, assuming my nose had been running from the cold, but a dark streak stained my skin. Blood.

"Here," Max offered me a tissue from his coat pocket.

As I blotted at my nose, Max shrugged out of his coat and wrapped it around my shoulders. I slipped my arms inside, grateful for the warmth. Despite my temperature running higher than humans, I shivered, something my body rarely experienced, unless from Liam's fingers.

My eyes lifted past Max, taking in the road stretching out on either side of us, the cluster of trees bordering the street, and the sign to our right. I was fucking outside.

The dream had been real. Sort of.

I didn't know if what I had experienced would be classified as sleepwalking. Perhaps, but it had been driven by my magic. The tingles of power lingered in my veins. What kind of fucked-up reality crossover vision was this?

"Did I walk here?" I asked, already knowing the answer but needing him to confirm my suspicions.

Max nodded, dark shadows on his face. It looked as if he was concerned about me and made me fret. "I saw you walk out of your house and followed you."

My confusion shifted into anger. "Why did you let me go this far?" It wasn't his fault, but he was here, which meant he got the brunt of my tongue.

Mist chilled around his face. "I tried to stop you, but you were in some kind of trance like you were sleepwalking. I couldn't wake you up, and when I tried to physically pick you up, you went ballistic and attacked me."

I clung to Max's jacket. "I attacked you?"

"Got the claw marks to prove it." He held out his arms, sporting fresh red lines all over his skin. "I didn't want to hurt you. It was as if you were on a mission. I figured the best thing I could do was make sure you didn't get hurt and let you finish what you had to do."

My fingers raked through my windblown hair. "Fuck." This shit was escalating, and I had no idea of how to get a grip on my powers.

"Is everything okay with you? Does this happen often?"

A chill rippled down my spine that had nothing to do with the brisk wind. "No, not since..."

"The heir prince started avoiding you," he completed, voicing his guess.

I swallowed. "Before," I admitted.

He took the tissue clutched in hand and gently dotted it at my nose. "Are you okay?" he asked with mildness.

I nodded. "Yeah." For tonight I'd be fine. I couldn't let myself think beyond that. "Do you plan on telling my father?"

Max more or less was on the same page. "Let's worry about that tomorrow. Right now, we need to get you home."

I allowed my guard to steer me away from the sign, and I pressed the heel of my palm into my chest, right above my heart where the ache pulsed. "Thanks for following me." It might be the only time I ever thanked him for anything.

"I've never met a girl with as many secrets as you."

My lips twitched. "You need to get out more."

"You need to stay home," Max countered.

"Touché." A pebble jabbed into the underside of my foot, and I winced, remembering I was barefoot. Hobbling, I glanced up at Max. "Any chance you followed me in a car?"

He scowled at my feet. "Sorry, duchess. Your ass is going to have to walk back, but at least you'll have me to keep you company."

"I'd rather be sleepwalking again," I mumbled.

"I can carry you if you prefer?" he offered.

I was so damn tired I contemplated letting the lug do just that, but the only wolf whose arms I wanted to be in was miles away. My feet were going to have to toughen up.

EXHAUSTION FOLLOWED me the next day. Too sleepy to drive home, I handed the keys to Max and climbed into the back seat of my car. Quietness filled the interior like a fourth person, but I couldn't muster up the mental capacity to speak. As we drew closer to Riverbridge, butterflies fluttered in my belly.

As if Max worried I might throw myself out of the car, he continually checked on me in the rearview mirror the whole trip. I flipped him off the last time our eyes met in the mirror. He just shook his head.

Even Nana appeared worried, but she was better at checking on me, making it less obvious than my guard.

I rested my cheek against the glass in relief when we entered the borders of Riverbridge and crossed over the bridge, but it wasn't enough to just be home. I had this piercing urge to see him, to hear his voice, and to breathe in his scent.

I considered reaching out through our bond, but I had a streak of stubbornness that refused to let me become a clinging mate. As hard as it was, I would respect Liam's choice to take a break from me. Even if it killed me.

Throughout the rest of the day home, I kept getting little spikes of tingles, and I'd run to the window, only to be disappointed when Liam was nowhere to be seen. If the heir prince was out there lingering in the woods, he stayed out of sight.

I hated how eager I was to catch a glimpse of him.

By Monday morning, conflict battled in me. I didn't want to get out of bed, and yet, if I went to school, Liam would be there. The pull to see the heir prince prevailed, but disappointment persisted through my first few classes.

Yawning, I rested my forehead over my hands lying on the table in my study hall class. Did I have homework I should be tackling? Yes. Studying for finals? Probably. But the lack of sleep caught up to me, and my mind and body were mush.

Liam had his physics class this period, only two doors away from my study hall, and our bond was happy about the proximity. So much so that it felt as if this was the first time I'd been at ease in days. Hell, weeks even.

I couldn't stop from closing my eyes and giving in to the sleep nagging at me. His face was the last I saw before I dozed off.

TWENTY-TWO
LIAM

"Have you seen her?" Riven asked as he pushed off the wall and walked beside me down the halls. It was obvious he had been waiting for me, which meant he had something on his mind, and apparently, that something was my mate.

I shrugged, not wanting to discuss Kelsey when it took all my effort to not think and worry about her every second of every hour. "Not yet."

Someone tossed a football down the corridor, nearly hitting a girl in the back of the head, but Riven was unfazed. Shenanigans in school were what he lived for. "You need to do something," he said, sounding more serious than I'd heard from him in a while.

My chest tightened. "Why? What happened?" If Kelsey had been hurt or in danger, I would have known, yet it still didn't stop the spike of concern.

"She isn't well. That's what. She's like lovesick or something," he explained, his green eyes troubled.

I shook my head. "That's not a thing."

"We also thought being Moonstruck was a fable."

He had a point. Unusual for Riven to be reasonable. He wasn't a deep thinker.

Riven rubbed at the bridge of his nose, and I glanced at him, seeing

the toll all the extra work he and Colsen had been putting took on him. Guilt gnawed at my stomach. "I can't explain it," he said, shooting a sidelong troubled glance my way. "But I feel as if the life is sucking out of her. She isn't Kelsey anymore, and I miss the girl who wouldn't think twice about telling me off."

I hated hearing she suffered. It was the last thing I wanted, and it only made it worse knowing I was the cause. "We only have a few weeks left."

We arrived at our physics class and strolled through the door of the already full room. "December's going to be the longest month of our lives at this rate," Riven grumbled.

He had no idea.

I weaved around the row of desks, heading to the back row, and took my seat. Riven occupied the one beside me. My fingers fumbled with a pen, twirling it around, as the bell rang and Mrs. Bloom started in on today's lecture which I had no interest in.

Having Kelsey back in Riverbridge was sending my wolf into a frenzy. I had to shift tonight or go crazy, but I was half afraid of what he would do if I let him loose.

I mindlessly tapped the end of my pen against the table, not hearing a single word coming out of Mrs. Bloom's mouth. It wasn't a hard class. Mrs. Bloom tended to be one of the more lenient teachers. I would have to go through the text later tonight to read what I missed considering I couldn't borrow Riven's notes. He never took any.

Shaking my head, I attempted to tune into the lecture, picking up bits and pieces about magnetism and the physical attributes.

How ironic this was the physics chapter we were learning.

I sighed and slouched lower in my seat as an image of Kelsey flashed in my mind. Nothing new. I'd done nothing but think of this girl for months. She crowded out any other thoughts.

Except this image of her was vivid, wildly so.

I stared down at my desk, and yet I didn't see the wood grain covering the top. I saw Kelsey walking toward me, a faint smile on her lips and her long, thick lashes lowered slightly.

I dragged my eyes over, taking in what little clothes she wore. *What the—?*

A black lace bra that hardly covered her full breasts. Cheeky panties, and I was sure if she turned around I'd get an entire view of her ass. Silky stockings stretched up to her thighs.

Okay, this was not an appropriate time to have a sex dream about Kelsey, and yet my mind seemed hellbent on doing just that.

She climbed onto my lap, her legs flanking either side of me as she sunk into me. I was no longer in a classroom full of people but alone with my mate in a chair that looked like a throne fit for a king.

Her fingers slid up my chest, settling on my shoulders, those violet eyes glazing a bit with mischief.

"What are you up to, pup?" I asked, still trying to figure out what this was.

My doing? My imagination?

Hers?

Ours?

This did feel a tad like something my reckless mate would conjure. If this wasn't *my* sex dream, then...it was...*hers*.

Leaning forward, she brought her lips to my ear and whispered, *"I missed you, princeling."*

Swallowing, I closed my eyes and then realized what a bad maneuver that was. I fucked up. It made the whole dream or fantasy, whatever it was, so much more immersive. Her fingers climbed up my neck and into my hair, setting my nerve endings alive and little currents of electricity thrumming through my veins.

"Touch me. Please." Her voice sounded so damn hypnotic. So desperate that if I didn't put my hands on her body the agony she felt would continue to plague her.

I shouldn't. The logical part of my brain deduced that even if this wasn't real, it fucking felt real and would mess us both up. How could I stay away from her after having my hands on her? My lips?

I forced my eyes open even as my arms moved, lured by the plea in her voice, despite my brain attempting to be reasonable. The rest of me didn't care and ignored all logic.

I slid a hand over her bare waist, my pinky skimming the lacy hem of her black panties, while my other hand glided up an exposed thigh. *"Your skin is so damn soft,"* I murmured.

She chuckled, her breath a tingly brush of hot air on my ear. Her hips shifted, rubbing against my growing dick, and the glint in her eyes gave her away. The maneuver had been intentional. *"You're definitely not soft."*

My blood sang, along with other parts of me, making it damn difficult to deny my desire for this girl—my girl. *"What are you doing?"* I demanded even while my fingers inched higher up her thigh. My tone had gone rough.

She leaned back, gazing into my eyes with a twisted feline smirk. *"Isn't it obvious?"*

Yes. She was trying to seduce me.

And it was working.

I wished her timing had been different and I wasn't sitting in a class full of people. Perhaps it was better I was. I would be less likely to act on my impulses.

Or so I thought. Assuming I didn't forget where I was.

But if she kept going...

She licked her lips, leaning into my touch and pressing closer into me, the glow in her eyes mesmerizing. I couldn't look away.

"Kelsey," I growled, yet it turned into a moan as she skimmed the edge of my jaw with her teeth and tongue.

In my head, my hands were on her body, but in reality, they gripped the edge of the desk. It was becoming difficult to separate the two. My eyes wanted to close and only bask in the daydream.

"Hey, are you okay, man?" I heard Riven ask from beside me. "Your eyes are..."

He didn't have to say it. I knew. I felt the wolf push to the surface.

I had to get out of here.

Shoving out of my seat, I grabbed my shit off the desk and walked out of the room without saying a word. Mrs. Bloom's lecture broke off at my disruption, and everyone's eyes were on me. I didn't give a shit. Riven would cover for me.

Outside in the hallway, I pressed my back against the wall, the vision of Kelsey centering behind my eyes again.

She paused at the edge of my lips, her fingers toying with the ends of my hair. *"You can do whatever you want to me here."*

"Is that so?"

A single dark brow arched. *"Should we test the waters first?"*

God, I want her so damn much.

Would it be possible to find satisfaction in a dream or a vision, whatever this was Kelsey created?

Or would it only make me want more?

I was barely holding on as it was without seeing her.

If this continued...I might snap.

And I wouldn't give a damn where we were.

Or who saw.

Clouded with the force of lust I had for Kelsey, I'd risk exposing not just me but my whole damn pack.

I ran my hands up her thighs, cupping her ass. She traced the outline of my lips with a nail. I couldn't help from closing my mouth around her finger and flicking my tongue against it. She tasted sweet and like pure pleasure.

My dick grew harder, pressing against the front of my jeans. *Fucking hell.*

I slid down to the floor. *"This isn't funny, pup."*

"Neither was it when you demanded I stay away from you. This is what you asked for." She withdrew her finger, brushing her mouth across mine in a teasing light kiss.

"You know it isn't." Yet as the admission left me, my fingers pressed firmer into her flesh, and I ground into her, destroying myself with the feel of her softness rubbing on my hardness.

She purred at the contact. *"I guess you should have been clearer in your terms. I mean, we're nothing but a contract anyway."*

"That's bullshit, and you know it." The more we argued, the hotter this thing between us burned.

"Perhaps, but at least I had the balls to take what I wanted," she said breathily in my head. Her hand wrapped around my shaft through my jeans.

"Kelsey," I groaned. *"Stop this."* But my body displayed the exact opposite of my words, growing thicker and harder in her hand.

"Do you know what I want right now, princeling?" Her voice was husky and sultry like I'd never heard before.

"Don't. Don't say it," I warned, my back pressing heavily into the wall, losing all notion of the real world.

She didn't just say the words; she showed me. Every fucking glorious detail in my head. I didn't understand how she did it, her gifts no doubt, but I was going to catch fire and burn right in the middle of the hallway.

Her hand stroked over me, and a near silent growl vibrated through my throat. *"I'm going to kill you, pup."* What I really thought was *I'm going to kill you if you stop.*

Her teeth attached to my ear, scraping down the lobe before sucking it between her teeth in a maneuver that made me shudder. *"Is that all you're going to do to me?"* she taunted.

"Roof now," I ordered, the vision no longer enough. I wanted the real thing. I wanted her.

A wicked, husky laugh grazed my ear. *"Sorry, I can't afford another detention. The dean said if I step out of line again within thirty days he'll suspend me."*

"I don't give a wolf's ass what the dean says."

"Are you trying to get me suspended? It would work in your favor. You wouldn't have to see me at school for a week, but it wouldn't stop me from getting inside your head, princeling."

She licked up the column of my neck, right over the spot where she had claimed me.

It almost undid me.

I clamped down on my lip hard enough to draw blood, my canines piercing through my skin. The sharp taste hit my tongue, and I wished more than life itself that it was Kelsey's blood I tasted instead of mine.

Fuck it.

It already felt as if I was burning in hell. I might as well fully commit and ride this train straight to the underworld, consequences be damned.

I shoved aside the edge of her panties and slipped a finger inside her wet folds. She was so damn ready for me. A long moan pulled from her lips. Her eyes landed on mine, the rare shade of violet shimmering brightly.

She arched her back, lifting slightly only to sink farther onto my finger, those bright eyes never leaving mine.

I took her nipple into my mouth, using my teeth to apply a bit of pressure through the lacy material of her bra.

Her head dropped back as my fingers continued to work her, taking her to the verge of bliss. My thumb stroked over her clit, and she groaned. She was so damn close, and I had to feel her orgasm clasp around my fingers. I had to—

Buzz. The bell fucking blared through the school, and my finger slowed its movements, knowing at any second these halls would crowd with my peers. I was in a state.

Kelsey grabbed the back of my neck. *"Don't you stop,"* she growled, her nails digging into my skin.

My lips curved. I had no intention of doing any such thing. The fucking school could be blazing around us, and I wouldn't stop fingering her until she tumbled over the edge, her pleasure satiated.

Her hips moved again, riding my fingers harder and faster. The bulge straining against my pants throbbed. She was so close, her inner walls clamping around me, and then—

The vision disappeared.

I blinked, certain this wasn't happening. Not right at a pivotal moment. Not when I was about to make her scream.

A deep groan reverberated through me born full of frustration. Surging to my feet, I scanned the horde piling into the halls, Riven among them, but he wasn't who I searched for. I only had eyes for one person.

Where the fuck is she?

Her class was only a few doors from mine. I couldn't wait.

My feet moved, heading toward her classroom. I burst through the door, everyone standing and heading my way. My eyes went straight to Kelsey.

TWENTY-THREE
KELSEY

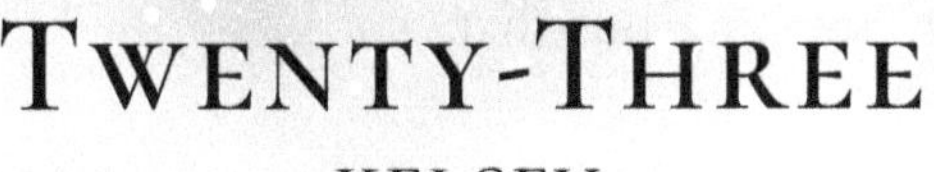

Buzz.

The bell jarred me from sleep, and I jerked upright, trying to figure out what the hell was going on, where I was, and why I was alone. I wiped a dribble of drool from the side of my mouth, lifting my head. I sat at my table for a few disorientating seconds.

My body flamed, and shifting in my seat did nothing to alleviate the throbbing between my legs.

Around me, people shuffled out of their chairs while I sat figuring out why I was at school instead of in Liam's lap about to have a mind-blowing orgasm.

I could still feel his damn fingers moving inside me.

Did I really have a sex dream during study hall?

Embarrassment stained my cheeks.

"Must have been a doozy," Leith commented as he passed by with a wink, pausing in front of my table to wait for me.

He and Colsen had guard duty until my next class.

I felt the color deepen on my face. "You have no idea," I replied under my breath, combing my fingers through my flat hair. I wouldn't be surprised if I had an imprint of the desk on my face. "Just tell me I wasn't snoring."

A corner of his mouth lifted. "Not loud enough for Professor Stein to notice."

"Fabulous," I replied, my mouth pressing into a thin line.

I gathered my bag, doing my best to maintain some sort of composure when inside I was a mess. My blood tingled with magic, and as the sleep slowly faded and clarity took over, I suspected the dream had been anything but that, not when my blood was full of power.

A vision.

Did that mean sometime in the future, Liam and I would end up getting sexy on a throne?

Weird.

But stranger things could happen.

I had my belongings in my hands and had stood from behind the desk when the door to study hall burst open. The heir prince loomed in the door frame, his features dark like he was seconds from murdering the entire class, the teacher included. Perhaps me too, but his fierce scowl didn't intimidate me. Just the opposite. I loved it.

Holy shit. His eyes.

They were glowing like the goddamn Northern Lights.

Leith stiffened at the sight of his brother, the smirk disappearing from his lips.

At the front of the room, Professor Stein pushed his wire-rimmed glasses up the bridge of his nose, peering at Liam through the thick lenses. "Mr. Castle. Is there something I can help you with?"

Liam's eyes never left mine as he said, "I need Kelsey Summers."

I choked at his word choice. There was no way he knew about the vision. Right? Not unless I'd done something utterly stupid and projected it through our bond like a fucking drive-in movie. *"I just bet you do,"* I retorted through our bond, earning me a wicked scowl from the heir prince.

"Save the antics for when we're alone," Liam answered.

My hand gripped tighter on my laptop. *"We can't be alone. You're rules,"* I reminded.

A muscle along his jaw ticked. *"Get your ass over here before I haul you out of this room myself."*

"I dare you." Maybe not the wisest decision, but of course, he would call my bluff to prove a point.

Liam strode in with purposeful strides straight for me, those lingering in the rows hurrying out of his way or rushing out of the room. A few stayed to see what would happen next, including the professor.

"What did you do, Kels?" Leith asked, watching his brother, unaware of my mental taunt to the heir prince.

My gaze pinned on Liam's, I scrambled around the table, using it as a barrier, a poor one, but I felt better with something between us. It gave me the chance to escape.

Not that I wanted to.

"Mr. Castle," Professor Stein called sternly, but no one listened.

This was the most attention Liam had paid me in weeks, and in some twisted way, I enjoyed pissing him off. He'd hurt me. He deserved to suffer.

I dropped my laptop back onto the table, waiting to see which direction he would go while Leith stared at us like we'd lost our godforsaken minds.

Instead of choosing left or right, Liam took the edge of the table and flung it out of his way.

I scowled at the prick. *"Not fair."*

Multiple gasps echoed through the room. Leith groaned, smacking his forehead.

"Exactly," Liam fired back.

Color stained my cheeks as the heir prince literally snatched me the second my feet moved. His arms went around me, and I squirmed, refusing to make it easy. I would not be a compliant hostage.

"Don't touch me!" I seethed, shoving at his chest and shoulders as Liam lifted me off the ground.

The bastard easily tossed me over his shoulder. *"Too late, pup. My hands are already on you and have no intention of letting go. This is what you wanted, isn't it?"*

I stared at his back, fuming and contemplating how I could connect my foot with his balls. Oh, I vowed to pay him back for making a scene at school, and I looked forward to his torment.

Someone in the classroom squealed.

A few snickered.

"Leith, grab her shit," Liam barked.

Professor Stein was one of those teachers who liked to use formal names with his students, always referring to us by our last names. "Mr. Castle, this isn't the place for..."

Liam was already gone and out the door, carrying me with him.

A curtain of my dark hair fell forward, swaying back and forth with the heir prince's long strides. The murmurs and whispers started before we got into the hallway and amplified as Liam carried me down the halls.

Being this close to him for the first time in weeks wreaked havoc on me, and yet at the same time quieted the constant buzzing of my power. The lull was like a weight being lifted off me. My mind didn't have to think about containing it every second of every day.

And God, why does he have to smell so damn good?

He was like my own personal brand of booze. I was the recovering alcoholic, and he was tailored just to fuck with me, to tempt me to fall off the wagon.

The angle at which I dangled gave me a perfect view of his firm ass.

Principal Miller lingered by the front exit, monitoring it for students skipping class. He cleared his throat as Liam approached the double doors with me slung over my shoulders clearly resisting. "Where are you going?" he asked Liam with less authority required of someone in his position.

"Family emergency." The heir prince grunted his response, not in the least bit intimidated by him.

"Do I need to call your father?" Principal Miller threatened as if Liam would fall into line at the mention of the alpha.

Liam sneered. Nothing about his body implied he found Principal Miller frightening. If anything, he laughed internally at the principal's attempt to stop him from leaving school. "By all means, please. I'm sure he would love to hear from you," he replied sarcastically and proceeded to stroll through the doors.

Cold air slapped at my ass, lifting my shirt so anyone outside would have gotten a show and some popcorn. "You're going to get me expelled," I gritted out, thinking I couldn't afford another detention.

"Me?" Liam spat, adjusting his hold higher up my bare thighs, a fact I scolded myself not to think about. "What about that stunt you pulled? You don't fight fair, pup."

"I wasn't trying to fight with you," I defended, being reasonable unlike him. "I fell asleep in study hall."

"Are all your dreams so…explicit or just the ones with me in them?" he asked.

"Fuck off," I snapped.

"Do you feel better?"

Color stained my cheeks. "*Fuck no!*"

His chuckle in my head only proceeded to infuriate me further. "I think we have some unfinished business."

"What? Here?" I shrieked, staring at the parking lot.

He stopped in front of his truck, setting me on my feet but making sure to block me in with his body so I wouldn't bolt. "You didn't seem to have a problem doing it in the classroom."

Ugh. So, he had seen my dream. I lifted my chin despite the color deepening on my face. "Fine," I retorted, curious if he was bluffing or if he would really pick up where we had left off. I hated to admit the prospect excited me. My blood still hummed from my dream, and damn, if my body wasn't thrilled at the idea of Liam's hands on me again.

Without a speck of doubt, he swooped in, pressing me fast and hard against the car as his lips took full dominance of mine.

It wasn't a gentle kiss, but I didn't want sweet. Rarely did when it came to Liam. He unleashed himself on me, wild and unchecked, for once not restrained by his unyielding control.

Holy crap.

It took my mind and body a few moments to catch up with the fact that this was really happening. Liam was kissing me.

This was exactly what I needed.

Our tongues danced, and the taste of him was one my wolf savored. She purred within me happily.

Home. He tasted like home. Like I belonged by his side.

His mouth slanted over mine, deepening the kiss further, and he groaned, the sound reverberating all the way to my bones. One of his hands pressed against the car moved to my shoulder, pushing aside the collar of my sweater to expose my skin.

Liam's wolf might not have claimed me, but his mouth had, and he continued to kiss me as if my lips were more vital than his next breath.

"I need you. God, I need you, pup."

If he expected anything but compliance from me, he wasn't going to get it. I was ready to strip down naked in the parking lot and let him have his way with me, onlookers be damned.

His fingers moved to the door, fumbling with the latch, and we tumbled into the back of the car all groping hands, fervent kisses, and unparalleled heat.

Like in my dream, I straddled Liam, bringing our bodies together, and I sighed at the way we fit perfectly. For the time being, I thought of nothing else but right now. No hunters. No secrets. No fear. There was only Liam and the pleasure we felt, the desire no one else could come close to making me burn with.

I fiddled with his button and zipper as I worked to free his hard length. His head fell back against the seat when my fingers wrapped around him. *"Jesus, I've missed the taste of you."*

I absolutely loved hearing the sound of his voice in my head when we were wrapped up in each other.

His mouth was on mine again, making me feel more alive than I had since than last time he kissed me. Weeks ago. Too long.

Thank God, I wore a skirt today, which made this a whole lot easier. Neither of us had to get fully naked, and truthfully, we were both too impatient for that. I had to have him inside me now.

I stroked him from root to tip keeping Liam right where I wanted. On me.

The guttural groan from him went straight to my core, the ache between my legs intensifying. I answered the searing of his lips with a demand of my own, my tongue brushing his.

The dream had been so real, but this...

Nothing came close to the feel and taste of the heir prince in the flesh.

My sweater was flying over my head, discarded somewhere in the truck. Liam's gaze dragged over my mostly exposed body, and I imagined to anyone else I might look like a mess with my skirt shoved all the way up my legs, only on a bra covering my chest, and my hair tangled, but the way Liam looked at me, I never felt more beautiful. Or wanted.

"God, you're gorgeous. It hurts to look at you sometimes." Liam wasn't overly romantic, but my heart tumbled at his words.

"Liam," I whispered.

His stormy eyes lifted to mine. Then his hands were skimming up my body, gliding to the clasp at my back. It snapped open, and the bra fell away. "It's red not black," he murmured, tossing it out of his way.

"Are you disappointed?" I teased, nipping the scar on his bottom lip.

A scoff breezed through his nose. "Nothing about you would ever disappoint me. Certainly not the color of your undergarments."

My breasts ached, becoming full and heavy in his hands. He swiped the pad of his thumb over a nipple, and magic tingled in my blood, but when he lowered his head to take a tiny bud into his mouth, raking his teeth along the sensitive spot, my power swelled, humming brighter.

He made me feel as if I was glowing from the inside out, and I couldn't take it anymore. I had to have him. "Now," I said, rocking against his hard length pressed into the material of my underwear. They had to go. "I need you now."

Reaching between our bodies, he hooked a finger into the thin band of my panties. "These need to go."

I fucking couldn't agree more.

My hips lifted slightly but I didn't get far.

Rip.

Material shredded as he tore them off my body, and before I could catch my breath, his dick was eagerly at my entrance as he positioned himself between my thighs.

Screw waiting.

Neither my wolf nor I could survive another heartbeat without him inside me.

I sank on top of him, and he slid in, my body consuming him.

"Fuck me, pup," he moaned in a swear not a command, his head falling back against the seat.

My lips twitched as I ran my hands down to the hem of his shirt, realizing he had too many clothes still on. "I am," I purred, inching the tee up his flat chest for my fingers to explore.

He shook his head, those aqua eyes glowing bright and clouded with lust. "I don't know what to do with you."

I rolled my hips. "I think you're figuring it out just fine, princeling."

The windows fogged up, offering a frosting of coverage. "God, I could live inside you all day. I don't ever want to stop."

"Please don't," I part moaned, part pleaded, our bodies moving together in synchronized thrusts.

Feeling so much emotion and many sensations overwhelmed me, and tears stung my eyes. I'd wanted this, wanted him, for so long my bond to him sang. I didn't know what was wrong with me. Who cried during sex? But there was something so breathtaking and beautiful about being connected to Liam in this way.

It was almost as if I loved—

"Damn it, Kelsey. I'm going to bite you," Liam moaned, determination etched into every line of his face. His canines gleamed, and my heart thrummed in my chest.

I wanted this. Wanted him so badly to claim me.

But he couldn't.

Not yet. And the knowledge of it broke something inside me.

I shook my head, capturing his face between my hands. "No, you won't, princeling. I trust you. I've always trusted you even when I hated you."

His eyes zeroed in on the column of my neck, a primal hunger in them I understood. "If you were honest with yourself, pup, you would realize you never hated me." He didn't stop moving inside me, his fingers gripping the sides of my hips.

With my hands on his shoulders, I kept a bit of space between us, my knees on either side of him. "Perhaps. Here..." I grabbed a piece of gum from the cupholder in the door and unwrapped it. "Chew on this."

"I'd rather—"

I shoved the gum into his mouth. "I know what you would rather bite." I clamp my inner muscles around his dick, filling every inch of me, and swivel my hips to bring the focus back to our bodies. "Now will you please shatter my world?"

And damn, did he deliver.

As much as I wanted his lips, I didn't dare risk kissing him for fear he would bite me. The muscles underneath me were solid and tense as together we chased the building pressure created by our bodies. Liam's wolf wasn't the only one who fought their way to the surface. Mine wanted nothing more than to nuzzle her mate.

Power crackled and sparked in my veins as I drew closer to the edge, the air in the car trembling. *More. Give me more.*

And then I was flying, pulsing and tightening around him as he emptied himself into me. I shuddered, dropping my forehead to his, my breath coming out in hard pants. Liam curled an arm around me, keeping our bodies interwoven as we rode the wave of pleasure that felt as if it would go on forever.

I fell limply against him, the side of my cheek brushing his. A feeling of completeness came over me again.

Home, my wolf purred. Liam was home.

Neither of us moved for a full minute, and when I finally sat back slightly, Liam's eyes were hooded with thick lashes. Suddenly, I didn't know what to do or say. This hadn't been planned.

What I wanted to do and what I did were two different things. I wanted to kiss his scar softly. Instead, I untangled myself and shifted onto the seat beside him.

I scooped up my panties from the floor of his car. It only took me a few seconds to realize they were useless. It looked like I would be going commando the rest of the day.

Twisting my skirt back into place, I slid a sidelong glance at Liam. He finished buttoning his jeans. Tension mounted between us, and I hated it. Why did things have to be so complicated?

Liam dropped his head onto the back of the seat and turned toward me. "This can't happen again," he said. "I nearly claimed you. If you hadn't come to your senses..."

"How did I know you were going to say that?" And my heart still had the audacity to sink.

"Because the risk is too high. No more projected fantasies." His fingers raked through his disheveled hair. "What's the point in staying away from you when you do shit like that, pup?"

I lifted, reaching over the seat in front of me to grab my sweater. "How do you expect me to control them? It's not like I woke up this morning and plotted to have sex with you in the school parking lot."

Worry set in the area between his brows. "I don't know. Your power is a mystery to me."

"We're not meant to be apart, princeling," I said softly even though I didn't believe anything I said would change his mind, the hardheaded jerk.

"Maybe so," he agreed. "But I can't be around you. When I'm not with you, I feel like I can't breathe. But I don't care as long as you're breathing. You're all that matters."

"If that was true, you wouldn't push me away," I reasoned, knowing it would do no good but unable to stop.

"What do you think the king will do if we break the treaty? I'm not even certain he isn't also involved in wanting your power. He could very well be working with my father or ordering him. We don't know, and until I do, the best thing is to follow the rules."

Rules and order were important to the heir prince. I got it. I just wished his principles didn't cause me pain—cause us both pain. "It would be very easy to blame someone else. I get it. He's your dad, and I hate that you're stuck in the middle, but is the best thing for either of us to be apart?"

He held my eyes, his expression full of all the emotions churning through our bond. "It's just a little longer."

I shifted in the back seat, facing him. "Is it? Because I can't shake this feeling that if we don't complete the bond soon, we won't get the chance. It will be taken from us."

Liam's brows drew together, his aqua eyes going dark. "What does that mean? Taken? Have you seen something?"

Frustrated, I let out a long sigh. "Only a dozen different times with just as many endings but none of them good."

He took my chin between his finger and thumb. "I'm not going to let anything happen to you."

I snorted. "Famous last words in every story. The hero never intends for the girl to get hurt, and yet the villain still manages to do so. Sure, the hero might come through in the end but not before the love of his life suffers."

His aqua eyes went stormy as did his tone as he replied, "Maybe in our story, I'm not the hero. Maybe I'm the villain."

What did that mean for us?

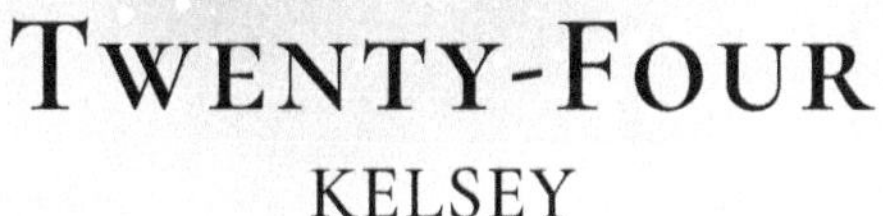

Twenty-Four
KELSEY

I savored the high of being with Liam, but it didn't take long for the glow to wear off leaving me desperate for another fix.

Hope and I made plans to hang out on Saturday because I couldn't take another weekend alone. We were going to get a bit of Christmas shopping done because, holy shit, the holidays were right around the corner, and I'd done nothing. I did, however, promise Nana I'd help her get out the décor on Sunday. It gave me something else to look forward to and would keep me occupied.

All good things.

Now if only my emotions would cooperate. I wanted this weekend to be fun. I needed a fun, Liam-free weekend with my best friend. And Max.

Can't fucking forget about my damn guard. I'd already given him a lecture about ruining my girls' day.

I pulled into Hope's driveway, my overnight bag in the back seat. My tires crunched over loose gravel, and through the cracked window, the wind carried wisps of damp leaves and wood burning. Hope's driveway was long. Beside me, Max assessed the property, his sharp eyes taking in every detail.

As we rounded a bend in the weaving driveway, I got a glimpse of

the rustic cabin-style house. The last thing I expected to see was Gunnar on Hope's porch with his lips attached to my best friend's. He had a hand tangled into her long brown hair.

"Holy shit," I mumbled, blinking to make sure my eyes didn't deceive me.

"Isn't that...?" Max asked.

She was truly kissing the enemy. Like full-on, lip-locking smooching that could lead to something a whole lot more if they were alone.

What the hell?

Who makes out with the guy responsible for drugging and kidnapping them? Who lied to them for years? And I didn't give a crap about the we-were-friends-first defense.

Hope had some explaining to do.

I slammed my car door shut, and the two sprang apart. I was surprised they hadn't heard me until now. Unusual for both considering their hearing abilities. If they hadn't been so absorbed in each other, they would have heard my car coming up the driveway.

Hope's cheeks burned red, and it had nothing to do with the chilly air.

Gunnar shoved his hands into his front pockets and trotted down the porch steps. He met my harsh eyes, the frown on my lips deepening, but he didn't flinch under my disapproval.

"Let me guess. Liam ordered you to come over here and make out with his cousin," I greeted, my voice like glacial ice.

"Liam doesn't know I'm here," Gunnar said. "He isn't the only one with people to protect."

A brassy snort left me. "This is my I-don't-give-a-shit face."

Max snickered.

I whirled my glare on him. "Get lost. Go walk the perimeter or whatever guard shit is part of your duties."

Max lifted a brow at Gunnar, straightening his shoulders so his sweater stretched over his broad chest. "I'm not leaving you alone with him."

It took everything in me not to roll my eyes at his obvious display of machismo. "Don't worry. The hunter was just leaving."

"It's not what you think," Gunnar defended, something akin to panic sparking in his eyes.

What did he think Liam would do to him if the heir prince found out he had an intimate relationship with his cousin?

He probably had a good reason to be worried. If I gave a shit, I might feel bad for him, but the only person I cared about in this situation was Hope.

I wouldn't do anything to hurt her.

Even rat Gunnar out to the heir prince.

He'd find out soon enough on his own.

"Oh, really, because it looked as if your lips were devouring my best friend. *Your* best friend," I pointed out.

Gunnar's body stiffened, and I swore, behind those dark eyes, I saw a flash of ruthlessness. He often hid himself behind the loner-boy façade, but I knew who he really was. "I care about her," he stated.

I snorted again. "You have a funny way of showing it."

"Not if you separate work from personal life," he argued softly.

"I can't just flick off my emotions like a job," I snapped.

Gunnar sighed. "The real person you should be worried about in this situation isn't me. If anything happens to Hope, I'll hold you responsible."

Did he just threaten me? Me? The girl he shot! The girl he tried to abduct on more than one occasion!

And I'm the dangerous one.

He did have a point, but I refused to let him know he wasn't the only one who worried about me being alone with Hope. It was stupid and silly to think I'd hurt her, but Hope being in my company at any time was a hazard.

My eyes narrowed, and I took a step forward. "Do you know something I don't? Has anyone contacted you? Are they coming?" A lash of panic whipped through me.

A sad expression took over his features, causing a chill to skate down my spine. "They're coming. I don't know when, but we'll both be in hot shit when they do. You're not the only one on their radar now that I've gone rogue."

More like forced to go rogue. "If you want me to feel sorry for you, you're barking up the wrong tree."

His lips twitched at my choice of words. "I'd make a better ally than an enemy," he said before walking to his truck.

I stared at his retreating back, an ominous feeling shadowing what was supposed to be a carefree day with my friend. No trouble.

Fuck.

This was not the mood I wanted to start my day with. I didn't want this to affect my time with Hope, and to ensure it didn't, it was best to be direct and get rid of the awkwardness.

"What was that all about?" Hope asked as I walked up to the porch where she waited for me. Lines of apprehension appeared on her forehead.

I lifted a brow as the engine of Gunnar's car purred to life. "I could ask you the same."

Peach, Hope's little fluffy Maltese barked rapidly at Max. My guard growled lowly, and the pooch whimpered, running and hunching behind Hope's feet.

I scowled at Max. "Don't terrorize the dog." Then I faced Hope, crossing my arms. "Did I just see what I thought I saw?"

Hope rubbed at the back of her neck, fidgeting. "Depends on what you think you saw."

"Uh, you kissing the hunter. Although, I'd rather unsee it."

"Oh, that," she fumbled, clearly uncomfortable that I'd seen her with Gunnar. "We're sort of testing the waters."

"With his tongue in your mouth."

She winced, her perky little nose wrinkling. "Yeah, pretty much."

Traces of my anger left me as I exhaled. "Were you ever going to tell me? How long has a thing been going on between you?" I was genuinely curious. Had they been sneaking around right in front of us while I'd been too wrapped up in my shit to notice?

She toyed with the ends of her sleeves, a comfy oversized sweatshirt I was pretty sure belonged to Gunnar. "I was going to tell you, and it just happened. I wanted to wait and see if it would become a thing before I told anyone."

I adjusted the strap over my shoulder, the weight in my bag getting heavy. "Is it? A thing?" I asked as Max stepped behind me and took my bag from me.

She chewed on her lip. "Don't tell Liam. I don't want him to know."

Everyone wanted me to keep secrets from my mate. "Why?"

"You know why. He won't understand," she insisted, reaching out to take my hand as she pleaded with puppy-dog eyes.

Liam would kill the hunter most likely, but honestly, I kind of wanted to kill him myself. "I don't know if I understand, but our opinion doesn't matter. I want you to be happy, but I also don't want you to get hurt. *Again,*" I added in case she temporarily blocked out what happened Halloween night.

She looped her arm through mine. "How about we make a pact to forget about boys for the weekend." The colder weather made her limp more prominent as she led me inside the warm house.

And we did. We were good on our agreement, not mentioning any of the boys for the rest of the night.

It was wishful thinking to think I wouldn't have any nightmares while at Hope's. Attempting to drown dreams with bottles of wine from her parents' liquor cabinet did nothing to keep them at bay. If anything, it might have done the opposite, loosening the rein on my abilities and welcoming the visions.

I no longer steered my powers. They took me where they wanted me to go. I was a passenger along for the ride, gripping desperately to the oh-shit handle and praying I made it out alive.

On a gasp, I jerked upright from the clutches of my ritual dreams. There was nothing new about the death, horror, and destruction that waited for me in the future, but the scent of burning bodies, singed wolf hair, and the sharp smell of blood thick in the air followed me from one world to the next. It lingered in my nose, reminding me the dreams were far too real.

Having consumed more than my fair share of booze tonight, I woke up parched, my throat dry and in need of water. Sneaking a glance at a still dozing Hope, I snuck out of bed, careful not to jostle the mattress too much.

I took one last look at Hope sleeping and envied how peaceful she looked before slipping from the room. I tiptoed down the hall to the bathroom.

Reaching for a disposable cup, I put my other hand on the faucet ready to turn it on when I heard something. My hand paused, and I listened in the dark. A deep voice belonging to a man crawled under the door.

Knowing me, I didn't bother listening to internal reasoning, and I put the cup down and zeroed in on the voice, on where it came from. It was too faint to be from inside the house. My guess was they were standing somewhere outside.

Was it Max?

If it was, I was even more interested in who he was talking to.

Hope's parents' bedroom was located on the first floor. I had to be careful not to wake them. Maybe I could open a window in one of the spare rooms upstairs. I only needed to get a little closer to make out what they were saying.

I couldn't sense the presence of another wolf, but I wasn't all too sure how much I trusted my wolf instincts at the moment. My unstable magic made me unreliable.

Creeping into the room across from the bathroom, I stared at the window opposite the entrance and crossed the floor. This side of the house faced the front.

I twisted the blinds, parting them slightly, and a curl of moonlight spilled into the room behind me. Pressing my palms to the glass under the blinds, I carefully pushed up, cracking the window an inch. The cold instantly hit me, sending curtains framing the sides of the glass twirling and dancing around me as the December nightly wind howled.

I put my ear close to the opening and listened, hearing only the rustling tree branches as the breeze knocked them into each other, sending the scarce leaves remaining tumbling to the ground.

Did they leave?

Am I hearing shit?

My wolf senses still didn't pick up any traces of undetected wolves or humans for that matter.

And then someone said, "He's wearing the collar."

Holy shit!

It was the beta's deep burly voice. There was no mistaking it. And I only knew one person wearing a collar. Gunnar. *And* the hunter had been hanging around the beta's daughter tonight.

He'd seen the collar.

My blood pressure spiked.

"Yes, I'm sure. How did he get it if you didn't issue the order?" the beta asked.

I did my best to control my breathing while I waited for him to say something else. If he heard me or became suspicious, I'd be in trouble.

"I don't think Hope knows anything," he said, his tone lowering.

Was he speaking to Rowan, Liam's father? It would make sense if he was. The only person interested in the collar had to be the one behind the attacks. Did that mean Hope's dad was involved?

I prayed for my best friend's sake he wasn't.

I didn't know Jacy, the beta, well. We'd only met a few times, and today was the first time we'd spoken for more than a minute or two. Despite him being Rowan's younger brother and the size of a tank, I found Hope's dad to be less intimidating than Liam's. He was easier to talk with once you got the pleasantries out of the way.

"What are you doing?" Max's raspy voice filled the dark, abruptly interfering with my internal thoughts.

Squeaking a bit in surprise, I whirled to find Max sitting up in bed, watching me. I put a finger to my lips and glared at him, telling him to shut up with my eyes.

I kept my glare on Max but listened intently to make sure Hope's dad hadn't heard me. A minute went by and then another before I gave up and slid the window closed, pressing my back into the wall. "What the fuck, Max," I hissed at him, keeping my voice to barely a whisper.

He blinked sleepy gold eyes. "Would you care to explain why you're in my room? Or why you're eavesdropping on the beta's phone calls?"

"No, not really," I snapped back. Explaining to Max would involve him, but honestly, him being my guard alone was enough to entangle him in my mess. My curiosity was piqued. How much had Max been able to piece together during his time as my guard?

Probably too damn much.

His jaw ticked. "How much longer are you going to keep secrets from me? I thought I had your trust."

My gaze narrowed. "Guilt won't work on me."

"Then let me ask. Are you safe here?"

Fuck. He knew the right questions to ask. I chewed the corner of my lip and shrugged. "I don't know. I'm not certain there's anywhere I'm safe."

The tiredness vanished from his eyes. They were alert and ready to respond if a situation arose. "Say the word, and I'll get you out of here."

I shook my head. "It would look too suspicious." But there was no way I could go back to sleep. I padded as quietly as I could across the floor to the bed. "I think Hope's dad is involved. I need to tell Liam."

Max's eyes tracked me as I sat on the far edge of the mattress, leaving plenty of space between us. "Involved in what, duchess?" he asked.

My nose scrunched. "Stop calling me that."

He lifted a brow. "Do you have another name you would like me to use?"

"Yeah, mine," I replied with tight lips.

The corner of Max's mouth twitched in the dark. "I like duchess. It suits you."

"Well, dumbass suits you, and yet I somehow refrain from calling you that."

A faint chuckle rumbled his chest—his bare chest.

I ripped my gaze from his upper body, staring at his nose. It seemed the safest place on his face. "Please tell me you're not sleeping naked at my friend's house," I groaned.

A slow smile spread over his lips. "Would you like to find out, *duchess*?"

"Ew. Gross. You're going to make me sick."

Amusement slipped from his face, the gold flecks in his eyes flaring. "When we leave this house, you're going to tell me what the hell is going on."

I swallowed and nodded.

Cue the doom music.

I HAD no intention of telling Max shit.

At least, that was what I told myself last night, but now with the sun shining so god-awfully bright and my eyes so damn droopy and sensitive, I blamed everything that came out of my mouth on delirium.

And the wine I drank.

The heir prince would be pissed when he found out, but the rational side of me argued it was better to have Max on our team. Wouldn't it make more sense that he knew what we were up against and the suspicion of betrayal within the pack?

Liam would hate having an outsider involved in pack problems, but this went beyond just the Riverbridge wolves.

"Start talking, duchess," Max ordered while handing me a cup of coffee. He'd gotten one for himself as well.

I took the drink as he got situated behind the steering wheel and started the car. "Bribes won't work," I mumbled.

"It's just coffee. You look like you need it. I know I sure as hell did. Someone kept me up all night." He lifted his coffee and took a sip before placing it in the cupholder between us.

"Isn't that part of your job?" I pointed out, letting the sides of the paper cup warm my hands.

He pressed the start button on my car, the engine purring to life. "Your distraction tactics won't work on me."

My lips twitched in a sleepy manner. "Touché." A long sigh filled my chest before expelling. Max turned the heat on, but it still felt nice to have the hot coffee warming my insides as I sipped. "Before I say anything, I need your assurance that you won't go running to my father. At least not yet. It could ruin our chances of uncovering who is after me."

"I don't love the idea." His admission came out clipped. "But I understand," he added, guiding the car onto the road. "You have my word unless your safety is in jeopardy. Then I'm required to tell him."

"If it gets to that point, I'll probably need my father's support," I admitted. I glanced out the windshield and blinked as the first snow of the year began to fall, sprinkling from the misty clouds overhead. It was beautiful. There was something so innocent and fresh about seeing the white powder sticking to the bare trees and the brown grass.

While he drove and we consumed coffee, I explained what happened on Halloween night, about how it had been Gunnar hunting me those first few weeks when I came to Riverbridge. He already knew what Gunnar was.

"Why you?" he asked.

Staring straight ahead, I watched the snowflakes hit the road in front of us and then disappear. "This is the part that's easier to show you than tell you. Pull over."

His head slid to me, suspicion furrowing his brows. "What? Now?"

"You want answers. It's now or never, Max. Your choice."

"Shit," he mumbled, steering the car to the shoulder.

With regret, I set aside my coffee after taking a long swig and got out of the car. "It would be best if we walked a bit into the woods for coverage. I don't want anyone to see us."

The suspicion within him was palpable. "You aren't going to murder me or something?"

I snorted. "Not today. Maybe tomorrow. Depends how much you irritate me after this." I stepped off the shoulder of the road and into the woods.

Max cursed under his breath and followed. "Okay, what is it that you had to show me in the woods with no one around, duchess?"

A sharp ache of uncertainty stung in my chest. I prayed I was making the right choice. "It's the reason why I'm hunted so ardently, why my father took patrolling our borders so seriously."

"We've always known it had something to do with his family. It's you?"

I nodded and flipped my hand over, palm up, and a globe of violet energy appeared, hovering slightly above my fingers. It had more of a solid form than the protective barriers I created in the past like electric threads woven together, flickering and sparking in a tangled sphere.

For a few moments, he said and did nothing, just gawked at my hand. A range of emotions crossed over his features. "Holy shit, Kelsey."

I wiggled my fingers, watching my power move with me. It was different than it had been growing up, the color bolder and the strength more potent. "I know."

"You have magic," he muttered in utter disbelief and a touch of awe.

Flakes of snow gathered in my hair as I made a circle with my fingers in front of my face, watching the energy form a ring. "It's hard to be enthusiastic about something that has been nothing but a burden all my life."

Max circled me, ogling the electric circle. "And this is why the hunters want you? Not to kill you but to take your gifts."

"Something along those lines. Gunnar could probably tell you more about what they have in store due to him being a meta hunter."

"You believe they want to do the same experiments with your powers by giving them to other wolves?" he guessed, his focus still on the humming violet power. His expression was one of intrigue and interest now as if he longed to reach out and touch it.

"Scary, huh?"

His gaze finally found mine again. "Shit. And the heir prince knows about all of this?"

I nodded, a somber ghost of a smile on my lips. "He does. We have no secrets."

"What will happen if I touch it?"

It was difficult to keep my lips from curving. "Why don't you find out?" I encouraged.

He frowned but didn't lift his hand. "This feels like a trap."

"You won't know unless you try," I said, baiting him.

"I'm going to regret this." Max stretched out his hand, fingers fanning out and hovering dangerously close to the ring of magic. "It makes my skin tingle." Becoming a bit more daring, he slowly inched his fingers forward until they connected with the violet circulating strands. A second later, he sailed through the air, landing feet away from me on his ass.

Max glared up at me, not hurt except for maybe his pride from being flattened by a girl. "You did that on purpose."

I chuckled. "What did it feel like?" I asked, genuinely curious. I'd never zapped anyone before.

"Like I'd been electrocuted. I think you singed my eyebrows." He rubbed at the spots above his eyes and shoved to his feet.

After I banished the energy, the smirk on my lips faded as I stared at Max. "I've spent my life protecting this secret. You can't tell anyone."

"I won't," he swore. "But you might be coming to a point in your life where you can no longer keep your secret hidden."

That's what scared me.

Given the visions of late, it was obvious a war brewed in the future. I might have no choice but to expose my gifts to save those I cared about. What did it matter anyway? Someone already knew what I could do, and they were hellbent on taking it from me.

Max drove us the rest of the way home as I stared out the window, chewing my nails, while wondering if I made the right choice.

Regardless of right or wrong, it felt good to no longer lie to Max as long as he didn't betray me. It was a risk I'd been willing to take. Having a wolf like Max on our side was a valuable asset.

I couldn't stop thinking about what I'd overheard last night. Was the beta involved? Did this prove Liam's father was behind Gunnar's orders to take me?

"Are you expecting company?" Max asked, pulling me out of my head. I glanced at him, noticing he'd gone straight into guard mode, his muscles tensing behind the wheel.

We pulled into my driveway where a familiar car sat but I couldn't place it. Maybe it was one of Nana's friends. "No," I replied, my gaze moving to the porch where Nana sat with someone on the swing, sipping something hot. Probably tea.

I couldn't see their face from this angle. Nana blocked them. She turned toward us and smiled.

Max opened his door and stepped out before me. "It's a wolf," he muttered. His brows pinched together as I climbed out of the car, closing the door behind me.

The wolf's scent hit, recognition whirling through me.

"It's..." Max started to say but the rest of his statement was drowned out by the buzzing of denial in my head.

Why the hell would he come here?

I blinked, not wanting to believe what I saw as the wolf stood from the swing and walked to the porch steps, jumping past them to the ground.

Fuck me.

This was not happening.

But sure as shit, it was.

Huntley Doven strutted toward me. My fucking ex-boyfriend.

Feet planted, I waited with my arms crossed over my chest until he was in front of me. "Huntley, what are you doing here?" I hissed, clearly not as happy to see him as he was me.

He tried to come in for a hug but backed off when he noticed my face and the sharp edge to my tone.

Max shook his head, giving Huntley a sympathetic look. Being that Huntley was part of our pack, he knew who he was. "I'll give you guys a few minutes alone."

I nearly called Max back as he retreated to the porch with Nana, ushering her inside where it was warm. I didn't exactly want to be alone with Huntley or have the awkward conversation that was about to follow.

My eyes returned to Huntley's. The happiness that had been there seconds ago dropped and showed his real emotion as if he'd worn a mask. Sadness and anger glittered in his blue eyes.

"Did you claim him?" That was the first thing he said to me. He hadn't changed. Not the shaggy auburn hair. Not the graphic tees he loved to wear. Although, he might have grown an inch taller.

My spine stiffened. "That's none of your business. We're not together. Remember?"

His gaze bore into mine. "It's only been two months since we broke up, baby."

"Three," I corrected. "And I'm not your *baby*. Not anymore." Not ever really, but I didn't want to hurt him more than I clearly already had. When we started dating, I had made it very clear that it had only been for fun. Nothing serious could ever come from our relationship. I'd never lied to Huntley. He'd always known I was promised to another, and he still let his feelings get tangled. "You shouldn't have come here."

Color deepened in his cheeks. "I had to see for myself."

"Then you have your answer. It shouldn't be a surprise, Huntley. You knew why I left and what I came here to do." I implored him to understand, to not make this a thing.

"I just thought you would have fought harder. Instead, you claimed him before the ceremony." His voice rose with anger.

I bristled. "I don't have to explain myself to you. I get you're upset, and you have a right to be, your feelings are valid, but you know I never felt the same way. And as I said before I left, I'm sorry. I truly am. But you need to leave. Coming to see me unannounced isn't helping." In fact, it could get him in trouble with the Riverbridge pack. I didn't want him to hurt more because of me.

I started to walk toward the house, but Huntley grabbed my wrist, stopping me. He opened his mouth to say something, but his eyes sharpened and stiffened, his gaze swinging down the driveway. I heard it then. The arrival of another car.

What the fuck is even happening right now?

Liam's truck came into view.

Fuck.

Twenty-Five

LIAM

I hit the brake as I stared at some asshole with his hands on my girl. What was I to make of the situation? Kelsey wore a frown, annoyance lines crossing her forehead.

The guy who was about to die eyed me through my windshield, his eyes flashing with irritation. *The feeling is mutual, asshole.*

I turned off my truck's engine and got out, and my gaze connected with Kelsey's. Surprise filtered in them. She hadn't known I was coming. Why hadn't Maxtyn said anything? Not that it mattered, but I didn't want her to get the wrong idea, and I could see from the kernels of hope twirling in our bond that she assumed I was here for her.

The last thing I wanted was to put disappointment in those violet eyes or see them flash with hurt. She wouldn't be the only one in agony. Being this close to her and not pulling her into my arms killed me. So much so that I would gladly rearrange this guy's face to release the pain.

It wouldn't help. Not in the long-term, but it would help for a few minutes.

I swore as I drew closer tiny silver stars appeared in the center of my mate's eyes, and my breath caught. I curled my fingers at my sides to keep them from flying into this guy's face before I found out who he

was. My wolf senses made it clear he was one of us but not part of my pack.

So, who the hell is he?

I turned my glower onto the jerk who had the balls to put his hands on what wasn't his. "Why the fuck are you touching her?" I fumed, forgoing any pleasantries.

"Shit," Kelsey muttered, blinking as if she'd forgotten another guy had his fingers wrapped around her wrist.

If he didn't let her go in the next three seconds, I'd break every one of his fingers, including the ones on his other hand.

"No one. He was just leaving," she answered for him, shoving at his chest.

He cocked a brow at me. "Is this him?" the asshole asked, eyeing me as if I wasn't anything special, as if I couldn't flatten him or have him whimpering at my feet with a single growl.

"Huntley," she warned, her tone dropping. "Just leave before you get yourself killed."

Huntley? The name registered in my memory. *The ex-boyfriend.*

I stepped up. "If you're referring to her mate, then yes. That would be me."

Kelsey wedged herself between us. "We're not doing this. Not in Nana's front yard." She stretched her arms out on either side, tingles of magic sparking over her fingertips. "Why are *you* here?" she directed at me.

Not liking the position she took, I put my hands on her waist and pulled her in front of me so her back was flush with my chest. *"To see Maxtyn. We're doing some training with the hunter,"* I sent through our bond, unwilling to share any info with her ex.

Her body tensed at the mention of the hunter. "Gunnar's coming?" she whispered.

"Yeah, he should be here in a few minutes," I replied close to her ear. Too damn fucking close. The sweet scent of her hair swirled around me, and it was all I could focus on. I did the stupidest thing possible.

I inhaled deeply, breathing her in and holding on to her unique scent. If I could bottle her essence, I would carry it with me.

"Who's Gunnar?" the ex asked, his sharp blue eyes accusing Kelsey of something.

Did he honestly believe she was hooking up with multiple guys? He reeked of jealousy.

Kelsey stiffened against me.

"None of your business," I hissed. "She asked you to leave nicely. If I have to ask"—I let the threat of my tone linger before I finished what clearly was a threat—"it won't be as gentle."

"Liam," she gritted at me under clenched teeth, her head turning over her shoulder, and she glared at me. She sighed after a moment and faced Huntley. "You need to leave. Now is not a good time for us to... talk. Go home, Huntley."

He took a step forward toward her, and I growled in warning, the wolf flashing in my eyes.

A twig cracked in the woods bordering Kelsey's house, and my heart stopped as I listened. Nothing at first, but as I was about to let my shoulders relax, I heard an arrow being nocked into a bow and the string being quickly pulled back.

Shit!

My arms encircled my mate, taking her to the ground and shielding her with my body. "Get down!" I ordered at her ex, letting the power of my wolf affect my voice so it was a command he couldn't ignore.

If anyone was going to kill him, it would be me, not some hunter who ambushed us from the woods.

The ex was a tad slower than I would have liked but managed to avoid narrowly being hit by an arrow. It sailed over our heads, submerging into the ground behind us.

My breath abandoned me as I made sure Kelsey was safe. "Maxtyn!" I bellowed after lifting my head, and I scanned the trees, searching for the culprit.

"They found me," Kelsey whispered with horror, but it wasn't fear for herself. She worried about Nana, her gaze darting to the house. "Nana!" she sobbed, jumping to her feet.

"Kelsey, no!" I growled, my arms looping around her waist and lifting her off the ground. Her fear was valid, but that didn't mean I would let her run straight into danger, no matter how much she might despise me for it. She meant too damn much to me, and I couldn't live if something happened to her. I couldn't survive without her.

Kicking and fighting, I hauled her ass behind the first car for a bit of coverage. "If you run, you become a target," I hissed, doing my best to reason with her. How many were out there?

It took her a moment, but she calmed down, just not enough for me to release her. Her ex took cover beside us, but I paid him little attention. "I need to get you somewhere safe," I told Kelsey.

Her guard burst through the front door and immediately surveyed the situation, seeing us huddled behind the SUV. I jerked my head in the direction in which the arrow had flown from, the west woods. Maxtyn nodded and took off, vaulting over the porch railing. When his feet hit the earth, he stood on four paws, covered in fur. His wolf raced to the trees. I prayed he'd be able to pick up his scent, and if it was only one hunter, the guard shouldn't have any trouble dealing with him.

I wanted to go with him. The wolf within me snapped and snarled, clawing to get free, to kill anyone who threatened his mate, but I had to stay and protect her.

"I know you're worried about your grandma, but you can't help her if you get hit. I need you to wait until I say run, and then you take off to the house. Don't hesitate." I took her face between my hands, forcing her to look at me. "Do you understand?"

"Did you forget I have magic? I don't need your protection," she replied through our bond.

I gave a slight shake of my head. *"Not in front of him."*

"What about Max?" she muttered, eyes on the spot where his wolf disappeared. "He's out there alone."

"It's his job, pup," I reminded, my lips grazing her cheek. Gunnar was almost here. Lifting my head, I glanced through the windows. I just needed to get her to the house. A gamble, but we were fucking sitting ducks out here.

Huntley let out a shuddering breath, his eyes wide, staring hard at the arrow in the ground. "What's going—?"

A truck pulled up behind mine, the engine roaring before it was cut, and silence returned, leaving only the racing of our hearts.

I stared at Gunnar, every one of my senses on high alert, and this seed of dread sprouted in my gut.

Kelsey's whole body locked up. She tracked his every movement as he slipped out of his vehicle and crouched low, moving toward us.

"Another attack?" the hunter asked, seeing the tension in our faces, and reading the situation. "Did someone die?"

"Not yet, but the day is still young. Where were you?" I demanded, an inkling of mistrust finding its way inside me.

He lifted a brow, his keen eyes surveying the area and landing on the arrow. "When?" he asked.

"Like five minutes ago when we were being ambushed by your buddies," I snapped, the reins on my anger loosening.

Gunnar's brows furrowed this time, taking in what I said. "I was driving. How do you think I got here?"

"Was it you?" I hurled the accusation.

"You can't possibly believe I orchestrated another attempt to capture her. Have you forgotten about this?" His fingers rimmed around the collar still attached to his neck.

"I overheard Hope's dad talking about Gunnar's collar last night," Kelsey said, volunteering information I'd already considered.

Uncle Jacy could be helping my father. They always schemed and plotted together. It didn't seem likely my father would coordinate this whole ploy alone. "No more sleepovers at my cousin's until this is over," I gritted out through the side of my mouth.

"Will it ever be over?" she asked, dejection in her features.

"What's going on here?" the ex interjected. I'd forgotten about him. He was an insignificant problem that didn't belong here.

"Go home," Kelsey and I said in unison.

Kelsey sighed, softening her features and facing her ex. "It's not safe here right now, Huntley. You need to leave."

A glint of steely determination shone in Huntley's eyes. "Let me help."

"No," my mate and I said, again in sync. Neither of us wanted to be responsible for another wolf getting hurt.

"Who is this yo-yo?" Gunnar asked, staring Huntley down.

"Her ex," I remarked.

Gunnar rubbed his hands together and grinned. "Oh. This should be interesting."

Kelsey shot an elbow into the hunter's gut with enough force he winced, clutching his middle.

"Shit," he groaned. "You pack a hell of a punch for a girl."

She leveled him a look that said she wanted nothing to do with him. "Keep your mouth shut, or I'll actually put effort into hitting you next time."

My lips twitched, but the humor didn't last long. Not with someone or several people in the woods threatening my mate. "I need to get Kelsey to the house. Got any weapons in your truck?"

The hunter's gaze narrowed, and he tilted his head to the side. "There's no need. They're gone."

Like I would trust him. This could be a fucking trap. He could be involved. He could have set this up. "And how would you know that?"

"Just because *you* can't sense us doesn't mean I can't," he replied.

I pinned him with a glower, baring my teeth. "You're just now sharing this information?"

Gunnar shrugged and pushed to his feet. "You didn't ask. He took off in the northwest direction toward the road," he informed, sounding confident as if he knew what he was talking about, which could all be a show.

Kelsey looked at me hesitantly, and I could see in her eyes she didn't trust him. "They know where I live," she murmured. The terror in her tone wasn't for her. It was worry for the woman inside the house who meant everything to my mate.

"Yeah," Gunnar said gravely. "They do."

Motherfuckers.

Maxtyn's wolf appeared at the tree line, and I didn't need to be telepathically connected to him to see the hunter had gotten away.

If the new menace was anything like Gunnar, it was no surprise. Meta hunters were faster, highly trained killers who could mask their scent, pretty much leaving us at a disadvantage.

With my eyes on the wolf, I ordered Gunnar to get rid of the ex, and then I turned to Kelsey. "You should probably check on your grandmother. Just to be safe. And I'll station extra guards around your perimeter."

"What about your father?" she inquired.

"He won't deny you protection, not when it's coming from me," I assured.

She chewed on the corner of her lip, something she did when she contemplated a problem. "You're not getting rid of me. I'll be back."

I watched her take off toward the house at a full sprint. Gunnar and I waited while Max went to put on some clothes and to make sure Huntley left. I called Riven and asked if he would mind escorting the ex out of town. I didn't need any trouble lingering about. He promised to take care of him.

When Gunnar, Maxtyn, and I were finally alone, I shook my head, raking a hand through my hair. "We need to do something. This must end."

The tension in the guard's folded arms told me he was really starting to get the gravity of his position. "I agree."

Gunnar shifted his weight. "What are you suggesting?"

And so, the guard, the heir prince, and the hunter plotted. Sounded like an opening line to a bad fucking joke.

Sadly, it wasn't.

But the time for defense was over. We needed to go on the offense before someone died. Before I lost her.

I had to uncover the truth before Kelsey's birthday. My fear was if I didn't the treaty might never be fulfilled. If they wanted my mate, it made sense for them to abduct her before I claimed her.

I had to get to them first.

☽☽●☾☾

Despite Maxtyn clearing the area, I didn't want to leave Kelsey alone, so Gunnar and I stayed to work on some training as planned.

"I want to know more than the basics," I told the hunter. "I want to know everything."

He nodded.

And we began.

Two hours later, I picked up the approach of another car, and my first thought was Huntley had returned. There were no second chances. I'd asked the first time. The second, I'd kick his ass.

Leith's Jeep came around the bend, and I exhaled, the mounting anger in my blood cooling. Leaving Maxtyn and Gunnar in the open space to the side of Mrs. Nightingale's house working on technique, I walked to the driveway as Leith bounded out of the car. "What are you doing here?" I demanded, wiping the cold sweat from my brow.

My brother glanced me over before his gaze shifted passed my shoulder. "I could ask you the same. It looks like you're having a party without me."

"Funny. I know how you feel about training."

"Is that what you call this?" His head inclined to the clearing, just short of the woods where Maxtyn had Gunnar in a headlock. "I thought the three of you were trying to kill each other."

The possibility wasn't completely dead. "You never said why you're here? Is everything all right?" I asked, changing the subject.

"As far as I know. I'm here to hang out with my sister-in-law." His lips curved into a grin that made me want to practice my hunting skills on him. Maybe knock out one of his pearly teeth he was so famous for flashing. "I can see that got under your skin. Good," he winked. "At least you still give a shit about her. I was beginning to doubt you had a fucking heart."

My sigh was long and disgruntled. "I don't need your shit, Leith."

He made himself comfortable, leaning on the Jeep's front bumper. "Well, someone has to tell you when you're being a stupid asshole."

I snorted, the sound stumbling off my lips sarcastically. "God, you really want me to hit you."

Humor winked in his eyes. "Will it make you less of an ass?"

"What do you think?" I replied dryly, sporting a frown that had been stuck on my lips since I showed up at Kelsey's house.

"I think I'm grateful I was born second." Leith's gaze shifted to Maxtyn and Gunnar again sparring. I heard a thud like a body hitting the ground, and my brother winced. "Do you really believe it's Dad?" he asked quietly.

I dragged a hand over my face, the light stubble I'd been too preoccupied to shave scratching my palm. "My gut says it is."

Keenness crinkled at the corner of his eyes. "Good. You're finally paying attention."

Taking a step back, I flinched, my eyes narrowing slightly. "What does that mean?"

"That our family has secrets, and it's about time someone exposed them. You know how much I love a good show, but you need to tread carefully," he warned, sounding too serious for once.

"You think Dad is involved?" I'd never been sure how Leith would take it. They had a more complicated relationship than I did, in the sense that our father more or less ignored Leith most of the time. He spent his attention on me, training me to be the heir worthy of him. And because of it, my brother had always been closer to Mom.

Leith nodded. "I've never been delusional about who our father is or his ambitions, but I'm also not the son he's been grooming to take his place."

I leaned against the car beside him, letting my weight sink into the front end. "This feels like a fucking nightmare."

He put a hand on my shoulder. "Welcome to the dark side, brother."

I shook my head, glancing at the house and letting my thoughts drift to the girl inside.

Leith casually bumped his shoulder into mine, pulling me out of my head. "All jokes aside, what are you going to do?"

Uneasiness nagged at my chest. "I'm working it out, but I don't want her involved." My gaze remained on the house, specifically her bedroom window, where I sensed her.

"Is this your way of asking me to watch out for her while you go off and do something stupid? I do the dumb shit in this family. Not you."

"Maybe," I said.

Shadows crept into Leith's features. "Just don't get yourself killed. I don't want to be the one to have to tell her or watch her fall apart."

Shit could always go wrong. I slid a glance at him. "But you will be there for her?"

"Always," he replied without hesitation.

That was good enough for me. My brother might be a lot of things, including a shithead, but he was fucking dependable when push came to shove.

Twenty-Six

LIAM

Everything was set into motion. In just two days, I'd have to make the hardest choice I'd ever had to face in my eighteen years. I was about as ready as anyone could be.

All the secrets and lies would be exposed.

Tonight was the cold moon. The final full moon of the year.

And the last place I wanted to be was at school. I had too much on my mind, going over every detail Gunnar, Maxtyn, and I set into place, including asking Hope for help.

I hated the idea of putting my cousin at risk, but we needed a decoy, someone to wear Kelsey's scent and be convincing enough until it was too late—until the truth was uncovered.

My stress levels were too high to concentrate on school, so when the bell rang, I jumped out of my seat and dashed out the door before anyone else. I needed a moment to breathe.

Solitude greeted me on the roof. I leaned against the ledge and glanced down at the sprawling grounds. I used to own this place. Being that guy—the one every guy envied and every girl wanted—had felt important then. I was the alpha's son. I was expected to show dominance in every aspect of my life. School. On the football field. Within the pack.

I relished being the popular guy, all the while knowing there was a deadline to my freedom. And here I was months later happily willing to give up my life for the girl I'd once considered a prison sentence.

I didn't know who to blame for the problems on my doorstep. Kelsey. Gunnar. My dad. The king. Me.

Hope rushed through the roof door, her eyes wide and slightly out of breath, jarring me out of my thoughts. Her cheeks were flushed, yet her skin was paler than usual, making the pink tones bolder. "I knew you'd be up here. Have you seen Gunnar lately?" The words scurried out of her mouth, flying off her tongue.

"No, why?" I asked, not thrilled with how concerned she was about the hunter.

Worry pursed her lips. "I can't find him."

I didn't want to deal with this, but the hunter was my problem. "And you think something happened to him?"

She rolled her eyes. "That's why I came to find you."

"When was the last time you saw him?" I asked, gathering details and hoping to calm her down. She was visibly upset.

Chewing on her lower lip, she shifted her weight from one foot to the other. "I don't know. A few hours ago. Lunch, I guess."

I spotted my brother, Kelsey, and Colsen coming out of the stairwell together. I caught his eye. "Have you seen Gunnar?" I asked.

Leith scratched his chin. "Now that you mention it, he wasn't in woodworking."

Kelsey stared at Leith, her eyes avoiding mine. "I can't imagine you carving wood."

Leith shot her a lopsided smirk. "I like to work with my hands."

My mate rolled her eyes. "I bet you do."

A twisted feeling knotted in my stomach. "If the two of you are done flirting, we need to get Riven and Maxtyn."

"He's jealous," Leith whispered in her ear.

"Did you try his cell?" Kelsey offered, blinking at Hope.

My cousin chipped at her black nail polish. "Only like ten times. He didn't answer. Something's wrong, Liam. I can feel it."

I didn't want to know why she could sense anything about the hunter—didn't want to think about it either. The idea of my cousin and Gunnar being anything, even friends at this point, made me sick.

Tracking him days before setting the trap was the last task I needed, and finding him wouldn't be simple, thanks to his annoying ability to conceal his scent.

Kelsey's hand flung out to the edge of the roof, steadying herself. Recognizing the glaze in her eyes, I moved, rushing to her side. I pulled her against me because the last thing I could deal with was her tumbling over the roof's edge while in the throes of a vision.

She leaned against me, her body sinking into mine while her fingers clung to the front of my shirt.

"It's happening again?" Hope murmured. "They're getting worse."

This one didn't last long, thankfully.

"They have him," she whispered. Kelsey blinked, the vision fading as her eyes cleared, and she looked up at me.

"Who has him?" But I had a sick feeling I already knew.

She shook her head. "I couldn't see their faces. They're going to kill him."

Hope gasped. Leith was at her side, putting a hand on her shoulder, but she shook him off. "We have to do something! We need to save him!" she pleaded, an unruly glint in her eyes.

I did my best to keep my voice level and calm. "Hope, I understand you're worried, but this was a risk Gunnar took when he became a hunter and accepted the job."

"He didn't have a choice. Not any of it. You of all people should understand what it's like to be forced into something." She referred to my betrothal to Kelsey.

It was true I didn't want to be in an arranged marriage, but in my case, fate intervened. "He's a hunter, Hope. Or have you forgotten he hunts our kind?"

"Liam," Hope implored, my name a broken sob on her lips.

Fuck, I hated being in this position. "He tried to take my mate. I can't risk it."

Hope's wolf flashed in her eyes, the hue of brown in them going gold. "If you won't help me, I'll do it my damn self."

I jerked my head at Colsen as Hope spun around. My friend moved in front of the door, blocking my cousin from leaving.

She glared up at him, her nails digging into her hands. "Get out of the way," she seethed.

Colsen stood his ground. "I can't do that."

Hope whirled on me, knowing if she wanted to get anywhere she had to deal with me. "How can you do this after he's done everything you commanded him to do? You've treated him like a dog. Then you have the nerve to ask for my help when you won't lift a finger for me?"

"What's she talking about?" Kelsey directed at me, everyone on the roof going silent. I swore a pin could drop and it would sound like a bomb going off.

"Oh, right. Shit. I forgot. It was supposed to be a secret. Oops," Hope retorted sarcastically, clearly retaliating for my refusal.

Before I could respond, Kelsey stepped forward. "Hope, I'll go with you," she offered.

"The hell you will!" I bit out.

Kelsey finally lifted her eyes to me. Fire and valor were in her features. "If you won't do something, then I will. I have to," she insisted. "I thought we were done keeping things from each other."

Nothing would stop her, which backed me into a corner. A long exhale left my lungs. "No. I'll go. *You* stay here with Leith," I said.

"Fine."

My eyes narrowed at the snap of her voice. When she said fine, what she meant was the moment I took my eyes off her she would go out on her own. "Damn it, Kelsey. I can't be out there worried about you. If they have him, this could be a trap."

Her jaw set into unmovable determination. "You won't find him without me."

"If we don't die tonight, I'm going to kill you." Hell, if we found Gunnar, I just might kill him too. Someone was definitely going to die.

Snow had been falling for most of the day, blanketing the woods in what looked like a winter wonderland, beautiful and untouched. I had no plans to let Kelsey out of my sight. Pairing off, we set off into the section of woods not far from where the cabin was. Colsen and Riven, Leith and Hope, Kelsey and me, and Maxtyn on his own. The guard and I wasted too much time arguing over which one of us would accompany Kelsey in the search for Gunnar.

I won.

He might be her guard, but no one would or could protect Kelsey like I could.

"Don't even think about locking me inside the cabin's cage," she threatened as we headed east, taking our quadrant of the woods.

I followed her gaze to the rickety house concealed by the overgrown brush and trees surrounding it. If you didn't know it was there you might walk past. "It crossed my mind," I admitted, but of course, she would know that.

In her vision of the hunter, Kelsey had seen a flash of this cabin. It gave us a starting point. The snow would make tracking footprints easier, but it continued to fall, coming down harder, covering the clues we desperately needed.

Leith and Hope went inside to scope out the cabin and make sure Gunnar wasn't inside or locked up again. Kelsey and I were only a few feet away when I heard Leith's voice through our pack bond. *"He's not there."*

I hadn't thought he would be, but it was better to check out every possibility. Internally I still wrestled with the decision of whether this was the right call. Would it be so bad if I let the hunters have him? But if I did, I couldn't use him as bait to help trap the pack traitor.

At some point, my loyalty had shifted from the pack to Kelsey. I didn't know when, but I would put her safety above those who I was to rule someday.

And that meant I had to find the hunter.

It would benefit both the pack and my mate, but it was only Kelsey I gave a shit about right now. She was all I could think about, and the idea of having her taken from me froze my blood and made my wolf pace inside me with panic.

"Stay in touch," I sent back to the others. Only Max and Kelsey weren't connected to the pack bond.

Kelsey climbed up on a fallen log and scanned the thick patch of evergreens from a slightly higher advantage. This part of the woods was home to more pines than leafy trees. "What's the plan? Would it be easier if we shifted?"

Taking a beanie from my back pocket, I tugged it over her head. "I was thinking the same thing."

She tensed, stretching her neck to the side. "Do you hear that?"

Before I could say anything, she took off, sprinting through the trees toward a sound my ears didn't pick up.

I cursed under my breath and went after her. This was exactly why I didn't want to bring her. She reacted before thinking or considering what might be out there.

"Kelsey, damn it. Slow down."

"Can't keep up, princeling?" she tossed over her shoulder as I stared at the dark strands of hair flying behind her.

God, is she maddening.

"Did you ever think it could be a trap?"

One minute she was in front of me, and the next, the ground swallowed her whole. Her scream rang out over the valley, and my nightmares had come true.

Are you fucking kidding me?

This must be a joke.

But my heart hammering against my chest and the horrible feeling in my gut said this shit was real. A clammy fear turned my blood cold as I shoved harder off the ground, racing to the spot where she'd disappeared. The snow made the earth slick under my feet.

"Kelsey!" I yelled, leaping into the hole, only thinking of getting to her.

I fell and fell, darkness pressing in around me. It had been stupid to jump without investigating first. Kelsey's recklessness was rubbing off on me. My eyes lit up in the hole, my wolf seconds away from taking possession of my body.

Thud.

I hit the ground, landing crouched beside Kelsey who looked less than pleased to see me. She had dirt smeared on her face, and her bright violet eyes glowed annoyingly.

I groaned, my feet shrieking from taking the bulk of the impact, but nothing felt broken. Any injuries I sustained would heal, as would hers.

"Are you okay?" I rushed out, quickly scooting closer to her so I could see for myself.

She shoved a curtain of damp hair out of her face, blowing out a breath. "Did you really jump in after me? Now we're both stuck down here."

"I couldn't very well leave you alone in here. I panicked when you disappeared, and then you screamed."

Her fingers brushed at her clothes as she stood, glancing up where a small light seeped into the hole. "So, the heir prince can act before thinking. You chose the worst time to be reckless."

I stretched beside her, the bones in my knees cracking. "You're the one who fell through the ground. If you hadn't taken off and we stuck together like I said, we wouldn't be in this mess."

"Are you really giving me the I-told-you-so speech right now?"

"You drive me insane."

Her lips twitched. "In all the best possible ways." Only Kelsey could find something amusing about our dire situation.

I craned my neck and spun, looking for a way to escape. It didn't look good. "How the hell are we going to get out?"

"Was this grave always here?"

"Not funny. This isn't a grave."

"It's a trap," she said gravely. "And *they* got us both."

Her words made too much sense. It scared me. True fear.

Moving to the edge of the hole, Kelsey laid her hands on the dirt walls. "I've been here before," she murmured.

Our backs facing each other, I continued my inspection, glancing at her over my shoulder. "In a pit?"

"Yes." Then she shook her head and faced me. I didn't like the expression she wore. "No, in a vision. It's happening. Tonight. They're coming, Liam."

Yup. That's what I was fucking afraid of. "We have to get out of here."

"No. We can't. We're not going to win. They slaughter us, the entire pack." She swallowed over a lump of emotion in her throat, and something changed in her tone. "I watched you die. I refuse to let that happen."

"You expect me to sit in this hole while my pack...my family...my friends die?"

Her back pressed into the dirt as she sank against the earth. "You're not the only one who will lose people you love. But I can't lose you," she whispered. "Without you, I'll wither away. I'll be dead inside."

I grasped the one kernel of hope in what she was telling me. "You live?"

She realized she made a mistake, exposed too much because Kelsey knew I would gladly give up my life to save hers.

"No!" she said sternly. "No." Her head shook furiously back and forth.

"What happens to you after?" I pushed, stepping closer to her.

Her back was already to the wall. She had nowhere to go. Her lips clamped shut, a streak of stubbornness in her expression. She wouldn't tell me, sparing me from the agony. "You can't leave me alone."

My head tilted to the side as I considered what it would mean if I died, what she wasn't telling me. Without me to protect her, did that mean she'd become a lab rat? Had that been what she implied about withering away? A chilling fucking thought, but I started to see why I couldn't give my life up to save her because my death might be her undoing.

Tears shone in her eyes, fear making them bigger than usual. "Don't you see? You're not a threat if they capture us both. You've been the biggest obstacle standing in their way. Protecting me."

I reached out, cupping the side of her cheek, stroking over the soft skin with my thumb. "I'm not going to let them hurt you. We're getting out of here," I vowed.

Her face leaned into my touch, and she closed her eyes for a heartbeat before opening them again. "How? I can't believe you literally jumped in after me."

"What did you expect me to do? Leave you down here?"

A small, gentle hand covered mine on the side of her face. "Yes, if it meant getting help."

I pressed a kiss to her mouth. "I couldn't. I won't leave you. Ever."

Her body arched into mine, both hands flattening on my chest. "As noble as the notion is, princeling, now we're both stuck here and in danger."

"Colsen and Riven will find us. I'll tell them to circle back." Except...nothing happened when I reached out to touch the connection I shared with my pack.

What the fuck?

I tried again to reach the thread tying me to my friends and hit a wall. My brows slanted together.

Kelsey watched my face, seeing the tapering of my eyes. "What's wrong?"

"My pack bond is blocked. Like something is interfering."

"Can you hear me?" she asked through our mating link.

I nodded.

Kelsey lifted a hand and spread out her fingers. A tingle danced over the back of my neck as a dusting of her power floated in the air. "Someone put a barrier in this pit. It's probably obstructing your connection to the pack."

A muscle in my jaw ticked. "Are you shitting me? That sort of magic is banned."

"So is the collar, and yet you still had access to one," she reminded.

My lips press together. "Point taken."

"Your family seems to be in possession of forbidden shit," she muttered, and I couldn't argue with her.

I scowled up at the sky through a ten- or twelve-foot-diameter opening, dirt walls surrounding us. "A mental bond isn't the only way to reach them." My eyes met hers. "I could shift and send out a distress howl."

"That's the best idea you've come up with." Despite the sarcasm, she shivered.

"You're cold." Concern made my voice husky.

"I'm fine," she insisted, lifting her chin and tucking her hair behind her ears.

The air smelled like wet earth and iron. "Is that why your teeth are chattering? Come here. I won't let you freeze to death." I reached for her, grabbing her hand and pulling her into me.

"Just body heat," she said, drawing an invisible line between us that I had no intention of honoring.

My arms banded around her waist, using our combined heat to stay warm. The snow had stopped, but our damp clothes weren't helping. She settled against my chest, her sweet and sugary scent enveloping my senses.

We probably shouldn't be wasting time, but I couldn't deny the chance to have her in my arms. She nuzzled into my chest, her breath a hot rush of air on my bare chest.

It was a bad idea to breathe her in, to let the tip of my nose trace behind her ear, to press my lips to the beating pulse throbbing in her slim neck, but refusing...was impossible. Those simple touches were as natural as inhaling and exhaling. My body did them without thought.

She was mine.

Claim her, I swear the blood in her veins whispered to me, beckoning the canines I banished only moments ago.

Her neck moved, tilting toward my mouth, the exact opposite of what she should be doing.

I had to pull away. Now. Before madness took me. I was so damn close to giving in, letting the wolf have his way. So close.

Clearing my throat, I stepped away from her. "I should probably shift and see if I can get someone to find us." I slipped off my shoes and stuffed my socks into them, cold dirt squishing between my toes.

"What if *they* come to retrieve us before our friends do?"

A boulder lodged itself in my throat as I lifted my shirt over my head and handed it to Kelsey to hold. "We fight, pup." The words sounded more convincing than I felt.

Her fingers wrung the material of my shirt. "Tonight's a full moon."

"I know." I slipped off my pants, and she held those too. In only my boxers, freezing my ass off, I faced my mate, hooking a finger under her chin so she would look at me. "Everything will be okay."

She nodded despite her eyes brimming with worry. Her fingers rested on my bare chest, and that part of me that I'd suppressed for weeks came flaring to the surface, growing brighter and clearer.

Claim her.

Claim her.

Claim her.

Just a single innocent touch shattered me, and suddenly I had other concerns than just getting us out of here. If I didn't put space between us soon, I would do the very thing I'd worked so fucking hard at avoiding. I'd hurt her. I'd caused her pain. I'd pushed her away when it was the last thing either of us wanted.

And for what?

To end up breaking the treaty after all because we fell into a trap?

"Liam?"

I blinked and took a step back. There wasn't a lot of room to maneuver especially once in my wolf form, but I didn't see what other options we had.

The shift came naturally, easier today than others due to the moon's aura even when it wasn't yet present in the skies. I welcomed the stretching of my muscles and skin, the reforming of bones, as the wolf took ownership of the man. White fur blanketed my body, completing the last part of the transformation.

Shaking off the shifting tingles, I angled my head toward Kelsey. She stood staring at me, a glint of awe in her gaze I understood well. It was the same way I felt when I'd seen her in her wolf form. Amazed. Drawn. Breathtaking.

She stepped toward me. It only took one step to reach me considering how much smaller the space became after I shifted. Her fingers spread into the fur along my neck. "God, you are a beautiful wolf."

My head bent, nuzzling the side of her cheek with mine. I had trouble remembering what I was supposed to be doing with Kelsey's scent so strong in my nostrils and her fingers running through my fur.

I forced my hind legs to back up, my front following before I tossed my head back and howled, a deep guttural cry echoing through the tunneled pit up into the forest beyond.

I hoped it would be enough. It had to be. With the number of allies we had in the woods, Max, Hope, my brother, and my friends, one of them would come. Hell, I expected all of them to show up.

It was what we did.

We were a pack.

We were family.

We came when one of us called.

The hole suddenly became too quiet, the dirt pressing in around me, loose pebbles crumbling off the walls. A faint vibration quivered under my feet.

Something was wrong. My chest squeezed against my heart as I turned my head toward Kelsey.

Her eyes...

They were unfocused, but it wasn't just that. Her pupils were gone, only the eerie glowing violet of her eyes visible. The air trembled with her magic, making the hairs on my back feel electric.

"Kelsey?" I sent down our bond, but my voice bounced back like an echo in my head as if the power creating the vision rejected my summons.

I didn't know what to do in this situation, when she was lost to me, her visions capturing her. Was I supposed to pull her out? Did I let the vision run its course?

Blood dripped from her nose, trailing onto her lips.

That couldn't be good.

Her eyes started to shake, and my worry climbed within me.

Banishing the wolf, I shifted back into my human skin and yanked on my jeans, not bothering to zip or button them. In a single stride, I was in front of her. "Kelsey," I murmured, framing my hands on either side of her cheeks. Her skin was so damn cold.

I didn't know what else to do.

So, I kissed her.

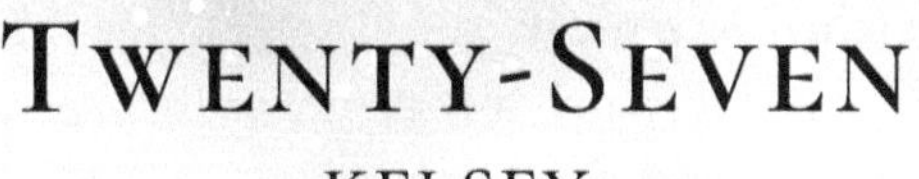

Twenty-Seven

KELSEY

My teeth chattered, knocking against each other uncontrollably. The cold cut through me, going straight to my bones, deep into my marrow. It wasn't the chilly night freezing my body. Ice traveled through my veins, and I began to tremble. I'd never felt anything close to hypothermia, but if I had to imagine, it would be what I was feeling.

The blizzard swirling in my blood wasn't the worst of it. The vision sunk its claws into me and refused to let go. Unlike the others, this held an air of desperation and realism as if I'd been plucked from the hole and dropped into the middle of a battlefield.

I'd been here before. Over and over again, but what differed this time was our clothes. Gunnar, Hope, Leith, Maxtyn, Colsen, Riven, Liam, and even me were all wearing the same outfits we had on right now.

Today.

The fight, the battle, and the meta hunters my visions had warned me of for weeks were finally here, and I couldn't be more fucking unprepared or scared.

Various degrees of panic scurried within me, and my sanity was slipping away. I didn't know what to do, how to save them, or how to stop

from losing everything. What good were the visions if they only showed me the horrible shit? What about a solution? For once, I would love my gift to reveal something wonderful, something to give me hope, not this murderous, sorrowful, cruel, unfair destruction of life.

I fell to my knees, icy tears tracking down my face, and screamed. I screamed for help. I screamed for the pain tearing my chest apart. I screamed as I watched Riven's head roll toward me on the ground, his mossy green eyes staring lifelessly up at me. I screamed as I watched my mate surrender to the enemy to save me.

I felt as cold as death. I felt numb. I felt—

A cascade of warmth flooded my cheeks, followed by a whisper. The heat moved to my lips, and the scent of something woodsy with a trace of mint filled my nose like winter in the forest. That's what Liam smelled like to me.

And it dawned on me that it was his scent tickling my senses. I held on to that scent, focusing on him instead of the mayhem surrounding me. His scent grew stronger, and with it, my other senses were touched by him.

His lips were pressed to mine.

"Liam," I mouthed against him in a soft sigh. My fingers landed on his chest, the heat from his skin immediately thawing the ice coating my hands. His body was like an inferno, and I instinctually moved closer to dispel the cold and hopefully any lingering remnants of the vision.

It worked. His warmth spread through me like I'd drunk a gallon of hot coffee, defrosting every crevice I had.

He brought me back.

And I was grateful, but the gratitude and relief lasted only seconds. "We're not alone," I said, staring off into space, watching the last frames of the nightmare vanish. "They're almost here."

"Who?" Liam gently prodded, his fingers running through my hair.

I stared at the scar on his lips, comforted by the sight of it. The scar was real. Liam was real. "The meta." My gaze lifted in time to see the worry flash through his ocean eyes before he banked it from me.

The hand in my hair fell to his side. "Fuck." The curse breezed out on an exhale. "Now? They're coming now?" he repeated as if it would somehow make what I'd seen less true.

If that was only the case.

Not that I couldn't be wrong. Or the future couldn't be altered. Both were true, but I wouldn't risk our lives on either. Nor our friends.

I nodded. "And they're bringing reinforcements," I added, delivering another unpleasant layer to our predicament.

"Rogues?" he guessed.

My eyes stayed on his. "Yes."

"How much time?" he prodded, gathering as much information from me as he could.

A howl echoed in the distance, and in unison, we glanced up at the sky.

My stomach pitched. The fear clutching me in the dream choked me. Our friends were out there with no way for us to warn them. "Not much."

Liam stiffened beside me. "We need to get the fuck out of here."

My thoughts exactly, but how? The question nagged at my brain over and over.

How?

How?

How?

It was like beating my head against the dirt wall on repeat. I shifted even closer to Liam, nearly plastering my body against his to chase the last few wisps of cold from my blood.

The maneuver drew his focus down to me. "Are you okay?" he asked, his body losing some of the hardness that had formed.

"No," I admitted, wanting to wrap my arms around him and bury my face into his neck.

He must have sensed my need to be held as one of his arms snaked around my waist and his other hand cupped the back of my head, guiding it to the space between his shoulder and neck. Our cheeks brushed, sending a zap of warmth through me.

That's what it took to dispel the last fragments of ice. I shuddered against him, taking a deep breath.

Outside in the woods, a battle brewed, and I was stuck in a pit with Liam, glowing inside from his touch.

It was fucked up.

And I knew it.

Our friends needed us, and I had to get my head on straight and not let Liam's naked chest get the best of me. Our bond would have to get on board and behave if we stood any chance of escaping.

I took my lip between my teeth, chewing on a thought. I had an idea, but getting Liam to agree would be a difficult task. "Let's say we get out of here. Then what? We're going to take on an army of hunters and wolves?" It seemed like a sure way to get killed along with our friends.

"What other choice is there besides fighting? If you suggest I let them take you in some heroic attempt to save everyone else, then we might as well wait here for the hunters to collect us. Where you go, I go."

They'd kill him, which could eventually kill me. A risk my captors might be willing to take, but I wasn't.

"It seems a little convenient that Gunnar went missing the night the hunters decided to invade, doesn't it?" I mused, mulling on this idea.

"You think he's part of it?"

"I don't think it is a coincidence, and we played right into their fucking hands." Anger flooded into me from our bond—Liam's anger. He blamed himself. Of course, he did.

"This is a setup. We're sitting at the bottom of a pit because of that backstabbing prick. I should have killed him," he fumed.

With Liam and me down here, we were useless.

Or were we?

This was the part that became tricky, but I had to try. What other options did we have? None I liked. "I have an idea, but I need you to be open-minded and not immediately shut it down," I told him. "I need you to think like an alpha and not my mate, okay?"

He frowned down at me, his hands resting on the small of my back. "I already don't like where this is going, pup. I'm not sure I can separate my feelings."

"Try," I insisted.

Taking a breath, I stepped back, putting space between us so I could better see him and his reaction. "You have the right idea. We have no choice but to fight. I won't run and leave our friends defenseless. I have something that might give us the upper hand."

Intrigue yet suspicion darkened his eyes to the color of the ocean during a wicked storm. "And what might that be?"

Here went nothing. "Me," I stated.

His lips carved out a deep, frightening frown. I didn't need to see his face to know how he felt. His absolute displeasure screamed through our bond.

"Just hear me out," I quickly added before he could shut me down, which he did anyway.

"No," he said firmly, his lips clamping shut afterward.

"Liam, open-minded," I groaned the reminder. "You're the heir prince right now. Not my mate."

"There is no difference for me." He sighed, shoving a hand into his disheveled hair. "I'm not going to like this, am I?"

I swallowed over the dryness in my throat. "When do you like any of my ideas?"

"Never," he agreed before releasing a long, suffering sigh of partial resignation. "What rules are we breaking tonight, pup?"

Only one that could put both our packs in jeopardy. "Claim me."

Twenty-Eight

LIAM

Claim me.

Her solution echoed through me, my wolf jumping at any reason to finally have what he wanted for so long.

His mate.

My gaze moved to her throat where her pulse hammered.

I blinked. "I fail to see how my biting you is going to give us an advantage."

The snow stopped drifting into the hole, but the sun would soon pass the torch to night, and the moon would rise. Kelsey chewed on her lip, contemplating. "Do you have a better plan?"

I didn't have shit except hope our friends would look for us. "I fail to see how claiming you will solve our problem, pup." But fuck me, if my blood didn't heat up at her solution. My body in whatever situation wanted her. We'd gone too long apart, and the wolf needed his mate like he needed air to breathe. "How does claiming you change the outcome?"

A ghost of a smile touched her lips. "There's something I haven't told you."

"You kept a secret." Our bond made it nearly impossible to hide

things from each other. Both impressed and annoyed, I stared at my mate.

"I had no choice," she reasoned.

"I'm waiting, pup."

"You know I've been struggling with my powers." Her finger touched her nose. The blood was gone, but the reminder of the toll her visions had on her body lingered.

"Yeah, the visions," I said, my stomach twisting. It was hard for me to see her lost, somewhere else where I might not be able to reach her. That wasn't how it was supposed to work with mates.

She nodded. "It's because I claimed you. My gifts aren't fully developed, not until I mate."

"You're saying if I claim you your magic will enhance, you'll be more powerful."

"My magic will be fueled by your strength. Right now, our bond is only half completed, but if you claim me..." She looked at me expectantly with specks of hope.

For me, it wasn't such an easy decision. It might get us out of here, it might help us fight, but I'd seen what the visions did to her, and my hesitation had nothing to do with not wanting her and everything to do with her safety. "Why does that sound dangerous?"

Her shoulders shrugged, trying to seem nonchalant. "What's life without a little danger?"

Now it was my turn to put my foot down. "Not happening. I'm not willing to risk you or your health."

She took two strides and reached for my hand. "What other choice do we have?"

A chill rippled down my spine. I wanted to whisk her away, far from the woods, the danger, the death to come. "You stay here, and I'll fight. If the hunters show up, I can ambush them."

Kelsey shook her head, her fingers squeezing my hand. "You're a fool if you think you can leave me behind or that I would stay put. I will always fight at your side, princeling. I'll never cower behind you or stay tucked away in a pit."

My features grew solemn. "Why do you have to be so fucking difficult?"

Her eyes were bright, glowing in the shadows. "Just as you would risk your life to save me, don't you think I would do the same?"

I cast my eyes upward, a prickle of uneasiness poking at my wolf. "I don't want to think about it."

"This is our best chance," she continued.

"Is that what your visions reveal? We'll win if I claim you?" I asked roughly, my gaze returning to her face.

"No. That's not what I saw," she admitted with a ruffled huff.

"Do you want to tell me what you did see?"

"Not really. I want to save not just us but our friends. Are you really going to leave them alone out there to fight?"

As if to drive her point home, a trio of wolves howled.

Perfect timing.

"Damn it," I growled.

Her fingers turned over my arm, exposing the moon marked on the inside of my wrist. She looked down at the symbol of our connection, now bolder on my skin. "I might not know if we survive the night, but I know that if we don't do this we won't stand a chance. Isn't it better to risk it than do nothing at all?" she proposed, looking up at me.

My face grew taut. "This plan of yours puts you at the center of the fight. I don't like it."

A sad smile touched her mouth. "You'll be at my side."

"And what if it's not enough?" I murmured. So many factors to consider. I didn't want to make the wrong choice. Not with her.

"You're enough for me," she whispered, and I swore stars flecked the centers of her eyes.

"This isn't the way I wanted it to be," I said, tucking a strand of hair behind her ear.

"What? You never dreamed about claiming your mate at the bottom of a creepy hole?"

I only stared at her, needing to memorize every line of her face before our world erupted.

"Jokes aside, princeling, I'm not trying to force your hand, and I also don't want this to sound pretentious, but I think I'm meant to stop them. This power was given to me for a reason. The fates picked *you* as my mate. We're Moonstruck, a bond so rare no one can remember the last pair to exist. And my power is literally fueled by our link. It can't be for nothing."

For once, I couldn't argue, but it didn't mean I fucking liked it. Why her? Why couldn't it have been someone else? Anyone else but the girl I loved?

I blinked.

The realization slammed into my chest.

I was in love with her.

Something I'd have to unpack later.

"Maybe so, but it doesn't mean I have to like it," I said.

"Neither of us asked for this. I didn't want you." She looked up at me with loving, violet eyes that sparkled under moonlight and starlight. "And yet it didn't stop me from falling in love with you."

My chest expanded, a light beaming inside me. I'd only just discovered my feelings, and here she was admitting hers. "Don't toy with my emotions, pup."

She pressed a hand to my wildly beating heart. "I love you."

The admission the second time stole the air from my lungs. How could this girl twist me up so thoroughly into knots? "You turn eighteen in ten days."

A snarl from somewhere deep in the woods snapped her attention upward as we both felt the pressure. I couldn't believe the chance we were taking, but I had to decide now. The clock was running out.

Shaking my head, I moved in closer, our eyes locked. They stayed affixed as I lifted the hair off her shoulder, pushing it off to the side and exposing her neck. The sun had descended, trading places with the moon, giving the sky a different, moodier glow. Tonight was a full moon, and as I drew my hand away from her hair, I saw the mark shining on my wrist brighter than any other night.

I reached for her hand and lifted it between us, flipping it around to expose the inside of her arm where the twin to my mark shimmered. I ran the pad of my thumb over the white moon, and it flared at my touch. My pulse raced. "I've wanted you for so long." My eyes lifted to hers. *"Kelsey,"* I murmured through our bond.

The vein on the side of her throat pulsed...a temptation. I didn't know if I was looking for any excuse to claim her or if this was our best shot to survive. It didn't matter anymore.

I leaned in, the light pressure of my teeth scraping against her neck in an erotic caress. "I want to make you mine," I murmured in a guttural voice that almost sounded as if I was in pain. In a way, I was. For weeks, I'd locked my need to claim her inside an internal prison.

"Nothing is stopping you now, princeling. Make me yours." Her voice cooed through our link.

She was the damn devil and angel inside my head. I pressed a nipping kiss to her neck, torturing us both. She arched her throat closer to my mouth, closer to my canines, as her fingers dove into my hair.

My control slipped entirely. I barely pressed my canines into her neck, and my whole world exploded the second a tiny drop of her blood landed on my tongue. I swallowed, never tasting anything like her in my life.

My body shuddered.

Deeper. Deeper. Deeper, my wolf urged. I clamped down harder, needing more. I had to have all of her. My canines pierced deeper as I pulled her blood, and she whimpered, her nails digging into my head.

"Yes. Yes. Yes," she chanted like a sinful prayer in my head.

Tighter and tighter our bond sealed, our wolves merging as much as our souls. With her blood on my teeth and on my tongue, I whispered, "You're mine."

The bond snapped into place, a flood of feelings slamming into me as our scents merged, our mating bond complete. My blood roared, or perhaps it was the wolf.

Inside, I radiated as if the full moon itself lived within my chest, lighting up every dark corner of my soul. Our bond had been a constant thread tugging and pulling at me, but it turned into a ribbon that wove us together until I couldn't tell where the end or the beginning of the ribbon was. It illuminated like nothing I'd ever felt.

Pulling back, I glanced into her eyes glittering like polished amethysts.

We were mated.

"How do you feel?" I whispered, swiping at a drop of blood slipping down her neck with my thumb. The link to her pack would have severed. She was part of my pack now, and every wolf would know, including my father, once we stepped foot out of this pit and the magical barrier no longer interfered with my pack bond.

Kelsey's lips curled. "Like I could destroy the world."

I chuckled, shaking my head at this beautiful, reckless girl who stole my heart. "How about we take that power down a notch and stick to the bad guys today?"

She laughed, a dazzling smile of happiness on her lips. We were trapped in a hole, and I could feel her elation. Her hands lifted, turning them back and forth and examining them as if she were trying them out for the first time.

In a way, I guess she was.

I imagined what it must feel like to harbor and wield such power, different than the power I inherited as an alpha, and through our link, I could do more than picture it—I felt it.

She was fucking magnificent.

"We fight together," I said with steely determination. Kelsey was my partner, my equal, and although my first instinct was to shelter her, I knew we were stronger side by side.

We exchanged a look. "Always and forever," she murmured.

I pressed my lips to hers in a soft kiss. We didn't have time to get swept away in the completion of our bond, regardless that my wolf demanded it. "As long as the moon shines," I vowed.

"And the stars twinkle," she added.

"I assume you have a master plan to get us out of here?" I inquired.

Color bloomed on her cheeks. "I have a thought."

"But..." I added because I sensed there was something she wasn't saying, her hesitation and doubt traveling through our fully formed bond.

She eyed the dirt walls with a thoughtful expression. "There is a chance I could create a landslide and basically bury us alive."

"Fabulous," I grumbled, dragging a hand over my face.

Slipping her arms around my neck, she tipped her chin up. "It's like a fifty-fifty shot."

I frowned. "Those aren't great odds, pup, not with your life."

She winked at me. “Have a little faith.”

“Shit.”

“Just in case, we should probably stay in the center. Put your arms around me,” she instructed, an order I could handle.

Stepping up behind her, I wrapped my hands around her waist. “Is this necessary?”

“No, I just wanted you to touch me,” she answered, the air already tingling with magic. She’d begun to use her sixth sense. Dirt and debris crumbled from the bottom of the pit, working up as her power carved and shaped small steps into the wall on a slight incline. Just enough to give us the height we needed to jump the rest of the way out.

I gazed at the makeshift stairs, circling upward. “Don’t tell me you could have done that the entire time.”

She shrugged, glimpsing over her shoulder. “Who knows, or maybe it’s your power that’s giving me the strength.”

“A nice thought.” I quickly tossed on my shirt and slipped back into my shoes, more than ready to get the fuck out of this grave. It wouldn’t be ours.

The moon hung heavy in the night sky, casting an eerie silver glow over the darkened forest as we emerged. Fighting was the last thing I wanted to do. What my wolf and my body ached for was a bed where I could be alone with my mate for hours. Hell, days or weeks, however long it would take to satisfy this insatiable need for her. I’d been a fool to believe it would lessen once we completed the bond.

I wanted her more if it was possible.

“I need to warn the others,” I advised as she shook out her hair, particles of dirt flying out. Now that we were free of whatever barrier prevented me from touching the pack bond when we’d been inside the hole, I should be able to give Colsen, Riven, Leith, and Hope a heads-up. I also needed to send an SOS to the entire pack. Tonight would require all hands on deck, but it would ultimately be up to my father whether the pack fought.

If a battle had been brought to his territory, he would know the moment they crossed into our borders, and judging from how close those howls had been, I was guessing they were already here.

So why wasn’t I getting any orders from the pack?

They would have also sensed the addition of a new member—my mate. Kelsey was an official member now that I claimed her, and everyone knew I'd broken the treaty. Was that why I felt nothing of the threat?

Kelsey laid a hand on my arm. "What's wrong?"

"I'm not sure yet," I replied, my brows drawing together in concentration, but we couldn't stand here. We needed to move. I'd keep trying to reach the others while we ran toward danger.

The fingers near the top of my shoulder dug into my skin. *"Liam, someone's coming."* Her voice whispered into my head.

My spine locked up.

Voices drifted from not far away. They carried through the trees.

"What's Hope doing here with your father?" Kelsey asked, her expression confounded as she looked to me for answers I didn't have.

"I don't know, but nothing good," I replied, listening and catching pieces of their conversation.

"You're sure they're there?" my father asked.

We couldn't see them, but her voice was unmistakable. "Yeah. I did what you asked."

I swallowed the massive lump in my throat, and tears burned in my mate's eyes, hurt projecting through our bond. *No. No. No. Not my best friend. Not the girl who made my first weeks bearable. How could she?* Those were Kelsey's thoughts, but I felt Hope's betrayal just as deep, if not deeper. She was family.

Only one answer made sense.

It was also the only reason I would ever betray my family or friends.

Love.

For Kelsey, I would sell my soul to the devil.

Kelsey's fingers suddenly gripped my arm, her head shaking as she backed up, dragging me with her. *"Something's in the air, Liam. It's wrong. Don't—"*

Her warning came too late. The threat had already entered our lungs, and within seconds, blackness swallowed me.

I'd been knocked unconscious a few times in my life. Always from fighting. Some had been Leith and I goofing off. Others had been pack members challenging me. There had even been the time a college guy hit me for kissing his girlfriend. I'd been twelve. But never in my life had I ever been rendered unconscious by breathing.

A fogginess and heaviness nagged at my head, making it hard for me to fully open my eyes. I struggled with the effect of the chemical screwing with my body.

I blinked slowly, my vision clearing at the pace of a snail. My temples throbbed, and I attempted to lift my hand to rub at the spot, but I couldn't move my arms.

The film of fuzziness over my eyes cleared, and I stared at a crack piled with dust in the floor. *Where the hell am I?*

"So glad of you to join me. I was getting a bit lonely," someone said sarcastically.

Ugh. That voice. My eyes lifted, landing on Gunnar chained to a chair same as I was. His head hung down until he felt my gaze on him, and he lifted it. His eyes were dark in the dimly lit room, the single overhead light swinging and casting shadows on the concrete floor. Dried blood cracked at the side of his mouth. A steady dripping sound filled the room. "Where the fuck are we?"

Gunnar's gaze did a sweep of the dingy walls. "Another secret lair. Welcome to hell, heir prince." A bleak smirk twisted on his lips.

"Kelsey," I hissed, fear working its way into my gut and clawing through me. I frantically turned my head, surveying the shithole room with a critical gaze before landing back on the hunter. "Where the fuck is she?" I demanded, the chains around my wrists and feet rattling as I tested their strength, trying to break my hands free.

The metal held.

For now.

But I wasn't giving up until I got out of here. Until I found her.

Gunnar's eyes shifted, and I followed his gaze to the massive iron door locking us in. "They took her."

"Who?" I growled, my wolf surging to the surface, seconds from taking control.

"You know who," he rasped.

Fear-laced adrenaline pumped hard and fast into my blood. He was right. I did know. I felt something around my neck, and my fingers lifted, encountering a familiar cool chain.

"We're both dogs now," Gunnar muttered, staring at me with hard eyes as I swallowed over a lump in my throat.

A collar.

I was wearing a fucking collar.

A different form of panic entered my veins, the wolf within me thrashing.

"It's only temporary," Hope said, her soft voice coming from the corner at my back.

Hope? How could she be a part of this?

Footsteps sounded, and I twisted my head, needing visual confirmation to what my senses already discovered. My cousin was in the room.

"Just to keep you from hurting yourself...or others," she added, coming into my view. "You'll be freed once they finish."

"Finish what?" I dared to ask, but I had a horrible hunch.

She favored her leg as she walked, her limp more prominent than usual. "With your mate."

"Kelsey," I reached out, but the bond was weak and foggy. I didn't want to decipher what that could mean. I refused to think of anything but finding her. "You're a fool if you think a collar will stop me from ripping out their throats. I won't stop until I hunt them all down."

"It would be better if you don't fight," she said sadly.

Anger expanded in my chest. "Hope, get me the fuck out of these chains. Now. I command it as your future prince."

"I can't," she sobbed, tears pooling and spilling over her cheeks. Her arms went around her body as she hugged herself. "I can't," she repeated, looking as if she might crumble to the ground at any second.

"Don't push her," Gunnar warned with an edge.

I ignored him. Worrying about other people's feelings wasn't high on my radar. "Where's my brother?" I snapped. He and Hope had been together when we set out to locate Gunnar, and I saw now what a fucking terrible mistake that had been.

"I-I don't know," she stammered. "You have to believe me."

My head shook, the damn collar heavy on my neck, not physically, because the chain itself was thin, but metaphorically, the necklace added an element of pressure. "How could you? You betrayed your pack, your family, for him?" I indicated with a jerk of my head at the hunter. "After everything?" I couldn't fathom Hope's choices. Why she was standing in a cell with us, unchained, unharmed, while Gunnar and I were imprisoned. I couldn't comprehend why she wasn't rushing to help us. Why she quivered in fear and was riddled with guilt.

"You're not the only one with people to protect. He threatened to kill Gunnar. He said this was the only way to stop the hunters from getting to him. I love him, Liam." Her voice cracked. "He's my mate."

I flinched. "Gunnar? Your mate?" The idea made a manic bubble rise in my throat.

She limped forward, her brown eyes beseeching me to sympathize with her dilemma. "You understand why. You would have done the same for Kelsey."

"That matters little to me now. I trusted you." Pain and betrayal vibrated in my tone.

"I didn't have a choice. I did what you would have done to save Kelsey. Why is it because I made the same decision you condemn me for it?" She tried to reason with me.

I bared my canines. "You don't know what I would have done."

The slow scraping of metal against concrete pierced my ears. I winced. The door to the cell opened, and Hope backed up a few steps, terror widening her eyes.

A shifter I'd never seen before scampered into the room. He was a wolf but not of our pack. Outcast? Rogue? It mattered little to me.

"I thought I heard voices," he said with a toothless grin. The spot where his canines should have been was empty like they'd been pulled out. The extraction of a wolf's canines was an old method used as punishment, stripping one of what was considered a vital element of being a wolf.

My chains clanged. "What did you give me?"

"Just something to muddle your link to the pack," he replied.

And my mate, it seemed.

"I think it's time for a second dose. We wouldn't want you to spoil our plans before we get to the fun stuff." He pulled out a needle from his pocket and grinned.

I couldn't let him stick me with that shit. "Only cowards use impairing agents. Fight me like a wolf, you pussy."

He tapped the needle as he advanced toward me. "Your father said you were clever."

I had seconds, literal seconds, to come up with a plan.

My gaze locked on Gunnar's.

We might both be wearing collars, but I still controlled him, and I would use that to my advantage. Holding Gunnar's gaze, I kept my voice low, nearly mouthing the command. "Kill. Him."

The hunter nodded the tiniest fraction, nearly not moving at all, but he understood.

Testing the syringe, the shifter stood in front of me, his back to Gunnar. He leaned down with rapt pleasure, and the hunter made his move.

Silent like a mouse, he rocked forward onto his feet, the chair bent around him as he crouched and spun, hitting the shifter with the back of the chair.

Wood splintered. The shifter groaned and stumbled a step. Then Gunnar slammed into him at full force, the pair of them plunging to the ground with a hard thud.

One of the legs on his chair snapped, not completely freeing his feet, due to the chain, but giving him a bit more leverage. The needle fell out of the shifter's hand, skirting over the cold floor and rolling a few feet away from Hope's boots.

This was it.

Our one shot.

We couldn't fuck this up, but I needed my cousin's help.

"Hope!" I roared.

She looked at me, her eyes wider than I'd ever seen them. If she didn't reach down and pick up the fucking needle now, we were doomed. This was our chance. Who knew when another one would present itself, and I refused to waste the opportunity. It was now or never.

The guard swore as Gunnar rammed his knee into his gut, not once, not twice, but three times in rapid succession.

"Hope!" I roared again, putting the power of an alpha into my voice. Gunnar would only be able to fight him off for so long impaired as he was, bound by chains.

Blinking, she dashed for the needle, scooping it up and twisting around toward the guard. He and Gunnar tussled on the floor, the hunter doing his best to use the chair to his advantage. He used the chain between his feet to wrap around the shifter's legs.

The hunter took a hit to the face, his head snapping to the side. The fool laughed and braced for another punch, which came. He was buying Hope time, distracting the shifter by letting him beat the shit out of him. Not exactly the move I would have gone for but effective, nonetheless.

Hope surged forward, plunging the needle into the back of the shifter's shoulder, pushing down the injection before she fell backward. The bastard growled, his hand moving to his upper arm, searching out the needle Hope left stuck into him.

His fingers fumbled around, finally enclosing on the syringe and ripping it out. "You're going to pay for that," he threatened, his furious, glowing eyes pinned on Hope.

Gunnar held him back with his legs, but he wouldn't be able to for long. A few moments at best. "Run!" he screamed at Hope.

My cousin scampered away backward on her hands and feet, butt scooting across the floor. I could smell her fear.

The shifter broke free and crawled toward my cousin, his arm extending toward her feet. She kicked, shrieking and crying. The order for her to shift was on the tip of my tongue when the drug finally worked its way into his system, and the shifter clonked to the floor.

No one did or said anything for five heartbeats. We sat there, staring at the lifeless body, the silence in the room deafening.

"Hope," I called softly, doing my best to keep my voice calm. I didn't need her to fall apart now, and regardless of how angry I was with her, I had to put that aside for later. "Get his keys."

Her vacant eyes stared at the body, and all I could think was we were screwed if she didn't snap out of it.

"Hope." Gunnar tried to get through to her, a tangle of chains and chair pieces around him as he did his best to sit up.

She blinked, the shock clearing from her eyes. Getting on her hands and knees, she crawled to the body, unhooking the ring on his belt loop, and moved to Gunnar. Her fingers shook the entire time, but after a few failed attempts, she managed to unlock his hands.

Gunnar took the keys from her, clasping her chin between his fingers. "It's okay. I'm okay. I got you," he murmured in a soothing voice.

She nodded as he unlocked his feet.

Slowly standing, Gunnar took Hope into his arms, and she sagged against him. As much as I didn't want to interrupt their little gagging reunion, I was still fucking chained, and Kelsey still missing.

I cleared my throat about to issue a command if the hunter didn't undo my chains immediately. He got the point, shifting Hope to the side as he crouched in front of me. "Don't blame her," he whispered.

"She's the least of my concerns right now," I assured, holding his gaze.

Gunnar gave a single nod, turning the last lock on my feet.

Rubbing at my wrists, I kicked the chains off my ankles and stood. I might be free from my bonds, but the links around my neck had a firm grasp on me. My wolf itched to claw it off, but it would do no good, not without the blood of the owner. I turned to Hope, my fingers clasping her shoulders. "Who put the collar on me?" I hadn't meant to sound so harsh, but the panic and fury within made me sharp and impatient.

The crestfallen expression that came over her confirmed what I presumed. "I'm sorry, Liam."

My fingers pressed deeper into her skin. "Was it him? Was it my father?" I needed to hear her say it.

"Yes," she affirmed, a single broken admission.

I whirled, bolting out of the partially open metal door and into a long corridor leading to another door. I whipped it open, taking a step back at seeing my brother on the other side.

"God, I found you. What the actual fuck is going on?" Leith

mumbled, looking as disorientated as I felt not long ago, rubbing the back of his head.

Not wasting time, I stepped outside and glanced at my surroundings. "They took Kelsey. We need to find her," I told him.

"Okay, clearly, I've missed a lot, and by the looks of you, shit definitely went sideways. We'll find her together." I had to give my brother credit. He caught up quickly and went right into warrior mode. "What is this place?" he asked, eyes scrunching at the cabin.

"Hell." Gunnar and Hope appeared in the door behind me. I spared them a fleeting glance. "We need to go." I didn't care one way or the other if the hunter and my cousin followed.

A faint shadow of a bruise painted the underside of my brother's eye. "Where?" he asked, understanding the importance of finding my mate.

I looked left and then right. "This way," I said, hoping my intuition was right. Finding Kelsey depended on my ability to locate her when she was in trouble. My gut said left. We went left.

We ran against the wind. I would have run in a tornado, a thunderstorm, or an earthquake. Nothing would get in my way. Hope and Gunnar trailed behind. I said nothing, surging forward on pure instinct and a desperate need.

Please don't let me be too late, I begged the fates. I'd drop down on my knees to the moon. Whatever it took.

It was a good three- to four-mile trek through the snow in the woods before I skidded to a halt, my connection to Kelsey buzzing like a live wire in my veins. "She's close. I can feel her."

Leith shook his snow-flecked hair. "There's nothing here. Unless they've got her underground, she's not here."

My head jerked in his direction. "What did you say?"

His brows furrowed. "That she's not here."

"No, the part about her being underground," I said, inspecting the area with a new perspective.

"Bunker," Gunnar said what I was thinking, our eyes meeting.

"Look for a hidden door on the ground." The snow still fell from the evening sky, blanketing the trees and grass, but if they had accessed it an hour ago, the area should show some signs of disturbance. That's what we were searching for.

The four of us spread out, combing the forest floor. I used my boot to clear and brush aside patches of snow, twigs, and wet leaves. Urgency propelled me to move faster, and a few times, I thought I heard my name whispered in the wind as it blew through the trees.

But that wasn't all I heard in the woods.

A howl cleaved through the night, and we all froze, glancing in the direction it had come. The cries, the warnings, the threats, and the snarls tormented us the entire time we had run. It was so fucking hard to ignore what else was happening deeper in the thicket.

Colsen, Riven, and Maxtyn were still out there. Alone.

Fighting a battle I should be fighting alongside them.

First, I had to get Kelsey to safety, and then—

"Here," Gunnar said, keeping his voice lower. There was no need to shout when we could all hear him fine. "I think I found it."

Scrambling to where the hunter was, I saw the hatch. I glanced at Gunnar and gave him a nod of thanks.

The two of us grabbed the handle and yanked, revealing a tunnel that went straight down several feet.

Fucking great. Another damn hole in the ground.

At the bottom, a light flickered like some horror movie. "You guys don't have to do this. I can go in alone," I said, putting my feet onto the rungs of the ladder.

My brother wasn't having it. "No fucking way. I'm going with you."

Gunnar glanced over his shoulder for a moment. "Fuck it. I'll take my chances with you."

"There's no way I'm staying up here by myself," Hope insisted. "Where he goes, I go."

And so, I descended into the bunker. My feet hit the hard floor, and a wave of déjà vu hit me as I stared down the long hallway. "I've been here before," I murmured.

Leith dropped down beside me. "What do you mean?"

There wasn't much space, and I stepped into the tunnel, making room for Gunnar and Hope. "I'm not sure. I thought it was just a dream. I was in my wolf, tracking Kelsey. I didn't realize it then, but I think it was one of Kelsey's visions. I saw it through our bond."

The corridor was only big enough for one person width-wise. I went first, my brother behind me. "You guys have some intense mating abilities," Leith muttered.

"You have no idea," I replied, keeping my steps light, trying our bond again, but it was still murky.

"Did you save her?" he asked after a few seconds of walking.

"What?" I whispered over my shoulder, coming to a junction of tunnels. This place was a damn maze.

"In the dream or vision, whatever it was. Did you save her?" Leith asked again.

I hooked another left, wondering why the hell we were having this conversation. "I don't know. It ended before I could see." The top of the tunnel wasn't high, seven feet max, and at times, it felt as if the walls were pressing in around me. My wolf hated being underground.

"Great. Just great. How are we supposed to know how this story ends?"

"This isn't a novel, Leith. It's my life." The burn in my chest expanded, crawling up my throat.

"All the more reason why the ending is so damn important," he grumbled. "But you have to admit, it would make a great book."

"I'd read it," Gunnar spoke up from the rear.

I'd heard this faint beeping when we entered the bunker, and it grew louder with each step. I took that as a good sign. "No one asked you."

"Maybe you should write it if we ever make it out of here," my brother suggested.

"Will the two of you both shut up?" I hissed, my fingers running along the wall as we passed door after door. "We don't know who else is down here." Not to mention, I couldn't hear myself think.

My cousin had been silent most of the way. For good cause. I didn't want to hear anything she had to say.

After what felt like hours but had only been minutes, I paused in front of a closed door identical to the dozen others we passed. A constant beep echoed from the other side, but it was her breathing, her heartbeat, her magic, her blood, her wolf, our bond, that summoned me.

For once, Leith and Gunnar were tight-lipped as I glanced at them. We shared a look, and then my fingers moved to the latch. I flung open the door, the vision of her lying pale and lifeless on a metal bed, hooked to a machine, tubes running from all over her body stained behind my eyes, but that wasn't what waited for me as the door swung open.

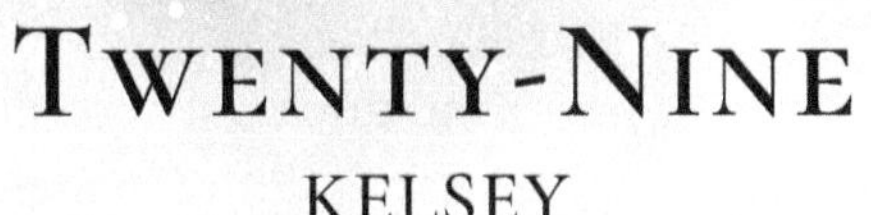

Twenty-Nine

KELSEY

Beep. Beep. Beep.

The incessant, annoying sound repeated in my head, and I followed it out of the deep heaviness that kept me in an unconscious state until I became aware.

But then, I wished to be back into the void of nothingness, where my mind couldn't put together the pieces and jump to conclusions. The more aware I became, the faster my heart raced, surpassing the rhythmic beeping of machines.

I didn't have a clear picture of what happened in the woods. Liam and I escaped the hole, then we began walking, and I remembered something odd in my nose, but after that...nothing.

I always knew I'd end up here, but no matter how many visions I had, nothing had prepared me.

Liam.

Pressure clamped down on my chest.

Where was he? Had they captured him as well? They wouldn't hurt him, right?

It wasn't him they wanted but me. And *if* his father was behind this, he wouldn't harm his son. I clung to that kernel of hope. I had no other choice, or I'd go mad.

With my eyes still heavy and uncooperative, I managed to wiggle my fingers, but it felt as if my body wasn't mine. The support under my back was cold, as was the room, and my arms prickled with goose bumps.

"Liam?" I called through our bond, desperately needing to hear his voice, to hear he was alive. My voice came out wobbly and weak in my head. I hated feeling so unsteady and sluggish.

I tried to reach out again to the threads of our link, but it wasn't there, or I couldn't find it. Either way, it didn't matter. The heir prince had been cut off from me. It could be the drugs in my system or something far worse.

I wouldn't consider the possibility someone had managed to sever my bond with Liam.

Panic burst in my chest, spreading like a disease. The air in my lungs felt as if it had been cut off, and I struggled to breathe. Gasping, I continued to drown, and yet I wasn't in water. In my mind, I flailed, desperately searching and grasping for anything to save me, to banish this horrible sensation of death's hands around my neck.

Squeezing. Squeezing. Squeezing until every last drop of life was sucked out of me.

Not life.

Magic.

I mentally shook my head, or maybe it was real. I couldn't separate the two, but one thing of certainty was I wouldn't let them take my power.

Mine. It's mine. The magic in my veins belonged solely to me.

So I fought back, grasping those tingles that represented more than my sixth sense. They were my life. They were Liam. They were our bond. My love for him.

Only a few sparks flittered, but that was all I needed.

They were like little molecules within me. One attracted another, doubling in numbers, I pulled the power into me.

My eyes flew open, and I gasped, greedily taking in air into my lungs as I fought to breathe—to live. Wetness gathered below my eyes, streaming down my cheeks. Tears, I realized. I'd been crying.

But I had a lot to cry about.

I stared at my reflection in the metal hanging over my face. My eyes glowed bright and full of malice. All my fear morphed into anger, and I was really afraid. Not just for me but for my friends—for Liam.

My fingers curled at my sides, awareness of my body coming alive and with it pain. Ice seared my veins—so potent I felt as if I'd just emerged from a frozen river. For a wolf whose body temperatures ran hot, this extreme cold was torture on its own—a different burn.

I'd rather be scorched by fire.

Teeth chattering, I couldn't subdue the violent shakes controlling my muscles. My whole body trembled on the metal table. I wouldn't even mind its hard surface under me if only the tremors would cease.

Staring at the dark ceiling, I did my best to level my breathing and slow my heart rate. Traces of damp earth and something like iron—some type of mineral. I was underground. Again. My wolf whimpered.

"You're awake," a woman with a soft, feminine, familiar voice whispered.

It couldn't be. No. It wouldn't be her face when I turned my head to the side. And yet...

Liam's mother came into focus.

Disbelief struck into my heart. Why was she here? Had Liam sent her? The alternative would hurt too much, that she was helping the wrong side.

Surprise shone in her eyes, but an emotionless expression quickly replaced it. "You shouldn't be awake." She put her finger to her lips, indicating for me to keep quiet and not speak. Her eyes hardened as I shook my head. "If you want to survive, you must cooperate," she whispered insistently.

I would do no such thing.

"I-I don't understand," I croaked, my throat scratchy like I'd been screaming. There was a good chance I had been, all things considered. "How could you...?"

Her hand flew to my mouth, shaking her head.

I tried to lift my hand to remove hers from my face, but they were restrained as was the rest of me I soon found out. A wolf didn't just value freedom, but it was essential to my state of mind. I went straight into freakout mode.

My back bucked in a worthless endeavor to loosen the binds around my chest. Whoever had restrained me had done a thorough job.

"If you don't stop, you'll hurt yourself," Sydney said with a levelness that made me wonder if she was the same shifter I'd gotten to know and love these last months.

Fear trickled in again, my emotions wavering. "Let me go," I pleaded.

She sat on a stool that rolled as she scooted toward a machine to the right of my head. "Neither of us are in a position to negotiate. Just don't do anything to make this worse. It will be over soon."

I allowed my gaze to roam the room with my limited movement. My captors had spent literally nothing on the space itself. The most expensive thing in the small room was the equipment surrounding me. As far as torture chambers went, it was in desperate need of some bleach and a mop. Or a grenade. I voted for the grenade. It needed to be blown up, all the stupid machines, the tubes, the shelves of jars full of... Shit, I didn't want to know what was in them.

I guessed those sterile white rooms from my visions weren't part of the plan tonight. "Why are you doing this?" I asked, not really believing I'd be able to understand her motives. Months ago, the idea of kidnapping someone seemed preposterous. Then Gunnar happened, so perhaps a small slice of me could sympathize to a degree. I just wished it wasn't me strapped to the table.

She checked the machine still beeping annoyingly in the otherwise quiet room. "I don't have a choice." She kept her voice so low I strained to hear her even with my heightened abilities. Who was she trying to prevent from overhearing?

"Of course, you do," I rationalized like the answers were black-and-white.

Sydney was determined to convince me they were gray. "If it were only that simple."

"What did you give me?" My body had this off feeling, so I continued to cling to the magic being siphoned out of me. It became like a lifeline. I had to hold on.

Her expression remained the same. Sad. "It's nothing. Just a sedative."

I scoffed. "What kind of sedative blocks my bond to your son?"

Her brows knitted together, something akin to surprise in her eyes. "Your link is gone?"

Nausea rose. "Don't pretend like that wasn't exactly what you wanted, to cut us off from each other."

She opened her mouth to respond, but the door in the far corner of the room opened, drawing her gaze away from me. Her lips pressed together as her eyes followed Rowan, her husband, but he only stared at me.

I stared back, frozen at the sight of him. Suddenly the depth of my troubles was too fucking real. "Kelsey, I'm sure this is confusing," he started in a gruff voice.

"Not really," I snapped, averting my eyes to stare at the ceiling. I forbid my eyes to look at him. This was his fault.

But his large frame took up too much of the room, making it cramped, suffocatingly so. "I thought you said she would remain unconscious," he directed to his wife.

Sydney swiveled in her chair, her unapologetic eyes meeting her husband's harsh glare. "She should have."

"Your son will find me," I interrupted, wanting to rattle his composure and unshakable arrogance. "He always finds me. It won't matter how much you drug me."

His beefy fingers reached out, sliding over one of the tubes attached to my body. There were many. "Then we better not waste any time."

Not the response I anticipated from him when the threat rolled off my tongue. Perhaps if I kept him talking, I could distract him long enough to keep Sydney from noticing I still gathered my power, pulling it back into me from the machines stealing it. "He knows it was you. Has known since his birthday when Gunnar tried to trap me. Your hunter gave you up. Loyalty is a lost art, it seems, among those who have been wronged." I sounded a lot braver than I felt, considering my vulnerable position, putting me at a disadvantage.

A flicker of a dark emotion crossed Rowan's features. "So you understand what we are doing?" he asked without being straightforward. Cagey. He wanted to hear how much I knew from me.

I didn't understand shit. "There's no saving you now."

"Touché." His focus shifted to his wife. "Well, this is a complication."

"It's nothing we can't fix. *I* can fix it," Sydney assured. She didn't tremble or shrink under her towering husband, and yet, I couldn't shake the feeling she feared him.

"You have no choice. Because if you don't, I will." Rowan pressed his lips together, a finality to his statement.

"Her body isn't reacting like you told me," his wife explained, but I doubted the alpha wanted explanations. He was after results. Quickly.

It shouldn't have been a surprise a doctor was needed to do what they were doing to me, but I wasn't exactly sure how they were sucking the magic from my veins. Hell, I was pretty sure I preferred not to know the details. I just wanted it to fucking stop. I wanted my powers back. I wanted the heir prince in my damn head.

"What's the problem? I gave you everything I recovered on Dr. Samael's research," he said.

Dr. Samael? Was that who turned Gunnar into what he was? I couldn't remember if he mentioned his name.

Sydney glanced at a screen, her features pinched in confusion. "I'm not sure. It just started to reverse on its own."

Shit. I'd hoped she hadn't noticed. I also wished she would have kept that information to herself.

"Fix it. Now," Rowan demanded, nothing loving in the way he talked to his wife. "We're running out of time."

Sydney winced. "She's fighting the extraction."

Rowan gave her a solution. "Give her a higher dose. She can't resist if she isn't conscious."

The fuck I can't.

The alpha leaned over me, his eyes glowing. "Don't make this harder than necessary."

My chin jerked up. "Why shouldn't I? It's not like you're going to let me walk out of this room now that I've seen you for who you really are." Venom coated my words.

Rowan cleared his throat, straightening to his full height, his head only inches from the ceiling. "You're right. Your comfort no longer matters."

Well, crap. That isn't what I meant.

"He'll kill you when he finds out. He'll know," I immediately retorted, not caring that I sounded desperate.

"He might try," he agreed.

"And this is worth it? The destruction of your family, the loss of your son? For what? Power? Power that isn't yours?" It was hard for me to make sense of his motives.

Rowan took two steps back and leaned against the wall. "And why do you think you deserve such magic? What makes you so special?"

"My fucking DNA," I spat.

"Exactly," he said with a cool expression. "To survive in this world, you need to be strong. To lead a pack, you need to be powerful. To rule a kingdom, you need to be unstoppable."

"What? You plan to kill the king and take his throne?" That would be a death sentence. To even get to the king, he would have to go through an army of wolves. His pack alone wasn't strong enough, but the addition of an artillery of meta hunters...

Fuck me.

And if the rogue wolves joined...

He would have a damn fighting chance to take the throne, and with the addition of my power in his arsenal, he would have the upper hand. Had I screwed us, screwed the entire shifter community when I convinced Liam to claim me?

The power of his son amplified my abilities, but Rowan didn't know that little fun fact.

Not yet.

"I can see you working out the logistics. Still think I don't stand a chance?" he asked with a cocky raised brow.

Horror drenched my veins. "I won't let you take it."

"You can try to stop me," he challenged with a tight smile.

"And then what? Will you kill me? What will you tell your son?"

"Horrible accidents happen," he replied with lethal calm.

"He'll see through your lies. He claimed me tonight, which you would have known if you hadn't muddled our link with your drugs."

"Don't lie to me," Rowan hissed, anger flaring in his eyes.

"What will happen to him if you murder me? Are you willing to gamble with your heir's life as well?" The thought he just might made me sick, but despite the alpha's thirst for power, I was banking on the possibility he loved his son.

His smile reminded me of a rabid wolf. "Perhaps I'll keep you down here. An induced coma should make you more agreeable for the time being."

My stomach recoiled, fear unfurling.

He pushed off the wall. "I didn't want things to turn out like this. If you'd only stayed asleep, you'd be my daughter-in-law instead of my prisoner." Rowan left with those heartfelt, parting words.

With my heart pounding in my ears, my eyes darted around the room. I had to get out of here. But how? Could I shift? Would I be able to snap the straps? The problem with shifting was a wolf couldn't open doors, but perhaps my powers could.

Sydney put a hand on my arm, her lips brushing close to my ear. "It will be okay," she said in the barest of whispers, her fingers touching mine and squeezing.

It happened the moment her skin grazed mine—a vision but not like my others. Eerie wasn't close enough to describe being smack in the middle of a vision that would occur only moments after blinking away what my gift revealed.

I was in the same room. Strapped identically to the table. Nothing was out of place except...

Sydney. She no longer sat beside me but stood over me, her face too close. "Use your powers," she said. "You have the ability to free yourself, to escape, to level this bunker if you so choose and everyone in it. You are strong. The magic is yours to command. Now command it, Kelsey."

I blinked, and Sydney was back in her chair, her gaze imploring mine like she was telling me to trust her. How the fucking hell could I do that? I was so damn confused.

"Are you ready?" she asked, raising a brow before she pulled back and lifted a syringe.

I thought so...but honestly, I could be misreading the entire situation. Perhaps my mind wanted nothing more than to believe Liam's mom was a good person and was on our side, was helping me.

The door opened, and two of Rowan's guards sauntered in.

Sydney's eyes flicked up before finding mine again. "Now," she mouthed. At least that was what I thought her lips said.

My power surged, rallying to strike. The machine beeping went crazy, and energy burst from me, the straps on my wrists snapping. I yanked up, breaking the restraints on my arms, and with a thrust of my hands through the air, the rest of me was freed. When I sat up, my head angled to the side as the door clanged shut behind the two guards.

"Shit," one of them whispered, stopping dead in his tracks as he gawked at me.

I twisted my wrist, palm up, and watched as the two guards went flying across the room, pinned to the far wall, feet levitating off the ground. Power rippled around me, the table underneath me shaking.

These motherfuckers.

I ripped the tubes from my veins, one after the other. Twenty in total, covering all parts of my body. My legs swung over the edge as I put weight on my feet.

No one stole what I didn't freely offer. And that included my magic and my bond with Liam.

They would pay. As soon as the room stopped spinning and I could stand without my legs collapsing underneath me.

Outside, footsteps came barreling this way. A growl rumbled from across the room. I turned back to the dangling guards, one hand braced on the table. His eyes were glowing, canines gleaming in his mouth as he snarled. A different form of magic joined mine. He was shifting, and I couldn't let that happen.

I brought my other hand up, snapping my fingers closed into a fist. *Crack*. Their necks lobbed to the side, their bones fracturing. Together, as if they were almost in sync, their bodies slumped forward, and I let my hand fall to my side. It was like puppet strings being snipped; the lifeless bodies smacked to the floor.

I winced at the sound, staring, half expecting them to move. *Did I really just kill them with a flick of my fingers?*

My heart stopped.

"Kelsey," Sydney whispered.

I glanced to my right, and my heart started working again. Her aqua eyes brimmed with tears. "You need to go. There isn't much time."

Without moving her head, she shifted her eyes to the corner of the room.

I followed her line of sight, careful not to be obvious, and spotted the camera. Someone was watching us. They'd seen what I'd done—seen that I'd escaped. Which meant trouble was coming.

"Come with me," I whispered.

She shook her head. "I can't—"

A hissing sound entered the room, and it was coming from the ceiling. Sydney and I both glanced upward. I couldn't see anything except what looked like a sprinkler system.

An awful thought infiltrated my mind.

This was bad. Very, very bad.

My gaze darted to Sydney's; the worst of my fears were confirmed in her forlorn expression as if she'd given up. A chemical trickled into the cell, and I didn't know what it would do, nor did I give a shit.

"Protect my boys. Now run."

I couldn't go. Not without her.

She had helped me. I didn't know her story, and she could very well be as much of a victim as I was. She was Liam's mother, and I could repay her with the same act of kindness.

Feeling a bit steadier, I stood on both feet and threw out my power, creating a shield encompassing Sydney and me.

The door burst open, but before he appeared, I felt him, our bond clicking back into place.

Liam, every crevice of me sighed.

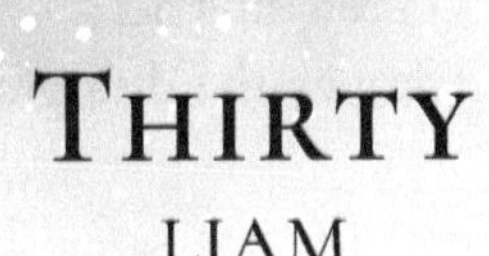

THIRTY

LIAM

What. The. Actual. Fuck.

I didn't know where to look first or even what the hell I was looking at. Two bodies lay immobile on the ground, their heads awkwardly angled. The light flickered over their faces.

Two of my father's guards.

In the center of the box-sized, windowless room stood a metal table. A dozen or so straps hung from the sides, dangling near the floor. They'd been snapped. Tiny tubes were discarded on the top of the metal table, and I could smell traces of blood.

My mate's blood.

Hope gasped behind me, but my gaze locked on Kelsey. My heart tripped out of my chest, and the entire world halted. She was here. Alive, and looking at me with confusion and disbelief as if she couldn't believe I was real.

My hand pressed into the wall, steadying myself. I didn't want to think about what happened in this room, why she looked so fucking pale, why two guards lay dead near her feet, why her eyes were glowing with power, or why my mother sat on a stool across from Kelsey, the metal table separating them.

Her eyes widened, wetting with tears, but the relief only lasted

seconds. A look of horror descended on her features, confounding me. Something was wrong. Really fucking wrong.

I went to take a step forward.

"No!" Her voice screamed through our bond before her hand flung out toward me, the door slamming shut in my face.

Did she just stop me from rescuing her?

Stunned, I blinked, staring at the dull gray metal in front of me. *"Pup,"* I growled.

"You can't come in here. It's not safe." Her voice wobbled, but through the shaky fear, I heard her resolve. She was as damn determined to protect me as I was her.

She wasn't the only one with a stubborn streak. *"Then I'm sure as hell not leaving you in there. Or my mom."*

"We're okay. I'm shielding us from the mist."

Behind me, Gunnar eyed the hallway, his hand intertwined with Hope's. *"Mist?"* I repeated.

"It's coming from the ceiling vents. I don't know what it is, but my guess is it's meant to knock us out."

"How long can you keep up the barrier?"

She didn't respond right away, and her hesitation made me want to break down the door. *"I-I don't know. For as long as I need to,"* she finally said.

But I wasn't buying it. *"What aren't you telling me? I can feel how weak you are, remember? We're fully mated. You might not want to admit it, but your magic will deplete."*

Gunnar grew restless, and I sensed his urge to leave. Understandably. This place had to dredge up a slew of bad memories for him, but my concern wasn't for him.

"I'll worry about that later. You need to get out of here," Kelsey pushed.

I pushed back, trying the handle on the door. No surprise it didn't budge. *"Not without you."*

"Liam, please."

"Save your strength. Nothing you say will make me leave." Not when I only just found her.

"Do you smell that?" Gunnar asked, his eyes narrowed at the door.

I slid him a sidelong glance doing my best to come up with a plan, and I didn't need his interruption.

Hope chewed on her nails. Her eyes never looked so big. "What's happening?"

"They're gassing her," Gunnar said, taking a step away and pushing Hope back at the same time.

He wasn't telling me anything I didn't already know. I cursed, my hand going to the handle and shaking it. "Kelsey, unlock the door!" I roared, the ceiling above our heads shaking.

She said nothing, but I could hear her breathing and the hissing of the mist as it continued to leak into the room.

Backing up, I surged forward, ramming my shoulder into the door. It groaned but held. "Help me," I ordered Gunnar.

The hunter gave me a not-so-pleasant expression but stepped up beside me, and together we slammed against the metal. This time it gave a little.

"Damn it, Liam. I'm trying to save your life," Kelsey grumbled.

"By sacrificing yours. Not going to happen, pup."

The third time, the door swung wide-open, and a cloud of mist came plunging into the hall. Lifting my arm, I used the sleeve of my hoodie to block my nose.

Before I could rush inside, a tingle of magic washed over me, the hairs on my arms standing up from the sudden charge in the air. Kelsey. She'd extended her powers, the shield encompassing Gunnar, Hope, and me.

Mom and Kelsey stumbled out of the door. I caught Kelsey, my arms secured around her. Gunnar steadied my mother, his hands gentle on her shoulders.

"Liam," my mate whispered as she sprang forward, launching her arms around my neck.

If I hadn't been prepared, we would have ended up on the ground. With my mate tucked against me, the scope of being separated from her moments after claiming her hit me hard. It was the sweetest torture.

"Can you walk?" I asked, still using our bond to communicate. My hands slid down, cupping her elbows.

"I think so. Your mom—"

"—is okay because of you," I quickly assured.

"You shouldn't be here," she said, her fingers following the curve of my jaw, a scratchiness in her throat I hated hearing.

My lips touched hers in a quick kiss, both of us needing the contact. "As if anything could stop me."

Gunnar cleared his throat. "As touching as this reunion is, we need to go. Company is coming."

Mom put her arm on mine, squeezing it. I hadn't processed or concluded why the hell my mother was here to begin with. "Find your father. You must stop him," she pleaded, a desperation in her tone. She held my gaze.

I stared at her. The depth of her words was penetrating, and yet, I had to be clear I understood what she was telling me.

I nodded. "Get them out of here," I told Gunnar. "If anything happens to her, I'm holding you responsible. I don't think I need to tell you what I'll do."

Gunnar rolled his eyes, his feet already moving back a step, eager to get to the surface. "The number of times you've threatened me, I have a good idea."

"No," Kelsey rejected. "I'm not leaving. Not without you."

"I need to finish this," I replied, willing her to understand.

She grabbed my hand, weaving our fingers together in a tight grip. "Then we finish it together."

"Kelsey, I—"

A siren sounded at the same time emergency lights flashed from the ceiling, cutting off my rebuttal.

"Now you've done it," Gunnar muttered under his breath. "They're getting closer."

"Move," I ordered the hunter, dragging Kelsey behind me.

Gunnar took the lead with Hope and my mother in the middle as we stomped down the hall. The doors lining both sides of the narrow passageway clanged shut, the locks clicking into place. We had no time to think about the security measures of the bunker. My only thought was getting Kelsey, Hope, and my mother the fuck out of here.

Gunnar came to a skidding halt at the end of the hallway, his body tensing. "The fun's about to begin," he muttered, cracking his neck.

A guard stood blocking our escape route, a gun pointing straight at us.

Instinct had me whirling, pulling Kelsey into my arms and pressing her into the wall, my body becoming a human shield.

The gun discharged, echoing in the hall. Time seemed to slow as I watched the syringe dart slice through the air toward us. *Boom. Boom. Boom. Boom.* Four more shots were unloaded from the gun in rapid succession.

The first hit Kelsey's barrier, pinging off the shimmering force field, and clattered to the ground. The second hit, and her shield wavered. Sweat beaded on her forehead. The third shattered our protection bubble.

"No!" my mate screamed, her hand lifting in the air and fingers closing into a fist.

The last two remaining darts came to a dead stop, floating midair inches from piercing Gunnar and Hope.

Kelsey exhaled, and the projectiles fell to the floor.

Gunnar's head whipped to Kelsey, eyeing her before he said, "Thanks."

We didn't have time for much else because this place was crawling with guards. At each corner, I half expected to run into the end of another gun. "Are you sure this is the way we came in?" I hissed at Gunnar.

The hunter sprinted ahead. "Do you want to lead? I can't believe I followed your ass down here to begin with."

A guard stepped out of a room in front of me, and before he could pull the trigger, I hit him in the face. His eyes rolled to the back of his head, and he fell to the ground like a plank. He wouldn't be unconscious for long, but hopefully, it would be enough for us to get out of here.

I helped Kelsey over his fallen body, and we raced down the hallway. The sirens continued to blare, my ears ringing, and the emergency lights flashed in a circle pattern, wreaking havoc on my vision as the tunnel in front of us wavered between bright and dark.

Another five minutes passed before Gunnar muttered, "We're almost there. I can see a light."

I didn't allow myself to feel relief. Not yet.

For good measure too.

The ceiling above us trembled, debris and dust falling on our heads. This was bad. "What are the chances this place has a self-destruct switch?"

"Pretty high," Gunnar shouted back to me.

Fuck, that's what I was afraid of.

My father wouldn't leave evidence behind. He was too smart, especially if the king were to get a sniff of what he was doing down here. Or all the other illegal items he had in his possession, two of which were currently wrapped around my neck and the hunter's.

The walls started to rumble. We had to move faster.

We were so close, and yet, I wasn't confident we'd make it.

"Gunnar!" I yelled. "Move your ass!"

Chunks of ceiling and wall were crumbling around us, but we ran, increasing our speed. My chest heaved as we got closer to the stairwell, the corridor not thirty feet behind us collapsing in a cloud of smoke and rubbish surging straight at us. Our boots pounded into the concrete.

We had a minute, tops, to haul our asses up the vertical ladder before this whole place became nothing but rubble. My grip on Kelsey's fingers tightened as we came to the exit, and I whirled to protect our backs. Gunnar ushered Hope and Mom up the metal rungs first, Kelsey next. I released my mate's hand. "Go, I'll be right behind you," I assured.

She hesitated, her gaze going past me to the storm about to swallow us whole.

We didn't have time for hesitations.

"Go!" I insisted. "Gunnar follow her up, make sure she doesn't fall."

Kelsey started her ascent, hands and feet flying up the ladder, Gunnar right behind her. I glanced up, judging how far she had to go and how fast the destruction pitched toward us.

The sirens stopped blaring and the lights went dark.

Oh shit, we weren't going to make it.

"Faster!" I demanded, grabbing the bars and hoisting myself up. The ladder under my hands and feet shook. It might not hold.

I had only three or four steps left, but it was too late. The tornado barreling through the bunker had finally reached us.

"Liam!" Kelsey screamed.

All I could think of was her—protecting her. Throwing myself up and out of the hole, I slammed into the ground with a jarring impact that stole my breath, Kelsey underneath me. Her head buried into my chest, my arms tight around her as the earth under us threatened to splinter.

When the world settled, I lifted my head, my breathing ragged and my heart pounding against my ribs. The ringing in my ears would linger for days, but we'd all gotten out, and from what I could see, everyone was alive. It didn't take me long to see why.

Magic glimmered over our heads in a dome shape almost as if a galaxy of stars embraced us.

Dirt smeared on Kelsey's cheek, and her sweet scent was tainted with traces of earth and metallic. *"You're okay?"* I asked for what felt like the millionth time today as the others started to stir and push to their feet.

A cloud of dust so thick swarmed us I couldn't see the trees only thirty feet away, and with my hearing fucked up, it was difficult to hear what was happening in the woods. I hadn't forgotten about the meta hunters or the rogue wolves they'd brought with them.

Kelsey's fear still pulsed through our bond, but her heart rate was slowly returning to normal. *"I'm good,"* she assured, dropping the ward.

A tingle washed over me as the magic dissipated. "It's not safe for us here. We need to keep moving," I advised, helping Kelsey to her feet before giving my mother a hand.

She was slow to get up, but like all of us, her sore muscles and scrapes would heal.

My main concern lay in getting the girls out of here, and I needed to reach out to my pack. I prayed my friends had fared better than we had.

Then I'd deal with my father.

"Liam," Kelsey said through our bond, and I didn't like the tone of her voice.

My gaze swung in her direction, noticing the sudden change in her expression—a dark, almost violent burn came into her eyes, but it was also shrouded with bits of terror. *"What's wrong now?"*

Someone gasped.

My mother?

Hope?

Hell, it could have been Gunnar.

Following everyone's gaze, I turned around and tensed as the cool evening air kissed my cheeks. My brother stood beside my father who had a gun at his side, clutched in his hand. It wasn't pointed or directed at anyone, yet the threat hovered. My father had his fingers on Leith's shoulder in a gesture that might have seemed loving to an outsider, but as I stared into his eyes, I saw the danger my brother was in.

"Leith." I inhaled sharply. "What are you doing here?" He was supposed to be far away, deep in the woods or something, fighting. Anywhere but here. I wanted to save him from this.

"Like I'd let you have all the fun," he replied in his usually carefree way, but the tone didn't match his eyes. Those said something completely different. A warning. A plea. A concoction of both.

"This isn't something you want to be a part of. This is between Dad and me, isn't that right, Dad?" I testily directed my focus to my father.

Dad's eyes were glassy with fury. "You have no idea what you've done. The years of research lost. The advancements destroyed." I'd seen bits and pieces of this side of my father throughout the years, but I still couldn't believe this was him. And yet, I could. My mind wouldn't decide one way or the other.

But, if a showdown was what he wanted, we could do this here. "I don't care about any of it. I've only ever been the son you trained me to be, but when it comes to Kelsey, I won't compromise her safety. She comes first." It was a blow to realize my father had never once put my mother above the pack or his ambitions. I would not make that mistake with my mate.

That's where we differed.

Everyone was careful to not make any sudden movements. We barely breathed.

"Our pack could have been the strongest. Don't you see what we could have achieved, the power we could have had, and your mate would have lived. We could have both had what we desired."

Through our bond, I felt Kelsey's heart skip. Mine mirrored hers, something we both had to get used to. "Her power isn't something you can take. It isn't meant to be shared."

His jaw ticked, the fingers on Leith's shoulder pressing deeper into my brother. "Power is *meant* to be conquered."

My gut told me to get Leith away from him. "I guess that's where we disagree."

Disgruntled, Dad shook his head. "I was securing your future as king. The throne would have passed to you."

"I don't want to be king," I snapped. Hell, to be honest, I didn't want to be a prince most of the time, let alone the alpha of a pack, but I was given no other choice in my future. Overthrowing the king was where I drew the line.

Mom stepped forward. "Rowan, it's over. Let it go."

He raised a hand, and before he could bring it down, I intercepted, my fingers wrapping around his wrist. "Don't think about laying a hand on her." Anger slithered into my chest. I was about five seconds away from snapping someone's neck.

The man who raised me tsked like I was the biggest disappointment of his life. "You're your mother's son. Weak. You let your emotions cloud your judgment."

"And you don't have any emotions," I shot back unapologetically.

"An alpha can't make decisions based on feelings," he spat, the centers of his eyes flashing.

Energy crackled at Kelsey's fingertips.

Dad's gaze darted to her, feeling the rise of power in the air. "Liam," he snarled, his wolfish eyes back on me.

I wasn't a child anymore. He couldn't bark my name and expect me to fall in line behind him. My lips curled, a growl sounding, except...

It didn't come from me.

Heads whipped toward the deep, low threat. Something sprinted in the woods, coming straight for us, and from the way they moved through the trees, I had a good idea. Wolves.

Rogue wolves to be precise.

Dad shoved Leith to the ground as a wolf lurched at him, barreling out of the darkness, fur as black as night so only his silver glowing eyes were visible.

And just like that, shit hit the fucking fan.

Dad rolled, exploding into his wolf as a roar peeled through the trees. I felt it in my soul, the call of the alpha—a summons for his pack.

Leith caught himself, his fingers digging into the frozen ground as I centered my body in front of Kelsey and my mother, my wolf ready to burst free.

Gunnar had Hope in his arms. "They're on their way."

Which meant we were almost out of time. The fight was nearly here.

Dad crouched, squaring off with the wolf and eyes deadlocked on the rogue, waiting to see what he would do.

Gunnar whirled as another wolf pounced feet away with lips curled and a bloodthirsty gaze. "I call dips on this asshole," the hunter claimed.

By all means.

"They're herding us," Mom whispered.

Dad and the rogue stalked each other in a slow circle, canines bared. The hackles on the back of his neck rose.

"Oh god," Hope sobbed as Gunnar barely avoided a second rogue wolf who lunged at his throat, snapping teeth scratching over his skin and leaving behind an angry line of red.

Thunderous, swift footsteps moved through the woods, and I glanced at Kelsey, seeing and feeling the panic traveling through her. They were coming. And they were pissed.

I was prepared when a third wolf appeared. He didn't charge like the others had but watched me from the shadows, eyes shining.

A howl pealed into the horizon, and that was the moment he struck. He went for Kelsey, but I intercepted, fingers fisting into his fur. I took him to the ground in a clean sweep. Wrestling both hands around his thick neck, I snapped it to the side, and the cracking of his bones was audible.

Adrenaline pumped into my veins. Rogue wolves I could handle. It was the meta hunters that worried me.

I turned to see Leith engaged with a wolf. Gunnar had taken down his first and moved on to two others. Dad had three on him now. Things were starting to heat up. If the numbers kept up at this pace, we'd be fucked, but I couldn't think about that now.

I had to stay alive and keep my loved ones breathing.

The rogue wolves prowled from deep in the woods, and my father sent another howl for aid. *"You're part of mine now,"* he said to Kelsey through our pack bond. *"Under my command. Use your gifts to end this."*

Hatred burned through me. I didn't want her used as a weapon, which was exactly what my father intended, among other things. Whether it was the girl or the magic, it didn't matter. He only saw what she could do for him. He didn't see my mate, not as a person or a wolf.

"You don't have to fight for him," I countered, using our mating bond, not the connection to the pack. What I had to say was for Kelsey's ears only.

She huddled next to my mother and Hope, the three defending each other. *"I'd be fighting for you."*

We were officially outnumbered, and I backed up as a trio boxed me in. *"Again, you don't need to. I'd rather die than see you become something you've avoided your entire life."*

Unable to stand by and do nothing, Mom shifted, putting herself in front of Hope and Kelsey. Her mocha fur gleamed in the dark, eyes the same color as mine radiating from her fur. Blood splashed on her paw as she raked her nails down a rogue's face.

"I've seen your death. I've seen mine. One way or the other, this needs to end," she replied, and I hated how ominous it sounded.

My eyes shifted to my father. *"And I know where we need to start."*

"Liam." Her voice broke.

The wolves closed in around me, and the familiar tingles of the shift prickled over my skin. *"Don't say another word. This is my choice."*

"And this is mine," she whispered.

Kelsey's hair blew back, the surge of her power humming in our bond as if her magic came directly from the full moon itself. Whorls of starlight, little sparks, and embers cut through the darkness toward the enemy, wrapping like silver cuffs around their ankles.

The mark on both our wrists illuminated, and a slight burn radiated against my skin.

With the wolves contained for now, Dad shifted, shedding his wolf coat, his body transforming into a man. I couldn't see the shackles of magic, but I sensed them. He fell to his knees, spitting blood from the side of his mouth, and I saw my opening. The mayhem surrounding me gave me the perfect opportunity, and I took it.

Hurdling over the wolves, I dashed through two large trees. So much blood covered the snowy ground, gleaming brightly under ribbons of moonlight through the heavy tree branches.

"Liam!" Leith called from my right.

My feet didn't stop moving as I glanced at my brother just in time to see him toss something at me. I caught the dagger by the hilt and skidded to a stop in front of my father.

Towering over him, I stared down at the man who'd always been larger than life to me, and before I allowed myself to think about what I was doing, I held the blade to his throat. "Tell me why I shouldn't end you right now?"

Triumph danced in his eyes. "You can't hurt me."

Confusion wobbled inside me. It was a pretty bold statement, considering I had a knife pressed to his neck. And then I felt it.

The collar grew tighter around my throat, and my hands dropped to my sides. For half a breath, I considered my actions. Could I kill my father? It wasn't even an unnatural notion among shifters. Alphas were challenged in packs frequently, even by family. The collar would make it difficult. One command from his lips and I could be rendered useless.

Kelsey's fingers flexed, and her magic tightened around my father, his features flickering in discomfort.

Hope began crying, shoving at Gunnar's chest, but the hunter held firm.

Regaining my composure, I returned the blade to the pulsing vein at his neck. "Swear you will give this up. Swear you will leave us alone, and no one else has to get hurt."

A husky chuckle slithered past his bloody lips. "You can't possibly hope to win."

I gritted my teeth, fighting against the power of the collar binding me. "And why not?"

A low, vicious snarl rippled from the dark, seconds before arrows rained through the trees. This night seemed destined to never end.

The meta hunters had arrived. The fight wasn't over. Not yet.

"Gunnar," I growled as my gaze immediately sought out my mate.

She stood between two trees, the pale moon slicing over half her body eerily. There was too much space between us, and I didn't even remember her walking away. Arrows speared into the snow, others into the trees, and many hit the rogue wolves no longer bound by Kelsey's magic. Her attention had shifted elsewhere. She raised her arms, and a blast of frigidness hit the air.

Gunnar ran toward the first threat, but before he reached the meta, the wind began to roar, stirring the air around me, and the mutated hunters noticed. It only took seconds for them to find the source, and that was when my mate struck.

The arrows sailing through the air froze as the trees surrounding her were uprooted, spinning wildly toward the hunters. They hit, one by one, knocking the meta senselessly to the ground before the trees fell on top of them, crushing bones.

He leveled me a cool stare, without an ounce of worry for his life. "You're wasting time. You'll kill us all. This is why we need to be stronger. To have an edge that gives us an advantage. We need her power."

Leith came up behind me, his presence like a wave of support. "Don't let him get into your head. You know what must be done. His actions have put the entire pack in jeopardy. If the king found out..."

Shaking my head, I dropped down beside my father so we were level and lifted the dagger, pressing it into his chest over his heart. Sweat beaded over my forehead as I fought against the collar's power. My hand shook, but I forced my fingers to stay clutched against the alloy handle. I didn't want our father's blood on Leith's hands—on his conscience.

It should be me.

It had to be me.

His eyes were hard. Cold. "You can't do it. I knew you didn't have it in you."

The coil of darkness tightened around my throat, and a scream of frustration trembled inside me. I loathed the control the collar had on my free will, and I understood the irony, considering it was what I'd taken from Gunnar.

"He might not. But I do." Leith covered his hand over mine and plunged the knife into our father's chest before I realized his intention.

The blade went in smoothly at first, and then he dug the dagger in deeper and deeper, making sure it pierced through his heart.

Horror widened in my father's eyes right before he gasped, and something in my chest cleaved open.

I forced myself to stare at him. I wouldn't look away.

Blood seeped from where the blade stuck out of his heart, hot and sticky as it wept onto my hand. "You." Dad wheezed the word at Leith.

My brother glanced down at our father with a tormented expression. "Didn't see that one coming, did you, Pops?"

My father said nothing. He didn't blink. He didn't move. He didn't breathe.

He was dead.

I continued to stare, unable to move, even as his body finally slumped to the bitter ground.

A soft hand touched my shoulder. *"Liam,"* Kelsey said through our bond.

On a shuddering breath, I stood and turned to face her. Her beautiful eyes bore into mine, tears filling them. She touched the side of my cheek, her expression brimming with guilt. *"Don't,"* I replied. *"This isn't your fault. I won't let you blame yourself."*

Tears streamed down my mother's face, and another piece of my heart cracked. *"It's okay,"* she whispered through the pack bond to Leith and me. "*You did what was right not just for your mate and the pack but for your father. His madness for power consumed him."*

I couldn't say anything.

This wouldn't break me, but my brother...

I grabbed Leith by the shoulders, holding his gaze. "You did nothing. Do you understand me? I killed him. It was my hand that held the knife. Not yours. Leith?" I prompted.

He blinked, focusing on my face. The haze of shock wasn't completely gone. "I don't want to be the alpha."

"Do you understand what I'm saying? It was *me.*" I held his gaze.

Leith nodded.

The wind howled through the woods. "Good. We never speak of this again."

Riven burst through the trees in his wolf form, blood dripping from his snarling mouth. His bright eyes accessed the situation. A moment later, Colsen came panting through, skidding to a stop beside Riven. *"You couldn't have saved one for head for me to rip off?"* Colsen said to Riven through our pack bond.

Kelsey blinked at them, and the haze of violet magic simmering in her eyes slowly faded.

My two best friends shared the same range of expressions as understanding arose when they caught sight of my father's body. The entire pack would have felt his death, and I still held the bloody knife.

Their heads started to lower.

"Don't," I said, pain and exhaustion evident in more than just my tone. *"Not tonight."* There would be plenty of time for formality, but for tonight, I wanted to go home and be with my family, mourn the loss of our father, not the obsessive alpha he'd become, for in my mind, they were two separate people.

I pinched the bridge of my nose with two fingers. These decisions were now my responsibility. It hadn't sunk in. And probably wouldn't for days, maybe weeks, that I was the pack alpha. I saw a lot of talking and politicking in my near future, but right now, all I wanted was my mate and some time alone to process—to grieve—to be thankful.

The path sprawled in front of me was shrouded in darkness and wound into the unknown. Once I stepped forward, there was no turning back.

I was no longer the heir prince.

I was *the* prince.

The Riverbridge alpha.

And I no longer feared or rejected my birthright. Not with Kelsey as my luna.

We fought together.

We learned to love together.

And now we'd rule together.

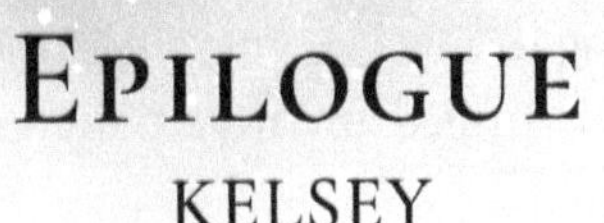

Epilogue

KELSEY

The next months were a grieving and healing process. Not fully, but a start.

What Liam had endured...

No wolf, no human, nor no meta should have been put in a position to choose between his mate or his father. The weight of his decision would bear down on Liam's shoulders for the rest of his life.

Mine too.

Leith might have shoved the blade into their father's heart, but they both suffered from scars that would never fully heal. Leith tried to save his brother from having more blood on his hands, knowing Liam's future as the pack's alpha would be filled with difficult choices every damn day.

I found Liam on the roof, sitting on the ground with his back pressed into the ledge as our peers and their parents ushered into the auditorium for graduation below. We should be down there, lining up, but he needed a moment away from the crowds.

Without saying a word, I climbed into his lap, resting my head on his shoulder. His arms immediately came around me, and we sat in silence, listening to the excited chatter and the bubbling river.

Words were unnecessary. Not when our bond revealed everything.

We'd learned so much about each other during these last few months. It was impossible not to when you were constantly in someone else's head, but we'd also figured out how to shield our thoughts when necessary. We were finding our balance.

His hand moved up my bare calf. "Where's your gown?"

My nose scrunched as a lick of warmth traveled up my leg. "It's hideous. I'm not wearing it."

Those lips that rarely smiled anymore twitched. "Why does that not surprise me?"

I lifted my head so I could look at his handsome face. "It's not like they won't give me my diploma if I boycott their silk robe. Besides, this dress looks killer on me."

His gaze ran over my body from head to toe. "We can agree on that. And I'm looking forward to taking it off," he said, lowering his voice.

I stopped his hand from going any farther up my thigh. "After."

Amusement sparkled in eyes brightened by the sun. "Love the boots."

I tapped the toes of my black combat boots together. "I thought you might. Turns out, I like goth Kelsey's style. She might stick around for a little longer."

His lips curved. "There's nothing sexier than you talking about yourself in the third person."

I rolled my eyes before letting my gaze drop to his lips and the tempting scar on his lower lip. "Are you sure? I bet I can think of a few things sexier."

"If you keep this up, we won't make it to the ceremony at all." He sucked his bottom lip because it drove me crazy, and my insides became liquid. I melted into him.

"I'm not complaining," I whispered, touching my mouth to his in a light kiss.

His fingers slipped into my hair at the base of my head as he took the kiss to a deeper place, leaving me breathless.

"Are you okay?" I asked softly. I couldn't help but worry about him. His life hadn't been easy before, but after his father's death, things got harder. His world changed. He was thrown into a position of leadership, something he'd trained for, but no amount of preparation could brace you for the actuality. “I wasn’t joking about skipping out if that’s what you want.”

“I’m better now.” He traced a finger down my spine, leaving tingles behind on my back.

“Should we get this over with?”

He leaned in for another kiss. “In a minute.”

I sighed, content to stay here on the roof with him forever.

Lacing our fingers, he stood and pulled me to my feet. Together we took the stairs inside and another flight to the first floor where Leith walked around the corner.

“Where were the two of you hiding?” The younger Castle looked me over and plucked something out of my hair. “Or I don’t want to know?” Leith did a good job of maintaining his carefree attitude, but I saw through the charade. I saw the shadows still haunting his eyes. I saw the pain he lived with—the heaviness of his choice. I just hoped it wouldn’t eat away at him. Only time would tell, but I was on Leith’s side. If he ever needed me, I’d be there unquestionably.

We were family.

“Whatever,” I replied with a smile, smoothing strands of hair Liam had messed up.

“You should be excited. Why aren’t you excited? Mom is already seated. So are your parents,” he said.

“We’re going,” Liam grumbled, leading me down the hall.

The weeks after the fight were a time for healing and mending. And boy was there a need for both. For some brothers, what Liam and Leith went through could cause a rift in their relationship, and for the first few weeks afterward, I’d worried about them, but somehow, the two were closer than before. I didn’t have the details of what went down. Liam only told me they worked through it and he wasn’t about to lose another family member.

Leith eyed me, a smirk slipping over his lips. “Nice getup. I might need to borrow it when I graduate.”

I elbowed him in the gut.

“See you inside,” he said, taking off toward the auditorium seats while Liam and I got in line.

“We’re supposed to be in alphabetical order,” I said.

The prince, now no longer an heir prince, lifted a brow. "If you can wear a dress instead of a graduation gown, then where we sit isn't going to make a difference."

"Are you breaking the rules?" I quipped.

"Only for you."

I lifted on my toes and kissed him.

"Do you ever stop groping each other?" Gunnar asked from behind us, sounding bothered.

Beaming, I turned and faced Gunnar. Hope was at his side. "Maybe you're not touching Hope enough. You ever think of that?" I shot back at him playfully.

Gunnar and Hope were still together, much to Liam's displeasure. Gunnar was Hope's choice, and my mate would have to find a way to accept it. He'd forgiven his cousin for her involvement in my capture. I would have done the same if I'd been put in Hope's position. In a threatening position, saving the person you love becomes the most important thing. There's nothing I wouldn't do to protect those I love. Who could fault Hope for that?

Liam didn't quite feel the same, but eventually, he came around, and the collar was removed. The prince still had trust issues.

Hope was still my best friend regardless of her questionable choice in mate.

The hunter gave me a shithead grin. "I don't stop ever thinking about her." They cut in line behind us, a few people grumbling, but no one would say anything, not with Liam there.

"Does that mean you're retiring from your hunting gig?" Gunnar might have recruited hunting shifters since the fight and his vow to Liam. They'd worked out a deal. No collar, and in exchange, Gunnar would track down other meta like him, offering them a place in his pack. It was a way to keep tabs on them, and in time, hopefully, we could find a place of peace with them.

There would always be hunters, people who didn't understand us, who felt threatened by what we were.

Gunnar slung his arm around Hope, pulling her close to him as his dark eyes glittered. "Talk to your boyfriend."

Hope rolled her eyes.

The teachers started to usher us inside to take our seats. I spotted Leith beside Sydney in the third row for guests. The doctor and I had an understanding. I didn't blame her for her part in Rowan's plan. She'd been as much a victim as I had been, and if he had forced any other doctor other than his wife, I might still be inside that bunker.

My parents, Nana, and little brother were sitting in the crowd, Noah waving enthusiastically at me. Mom shook her head when our eyes connected, disapproval tugging at her lips at my wardrobe choice. The ironic part was I'd inherited my rebellious streak from her. Dad only grinned, a glint of pride in his eyes.

Neither of my parents nor Nana were shocked when they heard what Rowan planned to do with me. They were relieved and grateful to Liam, realizing how incredibly difficult it must have been for him. Only Liam, Leith, Gunnar, Hope, and I knew the truth, that it hadn't been Liam who killed his father but Leith.

Liam continued to protect those he loved, and that included his little brother.

)))●(((

GRADUATION WASN'T the only ceremony on our to-do list. A few days after we received our diplomas was the full moon and our official claiming ceremony. Since nothing about our relationship had been done by the book, we figured why start now?

After fulfilling his place as the alpha, Liam met with the king to discuss the treaty. It was settled that Liam and I would still hold the claiming ceremony regardless that the deed had already been done to uphold pack tradition and honor the king's wishes to join our packs.

The two packs would meet on neutral ground, the king would attend, and I'd be officially crowned as the Riverbridge luna.

I stared at my reflection in the full-length mirror. The lacy white dress pooled over my bare feet and was utterly ridiculous, considering I'd be wearing it for a whole five minutes before shifting. And it was far too pure for my liking—virginal, which I definitely wasn't.

Nana stood behind me, pinning a brooch, a family heirloom

encrusted with amethysts and diamonds, into my hair. "There," she said, smiling at me in the mirror.

I twisted my head slightly, the stones catching the light. "It's beautiful, Nana," I said in awe.

The light in her eyes softened some of the anxiety fluttering in my stomach. "So are you, my dear," she said.

Turning around, I faced her, doing my best not to tear up. I'd applied way too much eye makeup to ruin it now. "I don't know what I would have done without you this year."

She fussed with my hair, brushing it over my shoulders. "I was thinking the same thing."

"I'm coming home every break," I said for not the first, second, or third time, but it was a promise I meant to keep.

"The door will always be open for you."

While we were away at college, Hope's father, Jacy, would be overseeing the pack in Liam's stead. He remained the pack's beta after Rowan's death. Liam would be required to attend pack meetings with the king while pursuing his college education. It was agreed upon that my abilities would remain a secret known by only a small group of shifters who had Liam's trust and Gunnar, of course.

I hugged her.

"He'll make you happy," she whispered, patting me on the back.

Something in her tone gave me pause. "I know." I wondered if we'd had the same vision, the one where I was happier than I'd ever been even with a baby boy on my hip. I still wasn't sure I wanted kids, but this version of Kelsey made me reconsider, especially knowing Liam was by my side.

Easing back, she swiped under her glistening eyes. "Shall we go and get this formality out of the way?"

I choked out a laugh, trying to not let my emotions get the best of me, and nodded.

A brutal winter had given way to a gentle summer, filling the woods with lush leaves, wildflowers, and little critters scampering about. The evening air had a trace of summer not too far off. Flickering torches lit the path to the circle, and I couldn't help feeling as if I was walking down the aisle to marry the man of my dreams except, I was too young for marriage and the guy waiting at the dais I'd once despised. Funny how fate had a way of intervening.

He stood in the center of the circle, a beam of moonlight slashing over the side of his gorgeous face. I didn't immediately lift my eyes to his, knowing once I did, I'd see nothing else. I wanted to take in this moment before I lost my head.

Dressed in all black, the prince looked dashing, and pride swelled in my chest. He was mine. My eyes were drawn to his wrist and the moon mark blazing as bright as the day he claimed me. It hadn't dulled a day since.

I wasn't sure if the intensity of the mark was any indication of our bond's strength, but if it was, then our connection was unwavering.

With a hint of a smile on my lips, I finally lifted my eyes, and a bolt of electricity ran through my veins. My wolf. My magic. My body. My heart. He had a grip on all of me, and I beamed inside.

I'd walked this path before during my welcome ceremony, but this time, the prince waited for me with an outstretched hand.

I laced our fingers, and he lifted our joined hands up in the air, flashing the twin moons on our wrists to the pack. Our gazes locked, and he gave me a quick nod. I took a step back, and we shifted into our wolves.

Shaking off the last tingles, I adjusted to my wolf while Liam circled me, waiting and eyeing the two packs. This was the moment another wolf could challenge either of us for our position in the pack. I held my breath.

Was there a wolf arrogant enough to challenge him? Me, perhaps, as I was the newcomer, but to challenge me would be to go against Liam. Huntley and Sabrina popped into my head. I spotted my ex in the crowd, his piercing blue eyes on me. My gaze narrowed. He would be a fool to fight Liam, but wolves were known to do dumb shit when it came to mates and love. In Huntley's and my case, unrequited love. He had to know I could never love him as more than a friend. As he stared at me, the fire in his eyes finally cooled to something like acceptance, and his shoulders sagged slightly.

The prince howled, indicating the period of challenge was over, and the wolves surrounding us bowed their heads one by one. The air in my lungs whooshed out.

It was done.

He was mine.

And I was his.

We had a long life in front of us. Together. We were in no rush. And Liam loved to show me just how much time we had to love each other.

His wolf stepped up to me, fur of the purest white covering his powerful form, and the moon made the ends of his fur shimmer in a sparkling light blue. He was by far the biggest wolf here, and dominance exuded from him in the way he held his head, the way his feet sunk into the ground, and in the sharp glow of his eyes.

Through our bond, I felt his elation—felt the way he saw me—and it never failed to leave me enthralled. *"Your fur is so dark. I swear you were born from a starless night,"* he sent down our link.

Amusement made me smile inside. *"I might have been."*

The tip of his wet nose brushed against mine. *"I'm so in love with you, pup. And it isn't only because the fates chose you as my mate. I fell for the reckless, wild, and headstrong wolf you are. You are everything I could ever want in a partner and so fucking much more."*

Eyes misting, I breathed in the scent of his wolf. *"I love you, princeling. Even if you're an alpha asshole most of the time."*

His chuckle sounded in my head. *"What next?"* he asked, firelight from the torches gleaming on his fur.

I nuzzled my head against the side of his. *"For once, I don't know. And I like it that way."*

THE END

ELITE OF ELMWOOD ACADEMY

Turmoil

USA TODAY BESTSELLING AUTHOR

J.L. WEIL

J.L. WEIL

USA TODAY BESTSELLING AUTHOR

WHITE RAVEN

RAVEN SERIES *Book One*

Stealing Tranquility

Dragon Descendants
Book 1

J.L. Weil

USA Today Bestselling Author

JOIN DARK DIVAS READER GROUP - My reader group is the best place to talk books and get up-to-date information. https://www.facebook.com/groups/1217984804898988

SIGN UP FOR JL WEIL NEWSLETTER - Get free books just for signing up. https://www.jlweil.com/vip-readers

FOLLOW ME ON FACEBOOK - Click the follow button on my Facebook page for notifications on what's happening. https://www.facebook.com/jenniferlweil

CHECK OUT MY SHOP - Get signed books and merch at my online shop! https://www.jlweil.com/shop

AMAZON - Click the follow button on my Amazon page and you'll get an email for each new release from me. https://www.amazon.com/stores/J.L.-Weil/author/B008A1AQGO

INSTAGRAM - I post pretty pics of my books and teasers. https://www.instagram.com/jlweil/

Check out my Amazon Author page for a collection of all my books available!

About the Author

J.L. Weil is a USA TODAY Bestselling author of teen & new adult paranormal romance, fantasy, and urban fantasy books about spunky, smart mouth girls who always wind up in dire situations. For every sassy girl, there is an equally mouthwatering, overprotective guy.

You can visit her online at: www.jlweil.com or come hang out with her at JL Weil's Dark Divas on FB.

Stalk Me Online
www.jlweil.com
jenniferlweil@gmail.com

www.ingramcontent.com/pod-product-compliance
Lightning Source LLC
Chambersburg PA
CBHW020248030826
48979CB00030B/2664/J

* 9 7 8 1 9 5 4 9 1 5 3 2 9 *